The Lies That Hide Within

Megan Boley

MIDNIGHT TOMES PRESS

ISBN paperback: 978-1-961529-05-2
ISBN hardcover: 978-1-961529-06-9
ISBN ebook: 978-1-961529-04-5

Cover: Trif Book Design
Editing: Cameron Montague Taylor and Nadara Merrill

First edition: March 2025

For every woman who has ever been told she was too much, too loud, too [insert whatever men find threatening here]...

You're perfect.

Eat the rich. Fuck the patriarchy.

Previously in The Darkness All Around Us...

After Rodney staged a coup in the Faction, Penny assassinated him and then teamed up with Agnes (formerly known as "Stella") to destroy Pharmatrox's HQ, take down the network, and dismantle Agnes's DNA editing machine.

Dr. Ingrid Hansen—the Leader, Agnes's mother, and the true mastermind behind the mind-control drug troxapine, aka "the dust"—is dead, killed by Penny and Agnes. Because of this, Penny has gained popularity among the Faction and is (supposedly) sharing leadership responsibilities with Malosi Olesa, the general of the resistance in the Capital and Kev's (the Faction's founder) number two in charge.

Penny is Quentin's sister and the user who set his house on fire, killing their parents and leaving him scarred. Driven by guilt and a thirst for vengeance, Penny ruthlessly pursued Agnes for months, mistakenly thinking she created troxapine and was the architect of her pain. Evie, Silas's sister, is the original creator of troxapine, but Pharmatrox used Agnes's machine to pervert her anxiety medication formula into something far more sinister.

In present day, the troxies have fallen back and the Faction is in search of more dionazole (detox serum)—the only way for troxapine users to quit without dying from withdrawal. Without it, troxapine is so addictive that users will use until they eventually turn into cannibalistic, zombie-like creatures.

"Team Outpost" consists of Lawrence (the lumberjack gardener), Tara (the feisty ex-military soldier and Stella's new best friend), Quentin (the goofy climbing-obsessed teenager), and Silas (Evie's brother and Stella's childhood best friend). Agnes and Derek have been in a relationship since the end of *The Darkness All Around Us*.

Penny and Mal, however...well. You'll just have to see.

1

P ENNY TWIRLED THE SEVERED thumb as she waited for the bodies to be devoured.

Right on cue, a slew of feral creatures staggered down the street and swarmed the piles of corpses stacked high. Flesh ripped from bone, guttural cries of turned echoing among the concrete buildings.

Waiting in the alley with the squadron of Faction troops, Penny pointedly ignored the looming presence of the hulking man behind her. He was pissed off, and she knew why.

"Are Mommy and Daddy fighting again?" Beside her, Raph, a sinewy man built for speed and sneaking, nudged her with a grin.

If she had her way, she'd be out in the Wilds hunting down Rodney's cult right the fuck now, but this was an opportunity for some fun she couldn't refuse.

Barely containing her eye roll, Penny said, "Just be ready with that light."

In response, Raph flicked his lighter, then shuffled to hide behind the dumpster near the glistening pavement at the mouth of the alley, his shoulders shaking with silent laughter.

Somehow, she felt the man's looming presence behind her grow even loomier. "Mal," Penny said through her teeth as she spun toward him, "stop glaring at the top of my head. What is your problem?"

Mal frowned at the severed thumb as she poked him in the chest with it. "Your plan is a bit theatrical, don't you think?"

"Theatrics is what I'm good at. That's why I'm here, isn't it?"

He grunted, which was more than she'd been able to drag out of him lately. Neither of them had spoken about their...moment in the woods after they'd taken down the Spire last month, defaulting to their usual pissed-off interactions.

Penny was more than okay with that. Whatever *feelings* had come over her that day had evaporated in the raging inferno of Mal's irritating personality. Not to mention, he was the general and she was the Faction's enforcer. Their partnership was about the mission, and there wasn't room for anything else. If she even wanted more. Which she didn't—something she routinely reminded herself any time he was near. Because while her mind was made up, her body didn't always agree, doing embarrassing things like *tingling* in his presence or when he looked at her just a second too long. Fucking idiotic. So she put on her argumentative pants to keep him at arm's length and mask the reactions she definitely should not be having.

At the weight of Mal's gaze on her, her skin *did the thing*, but she kept her eyes locked on the streets, searching. Rounding up the bodies had been a disgusting endeavor, but there was plenty of fodder after the last Faction raid on a Pharmatrox facility had gone bad. The Faction's clean-up efforts in the Capital had been mostly successful, and they were regaining more troxy territory every day, but with each facility they cleared, something felt...off. Pharmatrox had changed tactics. But to what, exactly, she wasn't sure.

"How much longer?" Penny asked.

Mal frowned as the hungry turned tossed torn limbs, old blood flinging in sludgy gobs. "Give it another minute."

Penny accompanied the Faction on raids and certain missions, pleased for a chance to stretch her combat muscles, but she left the strategizing and motivational speeches to Mal—another thing they argued about constantly. Sneaking a glance at him out of the corner of her eye, she had to admit, he was impressive. *But still a thorn in my goddamn side.* With his huge arms crossed in front of his massive chest, his stance screamed *powerful.* A few of his troops approached and asked questions, new ones she hadn't seen before, and he directed them on their way. Penny chewed her lip, stuffing the severed thumb in her pocket. *He should be the face of the Faction. Not me. At least he wants the job and is trained for it.*

Jerking her head at the unfamiliar faces, Penny asked, "New lackeys? Did your old ones run off?"

A muscle in Mal's jaw flicked. "There's high turnover right now. Since we have the upper hand, some are taking the chance to get out of the city. Can't say I blame them."

"Hmm." Penny nodded, but she wasn't so sure. "Could be Rodney's people picking them off."

The remaining dregs of Rodney's followers had fashioned themselves into a cult and were hiding out in the Wilds—the lands beyond the Capital's fortified perimeter. The Faction's patrol had reported people stealing supplies, but Mal wasn't convinced the cultists were behind it. This shit had Rodney's people written all over it, but without proof, Penny's protests were dead in the water.

"We have bigger issues," Mal said.

"For now—but *you* made the mistake of underestimating Rodney before." Mal glared at her. "And I did too. We can't ignore them forever."

She let the subject drop—how and when to deal with Rodney's cult was another of the many things they argued about, and she wasn't going to let it go. *Over my dead fucking body will I let those people immortalize*

Rodney as some kind of fucking messiah. "Any word from Chicago?" she asked.

"Not yet."

"Shouldn't we have heard something by now?"

With the network down, CLEOs and Patches were largely out of the picture, with long- and short-range comms resorting to satellite phones and radios. But their broadcasts to Kev in Chicago hadn't gotten any response, so word of mouth messengers had to be sent. Not ideal.

"It's only been a week. I'm not worried."

Yet hung unspoken in the air between them.

Movement at the far end of the street caught their attention. Mal straightened, gaze snapping to a band of troxy soldiers pouring out of the facility and marching for the turned. Penny didn't know what troxies did with the turned they captured. *Probably use them for deranged experiments or something.* She jerked to attention as Mal raised a fist to their troops.

Just a few more steps.

When the troxies reached the horde of turned and began firing their stun guns, Mal whistled to Raph, who tossed the lighter onto the wet pavement. A ring of flames erupted and raced down both sides of the street, encircling turned and troxies in a cage of fire.

"Now!" shouted Mal, charging for the street, everyone following. Shots and shrieks rose from inside the fire, but Mal projected his voice over the din. "Drop your weapons and surrender."

"Not a fucking chance!" one of the troxies yelled, firing his volt rifle.

Mal sighed as he dodged. "Raph? Try and reason with them. If not, give them the usual."

Shouldering his rifle, Raph said to the troxies, "Oi, put down the zappy blaster, buddy. It doesn't need to go like this."

As the Faction busted through the facility's glass front doors and filed inside, Mal said, "Should be minimal security."

The remaining troxies in the Capital were in hiding, so finding an empty entryway during a raid wasn't uncommon, but it still felt weird just walking into their buildings. While there were no drones, aerial bombings, or masses of troops filling the streets anymore, Pharmatrox was not inactive. They were up to something. She just didn't know what.

"Don't shoot unless they shoot first," Mal said. "If you find any scientists, bring them to me. Meet outside when you've cleared your floor."

As the Faction had been slowly working their way westward, something strange kept popping up—they hadn't found any Pharmatrox scientists. All the facilities were manned by guards, but no white lab coats in sight. And Penny wasn't sure what to make of that.

Mal and Penny took some troops to the basement level, as per Agnes's parting advice before she'd left for New York. *"Basement bunkers make great secret stash rooms."* Thinking of Agnes made Penny's thoughts automatically take a hard turn straight into the brick wall of *Quentin.* She mashed down the surfacing guilt that she hadn't made any progress on repairing their relationship. *Deal with it later. Always later.*

Penny took out the guard's thumb that she'd acquired in their last raid and pressed it against the steel door's reader. Troxy security relied on the network and Patch connection, but since Agnes and Silas had fried that, good old-fashioned backup measures were in place—retina or fingerprint recognition. After a cheerful chirp, the door swung open.

"Told you it would be useful," she said to Mal. "And you thought I just wanted to keep a trophy." Behind his stony exterior, she could *feel* him wanting to roll his eyes, and she smirked.

Pushing through the door, an expansive space separated into glass-walled labs greeted them.

As did probably every remaining troxy in the building—soldiers and low-level employees guarded the goods. *No lab coats. Weird.*

Penny slung her volt rifle around as Mal took point, his booming voice filling the enclosed space. "Hands up, everyone. You won't be harmed as long as you listen to instructions." He jerked his head, and his soldiers flanked out.

Penny's finger itched on the trigger. Were these the same people who had pumped her little brother full of experimental drugs to turn him into one of their brainwashed, obedient super soldiers? Or were they just cogs in the machine, following orders? *Or are they like Agnes? Like Mal?* The same questions plagued her every time they raided a new facility and came face-to-face with the very people who aided in creating troxapine. *But not all of them did.* Some of them could be like Agnes, people who thought they were working for the betterment of society.

It was hard to separate them in her mind. Painting Pharmatrox as purely evil was easier. *Growing a fucking conscience is so* annoying. *And time-consuming.* Because it meant that she no longer felt good about spraying a room full of troxies—regardless of their job descriptions—with bullets and moving on. She had to give them a chance to defend themselves; it's what Quentin would want.

But if it came down to a choice between her life or theirs, she'd choose herself every time, conscience be damned.

The sound of cracking glass brought Penny back to herself, and she said to the nearest troxy, "Smash all the troxapine vials. The powdered dust, light it up." She nodded at the Bunsen burner. The guards didn't move, hands reaching for their weapons. Penny fired her volt rifle at the ceiling, and everyone jumped. "Now would be good." Some moved to obey, but many did not.

Suddenly, a tall woman lunged for a panic button on the underside of the lab table. Penny shot her dead between the eyes before she could reach it. The woman froze, volts sizzling through her hair, and slumped to the floor in a heap.

Mal made a disgruntled sound, but Penny ignored him. "No heroes here today," she said. "I do remember Mal telling you to follow directions. He's kind enough to extend some amnesty to you fuckers. You can join our cause, get on the next convoy heading to Canada, or take your chances in the Wilds. But if you stay and have thoughts of retaking the city..." Penny pressed her volt rifle to the nearest troxy's temple and stuck her knife under his chin, drawing blood. "I don't think I need to tell you what happens next."

"Enough." Mal's voice rumbled from behind her.

She sighed. "You asked me to help. This is me helping."

His eyes flashed and his jaw muscle did that jumpy thing that meant his temper was seconds from detonating. She kept a running tally of how many times she could make it happen in one day. Her record so far was twenty-two—the last time they'd discussed Rodney's cult.

Mal's troops rejoined them, ushering a group of troxies and carrying crates of supplies. "Any dionazole?" Penny asked. With the increased number of users they'd been treating, their detox serum supply was running low.

Sanjali, another of Mal's best, nodded. "Think so. We'll take stock later."

"Any scientists?" Penny asked. "Only grunts down here." They'd need a scientist willing to defect if they planned to make their own detox serum. But Sanjali shook her head. *Where the fuck did they all go?*

"We've already stayed too long," said Mal. "Reinforcements could be on their way."

But before they could take a step, all the lights blinked out.

Penny latched onto Mal's arm, digging her nails in. "What the fuck?"

The emergency red lights turned on, bathing the basement in an eerie, bloody glow.

Forcing the troxies to their knees, the Faction surrounded them, weapons trained into the dimness. Then the sound of a steel door slamming shut interrupted the silence.

"Everyone, to the exit," said Mal. "Penny, get your...thumb." He broke off with a grimace, and they hustled down the hall.

Where a line of Pharmatrox's elite super soldiers awaited them.

A beat of silence, then all hell broke loose.

Bullets and volts flew in all directions as Mal shoved Penny out of the way. She rolled across the cement, rebounding to her feet and sprinting for the steel door. Ducking a soldier who took a swing at her, she elbowed another aside as she lunged for the biometric scanner. Slapping the thumb on the reader, the door hissed open—to be blocked by a slim, strong figure. The darkness obscured the man's features, but from the way he sank into a fighting stance with ease, she could tell this was no ordinary troxy guard. And he was no super soldier either—in the dim red lighting, his dark eyes looked almost black, but the clean whites of his sclera reflected red. *Not even a user. Just a man.*

Faster than a blink, he swiped at her with a curved knife, catching her across the cheekbone, and she hissed. *A really fucking dangerous man.* Ducking his next strike, she whipped out her sickle, sidestepping his repeated attacks.

"Penny!"

At Mal's voice, both Penny and her attacker turned.

A ferocious look plastered on Mal's face as he charged the remaining distance to her. In the seconds before he reached them, she could have sworn she saw her attacker *smile*.

Plowing into the man, Mal drove him to the floor and they rolled, struggling for position. Forgoing his volt rifle, Mal let loose a barrage of heavy punches. She'd never seen him unleash such unbridled aggression, striking with everything he had. The man was smaller, but no less skilled or tough, as he blocked Mal's relentless blows in a calm and collected way that reeked of a trained predator biding his time...

Then she saw the flash of curved metal slide into her attacker's palm.

"Knife!" she shouted, and Mal rolled, landing a kick in the man's side that slid him a few feet away. Around them, the labs' glass walls shattered as their forces struggled to hold off the elite soldiers. "Time to go."

But Mal ignored her, rushing her attacker, who had coiled into a stance Penny recognized from her Muay Thai days. Mal never shied away from a fight, but he always knew when to walk away. But something in the way he fought like a rabid dog had alarm bells going off in her head.

As Mal let out a visceral cry of rage, Penny realized.

Mal knew him, this well-trained predator. And apparently, they didn't have a good history.

Before Mal threw himself back into the fray, she caught his wrist and pulled him into her—or as much as she could manage to, anyway—and fired some volts in the direction of Mal's friend. "Whoever the fuck that guy is, he isn't worth all of us dying down here. We're going. Now."

Mal snarled, his muscles tensing as he towered over her. A tightly wound spring ready to explode in any direction—even hers. But she wasn't afraid of the big, bad wolf. She *was* the big, bad wolf, and he needed to remember that. Grabbing his shirtfront, she hauled him down to her level and pressed her sickle to his throat. "*Malosi Olesa.* I said now."

He bared his teeth, but Sanjali's shouts and the shattering glass snapped him out of it. These troxy super soldiers would blow through them in no time, and Mal knew it too. With a growl, he shouted, "Everyone, upstairs."

Laying down cover fire, the Faction took their hostages out to meet the rest of their group.

But Mal's friend wouldn't give up so easily.

He sprinted after them, firing volts that caught some of their retreating people. Mal helped them up and shoved them through the steel door, turning to face him.

But Penny was having none of that.

"Get your ass upstairs," she said, shoving him. "I'll handle it."

Mal made another frustrated sound but gritted his teeth and actually listened to her.

She smiled to herself. *I will never let him live that one down.*

When all of their people were out, Penny fired into the super soldiers and Mal's friend, corralling them. After pulling a grenade from her belt, she tossed it inside. In the split second before shutting the door, she made eye contact with Mal's friend. Even though he was about to be blown up, his self-satisfied grin cut through the darkness, branding itself in her mind.

It was the look of a man who had been presented with exactly what he wanted.

As she slammed the heavy steel door shut and hit the scanner to lock it behind her, she knew they hadn't seen the last of him, whoever the fuck he was. She raced upstairs, a muffled boom sounding from below.

Outside, their ring of fire had nearly run out of fuel, and Raph had talked some of the guards into surrendering.

"Everyone out of the building?" she asked him.

"All present and accounted for."

"Excellent. Back to the stadium." Glancing behind her, she half expected that man to have escaped the locked basement somehow and come walking through the flames, but she shook off the eerie feeling.

Half of their forces escorted the troxies out of town, while the ones who elected to defect came with Penny and the rest. As they ran the few miles back to the stadium, Mal was a flinty presence beside her. After a few minutes, she said, "That man—"

"Don't." He kept his eyes glued forward.

"*You* don't. You're going to tell me everything about the shit show I just witnessed."

"There's nothing to tell."

"Oh? So you didn't just almost get us all killed while you were preoccupied with a personal fist fight?"

His jaw muscle jumped. *That's three for today already.* "I don't have to tell you anything."

"Whatever. The next time you want to risk our lives to dance with your little friend, I'm leaving you behind." His eyes flicked to hers in a glare. "You'd say the same to me." His glare intensified, and his jaw fluttered again. *I am on fire today.*

She'd let him keep his silence. For now. But something had compromised their general, and she intended to find out what the fuck had gotten under his unflappable skin.

2

"WE SHOULD BE ABLE to clear the whole city in another month or so," said Mal as he stood in the Faction's stadium headquarters war room, addressing his best soldiers for the post-battle debriefing.

As he spoke, Penny posted up in the corner, cleaning her nails with a knife, and tried not to look bored. She was just there because Mal got pissy when she wasn't. Something about her shirking her responsibilities or whatever. But after another goddamn panic attack had kept her up most of last night, she wasn't feeling up to being center stage—not that she felt like doing it on a good day either. Ever since finding out Quentin was alive, old memories and fresh guilt bubbled up, thrusting her back into the panic attacks that had driven her to using the dust in the first place. And now with the pressure building from all sides, the episodes happened more often, making a good night's sleep impossible.

And if I can't get control of my own damn mind, how am I supposed to lead an entire revolution? So she attended the meetings and went on the raids, but that was the extent of her involvement, and that was how she liked it. Mal, however, did not.

"Badass idea with the fire cage, Penny," said Will, a handsome Black man around her age and Mal's former inside guy at Pharmatrox who had now officially joined their ranks. Inclining her head with a slight smile, she went back to her knife work as Will settled back into his seat with a smug look.

Mal just glared at her—an expression she had grown used to. She arched an eyebrow in a challenge, but he clenched his teeth and moved on.

"Next order of business," he said. "Still no word from Kev, but reconnecting with him is a top priority. He has eyes on the inside at Pharmatrox, and besides getting his intel, we need to make sure he's holding strong in Chicago. So if anyone wants to pitch in on Silas's satcom projects when he gets back, we're taking volunteers. Speaking of, his team returns from New York tomorrow, hopefully with news about the troxies' last remaining lab and server farm. Next up, a resources rundown. Sanjali?" Mal stepped back, allowing the willowy Indian woman to take center stage.

"We're almost done retaking the armories, but the troxies are holding out in the north," Sanjali said. "They've stuffed themselves into the SubTran tunnels below the old subway system. Won't be getting in there easily. They've boarded up the surrounding stations and have security patrols, but that's all we could get close enough to see. So good fucking luck with that."

"Falling back to the SubTran station? Seems unlike them," said Will. "They tend to favor big fucking buildings like the Spire and the cathedral. The SubTran is plenty big, but...I don't know. Maybe I'm being paranoid."

His statement hung in the air for a charged moment. Because while Penny wanted to brush it off, they'd all noticed Pharmatrox's changing tactics. And Mal had too—he caught her eye, something strange in his expression. But then he nodded at Sanjali to continue her report.

"Taking stock of the armory, we have sufficient volt rifles and guns," said Sanjali. "The hangar has a few jets and drones, but not enough fuel to use them much—only in emergencies. Acquired an extra EV today. Battery is in good condition."

"Your assessment of what's most pressing?" asked Mal.

"EVs. With our limited fuel supply, those rechargeable batteries will be game changing. Also, more radios—they're so old and hard to find, but until Silas comes up with anything better, that's all we've got for short-range comms."

"Make those items a priority on your scouting missions," Mal said to the room. "Thanks, Sanj. Lawrence?"

The big man stood, chair scraping across the concrete. Instead of the tactical gear that everyone else wore, his flannel and worn jeans afforded him a more lumberjackian look. "The gardens are holding up. I yielded a good harvest before the weather took a turn, and the greenhouse should be enough to get us through any unpredictable polar cold snaps. I'll do my best, but I don't want to waste all of our generator power on the few UV lamps I managed to find."

"Let me know what you need, and I'll do my damndest to make sure you have it." The two men shared a nod, and Lawrence reclaimed his seat. Mal looked tired, more tired than she'd ever seen him. "Any questions before we close?" Blood and dirt from the battle coated all of them, and they were eager to wash. The gash on Penny's face from that fucker's curved blade had begun to sting.

"I have a few." A tan-skinned woman with piercing caramel eyes crossed her arms as she regarded her general. "Someone tried to stab me just outside our walls last night."

Ooh, this is getting good. Penny put her knife away and settled in to watch the show.

"That's not a question," said Mal, pressing his palms into the table-top—a stance he only took when he was aggravated. Penny had been a wallflower at enough meetings now to know.

"My *question*, sir, is what the fuck are you going to do about it? Could be those black-eye tattooed freaks are running around having too much of a good time. Seems to me we should be treating Rodney's scourge as an enemy to be dealt with, just like the troxies."

Someone's asking the right questions, finally.

"I'm sorry that happened to you and I'm glad you weren't harmed," Mal said. "But we don't have proof of the cult's involvement, and until we do, we can't spare the manpower to go hunting in the Wilds. I'll up the patrols and make sure everyone has extra ammo. That's all we can afford."

After a moment, the woman gave him a stiff nod.

"If there's nothing else, everyone, you're dismiss—"

"Boss?" Raph, who had been securing weapons in the armory, barged into the war room, eyes wide. "Early morning patrol reported back just now—but Tara's late. She's never late."

At that, Penny lurched forward. The ramifications of Tara being missing twisted her stomach into knots. *Quentin cannot know about this.* "Has anyone tried her radio?" she asked.

Raph shook his head. "Nothing."

Fuck. Rounding on Mal, she said, "We need to find her. You heard what—" *Shit, I don't know her name.*

"Lupe," said the woman who'd spoken up earlier.

"—what Lupe said. Rodney's cult is growing bolder, if they've up-graded from stealing shit to stabbing. Tara could be in danger."

But Sanjali was the one who replied, expression wary. "You haven't had a lot to say at these meetings before, Penny." To her dismay, Penny saw the distrust mirrored in some of the others. "Mal's right—we don't know what's going on out there. Makes more sense for it to be troxies attacking our perimeter rather than a bunch of strung-out users."

"Maybe Penny's onto something," Will piped up, ignoring Mal's icy stare. "She knows Rodney better than any of us."

"Eh, Penny was late coming back from patrol last week," noted one of the men. Penny didn't know his name either. "She's still here and kicking. Seems like she's looking for any reason to take off after Rodney's cult."

Yeah, kicking your ass is what I should be doing. She opened her mouth to say it, but Mal cut her off.

"Enough," he said. "Tara is smart and she can handle herself. She'll get back soon. In the meantime, we'll keep an eye out for anything strange. See you for afternoon training. Dismissed." Everyone filed outside, murmuring uneasily, and Mal's expression remained troubled.

When they were alone, Penny said, "A word?"

He hung back, sitting on the edge of the table, arms crossed and brow lowered. She stood toe to toe with him, but even sitting, he towered over her. It was irritating.

"Thanks for the support," he grumbled. "Really makes us look like a united front when the face of the Faction lurks in the corner and glares at me every two seconds."

"You want to argue about that again? Fine." With the adrenaline of the battle still zipping through her, Penny was more than ready for a fight.

Mal's jaw ticked as he gripped the edge of the table. "After taking out Rodney, you agreed to us sharing leadership responsibilities. But part of sharing leadership is actually fucking leading sometimes."

"Thought I was pretty fucking helpful today. Didn't see anyone else bringing you a thumb or coming up with fire cages."

As he ground his teeth, she could see him mentally counting to ten. While she'd pitched in today, she couldn't say that was always true. But even so, his words stung more than she wanted to admit. They only served to remind her just how much she'd failed as leader of the Marauders and how much she was not up to the task of fulfilling her new duties as the revolution's poster girl. So she resorted to doing what she did best—bashing some skulls and wreaking some havoc. Mal was better at the leadership bullshit—although she'd never admit it to him. He didn't need her help.

"Lupe made a good point," she added. "The point *I've* been trying to make with you for the past week now, but seems like she and Will are the only ones who agree."

"You can't take a back seat whenever you feel like it and then expect everyone to agree with you when you finally speak up." Mal ran a hand through his hair, damp with sweat and blood. He looked like a badass general in his weapons harness, covered in the gore of battle. *He* was the one who should be the revolution's mascot, the rallying cry for their people, especially looking like that. Not her. She tried not to linger too much on the way his muscles nearly popped out of his snug shirt. *Focus, you idiot.*

Penny prodded him in the chest and took pleasure in the fact that his frown deepened. "*The point*—if you're serious about establishing a safe zone between here and Chicago, we'll need to clear out the cult anyway, so no time like the fucking present."

Mal curled his big hand around her wrist and lowered it to her side with a dark look. "You're too close to this. Your past shit with Rodney is fucking with your head and giving you a loose trigger finger. If we want to win this war, we need to reclaim control of the city first—and that means taking the fight to the troxies' new SubTran hideout."

Her jaw hurt from how hard she clenched her teeth, but somehow, she refrained from sinking her nails into his eye sockets. Going off on him, while satisfying, would be unproductive. But she changed tactics—she had more questions that needed answers. "If you recall, I only shot *one* troxy in the head today, which is a new record for my self-control. And you're still alive, are you not? One of my bullets hasn't found its way into your skull yet, although I question my restraint every day. Speaking of personal vendettas, who the hell was that guy in the basement? You've been distracted ever since."

"He's no one."

"Well 'no one' sure knew how to get you seeing red. Sounds like somebody also has some bad beef that might be affecting his ability to assess a situation objectively."

"You want to talk about objectivity when you don't seem to care if you 'accidentally' shoot our hostages?" Mal's expression slammed shut. "Zeln is none of your business."

"Ah, so the bad beef has a name." Mal flinched at his slip up. "Who's Zeln?"

Rubbing a hand across his beard, he conceded with a sigh. "He's an excellent mercenary, and if he's training their troops or helping them strategize, we're in trouble."

"He's just one soldier. Taking out one person isn't going to turn the tide in this war. It didn't work with Dr. Hansen, and it won't work now."

Mal's forearms flexed as he clutched the edge of the table and said through gritted teeth, "He's not just another soldier."

"Until you're ready to give me some fucking proof that he's not, that's how we're treating him."

Mal's eyes scanned her face as if truly looking at her for the first time, and his expression softened. He raised a hand to brush his thumb across the crusted gash on her cheek. "You're hurt. Was it him?" Murder burned in his eyes, and she looked away with a weird-ass feeling, like her breath was catching in her throat or something stupid.

"I can take it."

His lips quirked like he wanted to smile. "I know you can. Doesn't mean I don't want to kill the bastard for hurting you."

What the fuck is that *about?* She didn't like the mishmash of feelings his protectiveness stirred within her. But before she could say anything else, he blew out a breath, pulling on the back of his neck with a stricken expression that she'd never seen from him before. It had the question flying out of her mouth before she could stop it. "What the hell did he do to you?"

He was silent for so long she thought he wouldn't answer. Finally, he said, "He's the reason I defected from Pharmatrox. Zeln is a dangerous man, Penny. Seeing him today, knowing he's working for them again—" He broke off with a shake of his head. "Many powerful people owe him for the horrific shit he's done for them. If he starts calling in those favors, we're fucked.

"And yeah, you might be right that the cult is behind the weird shit that's been happening. But we also don't know enough about Pharmatrox's current state to know what they're capable of. With our resources limited, we need to aim them in a direction we *know* is a pressing threat. Something is regrowing in the SubTran station, and we must contain it before it becomes more powerful and spreads. Especially now that Zeln is involved. Because if we leave it unchecked? We could very easily lose this war." Mal looked at her with a challenge in his eyes. "Tell me I'm wrong."

Penny folded her arms with a surly look. "If Zeln is Pharmatrox's newest consultant, that explains their changing tactics. But it doesn't mean we should go into the SubTran guns blazing. We're doing well reclaiming the Capital, but we're not ready for that fight—you heard Sanjali. Don't let your past shit with Zeln cloud your judgment. And why didn't you bring any of this up in the meeting?"

"I'm still...processing."

Man, Zeln really has him fucked up.

"Rodney's cult, if left unchecked, could also be a huge problem," she said. "Just look at what happened with Rodney himself when we left him to his own devices. We know what inaction will cost us."

Mal exhaled in a gust, running a hand across his face. "We won't solve all of this today. Let's regroup tomorrow when Silas, Derek, and Agnes return from New York."

"I wish Derek was here to take my side. He loves ganging up on you," she said. But she let it drop for now.

"Until he gets back, looks like we're doing things my way."

"Every inch of that sentence makes me sick."

"Fine. Doing things *our* way—and that means you have to stop being argumentative just to annoy me."

With a saccharine smile, Penny said, "Who says I can't do both?"

3

Agnes

B EHIND AGNES, THE OFFICE exploded into a blazing inferno billowing through the hallway. She joined the throngs of troxies screaming and running for cover, the emergency alarms bleating over the din, as she scanned for the doorway she wanted.

There.

"Little bit too enthusiastic with the C4 there, don't ya think?" she breathed into her compact radio, dipping her head as she passed some guards. Nobody in the New York Pharmatrox facility would recognize her, but she didn't want to take any chances of running into an old coworker or something.

Derek's chuckle crackled through her earpiece. "Quentin would say there's no such thing as too many fireworks."

"Quentin has taken on his sister's propensity for dramatics. We barely survived his last experiment with tear gas bottle rockets."

"There's still time. I'm sure he'll blow us all up eventually."

She stifled her laughter. "Quiet. I'm supposed to be a panicked janitor. Si, I'll let you know if I find anything."

"Roger dodger," came Silas's voice through her comms.

Agnes clicked it off with a slight smile, grateful to have her best friend back, and approached the door labeled Experimental Pharmaceuticals.

More people flooded outside to evacuate—but none of them wore the telltale white scientists' lab coat. *Where have they all gone?*

"Wrong way!" a middle-aged woman yelled, elbowing past.

"Forgot my—" But the woman had already disappeared into the crowd. She slipped inside Evie's old office, the lab ransacked and fallen into disarray, much like the crumbling remains of the rest of the building. More than half of it had fallen during the Red Riots, and Agnes had—wrongly, she now knew—assumed the troxies would have consolidated their power in the heart of the only city still under Containment. But glancing around the wrecked EP wing, it was obvious that any insight she thought she'd had into Pharmatrox's power structure was completely incorrect.

And that was very bad news. Because it meant they were all flying blind with no idea what their enemy was up to.

After the few stragglers evacuated—*IT guy, a few managers, but no scientists. Mierda.* Agnes was alone. Approaching the lab table where a picture of her, Evie, and Silas was pinned to the wall, she ripped through Evie's already tossed drawers. They didn't hold anything of interest, but she dumped the leftover notebooks into her pack anyway. Silas might want his sister's possessions. But one of the drawers was biometrically protected and untouched.

Allí está.

Forgoing stealth since the room was already in shambles, she fired a couple rounds into the lock, and the drawer hissed open. A few holofiles and a digital notepad stared back at her, which she zipped away to take a crack at later. While Derek gathered whatever equipment he could stuff into his pack from Agnes's old lab and Silas rooted around the building's security grid to find Pharmatrox's server farm, she was rifling through Evie's office looking for detox serum or clues.

Somehow, the troxies were still making troxapine—the dust—even though Agnes had taken down the network, which was the national internet and the lifeblood of Pharmatrox's operations. Without the network, the labs were defunct and unable to access Pharmatrox servers, share data, or distribute orders. Or so she thought. But according to Faction splinter group reports, an increased number of users were packing the cities, which meant more turned too, since there wasn't enough detox serum to rehabilitate everyone.

For the troxies to be infecting people against their will en masse again, at least one lab was still active and had an emergency distribution process with direct access to Pharmatrox's server farm—which is why Agnes had made a case to come back to New York, the troxies' most organized remaining bastion of power on the Eastern Seaboard. If they did have a backup lab and a server farm, it could be here.

But the more of the rundown building she saw, the more she realized she might have gravely miscalculated.

Refocusing on her search for clues, Agnes picked through the remainder of the encrypted digital notebooks and holofiles—rudimentary digital filing backups. They were similar to a USB drive of the past but with data projection capabilities and only accessible by the person who held them. Between her and some troxy defectors, they could probably piece together what EP was working on. Hacking, coding, building machines, she could do. But creating a pharmaceutical like detox serum? That was beyond her expertise. In all of the labs they'd cleared, they'd yet to come across any scientific personnel. So either people were lying about their professions—which was possible—or something had happened to all of them.

I don't much care for the implications of that.

As a Hail Mary, Agnes had a hairbrained plan to modify her DNA editing machine she'd built for Pharmatrox to run simulations for detox serum formulas instead. That way, she could find the recipe and make the damn stuff herself. But that would also require hijacking a Pharmatrox lab, and she'd still need a scientist. With each empty drawer she opened, it was looking more and more like her wild Plan B was becoming the primary option, which didn't bode well.

Sighing, she zipped up her pack. *No detox serum here.* At this point, it was time to abandon this sinking ship. After snagging the photo from Evie's desk, Agnes pocketed it, then headed for the exit. She flicked on her comms and said, "I'm done. Meet you at the rendezvous."

The alarms continued blaring as she stepped into the hallway, where black-armored guards cleared each room. She turned heel and hurried away.

"You there! What are you still doing here?"

Joder. Agnes contorted her face into a panicked look and threw herself at the guard. "Oh thank god!" she said in a breathy voice. "I heard an explosion, and then I got lost. I'm new and this place is a maze, and I didn't know what to do, so I—"

"Okay, okay." The guard cut her off, looking equally as panicked at the thought of dealing with her hysterics. "Exit that way, and be quick about it."

"Thank you!" *Idiot.* She filed down the stairs to the underground garage level, where Derek and Silas awaited her crouching behind one of the transport vans. Flashing a smile, she said, "Nothing like the damsel in distress act—either makes them super uncomfortable or makes me appear less of a threat before I stab them. Either way, I win."

Derek laughed and dropped a quick kiss on her cheek. "Nice work."

Silas nodded toward the exit ramp at some armed guards. "That damsel in distress thing might come in handy."

"Don't need it," said Agnes, unlocking the nearest van with her Pharmatrox ID so they could climb inside. "Not if we just blow the checkpoint." Derek sat in the driver's seat and inserted her ID to start the engine, Silas and Agnes on the bench seat beside him. "We already blew up an office. Why bother sneaking out now?"

At the sound of the van starting, the guards turned in a chorus of shouts as Derek gunned the engine, heading straight for the ramp. Troxies fired at them as they roared past, volts shattering the windows. Agnes grabbed the rifle and climbed into the back seat, firing through the broken window. "Head for Lincoln Tunnel," she said. "Should be able to make it before they shut it down. Silas, cover us from the other side."

He'd been getting better with target practice, and he scrambled into position. "They're getting into vans!"

Derek cursed as he whipped around a sharp turn to avoid an oncoming troxy convoy.

"How much farther?" she asked, blasting more guards as Derek maneuvered them past Madison Square Garden.

"Few more blocks." He bounced the van over a curb and sped down an alley, sirens sounding in their wake. After a few more convoluted turns, the mouth of Lincoln Tunnel came into view. Rows of sandbags, fencing, and a slew of armed guards separated them from their escape route. "Ready with the tear gas?"

"Ready," said Silas, tossing several canisters at the guards. A few seconds later, noxious white smoke poured out just as the convoy screeched around the corner.

Derek plowed through the barricade, the windshield cracking from the impact, and drove straight through the guards. The remaining ones leapt for their own vehicles as they all blazed down the tunnel.

Agnes threw open the double doors at the back to get a better angle while Silas let loose the tire spikes hidden in his pack—another of Quentin's inventions for their trip, fashioned from nails and PVC pipe. The pursuing vehicles dodged, but some hit the tire spikes dead on, the rubber shredding on impact.

"Are we past it yet?" asked Agnes as she swapped out her volt rifle for a handgun to shoot out their tires.

"It's just up there, maybe a hundred feet," said Silas. In response, Derek pushed the engine faster. At the end of the tunnel, another line of troxy vehicles awaited them. A few seconds later, Silas said, "Now!" and pushed a button on a device in his belt.

A booming explosion ripped through the air, the ceiling of the tunnel collapsing behind them as they drove into the daylight and blasted through the last line of troxies, burying their pursuers in rubble. With any luck, the river would reclaim the tunnel and render one of the main thoroughfares into the city permanently sealed.

Derek gave a low whistle, a relieved laugh escaping him. "Where the hell did you get that much C4?"

"Penny gave it to me," said Silas, climbing into the front seat. "They found it in one of the armories last week. She thought we might find use for it on our trip."

After shutting the back doors, Agnes settled in beside Derek, and he slid a warm hand onto her thigh. "How long did it take you to set that up?" she asked Silas.

"Did it last night during the watch change. Easy. Except for the part where I almost got caught four times. Had to keep ducking back into the maintenance hallway every time a troxy drove by. So what's the verdict?"

Agnes sighed and shook out her bleach-tipped black locks. Once her hair got to chin length in another month or so, she planned to cut off the rest of the dye and go back to her natural hair. She passed her bag to Silas, and he sorted through the items she'd collected. "That wasn't their main troxapine production lab like we'd hoped."

Derek gave her thigh a squeeze. "We'll find it, Agnes."

She smiled at his use of her true name instead of Stella. "What about you guys?" she asked. "Find anything I can use to mod my DNA editing machine?" She *really* wanted an FPGA, a type of circuit that could be repeatedly reprogrammed and reconfigured to fit any of her needs. Without it, or something damn near close to it, her new machine would never work.

Derek shook his head. "Just some junky old lab equipment, but I did pull out some of the circuit boards. Dunno if they're useful or not."

"I can sort through it later," she said. "Thanks."

"Server farm wasn't there either," Silas said. "I checked the building's power grid and nothing was pulling enough energy to run something like that. Wherever their backup files are housed, it would need a reliable energy source, whether it's a generator or a direct pull from the grid, hydroelectric power, something like that."

"Makes sense they'd have their backup troxapine lab in the same place too," she said. "So New York is off the list, but that doesn't narrow it down much. Could be in any coastal city, or even near a large river."

As they headed south to the Capital, Agnes noticed a huge cargo ship docked at Port Newark. She poked Derek and pointed. "That's how they're able to keep New York functioning," she said. "But where are the supply boats coming from? Who would agree to work with them? Surely the world knows by now what they've done to our country."

Silas's frown matched Derek's. "With the network and all central comms down, I have no idea what propaganda they're blasting to the rest of the world. They've fallen back on the rudimentary radio comms just like us, but when we get back to the Capital, I'll try getting into the satellites again. That has to be how they're communicating with the outside world." He rubbed the stubble on his chin and stared out the window with a melancholy expression.

Agnes rested her head on his shoulder. "I'm sorry we didn't find Ivan," she said.

"It was a long shot," Silas said, patting her shoulder. "Wherever my guy is, I hope he's safe."

Derek's hand tightened around Agnes's leg, as if to assure himself that she was still there, and she planted a kiss to his shoulder. "Let's hope they had better luck back home," she said.

4

"Looser wrist," Penny explained as she threw a knife at the plywood target, lodging it home dead center. "Remember how Silas does it?"

Quentin moved his arm in a few practice throws as he held the knife by the hilt, tongue wedged between his teeth. "He always misses."

"Yeah, don't do it like him."

A quick smile flashed across his face but vanished in an instant. Penny frowned. She always caught Quentin doing that around her—censoring himself. But she didn't blame him. The fact he was even talking to her after…after everything was a miracle. Behaving like her old self around him had felt fake—the old Penelope didn't fit her anymore, but the specter of Penny that she'd created to handle her grief after the fire also felt wrong. She wasn't sure who she was now, but she knew for damn sure that she was a sister who missed her little brother.

For now, that would have to be enough.

From the other side of the stadium's field, Mal barked instructions at his soldiers as he ran through the afternoon's training exercises—weapons drills, sparring, and leg sweeps. Even though they'd already done a lab raid that morning, Mal ran a tight ship and never canceled sessions. When his gaze snagged on hers, his expression sharpened. She knew he would have some choice words for her later about how she'd sidelined herself again to work one-on-one with Quentin instead of leading group training like he'd wanted her to. It hadn't been the first time he'd suggested her taking over his training duties as a way to get to know their people better, and it hadn't been the first time she'd refused.

She didn't know the first thing about fighting in formation or any other military protocol. But that wasn't her only reason for declining—the idea of training people again made her think of her Marauders and the level of debauchery and heinous acts she'd allowed—even encouraged. No, putting her in charge of training was a bad idea. The kind of knowledge she had to share had no place in Mal's spick and span army.

But when Quentin had expressed an interest in wanting to learn hand-to-hand combat, she'd jumped at the chance to show him a few things and made a point to attend some of Mal's sessions. Training came more naturally to her than strategizing and chumming around with the troops anyway. Since the battle at the cathedral, her relationship with Quentin had been stiff and formal, so she hoped a shared interest would break the ice.

To her delight, Quentin had become a steadfast student. He maintained strict daily attendance and listened to her instructions with rapt attention, and he'd made great strides in just a few weeks. Throwing knives still evaded him, but he never gave up. He always stuck around well past the lunch or dinner bell to practice with her. Something about that made Penny smile.

"How many practice swings are you gonna take, Quent?" asked Mal as he approached, done with his session. Other Faction members milled about the field, practicing various leg sweep techniques they'd reviewed. "Gotta throw it sometime."

Quentin beamed at his big bulky hero. Bristling, Penny tossed another knife, sinking it into the target.

"I can't get the spin quite right," said Quentin, frowning at the bullseye. "Always end up hitting the target with the knife's butt. Or the flat of the blade so it just splats against the plywood like a plate of spaghetti."

That surprised a laugh out of Penny. She'd forgotten his quirky sense of humor. He gave her a half smile and raised the knife again.

"Try a tighter flick right as you're about to release," Penny suggested.

Quentin nodded and let the knife fly. It flew end over end—

And hit point-first at the bottom of the plywood, twelve inches below the target.

"Yes!" Quentin said, punching at the sky. "Finally!"

Mal rumbled a laugh, clapping Quentin on the shoulder. "Not bad."

"Good one," agreed Penny with a spark of pride.

"Now I just need to get the troxies to lay down first before I attack them," Quentin said. "Maybe I could run through them with a clothesline."

"I'm sure you could invent something that would do the trick," said Penny, slipping her extra knives into her belt.

Quentin's smile was full and genuine this time. "Can't wait for Stel—Agnes to get back. I want to know how my tire spikes worked."

As he jogged off to reclaim his errant knives, Penny's heart ached. She remembered when he used to be that excited to see *her* return home. *I'll get us back there.* Before the melancholy thoughts could pull her under, Mal's shadow fell across her, and she frowned.

"Still only offering personal training sessions?" he asked as he watched Quentin organizing his collection of mismatched knives.

Penny shrugged, busying herself gathering her weaponry. "He wanted to learn, so I'm teaching him."

"There's an entire stadium of people who want to learn. From you."

Scoffing, she shoved a knife in her belt as some people filed past heading to lunch, darting curious glances at her and Mal. "Seems like you're doing just fine without me."

Mal blew out a breath, tucking his massive hands in his pockets. "Arguing like this, especially in front of the troops, isn't instilling a lot of faith in our partnership. We won't get anywhere if you and I can't figure out how to work together."

"What do you suggest? I'm not hosting any campfire sing-alongs, so you can shove that idea in your suggestion box and burn it."

Mal drew himself up to his full height. She wanted to kick him in the fucking shins when he pulled that shit. "You could start with leading some training sessions. Maybe then you'd actually garner some support for your theories in the war room debriefings." He broke off with a frustrated grumble and turned a softer gaze to hers. "You're skilled and you have good ideas, Penny. I only lead this stuff because you refuse to and someone has to do it. But a lot of people doubt me and Will and others like us because we're from the troxy army. It's my association with *you* that is lending me any legitimacy. You're the one who took out Rodney, killed the Leader, and played a major role in winning the battles at the cathedral and the Spire. Add to that the fact that you're the only one who's ever quit the dust without taking detox serum and lived to tell about it—to them, you're not just a hero, you're a living legend."

Penny gave a harsh laugh. *Is he fucking joking?* "I'm not even in the same universe as those titles." The urge to pace like a caged animal came over her, but she held her ground. No need for him to know how unsettled she was. But not just unsettled—*afraid.* What if she took charge and royally fucked things up? What if she lost all of her people again, like she had with the Marauders? She hadn't really cared about them, so it didn't matter that they were dead. But now...her gaze lingered on Quentin. Now, she had a lot to lose.

At her thoughts, her chest tightened and her breaths began to wheeze. *Fucking hell. Not now.* Swallowing the familiar swelling feeling, she returned her attention to Mal. "I'm not leading the debriefings or the training, so stop asking. In case it isn't fucking obvious, I'm not exactly a people person. But if you want me to challenge you during meetings, that I can keep doing."

"I didn't say *challenge*—"

"Any sign of Tara?" Lawrence asked as he jogged across the field, throwing a wave to Quentin, who gave him a tiny salute and skipped over to join them.

Goddamn it. Penny made ixnay motions at Lawrence.

Quentin's eyes widened. "Is Tara okay?"

"Er—yeah," said Lawrence with a completely guilty look on his face. "She's...due back any time now."

Penny groaned internally. *Nice save, moron.*

Quentin turned a questioning gaze to Mal. Something about him defaulting to Mal and not her did funny things to her insides. "She's okay?" he repeated.

Mal looked to Penny before answering, and she didn't like the expression on his face. He looked guilty too. "She's running a little late coming back from a job," he said. "It's nothing to worry about."

Quentin straightened his newly acquired weapons belt—a parting gift from Derek—and puffed up his chest. "I want to look for her."

Penny glared daggers into Mal from behind Quentin's back, *I will murder you if you say yes* written all over her face, but he wasn't looking at her.

"Lawrence has a watch rotation later today after we get back from the evening armory run. You can join him. I'll go too," Mal said.

Fingers of apprehension tightened around her throat, stealing her breath. *Mal is fucking dead meat.*

"Actually," Penny said, forcing her voice to remain in the same octave and not sound panicked, "Tara had you working on some weapons mods before she left, right? Sounded kind of urgent." She mashed Lawrence's foot beside her with her own.

"Ow—yes! Yes, Penny is right," said Lawrence. "Tara will be really happy if you had a new toy for her to play with when she's back."

Quentin folded his arms and rolled his eyes, looking every inch the moody teenager. "I'm not a child, you guys. I know you don't want me to go. But it's fine. I'll work on Tara's project."

Penny hated disappointing him, but the thought of him going into the Wilds, even with Lawrence, Mal, and a band of soldiers was enough to make her tachycardic. Quentin was her responsibility. She'd be damned if she would be the one sending him off to be snacked on by turned—or worse. The budding anxiety hollowed out her chest, but she pushed the feeling down. *Just a few more minutes, then I can detonate in private.*

Mal, shockingly, was the one to save the day. "Hey, I could use a hand too with making more firecracker distractions for the patrols heading out tomorrow. Think you could do that for me?"

At that, Quentin brightened. "Sure, Mal."

Clapping him on the back, Mal said, "Good man. Get to it."

Quentin scampered into the locker room, eager to get to work.

Before she could open her mouth to let loose a string of curses at Mal for suggesting Quentin go out into the Wilds, Will approached, completely ignoring Mal and Lawrence. To her, he said, "Hey, Penny. I know you're kick-ass at Muay Thai, and I was hoping you could help me with my standup game. I don't think I've got my feet right when I do my sweeps."

Penny lifted an eyebrow. He'd flawlessly executed the sweep numerous times during previous training sessions that she'd actually attended, so she knew he didn't need help. Will flashed her an admittedly dazzling smile. Between that and his athletic build, the guy had every woman in their camp lusting after him. Penny understood why.

"Would you mind showing me?" he asked.

Before she could answer, Mal kicked Will's legs out from under him, catching his arm at the last second and yanking him back to his feet. "Any other questions, William?" he asked, hand clamped tighter than necessary around his friend's forearm.

At the exchange, Penny's eyebrow hoisted even higher. *What the hell is all of this male posturing about?*

Will laughed it off. "Yeah, okay. See you around, Penny." He waved and shot her another million-dollar smile before heading off, Mal's thunderous expression following him all the way to the locker room.

"You all right, Mal?" asked Lawrence. "Should I get a suture kit on standby for that vein in your temple that looks ready to explode?"

"I'm fine," Mal said through his teeth.

He's been on edge ever since he saw that Zeln guy. That has to be it.

Lawrence nodded at a cluster of newer recruits from across the field, who were nudging each other. "Looks like Will's not the only one who wants the attention of the woman who took down Rodney and the Leader."

Penny blanched. *I can't take any more of this fan club shit.* "See you gentlemen around," she said with what she hoped was an appreciative smile at Lawrence. He nodded but didn't return it, and she couldn't blame him for his wary treatment. But she didn't have time to worry about everyone's opinion of her, not when the panic was inches away from clawing through her thin veneer of normalcy. Before either of them could respond, she stalked across the field and through the main exit. By the time she made it inside, the cold sweats and shakes had already begun.

Shit. I'll never make it to my room in time.

Ducking into a side alcove, she huddled in the shadows to ride out the worst of her panic attack away from prying eyes. While her heart pounded against her ribcage, she hugged her knees into her chest. Squeezing her eyes shut, she tried not to let her thoughts spiral into rock bottom, but that was the thing. She spent most of her days a half step away from rock bottom. A desire for the dust shot through her, quick and bright, as always happened during these attacks, but she quashed it. Troxapine would not help—it was what had caused her life to fall apart in the first place.

But a few seconds later, the sound of heavy boots clomping down the hallway had her lurching to her feet, hand braced on the wall. *They can't see me like this.* She knew the panic attacks didn't mean she was weak, but she couldn't help but *feel* weak when her own fucking mind had her sweating and shaking on the floor.

When Mal appeared, she wanted to dissolve into the cinder blocks. As he took her in, his face creased with concern, and that about sent her through the floor. *I do not deserve his worry.* And so she reached for that comfortable, familiar companion: rage. Knotting her hand in the front of Mal's shirt, she pulled him deeper into the alcove and launched her scathing attack. "What the hell? Telling Quentin it's fine if he goes running around in the woods with a murderous cult and whatever else on the loose?"

Mal held up both hands, his concern shifting to wariness. "I would have been with him the whole time. And he's getting to be of an age where he can make his own decisions."

"That's not the point," she said, digging her nails into his chest, but the panic still had her in its grip. "It's not safe out there. Rodney's people could take him. Rodney—" She choked on the end of her sentence, her breaths coming in fast wheezes.

Rodney had taken so much of her humanity already, and to think of him reaching for Quentin, for her whole heart, from beyond the grave with his maniacal band of followers… It was too much to take. She couldn't be the cause of someone else she loved getting hurt. The faces of her parents, of her partner at the insurance firm, Lexa, looped through her mind on repeat. A high-pitch whirring sounded in her ears, only for her.

Shit. Not here. Not in front of him.

"Penny." Mal's voice anchored her somersaulting mind to the present, his hands finding either side of her face, thumbs tracing circles against her skin. "Pen, look at me."

Her darting eyes finally came to rest on his. *Sun-warmed whiskey. Tanned oak. Toasted walnuts.* Naming all of the colors in his eyes further grounded her in the moment, but her chest continued heaving.

"Deep breaths with me," he said, thumbs sweeping her face in their soft, rhythmic patterns. She took a long inhale with him, then they released the breath together. A few more slowed her runaway breaths enough for her to notice the weight of Mal's gaze and the intensity burning behind it. "Rodney is dead. You made sure of that. He can't hurt you or anyone else. You hear me?" He waited for her to nod before continuing. "And I'd never let anything happen to Quentin. You know that. He's safe with me." Another sweep of his thumb, this time just shy of her lower lip. "You both are."

Something in Penny cringed away from those words. Not about Quentin—she really did trust Mal with his safety. But about that sentiment for *herself*. Did she truly deserve to feel safe, or a sense of peace and belonging after everything she'd done? And not just the things she'd done since starting the dust. The long-lost horrors of her past zinged through her mind, jabbing straight to the heart of all the unsightly truths she held about herself. *Lexa.* She flinched. A name and a life she'd buried so deeply. But with every step forward, the memories of her mistakes with Lexa rippled to the surface. Add to that all of the shit she'd done in the past ten months, she deserved her own personal circle of hell. Certainly not the protection of this man, or of anyone else.

The closer she got to people like Agnes and Mal, the more the blood on her hands shone red. She never used to regret any of the blood she'd spilled since the Beginning. In her mind at the time, all of her kills had been justified. Deaths in pursuit of her goal of finding the Architect, of ridding the world of troxy influence. But now...now she doubted herself. Her past motivations. The whispers of the dead taunted her when she lay awake at night, staring into the darkness, longing to forget, to be someone else. To be a person who hadn't caused the murder of her best friend, who hadn't killed her own parents. To be the sister that Quentin deserved.

But did she deserve to be that person now? Would she ever?

"Penny, are you with me?" Mal's voice pulled her out of her reverie, and she blinked. He held her close, his breath tickling her lashes and the warmth of his hands on her face warding off the slight chill of the mild nearly winter air.

"I'm with you," she said, taking a half step back as a wave of goose bumps rushed over her. Mal let his hands fall, but regarded her with a watchful expression. "Aren't we heading to the armory across town soon? I should get my things." She moved past him, but he caught her by the wrist, his throat working as he searched for the right words.

"I have them too," he finally said. "Panic attacks. Nightmares. All of it." He gave her wrist a squeeze, then released. "If you ever want to talk…"

She dipped her head, uncomfortable with this man seeing right through to the dark core of her, to the ugly epicenter that she hid from the world, and offering her *compassion*. She didn't want it. Couldn't accept it. "I'll meet you out front."

But as she hurried away, a small, hidden part of her longed to stand bare before him, to spill every gruesome thing she'd ever done, every ugly thought she'd ever had. Because that small, hidden part of her wondered if he might be the only man who could truly *see her* and not run screaming in the opposite direction.

5

An hour later, Penny went with Mal and a group of Faction soldiers to the armory in Sector 9. She longed for the feeling of doing something useful; it was the only thing that helped her recover after one of her attacks. Busy hands kept her mind from wandering to dark places—and now, forbidden ones. She gulped as she thought of her encounter with Mal earlier. She'd never known the man could be so gentle. *Don't kid yourself. Of course you did.*

Vivid recollections of when she'd sustained her injury at the cathedral and of the way he'd remained at her side had taken up permanent residence in the secret compartments of her heart. And now he'd seen her in another of her most vulnerable moments and met her not only without judgment but with fucking *kindness*… If he kept that shit up, that secret space would be seeing the light of day more often. And Penny wasn't sure if it was something she wanted or not. Or was even ready for.

What am I even talking about? He's my general and we're in the middle of a fucking war. We have to stay focused. And it's Mal, for fuck's sake. There's nothing there.

Returning to the task at hand, Penny surveyed the street for danger. As they picked their way through the abandoned battlefront they'd only just reclaimed a week ago, the stocky concrete buildings shielded them from the mild November wind. In a world succumbing to global

"Let's take this shit to the troxies' doorstep," he said. "Everyone! Let's go."

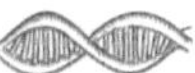

When their crew made it back to the stadium a few hours later, coated in the grime of battle, Mal directed them to the infirmary before disappearing. Miraculously, no one had died in the ambush, but many had sustained more than superficial injuries.

Penny was fine, but she was pissed. And—she didn't want to admit it—also fucking terrified.

She'd had her own turned army of sorts once but never had any real control over them. Dust and blood could point them in a given direction, but she didn't even know if they could reason or listen. But these new turned—they *listened*. They were a different breed. A new Pharmatrox creation. Something the Faction was unprepared to deal with—a true army of creatures that could be controlled, maybe even obey orders. That was somehow more frightening than brainwashed elite super soldiers on drugs. And with their forces combined? It could turn the tide of the war against the Faction.

In essence, a big fucking problem.

And how is Pharmatrox able to pull this off anyway? We cut off its head at the Spire.

But Penny knew the answer.

The hydra's head was regrowing.

Buzzing with buckets of emotions she didn't have time to process, Penny stormed down the hallway, ready to unleash her maelstrom in the direction that most deserved it: Mal's.

Turning the corner, she ran straight into Quentin, whose mouth popped open as he took in her bloody and disheveled appearance. "Penelope? What happened?"

Without thinking, she pulled him into a hug, needing to feel that he was breathing and alive and *safe. What if Quentin had been there today?* The thought skipped like a broken record through her mind. Then she pulled away, collecting herself as he studied her with an expression older than his years.

After a few moments, he said, "Agnes would come home like this sometimes. Before we started doing regular raids together, she'd say she had just gone out for a nice walk. She never wanted me to worry. Or worse, she never wanted me to *want* to join her. So, is that what you were out doing? Taking a nice walk?" He crossed his arms, and she didn't miss the unspoken challenge in his voice: *Will you try and keep me separate from this part of your life too?*

The words caught in her throat. "It's dangerous out there, Quentin. Even *I* feel unprepared to deal with it. I—" She broke off, clearing the emotion out of her throat. "I need to protect you from this."

Quentin shook his head, brushing past her, and her heart clenched. *I've disappointed him. Again.*

"At least Agnes finally realized that I don't need or want to be protected. I *want* to help." He walked away before she could call him back.

I never say the right things. But the thought of him facing off against literal demons had her stomach tying itself in knots. *He's at the center of this war now because of me. Because of what I did to our parents, he feels the need to play a role in every battle.*

By the time she reached Mal's room, she was supremely on edge, pushing the door open so it banged into the wall with a crack.

But when she saw Mal's bloody shirt plastered to his side, her steps faltered.

"Here to yell at me some more?" he said, fussing with some bandages in his locker.

Every angry word she'd prepared spilled out of her head as she took in the sight of him standing in the dim lighting of a camping lantern. *Shit, that's a lot of blood.* With an aggravated sound, she elbowed him aside. "You're getting the bandages all bloody. Shut up and sit down."

Instead, Mal leaned against the nearby table, and she grumbled. *Figures.* "Show me," she said, hooking a stool with her foot and sitting in front of him, ignoring the way he towered over her.

Black and red blood mixed on his brown skin, and she was sure she looked equally a mess. His mouth set in a grim line, and he refused to meet her accusatory gaze as he rolled up his shirt, exposing a bloody rent in his miles of muscle.

"You need stitches," she said, examining his wound, the scars from his years as a warrior slashing across his...admittedly impressive torso.

He shifted away. "I can do it."

"Yeah? How you gonna see it with your massive pec in the way? Don't be an idiot." Busying herself with the medical kit, she started on the stitches and kept her eyes glued to her work. Agnes had taught her a few things, so she could at least keep him from bleeding to death. After a few minutes of tense silence, she asked, "What happened today?"

"I fucked up. I know that. We don't need to have this discussion."

"No?" she said, yanking on a stitch, but he didn't even flinch. "Sure seems like it. This is exactly why I don't want Quentin going out there. What if he'd been with us today?" That skipping refrain took up presence in her mind again, threatening to spin her off in all kinds of catastrophic directions.

Guilt passed across his face before he smoothed it away, and he nodded to her needle. "Almost done?"

Biting her lip to keep from whirling into another panic, she tied off her work and affixed a bandage with quaking fingers. When she was done, Mal covered her hand with his, and her throat clicked in a dry swallow as she looked up at him, surprised at what she saw there. Anguish, tightening the lines around his eyes. "I'm sorry," he said. "It won't happen again."

He'd never apologized to her before, but there was no doubt he truly meant it. She gave a stiff nod and pushed her stool back, but he stopped her with a hand cupping her cheek. Her heart kickstarted against her ribcage, stealing her thoughts. This was the third time he'd touched her like this recently. What the hell was going on with him? And what the hell was going on with *her* that she didn't mind the feeling of his hands on her?

Brushing a thumb along her jaw, he said, "Thanks for fixing me up."

When she found her voice a few seconds later, she said, "I thought you said we shouldn't be 'involved' with each other." *Christ, where did that come from?*

At her words, he moved away, expression shuttered. It was the first time either of them had acknowledged their conversation a month ago, and she wasn't sure why she said it, only that his touch apparently made her lose all intelligence. But beneath the surface, a dark feeling churned within her. *Unworthy.* Detective Lexa Green's face flashed in her mind, reminding her that anyone who got close to her—friend, family, or otherwise—got hurt. And so she had reached for the protection of deflection.

"Yeah, I did," Mal said finally. "And I meant it." But that muscle in his jaw flicked, as if he had wanted to say something else. *Well that's not confusing at all.* His contradictory behavior sparked her temper because it highlighted her own conflicting feelings. Half the time she couldn't decide if she wanted to fight him or fuck him, and in that moment, she wanted to make *him* the uncomfortable and floundering one for once. So she took a bludgeon to the solid walls of his control.

"Kind of hard to tell what you mean when you bit Will's head off for talking to me. Lawrence seemed to think you were staking your claim."

"You are not anyone's to claim," he said. *Well, shit. That was a good answer.* And one that left her feeling even more confused than before. "And I'm not jealous of Will." But his nostrils flaring as he said Will's name gave him away.

"It isn't as though I have much time to carouse with him or anyone else. Or hadn't you noticed we're in the middle of a war?" More ice water on whatever was brewing between them. Mal made a sound of agreement and pushed away from the table, his mouth dipping into a frown. "I don't want Will," she felt compelled to add, for some fucking reason. *So much for making* him *the uncomfortable one.*

Mal didn't respond, but the tense lines of his shoulders relaxed slightly. *So it actually bothered him that he thought I was interested in Will?* Again, Penny didn't know what to do with that information. As he turned away to pull his shirt down, she noticed an angry scar on the upper part of his back near his shoulder. She reached out, but snatched her hand back, and he raised an eyebrow as he tucked in his shirt.

"You have many scars," she said, groaning internally. *What an astute observation, you absolute fucking doorknob.* After everything that had happened today, her brain felt like scrambled eggs. But at least she'd succeeded in changing the subject.

"Hazards of the job," he said, rubbing a hand over the old wound.

She ignored the way his arm flexed as he reached for it and noticed instead how his expression clouded. *More than one kind of past wound, maybe.*

"Is Zeln one of those hazards?"

Mal clenched his hand into a white-knuckled fist. "Something like that."

When it was clear that was all he had to say on the matter, she moved on to more pressing issues. "So about what happened with those...enhanced turned today—they wouldn't fucking die, and then that horrible feedback machine? Where are they even coming from?"

"I don't know. Pharmatrox must have some kind of organized presence, either here or somewhere else, capable of producing new turned and developing equipment to control them. And if we're facing problems like this here, who knows what Kev is dealing with in Chicago? With comms down and our messengers in the wind, he could have a shit show on his hands and we'd never know it. At the very least, maybe his inside contact at Pharmatrox knows what's going on. We need to get in touch with him somehow. It might even mean going there ourselves."

"If the troxies continue like this, we'll be overrun by an army of super soldiers, enhanced turned, *and* their regular troops. We'll be fucking obliterated, not to mention if Rodney's cult keeps acting up too. We need to shut that shit down."

At the last part, he looked askance at her, but he said, "Agnes might know something about this. We'll ask when they return tomorrow. For now, we'll up the patrols and spread the word about the enhanced turned."

"Fine. But if I find one more creepy ritualistic blood-drained body? I'm taking a crew and hunting down the cult myself." She squared up to the bruises forming around her throat, she winced, and his expression transformed into cold murder. "Who did this?"

She passed off the warm feeling flooding through her as the after effects of almost getting the life choked out of her, and not for any other insane reason, like the fact that Mal's first instinct was to hunt down her attacker, or the fact that she *liked* that.

"Give you one guess," she said, gesturing to the knife. As she swayed on her feet, she steadied herself with a hand on his solid chest, his skin hot beneath her touch. *Angry. You're angry.* "Zeln—or someone who uses the same exact knife—just tried to kill me in my own goddamn bed. In the one place I'm supposed to be safe."

His grip tightened at the nape of her neck, as if the thought of her in danger did...things to him. Releasing her briefly, he grabbed the knife and directed her to sit on his bed. She sat, but only because her legs were shaking, not because he told her to. Normally, she'd hate appearing weak in front of anyone, especially Mal. But something about how he was unsettled too had her feeling better. She was still fucking pissed though. "Your security seriously sucks," she said, hugging her arms to keep from shivering, the edges of another panic attack wavering in her periphery.

At her words, he tossed the knife away and knelt at her feet, hands braced on either side of her, as if he wanted to cage her in and fight off anyone who wished her harm. A dark cloud, something feral and primal, passed across his expression. "If you think for one second that I don't want to go out there and lay into every single bastard on watch tonight for letting him get past our perimeter, you're mistaken."

His intense reaction surprised an apology out of her. "Sorry," she breathed. "I didn't mean—look. I know it's not your fault."

Satisfied with her answer, he studied her for a few moments before grabbing a medical kit. He passed her a bottle of water, then sat beside her. She took a quick drink as he pressed a wet cloth to her neck. Wincing, she curled her hands into fists as he cleaned her wound.

"Are you all right?" he asked, bandaging her neck with a gentle touch.

"Yes." She felt dizzy and didn't want to meet his eyes, unsure of what she'd see there. "So if Zeln broke in, why would he come to my room and not yours? He doesn't even know me."

"Maybe he got the wrong room," Mal said with a frown, securing the last piece of medical tape in place. "Or maybe he was here to take out both of the Faction's leaders, but you fought back."

Penny hummed a noncommittal sound, but as he'd patched her up, she'd been thinking. If Zeln wanted her dead, she would be. She'd tangled with the guy and knew how ruthless, how precise, he was. A man like that didn't make mistakes. And then she remembered that *look* he gave her in the basement...

"Right before I tossed the grenade and slammed the door on him," she said, "he had this grin. It was unsettling. The only way I can describe it is cold, calculated...glee. Like the whole encounter had given him an edge in this fight against us." *And against Mal. Shit.* Then it dawned on her. "Maybe he saw how you protected me and misinterpreted it as—something else." She cut off, her throat suddenly dry, and took a gulp of water. "This was a message. A threat. He's rattling your cage, Mal. But why?"

Picking up the bloody knife, Mal turned it between his hands. She was grateful for the warmth of his massive, furnace-like body as the adrenaline leached out of her, leaving her chilled and unsteady. "He always did know how to get in my head. And attacking you—" He bit off the sentence and flexed his hands, as if he were envisioning strangling the life out of her midnight intruder. "Attacking you would strike a blow to the resistance."

"To the resistance. Right." But she thought it had more to do with striking a blow to a particular individual.

He blew out a breath and leaned back on his elbows, accentuating the ridges of his abs. Suddenly, she was aware of how close they were and how not clothed he was. *It's the oxygen deprivation.* Mal must have noticed her noticing, because he reached for a shirt and pulled it on. But she didn't miss the slight twitch at the corner of his mouth. Then it was back to business. "You're staying here for the rest of the night."

She blinked. "Why the fuck would I do that?"

"Penny. Zeln just tried to kill you in your sleep."

"Well he didn't do a very good job, did he?"

"Why are we arguing about this? Take the bed. I'll sleep on the floor."

"I can handle myself, Mal," she said, getting up and backing toward the door. She didn't know why she'd gotten so defensive all of a sudden, just that the thought of sleeping in the same room as Malosi Olesa sent all parts of her into a tailspin. She was too fucking fragile right now to maintain her necessary defenses and keep him at arm's length. "See you in the morning." Slamming the door on his protests, she hurried back to her room.

It would be a few more hours before camp began to stir, so she flopped onto her bed to think. There'd be no more sleeping for her.

Tonight's events had proven that Mal's judgment was severely compromised—enough so that Zeln could see it in a darkened basement and take advantage of it. And that was bad. Pair that with the enhanced turned, whatever was going on in the SubTran station, the cult growing bolder, Tara possibly missing...they'd have to go into the Wilds. Soon.

Clearing out the woods was the right call. Their messengers had been gone too long, and there could be a whole-ass war happening between the Capital and Chicago, or the cult offing anyone who wandered outside the city walls, and they'd never fucking know it because their god-damn radios only reached so far. While Zeln using her as a pawn in whatever shit he had with Mal pissed her off to no end, going after him in the SubTran station was a surefire way to end up dead. It would be playing into his hands, and—

A scraping sound. *In the hall, maybe against the door.*

Snatching a knife from her bedside table, she ripped the door open to—

Mal. Sitting in a metal folding chair parked in front of her bedroom door, arms crossed, glowering fiercely. "Back to bed," he said.

"What are you doing?"

"Slept enough already. Go on." He jerked his chin at her cot and settled his bulk against the wall. An immovable mountain. *Insufferable man.* But she left the door cracked, and her lips twisted into a smile as she climbed into bed.

She'd never tell him, but his presence outside her room that night was the only reason she'd been able to fall asleep after swearing she'd never sleep again.

7

Agnes

ARLY MORNING SUNLIGHT BLASTED into Derek's open garage as Agnes worked on modifications to her DNA editing machine, the smell of burnt plastic rising into the air.

"You're up early."

Pausing in her task, she smiled at Derek as he crossed the space and pulled her into him. Their kiss filled her with a bone-deep warmth, cutting through the chilly air, and she ran her hands through his sleep-rumpled hair, tracing her fingers along his tattoos. At first, touching someone like this felt foreign after closing herself off from other people for so long. But being with Derek, living in his house with Lawrence, Tara, Quentin, and Silas, she was coming back to herself. Or, building a new self. One that embraced all parts of Stella and who she'd been Before, and molded them with everything she wanted to be now.

But sometimes, she wasn't entirely sure who or what that was. It was hard to see beyond the horizon of war. *And,* she reminded herself, *victory isn't guaranteed.*

"Couldn't sleep," she replied.

They'd returned from New York late last night, but sleep had been an impossibility. Ever since killing Dr. Hansen, Agnes had felt adrift, and a dark inkling had begun gathering in the back of her mind. *What if I'm fucking all of this up? What if I'm making the wrong choices again and people die because of it?* And that train of thought always led her to the one core question she couldn't shake: How could she have been so wrong about Hansen? And how could she expect to trust her own judgment after falling for the woman's lies for *years*?

Every time she thought of her machine, a boulder fell into the pit of her stomach. No matter what anyone else said, she was partially at fault for what was happening to their country. Silas said the troxies would have found a way to achieve their goals without her work, but Agnes couldn't help feeling like she personally had a hand in accelerating their apocalypse.

So while it felt good to be transforming her machine into a tool to cure the users, it might not be enough to undo the damage it had already done. And if the Faction won the war—what then? Would she ever feel satisfied, like she had fully atoned for her role in aiding Pharmatrox's barbaric agenda?

Would anything ever feel like enough?

Derek's hand resting against her neck brought her back to the present moment, and she gave him a weak smile. "You're far away again," he said.

"Sorry," she said, gesturing at the bones of her machine. "Mods are hard, especially when I'm not a hundred percent sure this will work, *and* I don't have the parts I need."

"If anyone can figure it out, it's you." He kissed her nose with a smile. "But that isn't what you were thinking about."

She sighed. "Feels like the trip to New York was a bust."

"We don't know that yet. Silas crashed as soon as we got back and hasn't had a chance to work his magic on decrypting everything. Give it some time."

Penny rolled her eyes. "Zeln is playing games. That's it. I may not know the guy, but I know what he's doing. Because this tactic? I did that shit all the time when I ran with Rodney and the Marauders. When—" She cut off with a glance at Agnes, who paled, knowing Penny had been thinking of how she'd toyed with her in much the same way when she was hunting her down a few short months ago. Penny cleared her throat and went on. "He wants you to react emotionally and do something stupid, Mal. Going after him would be a bad move."

"Penny has a point," Derek said. "He could be trying to draw us into a blood bath at the SubTran station. Without any insight into their capabilities, we'd have no way to launch a successful assault."

Mal looked like he wished his eyeballs had laser beams as he stared a hole through Derek, but before he could speak, Penny said to Agnes, "I want to hear more about what you learned in New York."

Her eyes pinned Agnes like a butterfly to a board, and she felt like Stella again, cornered by a predator. Grabbing Derek's hand, she took a few deep breaths, then relayed what they discovered in New York. "Silas is still decoding everything."

"Should be able to hack into one of the satellites soon and get us some better comms, maybe some internet access, finally, but I'm having trouble getting a reliable uplink—"

"Silas, what did we talk about?" said Penny, her lips twitching, and Agnes bristled. Apparently, Silas and Penny had forged some kind of bond during their time infiltrating the Spire. It was unsettling, especially because Silas knew Penny's appearance in their lives had resulted in Evie choosing to meet death early. When she'd asked Silas about it, he'd only said, "Penny is different now. Or, she wants to be. I saw that firsthand."

Silas scratched his head. "Uh, right. Layman's terms. I can't get into the spinny contraption flying around in the atmosphere, but give me a week or so. Once I get a connection, I can use that to control the troxy drones, send some toward Chicago, maybe even spot a glimpse of our girl Tara if she's not back already."

At the mention of Tara, Agnes noticed Quentin squirm in his seat, but he kept quiet. *Please be okay out there, Tara. We need you.*

"And no luck finding any scientists?" Lawrence asked. "I could really use one to work with me on the farm's hydroponic system."

Agnes shook her head. "Not a single one. You?" She glanced at Mal and Penny.

"Nope," Penny said. "They have to be somewhere, right? They couldn't have all disappeared or fled the country already. It's only been a month since the Spire."

My thoughts exactly. "It's definitely strange. Pharmatrox is still manufacturing their poison, and they're getting better at it—the enhanced turned are proof of that. Finding their backup lab won't be easy, but we've narrowed it down to a location near a large body of water for hydroelectric power. I don't know what they're doing in the SubTran, but it's probably not set up for easily producing and shipping pharmaceuticals."

"We need eyes in every city on the lookout for this place, and not every Faction splinter group has long-distance comms, so we need to spread the word however we can," Silas added.

Before they could discuss any more, a knock sounded at the door and quickly turned into pounding.

"I'll get it!" Quentin said, zipping down the hallway.

"Why does he always run headlong into danger?" Agnes grumbled.

Derek nudged her side. "Sound like anyone else we know?"

A disgruntled female voice came from the entryway. "Why the fuck is the door locked? I thought that shit was broken."

Tara.

8

"T HANKS FOR SENDING OUT the cavalry to look for me. Really means a lot." Tara's tone couldn't contain more sarcasm if it had been directly pumped full of the stuff. The fierce woman kicked her booted feet up on the kitchen table as if she'd never left, although she looked like she'd gone through a high-speed blender with her tattered clothes, cuts, and bruises.

"We were going to send people today," Mal said, flicking a glance at Penny.

"Yeah, after we had a huge debate about it," Agnes chimed in as she pulled her best friend into a hug, the other Outposters gathering around to welcome her back. "Glad you made it back to us, tía."

Tara pulled a hand through her dirt and blood encrusted curls. But her wrists...they were freshly bandaged. "Sorry to worry you, tomatito," Tara said to Quentin, who had been glued to her side since she walked in the door. She tossed her radio headset device on the table. "That broke pretty quickly. Could use some more work."

"On it," said Silas as he scooped it up.

"What happened out there?" Lawrence asked, giving her shoulders a protective squeeze.

"I got separated from the watch group, and some turned showed up, so I had to detour into the Wilds, but I went too close to the woods.

And that's when they got me—Rodney's cult. Calling themselves the Chosen." Her voice shook with restrained rage, and she looked like she wanted to rip the cultists' heads off one by one.

Fucking knew it was the cult. Penny shot a glance at Mal, and he held her gaze briefly before looking away.

"They knocked me out, and I woke up somewhere deep in the woods at night. They slashed my wrists, tied me to a fucking tree." Tara took a shaky breath, the fear showing through a slight crack in her tough exterior. "I thought I was going to die."

Agnes reached across the table for Tara's hand. "You're safe now."

"I'm sorry we didn't come for you sooner," Mal said from his post against the wall. "It was the wrong call."

"Look, I was pissed at first and imagined clobbering you a thousand different ways if I ever got out of there, but there's no way you could have found me." Tara and Mal shared a knowing glance, the look of two commanders who knew what it was like to make unpopular decisions with their backs against the wall. "I don't even know where I was. The cult kept a bag over my head most of the time."

"How did you escape?" Derek asked.

A good fucking question.

"Someone brought me back."

The atmosphere in the room plunged to polar proportions. *Now that's an interesting development.* "Who?" Penny asked.

"Don't know. Didn't see or hear them. It happened late last night. The Chosen were draining me slowly. The diablos wanted my blood for some disgusting reason. Anyway, I heard sounds of an attack but couldn't see anything because of the lovely headgear. Next thing I knew, my bindings were gone and they dragged me through the woods. Sounded like at least ten people, but I was about to pass out, so I wouldn't trust that estimate.

Their camp was a few miles away from the Chosen. Whoever they were, they cleaned my wounds, gave me food and water. Kept the bag on my head the whole time though and wouldn't answer any of my goddamn questions. This morning, I woke up just outside of the city walls. They'd drugged me and dropped me off."

"Fucking hell," said Penny on an exhale. "This just opened up a whole new can of crazy." To Mal, she said, "Hate to say 'I told you so,' but looks like I was onto something with that drained body we found in the alley."

"You do *not* hate saying 'I told you so,'" Mal said on a growl. "But I would like to know what the fuck is going on out there."

"Oh, so you finally agree the cult is a threat worth paying attention to?"

"I *agree* we have a...situation."

"Why can't you just admit I'm right?"

"*Children,*" said Derek, cutting them off. "Let's focus, shall we? Tara, do you think you could lead us to the cult or this other mystery camp?"

Tara shook her head. "Not sure, but I'll go out with the groups you send to look. Maybe something will spark a memory." She chewed her lip, and if Penny didn't know better, she'd say their fierce warrior was afraid.

"I can blindfold you and tow you around, if you think the sensory deprivation will help jog your memory," offered Quentin. "I promise not to lead you directly into the creek or trip you at all." He held a hand to his heart, grinning.

"If I want to get wet socks, then sure, we'll do your idea," Tara said, bopping him on the head. Then she grew serious again. "But that's not all. There's something you should see."

warming, freezing to death in the wintertime was one less thing they had to worry about—unless you were unlucky enough to be caught in an unpredictable polar cold snap.

Beside her, Mal walked in silence but fiddled with the strap of his weapons belt—something he only did when his mind was elsewhere. Was he thinking of their earlier exchange too? Or was he still shaken over his encounter with Zeln that morning? He'd been clenching his teeth and flexing his hands more than usual—another thing he only did when he was agitated.

Jesus Christ. Why do I even know this about him? Those were things only someone close to him would pay attention to. *He has to be thinking about Zeln. Right?* She was convinced Mal was driven by his need to avenge whatever personal issues he had with the mysterious soldier. She understood well the compulsion to put on blinders and blaze a bloody trail toward a goal in the pursuit of absolution, and part of her didn't want to see Mal go down the same dark path. Not for the first time, she wondered what kind of twisted past they shared and if Mal was able to remain objective.

Before she could ask him what was up, Raph said from behind them, "Uh, I think I found something…?"

As Penny approached the gruesome scene, alarm bells went off in her head. A woman's body paler than any corpse she'd ever seen lay in an alleyway, the throat slashed in a way that reminded her of her sickle's signature. Mal knelt on the asphalt beside her, frowning as he touched the woman's boot—a civilian, from the looks of it.

"Drained of blood," Penny said. "Almost entirely. But there's no blood on the ground." Raising the question to the group, she asked, "Anyone ever seen anything like this before?"

"Nah, and I hope I never do again." Raph's umber brown skin was slicked with sweat, and he wiped a shaky hand across his forehead. Everyone exchanged worried glances, murmuring.

"Let's keep moving," Mal said with a grim expression.

"You really think it's nothing?" she asked. "This whole thing reeks of a ritual. You know who partakes in rituals? Cults."

"We know you have it out for Rodney's cult, okay? We get it," said one of the troops. "Maybe the rain washed the blood away."

"Could be a turned who had a taste for blood instead of flesh," someone else said.

Will scoffed. "Since when do turned act like vampires?"

At least one person is on my side.

"Rodney's people are too...erratic to do something this precise, right?" asked Sanjali.

Mal was silent a little too long before speaking. "Let's move out. But keep a sharp eye." He picked up a jog, and the rest followed suit.

Penny kept pace with him, fuming. She knew in her gut this was the cult, and it was proof they were ramping things up. But until they caught them in the act, Mal would never deploy troops to deal with it.

Unless Penny went rogue and decided to handle it herself—an option that was becoming more appealing.

A wild screech from the end of the street echoed between the buildings, interrupting her thoughts, and a chorus of other raw shrieks took up the cry.

Penny rounded on Mal, saying, "You didn't send scouts ahead to watch for turned?"

Mal blinked, the level of his fuck-up dawning on him. "I—"

More ragged voices joined the call, and Penny threw up her hands. "You never forget anything. What's going on with you?" She had a list of fucking follow-up questions, but something crashed into her from above, plowing her into the pavement and stealing her breath. Black teeth snapped in her face, hot saliva dripping onto her neck. The foul breath of the creature clogged her senses as she ripped her sickle across its throat, severing its windpipe. More turned jumped from a nearby window, and a dozen others rushed straight toward them.

The Faction fired volts, but while the former humans screeched in pain, they did not fall. *They're not dying... They're still fighting? How is this possible?* But the turned that had attacked her lay bleeding black blood onto the pavement from its severed windpipe.

"Forget the rifles!" Penny shouted. "Blades and bullets only."

Bullets didn't work either. The turned remained undeterred and fought with reckless ferocity and kept on coming. As if they were already dead and nothing could kill them.

What the fuck is happening?

Dodging the fray, Penny rushed at a turned with bullets in its chest, ripping her sickle across its neck in a vicious slash that sent its head flying.

"Blades only," she said to Mal, wiping the gore from her face.

"Right." He took a knife from his belt and lodged it in a skull.

They cut down wave after wave, but the din of battle and the smell of blood would draw more. "We have to go," she said. "The armory can wait. If we keep bleeding everywhere, this fight will just keep getting bigger."

Mal broke off with a curse, kicking a creature in the chest. He clicked his radio earpiece and said, "Sector 9 armory? It's a shit show out here. About two miles north of you. Fuck ton of turned. There's something wrong with them. Only blades will work, and you gotta damn near cut their fucking heads off before they'll die. We'll take out as many as we can, but we need to retreat. Be ready if they head your way."

He cut off the comms and threw himself back into the fight with a growl.

"I can keep this up all day, but I don't want to make you look bad," Penny said, whirling to pin another turned in the throat with her black-bladed knife. "I'm better with a blade than you are."

In answer, Mal slashed his knife across the nearest turned's throat, grabbed it by the shoulder and the jaw, and *ripped* its head clean off, black blood exploding in the air. "Don't need a blade."

Okay, I'm impressed. But she was still spitting mad. All of this was his fucking fault. He needed to get his head in the game before it all came crashing down on them.

The faraway screeches of more turned drew closer.

Mal let out a sharp whistle through his teeth. "Back to the stadium! Raph? The fire thing again, if you could."

"You got it, boss." Raph doused the nearest turned in lighter fluid from his hip flask and flicked his lighter, the flames eating up the accelerant in a burst of light and heat. The creatures screamed, churned into a frenzy at the bright light.

Suddenly, a high-pitched keening sound like microphone feedback filled the air, and Penny and the rest clamped their hands over their ears.

But the turned stopped in silence. Their panicked faces transformed into slack and serene masks, then they attacked with newfound vigor, ignoring the flames and the light. The Faction took down a few more, but the turned were too strong. Something had rejuvenated them, renewed their focus. Almost as if the troxies had found some way to control them too. Just like their super soldiers.

This is a new fucking level of bad news.

"There's a troxy-controlled sector a few blocks that way," Penny said.

him, pointing her finger in his chest. "And I don't care if you don't like it."

"If it comes to that...we can discuss it."

"I don't need your permission."

"We're supposed to be a united front."

"Then you better get quick about uniting with me on this."

Mal blew out an exasperated breath. "Don't go off half-cocked. Let's just...wait until we talk to Agnes tomorrow. Then we can decide our course of action from there."

"Good enough." She stood to leave, but Mal was there to stop her with a hand on the doorframe.

"Thank you. For having my back today."

He stood close enough to touch, and every inch of her skin felt alive with anticipation. "Sure." She ducked outside before her body decided to do anything else, like *gasp* or something embarrassing. *God, you'd think I never had a man's attention before.*

But with each fleeting glimpse behind his stone walls, she was realizing more and more that maybe she'd never had the attention of a man quite like Malosi Olesa.

6

ﾠ

A FTER TAKING A COLD shower in the locker room, Penny crawled straight into her cot, the late-night air seeping into her bones. Every day was a new battle—against the troxies and turned, but mostly with herself, and not just about how she felt unfit for leadership. As she sank into bed, the dangerous thoughts she only allowed herself to entertain in the moments before she succumbed to a fitful sleep danced through her mind.

Her encounters with Mal today had burrowed into her in a way she'd never be rid of. But she wasn't irritated or angry. She was...intrigued. *Fuck.* The constant push and pull of their relationship was as frustrating as it was invigorating—something she'd never admit in the revealing light of day.

But recently, they'd been having...different moments. Ones that stretched beyond their usual interactions and went in a charged direction. He'd supported her through her panic attack, something she usually locked herself in the bathroom to deal with on her own. He'd fought to protect her from Zeln in the basement. He encouraged her and *thanked* her. Those moments painted a picture of someone who cared for her, but paired with their usual cataclysmic daily interactions, she wasn't sure what to make of it. Or what she even *wanted* to make of it.

But all of it had her wondering what it would be like to be his.

On that note, it's time for some fucking sleep. She punched her pillow into a more comfortable position, but her secret thoughts wouldn't relent. As she lay there in the darkness, they took a more...divergent path. Mal using his brute strength to tear through a battlefield, his big body moving with the lithe grace of a skilled predator, his massive arms built to rip apart their enemies just as well as they cradled her gently against him. The feel of his fingers on her face, brushing her lips, maybe even caressing lower...

Nope. Sleep.

Rolling over, she pushed all thoughts of Mal and her troubles aside, but it was still another hour before she finally fell asleep.

The cold, familiar bite of a steel blade touched her throat. She knew the feeling; one of her Marauders had once tried to off her in the middle of the night.

Instincts took over.

Just as she'd done that night, she kicked out, placing one foot on her attacker's hip and using the other to sweep his legs out, flipping him to the floor and landing atop him—it was probably a him, due to the size and weight, but it could be a very jacked woman. Regardless, neutralizing the threat was priority number one.

Her attacker's breath whooshed out of him, but he reversed their positions in an expert move, raking the knife across her neck as she jerked back. *Shit, this guy is good.* She felt her skin slice around the blade's edge, and hot blood wept down her neck.

Grabbing his wrist, she beat his hand against the cement until the knife went flying, landing somewhere in the darkness. Reversing their positions, her attacker tucked her head under his armpit and locked his arm around her throat. She'd practiced escaping this position many times in her Muay Thai classes, but fighting from the ground wasn't her strong suit. And this guy was *strong*, the choke locked in. She tried to tuck her chin and roll them, but in the pitch-black room, she couldn't tell when her vision started to fade.

When she awoke, she was alone, lying on her back on the cold cement floor with no concept of how much time she'd lost. She touched her throat, sticky with blood, and her head pounded. *What the fuck just happened? And why am I not dead?* Crawling across the floor to her small shelf, she found the camping lantern and turned it on. Blood speckled the floor, and she located the attacker's knife.

A curved blade, just big enough to fit in her palm.

I know exactly who the fuck that was.

Then she stumbled her way down the hall.

Mal was about to get a fucking earful.

Heedless of the hour, she barged into Mal's room, the stadium's fluorescent hallway lights from the backup generator pouring into the darkness. He sat bolt upright, blanket pooling around his waist, his bare torso heaving with adrenaline as he searched for the threat.

Nice chest. He has a nice chest.

God, the oxygen deprivation must have made her loopier than she'd thought. She tossed the bloody curved knife at his feet, and it clanged against the concrete. "We have a fucking problem."

He was across the room in seconds, hands going to her neck, concern etching hard lines in his face as he examined her. When his fingers found

"But that's just it, Derek. There *is* no time!" Gripping the edge of the workbench, a sudden urge to sweep all of her work on the floor and watch it smash to pieces rushed through her, if only to get a moment's relief from the unending panic and frustration. "It's been a month since we took down the network and cut off Pharmatrox's facilities from one another. That was supposed to make things easier, and it feels like we're still in the same fucking position."

Derek tapped a tattooed finger against her temple. "I thought you'd been avoiding Penny, but you're sounding just like her. You might have more in common than you think."

"We don't."

"You're both recovering users. She's always saying we aren't doing things fast enough, and Mal is the one to rein her in. And now that Rodney—something dark from her past—is finally dead and she's thrust into a position she also doesn't feel ready for... I don't know, maybe you should talk to her."

Agnes gaped at him. "I'm barely able to be in the same room with her, let alone confide in her. She's the reason I killed—I mean, that my best friend died in my arms, and you want me to *talk to her*?" She'd told Derek about the extent of Penny's involvement in Evie's death, and she'd only just stopped referring to the situation as murder. The mental switch had been at Silas's suggestion so she could begin to forgive herself and move on. But it was slow progress. "You've been talking to Silas about this, haven't you?"

"I'm just saying," said Derek, shrugging. "Maybe she could understand something about what it's like to feel uncertain in the face of change. If anything, Silas seems to be friends with her, which is pretty fucking weird, honestly. But if he thinks she's capable of normal human interactions, maybe you should give her a chance. Maybe we all should."

"You don't know her like I do."

"And apparently Silas knows her differently than all of us."

Agnes narrowed her eyes and reclaimed her soldering iron, effectively shutting down the conversation. She tolerated Penny and no longer feared for her life around the woman, but they had a long road to go before she'd consider anything like *seeking out her company*.

A moment later, the door connecting to the house opened and a ginger freight train plowed into her. "Agnes!"

She laughed, wrapping her arms around her favorite kid. "Hey, Quentin."

"Missed you," he said, squeezing as hard as he could. She squeezed back, feeling better already.

Derek flapped a hand at himself. "I made it back in one piece too, in case you were worried. Where's my bone-crushing embrace?"

Quentin pulled away and wrapped his arms around Derek in a vise grip. "I *was* worried. If you didn't come back, who would teach me the incorrect way to fix a leaky sink? You're the expert at that."

"Hey, that was *one time* I used the wrong wrench," said Derek, wresting himself out of Quentin's obnoxious hug. Agnes snickered and he turned to her, indignant. "I'm a good plumber! I worked as a handyman for years!"

"I believe you."

"Your *smirk* says you don't."

"You'll have plenty of opportunities to prove me wrong this winter when the plumbing inevitably goes out at some point," she said.

Derek shuffled off, muttering about wrenches. "Come on," he said over his shoulder. "Mal and Penny will be here soon. Best wake everyone up."

Quentin froze, eyes darting to Agnes. "Uh, you should know—Tara hasn't come back yet."

She stopped in her tracks. "What?"

"She went on a scouting mission yesterday and hasn't reported in."

Agnes's mouth went dry and she locked eyes with Derek. This couldn't be good. But she didn't want Quentin to worry. "I'm sure she's fine." She led him back inside, Derek following. "But we'll go out looking for her today."

"You'll have to talk Penny and Mal into it," Quentin said as he hopped up to sit on the center island. "They threatened to glue my feet to the ground if I even thought about going out on my own to look for her." He swung his feet and smirked at the memory. "I still did though."

Derek rifled through the cabinets, opening jars and sniffing them before settling on a bag of stale pretzels. "Still did what?"

"Went out to look for Tara. Duh."

Agnes abandoned her coffee-making and whipped around to glare at him. "Quentin! It's not safe to go out alone. You know that."

"Agnes! I go out alone all the time. You know that."

She pointed her coffee scoop at him. "You're being a real butthead right now. Go wake up the boys and tell them to get ready for our meeting with your comic book superhero."

Quentin scampered off, delighted at the prospect of seeing Mal, and Agnes went to light a fire in the living room's hearth. If she was going to have to talk to Penny and deal with the world's most annoying teenager this early in the morning, she'd need multiple buckets of coffee.

An hour later, Agnes sat wedged on the couch between Derek and Silas, avoiding the red-haired woman leaning against the mantel.

Silas blew out a breath, buzzing his lips. "That's a fuck load of information. *We* were supposed to be the ones bringing *you* intel."

Mal grunted from his post against the kitchen table where Lawrence and Quentin sat. "Lot can happen in a few days."

Penny and Mal had shown up and word vomited all over the place, relaying how many troxy facilities were left to clear, reports about Rodney's cult, the enhanced turned, Penny's midnight attacker and Zeln's involvement, and how Chicago was still radio silent. *And Tara. Mierda, tía.*

"So what's our next move?" Derek asked, nodding at Mal. "You think the troxies are the biggest threat because of Zeln. But I'm guessing Penny doesn't agree because she usually doesn't."

"Damn right she doesn't," Penny said.

Mal's jaw flexed as he clenched his teeth. "We don't know who took over Pharmatrox after Dr. Hansen's death, but if they're hiring someone like Zeln, they're far more ruthless than Hansen ever was. He's the garbage disposal for powerful families and countries, and we should be concerned he's on their payroll."

"And he has some kind of personal bone to pick with Mal, which is why, newsflash, we can't trust the big guy's opinion on this one," Penny said.

"Sorry to interrupt the insult hurling," Derek said, "but I don't think either of you are capable of approaching this objectively."

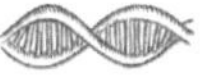

Tara led the group across McAdams Bridge, now under Faction control, toward the Wilds. Silas had remained behind to work, already halfway into his brainiac zone before they'd left the house. Quentin, of course, had wanted to come, and Penny didn't even bother protesting. It would only make him resent her, and Tara said they weren't going far.

Penny was glad for Tara's safe return, if only for the fact that it made Quentin happy. She didn't have a problem with Tara, but most of Team Outpost regarded her with cold suspicion, as they should. Shelving her rage and not immediately reaching for violence was taking some practice. Because knowing that Rodney's followers were still out there, using until they turned, forcing other people to use, maybe even sacrificing people and stealing them in the night—those thoughts made her murderous. And she wanted nothing more than to watch them bleed.

About two miles later, Tara veered off the road into the woods, carving a winding path. Another five minutes, and Penny saw it.

Well, *them*.

A man—very dead—with thick railroad nails pounded through his torso and hands, pinning the body to a tree, its throat slashed and coated with dried blood. Another body was nailed to the other side of the tree. As Penny looked up, something wet splattered on her face and she choked on her inhale. More bodies nailed to the tree limbs, almost all the way to the top. The tree hadn't yet shed all of its leaves before winter, shrouding the bodies in shadow.

"Looks like they were alive when they were bled dry," Agnes noted. "If the cult is into blood rituals like Tara said, then..."

Everyone exchanged concerned looks. She didn't need to finish the sentence. Penny was certain Rodney's followers were behind this.

Quentin was the first to break the stunned silence. "I'll climb up there and see...if we know anyone."

As he climbed, Penny's heart pounded in her throat. She knew he was good at climbing, but she never thought he'd be in a situation where he'd have to climb a demented Christmas tree decorated with dead bodies. *What kind of fucking world do we live in?*

A few minutes later, Derek called to him. "Well?"

"Maybe five or six bodies up here," he shouted. "Civilians, troxies, Faction, and—uh. We know some of them. I think their names were Hild, Smith, and...maybe Morales?"

"Moreno," Mal corrected, wiping a hand across his face with a grim expression. "Fuck."

The messengers they'd sent to Chicago after the first ones hadn't reported back.

Now we know the likely fate of those ones too. They'd never even gotten close to Chicago.

Then Mal voiced her next thought aloud. "And if Chicago—or anyone else, for that matter—sent messengers to us, they likely met the same fate."

"I was fucking *right*," Penny said as Quentin made his descent. "We need to end Rodney's trash bags *now*. How did your scouts not find this?"

Mal examined the gruesome scene with a hard look. "This body is the freshest kill, followed by the one just above it. Right?" he asked Quentin when he plopped beside him.

"Yeah, but the higher you go, the older the bodies are. Would be easy to miss seeing them, hidden in the leaves like that. Especially if you're not looking for a tree full of bodies."

"How'd you find this, Tara?" Lawrence asked, his mouth a tight line in his beard.

"I woke up here."

Unpleasant wake-up call.

Derek frowned as he paced, scanning for more evidence. "So your rescuers could have done this?"

"I don't think so," said Tara. "Why kill all these people and leave me alive at the scene of the crime?"

"Maybe they knew about it and wanted *you* to know about it," said Agnes.

An interesting point. "And they knew you'd tell us," Penny added. "Maybe this is their way of asking for help? Or—"

"Or what?" Tara asked with a sharp look.

"Or they're warning us about how bad things are about to get."

Tara leaned on her baseball bat, blanching at the implications of that. "How did my rescuers know that I'd even be able to help?"

"Maybe they saw something different in you," Lawrence said, tapping a foot against her unconventional weapon of choice.

"How would they know anything about me? They bagged me and refused to speak."

It was a good question. The Faction didn't wear anything identifying like a uniform; they donned stolen armor and gear from troxy armories, so Tara was not outwardly recognizable as a Faction soldier. *Unless...* As her eyes found Mal's, she knew he'd reached the same conclusion.

"We're being watched," Mal said. "Maybe even now."

"And they've gotten close enough to know you're high up in the chain of command," Penny said. "Influential enough to make a difference."

With a loaded glance at her, Mal said, "Let's head back. It'll be getting dark soon." As winter crept closer, the sun set early now, and while Penny was eager to get out into the Wilds, the darkness held more secrets than they could possibly imagine. Their search for the Chosen would have to wait until tomorrow.

Back at the stadium, Team Outpost had dispersed, and Penny didn't stick around long enough to hear where they went. Instead, she headed straight for the war room, dragging Mal with her. Once they were inside, she shut the door and pushed him into the nearest chair. He sat, looking grumpy about it.

"Do I get my scouting team now?" she demanded. She might not want to lead the Faction as a whole, but she had no problem taking a small strike team to root out Rodney's followers.

"You're the absolute worst person to send straight into the Chosen's territory. You killed their leader—you're a walking target."

"I'm the *best* option. If they want revenge, they'll come out to play. Then we follow them back to the source and wipe them out."

"You're suggesting I let you go out there as *live bait*?"

"I'm not suggesting you let me do anything. I'm telling you what I'm doing, and you're going to deal with it. I'm leading these searches myself." Culling Rodney's scourge—especially now that she'd seen what they were capable of—was her responsibility, and she would not rest until they were neutralized.

Mal surged to his feet, a thunderous look rolling across his brow. "The fuck you will. I need you here. Our people need to see you focused on our efforts in the Capital, not running around in the woods. I can't lose you. I—the Faction needs you."

Did he—? No, there's no way Mal almost just admitted that he needs me. At least, not like that. Right? Then she remembered him, parking himself in front of her bedroom door last night. He'd wanted to protect her, and—*fuck me*—she had wanted him there. It felt right, knowing he was outside her door. He'd always shown up for her. Even when he didn't agree, even when he was pissed, he'd always been there. So maybe he *did* mean something more than what his words implied. From the waves of agitation coming off of him and how he stood so close to her, close enough to see the fire in his eyes and catch the fresh scent of his soap, maybe he...

Jesus Christ. Now you're smelling him? You are off your shit.

She crossed her arms and tilted her head back to glare at him, which made her glare harder. She hated his fucking *massive size*. At least when she was trying to talk to his stupid face. The only time it was useful was during a battle. *Or when he's carrying your injured ass.*

Okay, enough.

"You got anyone else in this camp who is intimately familiar with Rodney's crew and their antics?" she demanded. "Anyone else who has tracked someone across the fucking country? It makes sense for me to do this."

"I'm going with you."

That did things to her heart rate that she didn't want to think about. "You're not. If we're both out 'running around in the woods,' people will think we've given up like you just said."

He balled his hands into fists but looked away, and she knew she had him. Squaring up to him, she said, "*I'm doing this.* I'll make contact with Tara's rescuers and convince them to help us take out the Chosen—because if they're this stealthy, I want them fighting on my side. Worst case scenario, we find out whatever they know and use it to take out the cult ourselves. Or, the cult shows face while we're stomping around, cutting down on our search time. Now say no to that fucking plan, Mal. And if you do, you're going to write me an essay about *why the fuck not* and cite your goddamn sources."

Mal held her gaze, nostrils flaring. She could feel him wanting to pick apart her plan, to rage and deny her. But when he spoke, he said two words she never thought she'd hear the man say.

"You win."

Now *that* was a good feeling.

9

1 YEAR, 6 MONTHS AGO

"**Y**ou win. I'll get you next time." Penny tossed her cards face up on the picnic table. "Big day today, Bill."

"You always catch the bad ones," said the bearded man sitting across from her as he gathered up the playing cards. "Thanks for breakfast, as always." He lifted the paper coffee cup in thanks and took a bite of the bagel sandwich she'd brought him.

"See you tomorrow."

She'd met Bill on the way to her first day at the insurance company five years ago. He'd asked for money, but she hadn't had cash, so she'd given him her breakfast instead. The next day, she'd bought two breakfasts, and thus began their daily routine. Sometimes she even made it by early enough to play a few hands of rummy.

Today is a good day. Work wasn't easy, but it was days like today that made the brutal hours worth it. Catching people who took advantage of the system was a reward on its own, but it was all to save up money so Quentin could escape the family farm and get far as fuck away from Uncle Hal. After the not-so-subtle gun to her forehead incident, she rarely went back home to visit. She'd discovered what he was wrapped up in, what he'd gotten her parents involved in without their knowledge, and now he was trying to suck Quentin into his orbit. She'd be damned if she'd let that happen.

Walking into the office, Penny went to her cubicle to wait for her boss to find her. She'd sent in her report earlier, and she knew he'd be ravenous to talk to her.

"Look at you! Office has been abuzz all morning."

Penny smiled at the petite woman who'd planted herself atop her half-height filing cabinet. She sported her dark hair in a pixie cut and wore a sundress with combat boots. "Hey, Lexa. Word spreads quickly, especially when you catch the big fish. What brings you here?"

"Following up with one of the other investigators about a cache of family diamonds that were just reported stolen," she said, wagging her eyebrows.

"Inside job?"

"My money's on yes."

Penny and the local detective had partnered on cases many times over the years, bonding over the odd hours and intense investigations. Partners in anti-crime, they liked to say, since they were in the business of weeding out fraudsters. Most cops shooed insurance investigators away, but not Lexa—she'd been too nice to tell Penny to beat it, and now they were attached at the hip.

"Anyway, good for you on the money laundering case," Lexa said. "Big boss will be barging over here any second to congratulate his favorite gal. Oh, speak of the devil..." Lexa waved and headed off as her boss made a beeline for her. Penny continued typing away on her computer, feigning busy-ness.

"I can't believe it. We've been after this guy for *months*. How'd you do it?"

"Oh, hi," she said, swiveling in her chair with a demure smile. "I see you got my report."

"Fuck yeah, I got your report. This will hold up in court too. He's going away for a long time." Leaning in, her boss said, "I know you're prone to more...unorthodox means of getting the evidence you need. Tell me if I need to be prepared to defend your 'methods' on the stand." Aka, lie.

Trespassing, questionable surveillance methods, and beating information out of people wasn't off of Penny's radar. And it didn't matter as long as she was never caught. Besides, she didn't see why she couldn't use every tool at her disposal, if it meant getting the truth and putting away the scumbags. Her boss never specifically asked her how she solved her cases, and she never told him, only relaying whatever information was strictly necessary in order to get a conviction or arrive at a settlement.

"Everything you need to know is in the report," she said.

Her boss nodded, clapping her on the shoulder. "Good work, as always. I think you're ready to swim with the sharks now. Familiar with that string of arsons?"

Penny sat up straight. *Fuck yes, I am.* She'd been following it for a year now. Different insurance companies, big payouts. Arson was nearly impossible to prove, but she loved a challenge. "Yeah, what about it?" she asked, keeping her composure.

"Well, one of 'em was finally ours." He tossed a file on her desk. "Warehouse burned down, and this time, we might have a lead on the guy."

"Surveillance photos?"

"Security cam footage. About ten possible suspects. Figured you and Lexa would want to take point."

"You bet your ass we do. And I already know it isn't him or him." She slid aside two of the mug shots.

He lifted a bushy eyebrow. "Doing some extra credit?"

"I was bored."

With a conspiratorial smile, he said, "If you take down this guy, you could be playing the big leagues in no time. This is your golden ticket, Penny."

Penny always got her man, and she had every intention of putting this asshole away for a long time. The fame, job prospects, financial security—all of that was secondary. She wanted to watch the bad guys burn.

And burn he would.

10

Frost tinged the early morning air as Penny and her crew headed into the Wilds for their fifth day of searching for Tara's rescuers. Despite Penny's protests that the cult and whatever else was haunting the woods would be more active at night, Mal had mandated daytime-only scouting parties. She was giving it one more fruitless day before she started at whatever time she wanted, Mal's wishes be damned. *And since when do I care what he thinks anyway?*

Her crew today was Derek, Lawrence, and Tara. Quentin, of course, had wanted to join, but luckily Tara had been the one to deny him, even though Penny had planned to. Silas and Agnes were back at Maple Street, working on the stolen files from New York and building Agnes's machine, but with the grumbling she'd heard between the two yesterday, they hadn't made much progress.

The group always started their search from the tree of bodies and branched out from there. At the usual spot, Tara froze. "It's fucking gone."

Penny looked up from her hand-drawn map of the Wilds. "What?"

Lawrence gaped at the tree. "The bodies. The nails. They're all gone."

Penny frowned, stepping up to get a closer look. Sure enough, the only evidence there'd been any bodies were the dried bloodstains. "But why?"

Derek tilted his head. "Smell that?"

"Smoke," Penny said. "Let's head back to the road, maybe get a look at where it's coming from."

"Or, we could just climb a tree and have a look-see." *Quentin* popped out from behind the nearest bush, grinning from ear to ear. "Anyone here who might be good at that?" He raised his hand. "Me, perhaps?"

At his appearance, Penny's panic ignited, and Tara grabbed him by the collar, yelling in Spanish. But Derek and Lawrence just sighed.

"Told you there's no way to keep Quentin out of things he wants to be involved in," Lawrence said, unable to hide his smile.

"I *thought* he didn't have a fucking death wish and would actually listen to me for once," Tara said, leveling a mean look at Quentin.

"Don't take it personally. I don't listen to anyone." His cheeky grin got even wider.

"He's here, might as well use him," said Derek, waving at the nearest tree. "Go ahead. Work your squirreley magic."

During the entire exchange, Penny had stood frozen, unable to shake the panic gripping her. *He's not Lexa. You're not in the warehouse. This is different. He will be safe.*

She blinked back into reality. Derek was right—Quentin would follow whether they liked it or not. But during their next mission, she'd handcuff Quentin to the bleachers if she had to.

"See anything?" Derek called. "If you say 'other trees and the sky,' you're getting a wedgie."

Quentin's laughter trickled through the treetops.

Penny's heart ached at the way these people had become Quentin's family. She was jealous, of course she was. But it was more than that. She grieved for the loss of the family she and Quentin were supposed to have. The one she'd taken from him. But even among the bad feelings, a seed of pure happiness bloomed. Their lives had all gone to shit in the past ten, eleven months, and Quentin had managed to surround himself with the best people. People who loved him. If Penny couldn't be that for him, she was happy he'd found it elsewhere.

Derek sidled up to her, breaking her out of her reverie, and nodded at the empty tree. "What do you think?"

Back to business, Penny ran through the possibilities. "I think we're about to find out what the Chosen's ritual is." But as she twisted her sickle's hilt in her belt loop, she had another thought. "This could all be a trap placed by Tara's rescuers. We're doing exactly what they presumably want—coming out here to investigate."

The group grew utterly silent. *Yeah, shit. I hadn't considered that until now. I've really had my head in the fucking clouds.*

"Maybe let's not mention that to Mal yet," Penny added. "I'd rather not fight with him."

Derek laughed. "Are you kidding? You *love* arguing with Mal. It's your foreplay."

"The hell is that supposed to mean?" she asked, ignoring the heat in her face.

"Anybody who's been in the same room as you two can see it. There's a thin line between love and hate." Derek waggled his eyebrows and Tara snorted. Even Lawrence joined in on the joke with a hearty chuckle.

"So everyone thinks this? That Mal and I are...together?" she asked.

"Nah, nobody thinks that," said Derek. "But everyone thinks that you *want* to be."

Dear god.

Before Penny could fully grasp the horrors of that revelation, Quentin hopped down from the tree. "Saw some smoke. That way." He pointed deeper into the woods. "I think we can make it there and back before it gets dark."

Lawrence rumpled his hair. "Good work. I say let's go." He glanced at Penny. "And we'll keep an eye out for anything that seems...wrong."

The group headed off, Penny taking point. This was her idea, and if anything jumped out at them, she'd be the first to hit it.

But hopefully it didn't come to that.

As they walked, her thoughts wandered to Mal, thanks to Derek's stupid comment. But they'd been heading that direction more often these days, especially after the way Mal had reacted to her midnight stabber. His protectiveness and primal aggression spoke to the dark, depraved part of her that hungered for the blood of her enemies. Mal had a streak of bloodlust in him too.

Only a person who truly enjoyed the fight, the adrenaline, the raw feeling of going to war with your own two hands, had that spark of something *other*. That night when she'd gone to his room, she could see that very spark in his eyes. And the way he'd cleaned her wound with a tender touch, big hands gentle with her but not holding her as if she was so fragile that she'd break... *He knows how to handle me. Maybe he's the only one who does.*

And seeing Zeln again had done something to Mal. Made him more reckless—in battle, and in his interactions with her. His mask was slipping...and she was insatiably curious to know what was behind it.

Even though it was early morning, little light reached them through the dense woods, lending their trek a gloomy quality. Penny held her sickle ready, tensing at each sound. The rattling of the wind through the branches. The crunching of dead leaves underfoot. The snapping of twigs. The chatter of leaves rustling in the trees. The breaths of her crew behind her. The smell of smoke getting stronger the longer they walked.

"How much farther?" she asked Quentin.

"I didn't have time to get out my protractor to measure the angle of the sun and plot our course with a piece of string and a stick."

She laughed, breaking out of her anxious mood if only for a moment. *Fuck, I miss him.*

His cheek dimpled in a quick smile before he guarded his expression. "Maybe another mile or so," he said, falling back into step beside Tara.

At least he's acknowledging me now. That's a start. But maybe I need to do more than teach him to throw knives.

Another ten minutes of walking, and the air grew hazy and thick with choking smoke that smelled of burnt hair.

Quentin gagged, pulling the collar of his shirt over his nose. "I think we're getting close."

"There." Lawrence pointed through the dense trees to a small group of rock formations where a smoking mound of...something awaited them.

"Is that...?"

As they approached, the source of the smoke became clear.

A smoldering pile of bodies, each meticulously placed in a circle with their heads touching and their feet spreading outward. In the middle of the pyre sat a pile of thick railroad nails. The bodies were charred beyond recognition, but she was willing to bet these were the same ones that had been nailed to the tree. Or, if this was a ritual the cult did regularly, maybe there were other body trees spread throughout the woods.

That's not ominous at all.

"I think I found something," Quentin said from beside the boulder pile. He ducked between a crevasse, clicking on his flashlight. The group followed him into the narrow space, the air dense with a rotten, metallic smell. When his light touched the walls, Penny nearly gasped.

Blood and death didn't bother her. Usually. But this ritual shit was bone-chilling.

The light illuminated a small cave-like space where buckets, bowls, and other receptacles lined the wall. Each was filled to the brim with a dark fluid. A few of the containers had railroad nails and smaller nails sticking out of them.

A tug on her sleeve. Quentin, pointing behind them, shining his light.

On the cave wall scrawled in a shaky hand, a dark liquid outlined a single word.

SALVATION.

"What is this place?" someone said, but Penny was too locked in on the demonic little room that she barely registered it. The only thought in her head was *I should have killed Rodney sooner.*

And she should have locked up Rodney's followers instead of allowing them to run free, thinking they would keep to themselves. But neither she nor Mal had realized what they were dealing with. That his followers would turn into...this. Whatever this was.

Setting aside her disgust and anger, the wheels of her mind turned to practicality. "Before I...stopped Rodney, he brainwashed his people, sucked them into his cult of personality. For his followers to still be working toward whatever goals he had for them, someone with as much power of manipulation as him must have taken over. It doesn't really matter *who* it is, but someone is leading these people. Nothing will stop them from expanding unless we completely eliminate them."

Derek tore his eyes away from the gruesome epitaph to stare at her. "So we kill all of them?"

"They're all users, and they'd all refuse detox serum—if we even had enough to offer them," said Penny. "This is a horde of turned waiting to happen. And we'd kill them if they were turned, wouldn't we?"

"We could force them to detox instead?" Lawrence suggested.

"Dionazole will neutralize the troxapine in their systems and prevent them from turning, but only if they quit using forever—which they probably won't," she said. "But the detox serum won't bring their minds back from the brink of Rodney's infectious bullshit. That part of their minds is forever rotted."

Then Quentin found his voice, surprising her. "There were cults Before. People were able to escape and re-enter society. We shouldn't just murder all of them."

His words lanced straight through her and she flinched. He was right. She was still thinking in absolutes. Rodney had made a habit of preying on the downtrodden, the susceptible, the emotionally fragile, and it wasn't necessarily their fault that they'd fallen for his tricks. Yes, the dregs of society were attracted to him, enjoying the free rein and debauchery with impunity, and they deserved everything coming to them. But some of his followers might be like she'd been when he first found her—lost people looking for any kind of direction in a world that no longer made sense.

It shamed her that it took Quentin saying it aloud for her to realize it.

"We'll find a way to handle this, but—do you hear that?" Penny lurched back outside. Nothing but the rustle of the leaves. But she could have sworn—

There.

A single, distant screech transformed into a chorus of *more*.

Closer.

They were coming. And fast.

"Shit. We need to go."

Everyone filed outside, running back the way they'd come.

A few minutes later, the sounds she'd attributed to the woods jostling around them manifested into harsh snarls and the quick sounds of feet trodding over the dead grass behind them.

She only had a few seconds to comprehend this before they were on them.

Glancing back, she saw a turned take a running leap straight at Derek. Without another thought, Penny threw herself into Derek, knocking him sideways, and they both plunged to the dirt. She pivoted with a slash of her sickle and the turned's head fell to the ground, Derek gaping up at her. "You saved me."

"Hopefully," Penny said as she swiped at other oncoming turned, helping Derek to his feet. "We still gotta make it out of this alive."

Tara stood at their backs, swinging her bat, and cast an unreadable glance at them.

"Where did they come from!" Quentin shouted, lashing out with his knife as Penny took aim with the volt rifle across her back. Lawrence took up Derek's fallen rifle and fired, tens of black, lifeless eyes glinting in the volt's blue light.

"Must have been drawn by the smell of..." She tried to look for a different phrase besides *cooking meat* but failed and elected to shut up instead.

As she and Lawrence fired with their only two volt rifles, none of the turned fell. *They're enhanced turned. All the way out here.* "Blades only!" she said. "These turned are different."

The group fell into practiced combat formations, and Penny surged to Quentin's side. But he surprised her, spinning in a move that she'd taught him, and a blip of pride went through her even in the chaos.

Time flew by in a blur, and then they were surrounded by bodies leaking black blood.

"More will come," said Penny, wiping her hand across her forehead. It came away bloody—her blood. *Must have gotten clipped.* "Everyone okay?" But she only looked at Quentin, and he nodded, what looked like claw marks raking across his arm. Lawrence held his side, and Derek and Tara sported various gashes, but they all nodded too. She'd take stock of her own injuries later. They had to get back before the blood attracted more turned—and apparently now they had to worry about enhanced turned outside the city walls. Which meant that they weren't confined only to the Capital.

They were spreading.

11

B ACK AT THE STADIUM, their scouting crew dispersed to clean up. But Derek hung back with Penny, brow pulled taut.

"You good?" she asked. The man looked constipated.

"About earlier," he said. "I didn't expect—I mean, I never would have thought—shit. Sorry. This isn't coming out right." Taking a deep breath, he fixed her with an oddly serious look that she wasn't used to seeing from him. "Thanks for having my back today."

Not accustomed to receiving any kind of gratitude because, really, she'd never done much to elicit that kind of sentiment, she could only nod. Derek returned it, then headed off, probably to find Agnes, who sometimes took breaks in the cafeteria. When Penny turned toward the locker room with a shower in mind—*fucking cut on my forehead stings*—Quentin leaned against the wall, watching the exchange. Startled, she said the first thing that came to mind. "Good job today."

Quentin's eyes narrowed in suspicion. "Thought you'd be mad at me for sneaking out."

"You were always sneaking out on your adventures when you were a kid too. Remember the corn maze?"

A genuine smile split his face, the sun shining through storm clouds. "Had that thing memorized in a few tries."

"And Mom would always yell at you for coming home with too many corn cobs in your pockets."

The mention of their mother brought them crashing back to reality, their laughter breaking off like a scratched record. *I will always disappoint him because I'll never stop being the person who killed his family. That fact will always be true.*

After another moment of excruciating silence, Quentin said, "You helped Derek." It sounded like an accusation.

Surprised at his non sequitur, she could only say, "Uh, yes."

"You don't even like him."

"I don't like anyone. Except you."

Quentin almost cracked a smile as he turned down the hallway. "See you."

An absurd feeling like she wanted to cry washed over her in a wave of pins and needles, and she retreated before she had an embarrassing outburst in front of him. In the Wilds, she'd lunged for Derek on pure instinct, but it had been a while since those protective instincts extended to anyone besides herself and Quentin. The old Penny would say she was going soft, putting herself at risk like that. But the way Quentin had almost thanked her had her feeling anything but soft.

Seeking the sanctity of her room, she shut the door on the outside world and breathed deeply into the darkness, the exhaustion finally catching up with her. She kicked off her boots and flopped on her bed until she could find the will to go wash off the filth of battle. Her heart rate spiked, but she took slow breaths through her nose and tapped her fingers against her leg, focusing on the feel of the material against her skin. When she felt more grounded, she turned her thoughts to what she was going to say to Mal.

Finding Tara's rescuers and dealing with the cult might be more involved than they'd thought. Why were enhanced turned in the Wilds outside the range where troxies could use their horrible feedback machine to control them? Maybe they were an experiment gone wrong, or had accidentally been let loose. Or maybe they'd come from a neighboring city and were flocking to areas with larger populations. Penny gulped around the sick feeling in her throat. *A larger food source.* And if that were the case, even more could be heading for the Capital at any time—if they weren't being manufactured within the city itself.

Agnes was right. They needed to stop the troxies at the source, whatever still-functioning lab they were using to pump these creatures out—right after they dealt with the cult. She didn't want either of those god-awful things anywhere near Quentin. But in the meantime, she could make sure he was prepared to face anything. Maybe he was old enough now that he could handle slaying his own dragons—and maybe she could teach him how. She knew of a few people who'd agree with her. *This could be my chance to make nice with more than just Quentin.* And maybe she needed to do more than just teach *him* how to smash some monsters...

Her mind churning with ideas, she went off in search of Tara and, hopefully, Agnes.

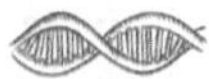

After asking around, Penny found them in the storage room rooting through tool boxes.

"Are we sure Derek doesn't have a hex driver at home?" asked Tara as she tossed a wrench into a box. "That man has everything, even if he doesn't know what it's for."

"No, I'm not sure, because like you said, he doesn't know half of what he has," said Agnes. "But at least his tools are organized, unlike this mess."

Clearing her throat, Penny said, "Hi."

The two women looked up, and Penny didn't miss the way they tensed before schooling their features into neutrality.

"Hi," Agnes said, face expectant, if a bit pinched.

The seconds ticked by before Penny remembered why she'd sought them out. "Oh, um. I wanted to...ask your advice, I guess. Both of you." *God, could I sound any more awkward?*

Tara leaned against the wall with her arms crossed, but her expression didn't hold the usual animosity as she lifted an eyebrow.

"We've encountered these enhanced turned a few times now," Penny said. "We're all good fighters and adaptable, but I'm not sure about the rest of our troops. Head shots are hard, and using a blade is even harder. We need to revamp Mal's training sessions to account for this new threat."

"We?" asked Tara.

"I was hoping you and Agnes would lead some of the sessions." *And act as a buffer so I don't have to be center fucking stage by my goddamn self.*

Tara and Agnes exchanged a look, then Tara shrugged. "We're in. We could start today before dinner."

"Oh, great." Penny didn't know what reaction she had expected, but quick agreement wasn't it.

"But you're leading the first one," said Tara.

Fuck. "Uh—"

"Mal would like it if you did." A sly smile tugged at the corner of Tara's mouth.

"Why the fuck would that matter?" Penny asked.

"We'll help out," Agnes said, interrupting. "I know the newfound fame makes you uncomfortable." That comment had a spark of gratitude flitting through her, but Agnes wasn't done. "Derek told me about what you did for him today."

"Don't mention it," Penny said. *Seriously, please do not fucking mention it.* She didn't regret many of her actions since the Beginning, but maybe she'd made a mistake with Agnes. With all of the Outposters.

"Well—thanks," said Agnes, looking equally as awkward. "It's—I much prefer Derek alive."

At that, Tara burst out laughing. "He'd make one hell of a ghost though. Bet he'd get a kick out of haunting Quentin. Maybe the invisibility would help him pull off a prank on tomatito for once."

"It might," Agnes said with a smile, the uneasiness passed. But the mention of Quentin reminded Penny of her second order of business.

"Ah, about Quentin—" *Just say it.* "I was wondering if you had any suggestions for how I could...make him happy." *That is the lamest thing I have ever said.* But she pressed onward, the words spilling out of her. "I've apologized, but I know that's less than worthless. I want to do more. He *deserves* more. But I don't know what to do. He and I are practically strangers now. And I...I don't have anyone else to ask."

Picking at her sleeve, she tried not to gnaw her lip as she awaited their response. These women owed her absolutely nothing. They should be spitting in her face. But they cared about Quentin, and she hoped that would be enough. This *vulnerability* thing was new, but if it meant getting closer to Quentin, she'd do whatever it took.

Finally, Tara spoke. "I've noticed you teaching him a few things one-on-one. That's good. But maybe you could invite him to join these new group sessions. He'd jump at the chance to train beside Mal and all of our soldiers. Make him feel more like part of the team."

Penny must have had a skeptical look on her face because Agnes quickly chimed in. "T and I both know the desire to protect him at all costs. But maybe we're coddling him too much—or as much as he'll allow us to, anyway. Kid has a history of going rogue—it's why I stopped refusing him. If we're all going on a raid and he wants to come, I let him. Keeps him from sneaking around, and it shows we trust him to hold his own. It would mean a lot if you asked him to join you on some scouting missions—ones that you think would be appropriate for him. And—" Agnes cut off with a sheepish look.

"And?" Penny prompted.

"Well...he's obsessed with Mal. Thinks the guy hung the moon, or at least catapulted it into the sky," Agnes said. "If you were to, I don't know, warm up to Mal—or at least not fight with him all the time—it might show Quentin that you're trying to forge a...friendly relationship with his idol. It couldn't hurt," she finished with a shrug.

Tara snorted. "At the look on your face, I can tell that was your least favorite option."

"Is it that obvious?" Penny asked.

"Just think about it," Agnes said with a smile that said she saw more than Penny wanted her or anyone else to.

"Thanks for the chat. I appreciate it," Penny said, unsure of what else to say, but she hoped it got across how much she truly meant it.

"Anything for our little payaso," said Tara. "Love him to death, even though I want to drop-kick his ass more than half the time."

"So, training in an hour?" Agnes asked.

"Sounds good," Penny said. "Make sure you drag Silas out of his science cave for this."

"I'm sure I can convince him to take a break from staring at a screen and entice him with staring at a shirtless Mal instead." Agnes waggled her brows and Tara snickered.

"That's a sight anyone would be interested in," Penny said, the joke flying out of her mouth before she could stop it. "I mean—I didn't mean me, of course. And he's usually clothed during training."

"Oh, of course." Agnes suppressed a smile. "But Silas doesn't know that. We'll meet you in the arena in a few."

Tara and Agnes headed off to spread the word, Penny staring after them and computing what had just happened. When she headed to their training session a bit later, she still hadn't quite figured it out. But whatever it was, she felt...good about it. Surprisingly good.

It was fucking bizarre.

"Everyone, choose your weapons." Penny nodded to the pile of variously sized knives, Pharmatrox-issue billy clubs, hatchets, a few random swords someone had found in an abandoned apartment, and a whole other assortment of crap that could be feasibly used as a weapon like garden shears, rakes, shovels, an old broom, a collection of sawed-off pipes—

"Where the hell did you get all of this stuff? Home Depot?" Mal asked as the first session of fifty or so people dug through the admittedly flea market–looking pile of items, Agnes and Tara helping to pass things out.

"I *might* have raided Lawrence's gardening shed," Penny admitted. "We didn't expect the first class to be so big and ran out of non-ammo weapons pretty quickly on short notice. We should get more on our next armory run—hopefully we get to actually do it this time, instead of getting a surprise visit."

At that, Mal crossed his arms, his demeanor growing intense. "Speaking of surprise visits, why did I have to hear from everyone else about what happened in the Wilds today?" Turning to look at her for the first time since they'd both arrived in the arena, he grew stormier when he noticed the gash she could feel on her forehead.

"Yeah, I know," she said, holding a hand in front of her wound. "It burns like a motherfucker, thanks for asking. I didn't have time to go to the infirmary. No point in wasting resources on something not important."

"A wound leaking blood down your face is not important?"

"Oh shit, is it bleeding?" she asked, patting at it with her tee shirt sleeve. *Only a little.* "It'll hold. Makes me look tough anyway." She waved him off, which only increased the pulsing of the vein in his temple. "Go make sure Raph doesn't take someone's eye out. He's pretty good, but he gets a little enthusiastic, and I'm worried about him swinging that rake around." She nodded toward Raph, who was twirling the rake over his head like a helicopter. *Actually, he's not bad.*

Walking over to the pile, Penny chose a new weapon for herself—a broadsword—but she'd mostly wanted to get some distance from Mal. His spotlight of protectiveness tended to scramble her brain cells, and she wanted to make sure this class left an impression with people—and with Quentin. He spent the longest digging around in the pile, examining each item carefully, a mischievous spark glinting in his eyes.

"Just pick something," Derek said, "before I die of old age."

"Shouldn't take too long since you're practically ancient with those creaky knees of yours, Gramps," Quentin said, choosing a pair of longer knives. "Was just thinking of all the cool things I could make with this stuff. If I attached that saw to a motor, maybe some knives too, I could make a deadly automated frisbee-type thing. Silas, will you help me?"

Silas nodded eagerly and opened his mouth, but clamped it shut at a glare from Agnes as she passed by. When she'd moved on, he ducked his head to Quentin, the two whispering conspiratorially.

"Remind me to stay far away from your inventions," Lawrence said as he grabbed the axe like Penny knew he would.

As Penny moved past their group, Quentin said, "Penelope—thanks for letting me train today. This is pretty cool."

She couldn't help the smile that spread across her face. *Pretty cool. A good start.*

Once everyone had selected something, Penny glanced at Agnes and Tara, who made encouraging gestures. Clearing the sudden emotion from her throat, Penny spoke up. *So much for avoiding the spotlight.* But with Tara's and Agnes's approval—and Quentin's studious attention—she found that maybe she didn't mind it so much.

"I'm sure you've heard by now the rumors about the enhanced turned. I don't want to alarm anyone, but their numbers are growing. Bullets and volts do fuck all, so don't waste your ammo. Only crushing the skull or decapitation will stop them."

"How can we tell them apart from the turned we're used to fighting?" someone shouted.

"Good question. You can't. If your bullets don't work, then you'll know. But that's why you're here now. We'll be retraining everyone on how to use weapons that don't rely on ammo. Anything can be a weapon—don't forget that if you're ever in a bind." Her nervousness constricted her throat, and the memory of an arm snaking around her neck had her thoughts jolting to her midnight fight with Zeln. "And for anyone who's interested, I plan to practice some hand-to-hand combat and basic ground fighting more regularly—because I could really use some work on that too." At the thumbs-up from Tara and Agnes, she knew her last-minute addition had been the right choice.

After separating everyone into smaller groups, Penny, Tara, and Agnes ran them through striking techniques for wielding an ungainly weapon.

"If you have something like a heavy sword—look, I don't know why you would, but you might happen to come across one at some point—or an axe or a hatchet, even a machete, these are bludgeoning weapons," Penny explained. "Same with a shovel or a hoe. It helps to know how to strike with them, but if all else fails and panic takes over, just beat the hell out of your opponent with it. That could be said for any weapon, really." *I'm rambling.* She'd never instructed a large group before, nor put herself in such a forward-facing position.

Agnes sidled up to her and whispered, "You know what you're doing."

Something about hearing the words from Agnes took her back to their own training sessions. While under much different circumstances that Penny wasn't necessarily proud of—like how she'd tricked Agnes into becoming a user—the means were still the same. She'd instructed people before, she could do it again. And this time, the cause mattered. Because it was all of their lives and the fate of the country at stake, not just fulfilling her own personal agenda.

Nodding in thanks, she projected her voice to the larger group. "Partner up and take turns. Speak up if you have questions."

"You heard her. Adelante!" Tara clapped her hands, and everyone got to it.

Walking around to each group, Penny observed and offered help when needed. But with Tara and Agnes, and even Lawrence, Mal, and Derek helping, she didn't need to do too much correcting; they were all good teachers and got along well with the soldiers. She couldn't help but feel like a bit of an outsider. Her own fault, really. Maybe this was her chance to get to know the people she fought beside.

Squaring herself, she made a point to interact with each group. She had thought it would feel awkward but it actually felt...good. Good in a way that training her Marauders hadn't. That had been a different kind of training. How to attack a sleeping camp, how to instill fear in hostages. But now, she was empowering people to protect themselves. And interacting in small groups was much better than standing up in front of an entire crowd. But she was kidding herself if she thought she was doing this for anyone but Quentin. Even so, she still hadn't worked up the courage to approach him yet, but seeing him happy was good enough. *Baby steps.*

Out of the corner of her eye, she noticed Mal helping Quentin with his dual knife wielding. It was a good thing too, because Quentin looked like he might accidentally slice his own shirt to ribbons. Seeing the two of them laughing and joking twisted some unknown part of her.

It was a fucking weird feeling, but not a bad one. But she didn't know what it meant.

I'm sensing a theme here of not knowing what the fuck is going on in my own head.

And she didn't like it. She'd always been sure of herself, of her convictions and actions. Even if she hadn't always made the right choices, she'd stood by them. But ever since she'd started spending more time with Quentin and his friends—and Mal, specifically—she found herself becoming something...other.

Maybe even something better.

But those weren't things she was ready to acknowledge yet, so she shoved them aside.

Penny noticed Agnes wander over to Quentin, watching with a bemused expression. "Giving you *one* knife is asking for trouble," Agnes said. "But two? We must all be insane. And Mal, you're putting yourself right in the line of fire."

"Don't worry, he's—hey!" Mal dodged as Quentin lunged with the butt of his knife for his ribs.

"You said to take advantage of my opponent's distractions," Quentin said with an innocent smile. "You were definitely distracted. So I took advantage." Quentin flipped the knife and caught it by the hilt—or he would have, if Mal hadn't snatched it out of the air at the last second and tucked it into his own belt.

"And another thing," Mal said. "Always keep a tight grip on your weapons. Would hate for you to get *disarmed*." Mal grabbed Quentin by the wrist and yanked him forward, making sawing motions across his arm while Quentin laughed, throwing fake punches. Penny found herself smiling at the exchange. The only side of Mal she'd ever experienced was the serious, broody general. This lighter side of him—well. She liked it. And she might even want to see more of it.

Finding her courage, Penny tossed Quentin a broomstick from the pile of unchosen "weapons."

"Yes! Vindicated!" Quentin said as he caught it and turned to thwack Mal.

"Hey!" Mal said with a chuckle, holding Quentin away with a hand on his forehead. "Easy on the shins."

Turning one of the most sincere grins Penny had ever seen from him in her direction, Quentin asked her, "Want to come over here and *sweep* Mal off his feet?"

Nearby, Tara guffawed from where she was helping a neighboring group. "Payaso," she said.

"No way," Penny replied. "You've gotta learn to fight your own battles." Which, really, was the true inspiration behind today.

"You mean I get to do this stuff every day now?" Quentin asked, still determined to take out Mal's legs.

"What, beat up Mal with a broom? Absolutely," Penny said, smiling at the mock glare Mal sent her while Quentin laughed. *This might actually work out.*

From nearby, Silas kept shooting glances at Mal, neglecting his partner. He looked disappointed to see that Mal was not in any state of undress, although his bicep tattoo was visible through the fabric of his tight white tee shirt.

I need to get a grip. I'm as bad as Silas now.

Catching Penny's eye, Silas smirked, beckoning her over. She rolled her eyes, but it was half-hearted. Silas was actually okay, even if he tended to go off on hyper-focused tangents about things no one else on planet Earth could understand.

"Enjoying the view?" he asked as he did another rep with his partner Ju Lee, a middle-aged woman who was pretty fierce with her fists. Penny also remembered seeing her working in the infirmary.

Scoffing, Penny said, "The only view I see is someone with a noodle arm attempting to take a swing at Ju Lee here, but he's only gonna end up hurting himself." Penny squeezed his elbow. "Tighten up."

"Try again, like you mean it," said Ju Lee.

He took another swing with his metal pipe—he must have been taking notes from Tara—and did better this time, although Ju Lee blocked. "Good!" said Ju Lee. "Again."

"Looks like you don't need me," Penny said, nodding at her with a slight smile, and she returned it.

After another half hour of drilling, Tara dismissed everyone to grab some dinner. Lawrence had promised them some semblance of herbed mashed potatoes, and people were buzzing with excitement, none more eager than Quentin. A small group, including Agnes and Tara, hung back for her sparring session, and when Penny asked for a volunteer, *fucking Mal* was the first to step up.

Goddamn him.

"Hip tosses are good if you're facing an opponent who outsizes you," Penny said, giving Mal a look, and the group chuckled as he puffed up his chest. "It's not as hard as it looks. It's all about leverage."

Snaking her right arm under Mal's and around his back, she cupped his right elbow with her left hand, stepped into him, and turned so her back was flush to his front.

Don't think too much about that.

Ignoring the heat of him behind her, she sank her stance and loaded his weight onto her back and hips, then flipped him to land on his side, his right arm still in her grasp. The group *oooh*ed, and even Mal looked impressed, sprawled on the ground at her feet.

Propping her knee on Mal's side and rearing back a fist, she said, "And then they're completely at your mercy." At her words, she saw something shift in his eyes. Something primal and all-consuming looked back at her. He saw the predator in her, and he did not shy away. But it was gone in an instant, replaced by a spark of mischief. In one swift move, he reversed their positions, trapping her legs with his own and immobilizing the use of her hips as he straddled her.

"If you get reversed like this," he said to the small group, "it's not a great position, but you can get out."

Penny's breaths came faster, and the familiar panic solidified in her chest as she remembered being trapped in a position with no idea how to escape. *Damn it, not now.* The last thing she wanted was to lose her shit in front of Mal again, and this time they had an audience. Sensing something was wrong, he moved to get off her, but she shook her head, clamping her hands on his biceps to keep him in position. "How do I get out of this?"

Watching her with a wary expression, he gave her waist a reassuring squeeze. "Make a frame against my hips. Left forearm across the top, keep your right elbow on the ground. Meet your hands at my hip. Good. Then push and curl to your right side, and sneak your leg through. All at the same time. This will get you back to your half guard position, and you'll have more control, or be able to escape from there."

Penny followed his instructions and completed the move, but she could tell he helped her by taking some of his own weight.

"Take some time to practice on your own, but then go get some dinner," Agnes said to the group. "Don't want to miss out on whatever Lawrence has concocted for us tonight." The comment was met with light laughter, and everyone branched off, some taking up the offer to make for the cafeteria.

Mal held out a hand and helped Penny to her feet. "Do you—"

"Again," she said, squaring up to him.

And he showed how well he knew her by not asking her if she was sure or suggest that she take a break until her hands stopped shaking. He knew she needed this even if he didn't know why, and he would give it to her.

They drilled the throw and the escape, and then moved on to other techniques for how to handle larger opponents. As they worked, the anxiety seeped out of her and she felt more in control. When she finally surfaced and looked around, she and Mal were alone in the arena, the fading sunset staining the sky ruby red.

"One more, then we'll call it a night," she said. Getting in position, she flipped Mal to land on his side, then slid her knee across and took the full mount position, straddling him. She moved to cut off his airway with her forearm, but he rolled them over, pinning both of her hands above her head, her legs wrapped snugly around his waist in full guard.

But the position shook something loose in her mind, a memory from before they'd taken down the Spire that she'd been thinking of more often now when she was alone at night with the darkness as her only witness.

She moved to shove Mal again, and he caught her wrists, eyes glinting. He backed her up against a tree, pinning her hands above her head. The planes of his body pressed against hers all the way down to her boots. Her chest heaved with fast breaths and she stared him down...

"Push me again, and you lose your walking privileges... Don't fucking tempt me."

Now with him pinning her again, muscles flexing, her skin flared like a live wire everywhere they touched. Trapped as she was, she wasn't aware she was arching up into him, pressing against his chest, drawn to him in a way she couldn't explain. His honey-brown eyes dipped to her lips, then back up, as if to say, *Don't fucking tempt me.*

Fucking Christ.

She wasn't sure if it was a curse or a prayer.

At her sharp intake of breath, the moment shattered and they rolled apart.

"Thanks for the help," she said, brushing herself off and keeping her eyes carefully away from him.

"We still need to talk about what happened."

At that, her eyes shot to his, and he held her gaze with unwavering intensity. After a charged moment that felt like an eternity, he said, "I meant about what happened in the Wilds. When you were attacked." His fingers brushed her forehead, light as a whisper. "You should get that cleaned out."

Am I...leaning into his touch? What is wrong with me? "I will," she said, taking a half step back. "Sounds like you already heard from everyone else what happened."

"I want to hear your assessment."

"Why? Derek and Tara are better at that logistical stuff than me."

"From what I saw here tonight, I'm not sure that's true. And your opinion matters to me."

Nope, not thinking about how that makes me feel. "The Chosen need to be neutralized, but I don't know that murdering all of them is the right choice. I'm not sure what else to do with them though. But I've been thinking more about Tara's rescuers, and we could arrange for a 'you scratch my back, I'll scratch yours' situation. We help them take out the cult, this mystery crew helps us retake the Capital. Then we can refocus on sending a small team to make contact with Kev in Chicago, hopefully with some newfound allies on our side. Maybe we could even raid the SubTran holdout together."

Mal nodded, considering. "We can send others to locate your mystery crew—maybe Derek or Tara could take over. You should stay here and continue training our people. It's good for them to see you involved like this."

Ah yep. There it is. While he might value her opinion, he always had his own agenda. "So other people are more expendable?"

Mal blew out a breath, rubbing his hands across his beard, saying, "With no news from Kev, morale is tanking. If I—*we* lose you, things will go downhill fast."

"I don't give a fuck about morale. Ending Rodney's cult is my responsibility. *Mine.* And you will not take that away from me, Malosi."

At the sound of his full name, his bright eyes darkened to sun-warmed whiskey. *There goes his jaw muscle again.* For an insane second, she thought he might reach for her like he had in the forest that night over a month ago now, when the turned had interrupted them. Whether to finish what they'd almost started or to pin her against the nearest surface until she relented, she wasn't sure. But for an even more ridiculous moment, she almost wanted him to do whatever that look in his eyes promised.

But instead, he clenched his fists and said, "You've got one more week, and then I'm handing the reins to someone else."

And just like that, we're right back at it. "You can't unanimously decide something like that. This is *my* idea."

He ground his molars together and bit off whatever he'd been about to say. "One week, Penny. Make the most of it."

Seething, she said, "How generous." Turning on her heel, she headed to the showers to clean her forehead wound. And maybe stuff her head in a locker to let out some frustrated screams.

Before she reached the arena door, she snuck a look over her shoulder and watched as Mal paused at the men's locker room, rubbing a hand through his hair. He tilted his head to the sky and closed his eyes, as if begging for divine intervention. But even from a distance, she could see the slight smile pulling at his lips before he pushed through the door.

It was the same kind of smile she found on her own face when she looked in the locker room mirror a few minutes later.

I guess we're both happiest when we're butting heads.

12

Agnes

AGNES AWOKE IN DARKNESS, a set of piercing blue eyes framed by silver hair emblazoned in her brain. A bloom of blood on a white lab coat. Dr. Hansen's blank stare as the life left her eyes, a black-bladed knife point through her neck. Agnes's breaths heaved in her chest, her heart kicking against her ribcage in the wake of the nightmare. Or memory.

Since that night on the cathedral's front lawn, Agnes hadn't dwelt much on it, opting to shove everything down. Which was probably the reason for the nightmares. And the heartburn. But at night when the darkness came for her, so did the vivid recollections of every moment leading up to Dr. Hansen's death, playing on repeat. And one key part always stood out to her—the black-bladed knife. Penny had yanked the knife from her own wound, risking bleeding out, to stab it through Dr. Hansen's neck. Whether it was in revenge for what Hansen did to Quentin or to keep them all safe, Agnes didn't know, and she'd never talked to Penny about it.

But after Penny had approached her and Tara almost a week ago, Agnes had begun to believe Penny's motivations for many of her recent actions truly were all with Quentin in mind. She hadn't been sure of Penny's ability to be anything other than the bloodthirsty woman she'd known. But this new side of Penny, a sister desperately trying to reconcile with her brother and make up for all the wrong she'd done, Agnes could relate to that. The compulsion to scrub out the dark marks on her past, but not just to alleviate the weight on her conscience—to do it out of a desire to be a better person. Agnes loved Silas and Evie like they were her siblings by blood. And now, she loved Quentin, Tara, even Lawrence and Derek—*mierda. That's maybe the first time I've even considered that about Derek.* There was nothing she wouldn't do for these people. Her family.

If Penny felt even a fraction of that for Quentin, which Agnes really believed she did, then maybe there was a path for Penny and Quentin to reconcile. Maybe even for her and Penny to find common ground too. She wasn't ready to consider that yet, but if Penny wanted to make Quentin happy, Agnes was more than willing to help. Tara didn't trust Penny farther than she could hurl her, but she'd begrudgingly agreed that Penny extending an olive branch wasn't entirely unwelcome.

In bed beside her, Derek stirred, wrapping an arm around her waist and nuzzling into her neck. "Bad dream?" he murmured against her skin.

"Yeah," she said as she snuggled into him.

"The cathedral again?"

"The cathedral again." She chewed her lip. After a moment, she added, "I was thinking about Penny."

"Oh?" he prompted, tracing his nose up the side of her neck and pressing a light kiss below her ear.

"Yeah, and about what you said. How maybe she deserves a chance to be different."

He made a sleepy sound of acknowledgment. "So you're telling me I'm right."

"Don't get used to it."

A chuckle vibrated through his chest. "Never."

She felt his smile against her throat and leaned into him, an overwhelming sense of *rightness* shining through her. In a world where she'd thought security was a thing of the past, being wrapped up with him was the safest she'd ever felt. "I couldn't do any of this without you."

He snorted, saying, "Of course you could. You *were* doing all of this, and more, before we met."

Tangling her fingers in his hair, she pulled his face back to look him in the eyes, tracing a thumb across his perfectly shaped brows. She always complimented his bone structure, and he always brushed her off, but he truly cut a striking profile. "I mean, I wouldn't *want* to go through any of this without you. I—you—I'm grateful you're my partner." These kinds of words didn't come easily to her, and she wrinkled her nose at the stilted delivery, but he pressed his forehead to hers with a genuine smile.

"I've got you, Aggie," he said, planting a kiss on her forehead. "You sure you don't want me to go with you today?"

"I'd feel better knowing Quentin has some additional supervision on this nighttime scouting trip."

"He does have a knack for finding trouble. But he'll be fine. We've got a good crew. Let's get a few more hours of sleep before we have to face the day." Derek tightened his arm around her, dipping his lips to hers. A sound of contentment escaped her at the silken feel of his tongue, and the kiss took on a more heated edge, all thoughts of sleep fleeing her mind. Hands sliding to her hips, he pulled away with a devilish smile, adding, "But I have a few ideas of what we can do first."

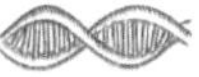

"Basement should have what we need. Can you get us in?" Agnes asked Mal as they surveyed the ten-story building. The lab was on the edge of the last few remaining Pharmatrox-controlled sectors, just a mile or two from the SubTran station. Which was probably why Mal was wound up so tightly today. His jaw had been extra hard from repeatedly clenching it. *I wonder if he has regular migraines.*

"I'll get you in," Mal said, then added, "Could have really used Sanj and Raph today, but they volunteered to go with Penny." Another jaw clench. *Guess they're fighting again.* "We should have enough manpower to clear the facility, but with it being this close to the center of troxy territory, I don't like taking unnecessary risks. Especially since we still don't know what the fuck they're up to." He scanned the streets and the troxies orbiting on patrol, trucks Agnes had never seen before passing by on regular intervals.

"We could come back a different day?" Silas asked. But he knew as well as Agnes did that they needed to get into this facility *now*. Their list of users that needed rehab was longer than the amount of detox serum they had left—not to mention that some people required extra doses to have the same effect. Which could only mean one thing. What Dr. Hansen had done to Quentin at the cathedral—given him a strain of troxapine that required a specific formula of detox serum—was happening to other users. Soon, their supply of detox serum might not even work at all.

So she'd come here in search of an FPGA to reprogram her machine to find a universal detox serum formula that would work for *any* version of troxapine. If she found a scientist to help her actually *make* the detox serum, all the better. But she wasn't holding out hope.

Silas, at least, had finally been able to crack some of the holofiles from New York. After he'd established a satellite connection—albeit, an inconsistent one with spotty internet—he'd decrypted everything except Evie's holofiles and digital notepad, which required a Helix Key to access. Agnes hadn't seen one in Evie's office, nor had she *ever* seen the woman in possession of one, so those were a dead end.

From the other files, they'd confirmed their earlier theories—Pharmatrox had consolidated their scientific operations into a secure black ops facility. Due to Silas's experience working for similar tech conglomerates, he figured this lab housed all of their "in case of catastrophic emergency" things like their server farm and enough capabilities to keep troxapine production on life support. But even if this doomsday bunker was off the grid, there had to be some kind of natural power source, not to mention a digital or paper trail leading to it—they'd have to coordinate shipments across the country to transport the drugs and get incoming supplies.

But we still don't know enough.

As Mal locked in on one of the guards—a medium-build man with dark eyes and brown skin—something in his face changed, and he snapped his fingers at the troops waiting in the alley. They'd brought a force of about thirty or so, which was plenty to handle the smaller facility. But the expression etched into Mal's face worried her. It was the same one Penny wore whenever she faced anyone she deemed an enemy.

Mal was out for blood.

Understanding dawned on her. *That must be Zeln.*

"Don't lose your head," Agnes told him. "This is an easy battle. We outnumber them. Don't blow it over something like this."

Mal studied her with a piercing gaze as she stared unflinchingly back. "Zeln's been quiet lately, but I don't trust it."

"I know you don't want to give Penny the satisfaction of flying off the handle and proving her right about your inability to remain objective."

That did the trick. Mal gave her a firm nod and whistled low to their people, who fanned out, weapons raised and gas masks on, as he pulled a small device from his pocket.

Earlier that morning, Quentin had rigged the street with some explosives and stink bombs that could be remotely detonated to cause "a delightfully annoying and smelly distraction," as he'd put it. Quentin would be leaving with Penny, Derek, and a few others to scout in the Wilds in about an hour—just the time they planned to be finished with the lab raid. She didn't love the idea of them facing unknown assailants, but the sooner they found the mysterious crew and cleared the woods of the cult, the sooner they could make contact with Chicago and get everyone scouring every city for Pharmatrox's doomsday bunker.

Mal clicked the button and the windows in every building shattered in a massive explosion, noxious gas dumping into the awaiting troxy guards, who coughed and clutched their throats. A few seconds later, troxies poured outside to meet the threat, falling victim to Quentin's stink bombs. At Mal's signal, everyone charged into battle.

As she ran for the door, Agnes cast a look over her shoulder and saw Mal zero in on Zeln, who powered through the fumes as if they didn't affect him. She opened her mouth to shout at Mal to make sure his head stayed out of his ass, but Silas grabbed her, hustling her inside.

"He can handle himself," said Silas, taking aim with his volt rifle and shooting some stunning zaps at the troxies flooding the halls, who dropped like flies, as the force of Faction troops rushed in behind them. "He's not an idiot."

"I can think of at least one person who disagrees with that statement on principle," she said, shooting her stun gun into the crowd.

"Agreeing with Penny? Derek said you'd been doing that more often lately." Silas grinned at her as he shoved a troxy aside.

Choosing to ignore that jibe, the two plowed through bodies toward the basement, and when they reached the door, Agnes scanned her thumb on the reader. The door gave a cheerful beep, swinging open to reveal an expansive warehouse-slash-lab.

But it was completely void of people. No personnel, no scientists at work, no orderlies running around.

She and Silas exchanged a glance as they wandered through the maze of shelves—then ducked back. At the far end, a few guards milled about a metal door with a serious looking latch. Something important had to be in there for the guards to maintain their post while all hell was breaking loose above.

Silas nodded, and together, they took off. After a brief altercation, the guards lay sizzling on the floor, incapacitated but alive.

Swiping one of their access cards, Agnes slapped it against the reader on the door and it swung open, admitting them into—

"An empty walk-in cooler? What the fuck?" Silas said, looking around the refrigerated room packed with shelves.

Agnes shrugged as she walked into the room the size of a small office. "All the containers are empty," she said after looking through her tenth barren one.

But in the back corner, something caught her eye. A shelf sat askew with fewer containers than the others. Examining it, she noticed a pinhole in the wall's sheet metal. A pinhole like the elevator card reader in the Spire, the one that went to the secret floor. Waving the guard's keycard in front of it, the metal slid back to reveal a dank, dark room reeking of sweat and dirt. A lone lightbulb hung from the ceiling, but its dingy glow hardly penetrated the expansive space.

"Si, I think I found something," she said, moving the shelf aside and taking a small LED flashlight from her belt. Shining it into the space, she nearly choked at what she saw.

Madre mía, did I find something.

"What—oh shit," Silas said. "How did they—what are they all doing here?"

"We can talk, you know." One of the ten or so people huddled in the room stood, walking into the circle of Agnes's flashlight. A middle-aged woman with black hair streaked with silver, her angular face twisted into a scowl. "So which ones are you? Can't be feeding duty. We just ate. Too soon for another interrogation. Maybe you're the good cops, here to convince us to work in the labs again with promises of freedom. Or maybe you're here to force us."

What the hell is going on? Glancing behind the woman, the other people in the room ran the gamut as far as age, but all wore dirty, dark blue scrubs. "Uh, we're not with Pharmatrox," Agnes said.

At that, the woman's eyes widened. "You mean—come on, everyone." She turned to the people behind her, who began gathering up their things—coats, shoes, small backpacks.

"Wait, hold on," Agnes said, blocking the door. These people clearly needed help, but she had some questions first. But then some of the woman's previous words registered, and Agnes's jaw dropped. "You're Pharmatrox scientists."

The woman's expression slammed shut, eyes narrowed.

"You already let it slip," Silas said. "Too late to deny it."

"So you're Faction, then," the woman said. "Fucking figures." In a swift move, she grabbed Silas's rifle and head-butted him in the face.

"Jesus *Christ*," Silas groaned, clutching his bleeding nose, but before she could move another inch, Agnes thrust a knife at the woman's throat. *A room full of scientists. Just what I need.*

"We're not here to hurt you," Agnes said. "Actually, I could use your help."

"Help? Ha! You probably want to *help* us right over the edge of a cliff," the woman said, eyeing Agnes's knife. "Bet your Kev would like to see us all dead. We have nothing to say to you."

"You can either talk to me or to our general," said Agnes. "And I don't think I have to tell you which of us is the nicer one." Mal had made a reputation for himself on the battlefield in the past few months, so most troxies knew they didn't want to face him.

But everyone kept their mouths shut.

For a wild second, Agnes almost wished Penny was there. *She is way better at being scary than I am.* It just wasn't Agnes's style. Pocketing her knife, Agnes stared down the older woman, who made a formidable opponent, especially after the move she'd pulled on Silas. After a moment, the woman shuffled off into the shadows and returned, dropping a box at their feet.

"We can't help you. But maybe something in there can."

Agnes knelt to investigate. "More digital notepads and holofiles for you to hack into later, Si."

"I hate those goddamn things," he grumbled, rifling through the box. "And why do there have to be so *many*—Aggie, oh my god." He thrust a circuit board in her face, waving it frantically.

"An FPGA, de puta madre, this is *perfect*," Agnes said as she cradled the equipment to her chest. "Now I can finish my machine." Turning an eager gaze back to the woman, she asked, "Where did you get these? And why are you all down here?" As her eyes landed on a petite young woman with round glasses, elegant dark brown skin, and a cute face, the older woman flinched. Sensing a chink in her armor, Agnes added, "Maybe we can help you, if you tell us what happened."

After a brief hesitation, the leader spoke. "About a month ago, Pharmatrox rounded up the scientists in this facility and anything related to our work. Shoved us all in here and locked us away. We're all that's left."

"What happened to the others?" Silas asked.

"Don't know. Never saw them again. In the event of a catastrophic emergency, Pharmatrox protocol is to 'protect' the scientists at all costs. We're the ones who know how to make their drugs, so they need us. But as you can see by our dwindling numbers, I'm not convinced protection is what they have in mind. Exterminating us to keep their information out of enemy hands is more like it."

"You—you think they're *murdering* all of the scientists?" Agnes asked. It sounded like exactly the kind of scorched earth policy Pharmatrox would implement in a last-ditch effort to protect themselves and their knowledge.

"Not all of them," the woman said. "Even after everything, some scientists remain loyal and are continuing Pharmatrox's work somewhere. No, the ones sent for 'advanced protection protocol' like us are those at risk of defecting or blabbing their secrets. They give us time to change our minds—they need as many of us as they can keep on board—but our time is running out."

"If you want to help undo this mess, I could really use you on my team," Agnes said. "If not, I can get you on a convoy to Canada. We're working on making a detox serum that will work for any new version of troxapine. I have a machine that can pinpoint the right formulas, but I don't have a lab or a scientist. Any chance there's some detox serum here?"

"They transported all materials and most equipment to a different lab when the protection protocol went into place. Only stuff that's left is whatever's in here with us."

Mierda. But at least we got some holofiles and that circuit board I need.

"It's admirable, what you're doing," the woman continued. "But we just want the nightmare to be over. I'll take a seat on that convoy." All of the other scientists nodded their agreement.

Agnes sighed, unsurprised. Who knew what Pharmatrox had put these people through? Asking them to stick around in a war-torn city inches away from the company that wanted them dead or at least imprisoned was not a demand she'd ever make. She'd once thought of running to Canada too, and if that's what they wanted, she'd make it happen. She could find another willing scientist somewhere.

"How do I know we can trust you?" their leader asked.

"We should trust them," squeaked the young woman with glasses. A few of her colleagues around the room pinned her with harsh glares, but some looked hopeful. "I remember you," she said to Silas, eyes wide with awe. "You helped me escape the Spire. In the stairwell. You and that red-haired woman."

Silas smiled and nodded. "I don't remember much about that day. I blacked it all out due to the insane amount of sheer terror I experienced, but I'm glad we were able to help you."

"You should know something about these holofiles and digital pads—"

"Enough," said the black-haired woman, but she forged onward.

"They're rigged to wipe as soon as they leave this room," said the younger scientist as the older woman sighed. "One of us will need to unlock them here and transfer everything to this." She pulled another digital notepad out of her scrubs pocket and held it out to Agnes.

Agnes eyed the woman. "Or all of you, if you're willing to help. The faster we do this, the faster I can get you out of here."

"They'll kill us for this," an older male scientist said. "We won't make it out of the Capital alive."

Silas's grip tightened on his volt rifle. "I'll make sure that you do."

The man grumbled, shaking his head and muttering something that sounded like *our funeral*. But at a reluctant nod from their leader, he and the others got to work unlocking the files and transferring the information.

"Can you tell us what you were working on?" Agnes asked the leader.

"Our directive was to alter the troxapine formula to hammer the reward center of the brain, making users more susceptible to manipulation and instruction." *Sounds like they're tampering with whatever they gave these enhanced turned.*

"Directive from who?"

The younger woman adjusted her glasses as she chimed in, "We don't know. Dr. Hansen has loyalists in the board of directors, so I think they're the ones calling the shots. Maybe Dr. Chun? No one has seen her since the Beginning though."

It could be Dr. Wanda Chun, the head of Experimental Pharmaceuticals and Evie's boss. That made the most sense. "How did you communicate and share your work with the network down?" Agnes asked.

"Satellite phones and manual delivery of holofiles," said the leader. "It was nearly impossible to coordinate without the network, but piecemeal requests were still coming through."

"Do you know anything about Pharmatrox's black ops lab location?" Agnes asked, knowing it was a long shot.

"That's kept on a strictly need-to-know basis," said the leader. "Meaning, probably no physical record of it anywhere. Top secret. If I had to guess, it's a drastically pared back facility, likely very small. Probably in one of the bigger cities like Houston, Portland, Chicago, maybe Seattle. Hard to say."

Agnes and Silas exchanged a dismayed look. It could be anywhere. *Like finding a needle in a stack of fucking needles.*

A few minutes later, the young woman handed over her digital notepad. "Done," she said. "Everything is transferred."

"Thanks. Let's move."

After escorting everyone outside and past the still unconscious guards, they regrouped with Mal and the rest, who had troxy hostages in tow. *No sign of Zeln.* The fumes from Quentin's stink bombs had dissipated, but a foul stench lingered.

"Got ten more for the convoy," Silas said, and the dark-haired woman inclined her head in thanks.

A rumble of thunder sounded in the distance, and Mal tilted his head to the sky, frowning. "Let's head out before this storm hits. It's going to be a bad one."

Hopefully Derek and the crew don't get caught in it.

13

"ONE MORE HOUR, THEN we're heading back," Penny said as she sliced through the underbrush with her sickle. "A storm's rolling in, so stay close."

"Aye, aye, Sis." Quentin saluted and marched ahead, scanning the woods for clues, the red beam of his nighttime flashlight bobbing in the darkness.

Sis. The thin threads holding her shredded heart together threatened to burst at the seams from the happiness flooding through her. He'd claimed her as his sister again, and over the past week, he'd been some semblance of his silly self around her.

"Don't think I've ever seen you smile that big before." Tara fell into step beside her, bumping her leg with her baseball bat. "Well, not since killing Dr. Hansen, anyway."

"Don't know what you're talking about," Penny said, rearranging her face into something more serious.

Tara barked a short laugh, shaking her head.

Tonight's search party was a smaller group. Lawrence had stayed behind to batten down the hatches at the greenhouses before the storm, and Agnes and Silas had gone with Mal on a lab raid for whatever sciencey things they were nose-deep into—she'd really have to go to Maple Street soon so she could maybe understand what the fuck they were talking about whenever they gave their weekly war-room progress reports. But from what they said at the last meeting, they'd been stagnant.

So that was great.

But at least Penny and her crew's search was starting to show some results. They'd yet to find any signs of Tara's rescuers—*the bastards are good at covering their tracks*—but the past few days, they'd been scouting at night and had come across more gruesome rituals like before. This time, though, they were fresh, the blood still dripping. Tonight, they'd finally catch someone in the act, Penny was sure of it.

A small but nearly undetectable trail had made itself known to her yesterday—boot prints in the dirt, faint but visible. It could be this other mysterious crew, the Chosen, or something else entirely. But if there were people walking around in the Wilds, she wanted to know what they were up to. And their clock was ticking. It was their last day of the week-long deadline from Mal to make contact with Tara's rescuers or draw out the Chosen—if she decided to listen to him, anyway.

Derek must have read her mind because he asked, "What happens if we don't find the Chosen today?"

"We keep looking," she said, illuminating the path with her red flashlight. They all had them—recent spoils from the armory resupply and perfect for scouting at night to maintain their night vision. But it was fucking creepy to walk around in the dark surrounded by the eerie red glow.

"Boss won't like that," said Raph, hacking through some low branches.

"Malosi Olesa is not my boss," she sneered.

From behind them, Sanjali laughed. "Damn right. I personally love to watch you wind him up. We could make a drinking game out of every time he clenches his fists."

"Or crosses his arms menacingly," Quentin helpfully piped up.

"Ha! Yes, next meeting, we'll keep track. What do you say?" Sanjali nudged Penny, who smiled, taken aback.

While Sanjali had warmed up to her during training and scouting sessions, the unfamiliar camaraderie still caught her by surprise. Begrudgingly, she had to admit that Mal was right about one thing at least—working with their people directly was doing wonders at uniting everyone. And Quentin had slowly begun to open up to her. The air around camp was more energized and hopeful, even in the face of all the new challenges. With a goal to train toward, everyone had a renewed sense of purpose. She'd had no shortage of volunteers to join her scouting missions, and Mal's soldiers were doing well on their raids.

But hope was a damnable emotion and one she couldn't indulge. Not after everything she'd witnessed in her life.

A few minutes later, Penny screeched to a halt at a familiar, harsh scent in the air. *Something's wrong.*

Everyone's red lights bobbed to a stop around her. Tara realized the problem right away and snapped her eyes to Penny's.

"Blood," Tara said, sniffing.

"Stay close," said Penny, pleased when Quentin fell back to her side. As one, they crept onward, weapons raised and alert for the slightest movement. Thunder rumbled in the distance, echoing her heartbeat thrumming in her ears, increasing with each step into the deep, dark woods.

"The sky is about to open up any second," Derek murmured. "We could get stranded out here if we don't head back soon. And I don't have to tell you what a fucking bad idea that is."

"Then why are you fucking telling me?" Penny hissed, then felt Quentin tense beside her. "Sorry. Yes, I know. Let's see if we can find the source of the blood, then we'll head back."

Derek lifted a brow at her uncharacteristic apology, but nodded, turning his light to scan for whatever was causing the stench.

The wind kicked up, rattling the branches and tossing leaves across the already difficult terrain. *Come on, there's something out here. We can all smell it. Where the fuck is it?*

But if they could smell the blood, the turned could too.

Derek was right, they needed to get the hell out of there. This was a bad idea.

"Come on, we should—"

There.

Just ahead, her roving red flashlight caught movement in the trees.

A *lot* of movement.

The group froze, transfixed by the sight.

So fucking many.

Bodies, suspended upside down from a dozen or more trees by ropes around their ankles, swayed in the wind. Mouths agape, faces twisted in fear, throats slit, blood *drip-dripping* into buckets and bowls beneath them.

A forest of blood and death.

Penny pulled Quentin into her, covering his eyes, but he squirmed away and approached the nearest body.

"What the fuck are you doing!" she whisper-shouted.

"Getting a closer look," Quentin said. "We didn't come all this way to not find out what's going on."

The kid had a point, even if watching him head straight into the dark gave her heart palpitations.

"Fine," she said, turning to the rest of the group. "Two minutes, find what clues you can, then we're getting out of here."

In response, the wind whipped up, swinging the bodies and roaring through the woods like a great beast, ready to devour them.

A storm is coming.

"Found something," Derek said, shining his light on one of the bodies a few trees over.

Penny had seen her share of bloodshed. But whatever vitriol Rodney spewed to his followers had manifested into some of the darkest shit she'd ever witnessed. Whoever was pulling the cult's strings now was just as depraved as he'd been, if not more so.

A cut sliced across its throat and the word "salvation" was cut into the torso's flesh, the wound weeping beads of fresh blood. On its forearm, the shape of an eye was carved in the same fashion, right where Rodney's followers wore their black-eye tattoos.

Throat clicking in a dry swallow, Penny approached the body—*fuck. He's still alive.* From his rattling breaths and heavy eyelids, the man didn't have much time left.

"Holy shit," said Raph, wiping a hand across his face. "This is so fucked."

"Where are they?" Penny asked the man, barely containing her rage. *I will end them all.*

But he was too far gone. With a glance at her sickle, he only managed one word: "Please."

Quentin shouldn't see this. But when she met her brother's wide eyes, he gave her a slight nod.

Knowing Quentin understood helped but didn't make it easier. She'd mercy killed before, but never like this. Never for something this...evil.

Steeling herself, she turned to the man, weapon drawn. "I'll find them," she promised, and sliced her weapon across his throat.

As she turned back to the group, stricken into silence, Tara was the first to speak. "We just missed whoever did this."

"And judging from the nearly full buckets, they'll be back soon to collect," Sanjali added.

Yeah, like that *thought doesn't make my own blood fucking curdle.*

"Branch out but stay close," Penny said, hanging back to keep watch as the five flashlights spread out. "Quentin?" she called into the darkness, and one of the red lights bounced back toward her, showing her brother's pale face. He was hiding his terror well, but his too-wide eyes gave him away and he remained glued to her side as they searched. *What was I thinking? This is no place for him. I don't even want to be out here dealing with this heinous shit.* But she knew exactly what she'd been thinking—she'd do anything to make him smile.

The wind howled, whipping Penny's hair behind her in a tangle, and the first few drops of rain pricked her skin. *Need to leave soon.* They swept their lights over the forest floor, frantically searching for clues before the storm raged through and obliterated any chance of learning anything from the scene.

Venturing away from the gallows trees, she glanced down and saw boot prints in the dirt that would soon become mud. *Where did you go?*

Beside her, Quentin's light swept over the bushes—

A cluster of black-booted feet attached to black-clad soldiers. *Troxies?*

Thunder crashed, deafening, and a fork of lightning split the sky, spearing into a nearby towering pine tree. An explosion rocked the air as the tree blew apart, igniting in flames and showering wood and needles everywhere. Penny shouted for Quentin and dove away, skidding in the dirt, a hunk of flaming wood narrowly missing her and landing in the bushes. The dead leaves caught the flames and spread quickly, pumping acrid smoke into the air.

Could really use some fucking rain right now.

Ducking away from the growing fire, she brought her light back to the place where she'd seen the boots. They'd vanished.

And so had Quentin.

No no no—

"Quentin!" she yelled, abandoning all sense of stealth as she tore through the trees in search of his red light.

There!

His light dancing in the distance. "I got them, I see them!"

"Quentin, leave it! Come back!"

But with the fire catching other trees around her and eating up the dry grass, seeing beyond a few feet was impossible. Her voice was quickly lost, the wind too fierce, the thunder too loud.

I will not leave him here.

Shouting his name, Penny raced ahead, screaming, searching, clawing her way through the bushes, choking on smoke and sobs.

She couldn't hear, couldn't see, couldn't think, couldn't *breathe—*

"Penny!"

Not Quentin.

Derek's voice reached her over the din.

"Penny, get your ass back here now!"

An impossible choice. Leave now and leave Quentin behind, or be ripped to shreds by the storm and the fire and whatever else awaited them in the woods. On top of everything, they were at a severe disadvantage on the unknown terrain.

The truth plummeted into the empty place in her chest, the vacant void ever since setting fire to her parents' house and realizing what she'd done.

If we stay out here, we won't survive the night.

Which meant there was a good chance Quentin wouldn't survive the night either.

But if they left now, they could come back at first light, maybe even sooner if the storm passed. And the storm would prevent the fire from spreading too.

The fear and guilt had her heart in a vise grip as she ran back to the cluster of red lights.

"Where'd you go? Where's Quentin?" Tara shouted, rain now pouring down in heavy sheets.

"He—he's—I—" *I can't fucking breathe.*

Tara's hand clamped on her shoulder and shook. "Tell me what happened."

"We saw some people. Dressed in black, looked like troxies. Then there was lightning and a tree exploded and fire everywhere and he must've run off and—I lost him." Her voice broke off in a wheezing gasp as she struggled to pull enough air into her lungs through the rain pelting them from all directions.

"Fuck." Derek pulled a hand through his wet hair. "Fuck!"

Before the group could process Penny's news, several people charged out of the darkness, weapons upraised, feral cries erupting from their throats. Slipping in the mud, Penny swung her sickle and a head rolled. In the red light of her flashlight, she caught a glimpse of their attackers. They weren't brandishing rudimentary weapons of people who'd been holing up in the Wilds; they had Pharmatrox-issued knives, billy clubs, and other riot gear. But that wasn't the most chilling part.

All of them had one word carved into their foreheads.

CHOSEN.

Rodney's cult, returned for their blood. And somehow, they got a lot of troxy weapons. Scavenged from the bodies of their victims?

Before she could think more about it, bodies thrashed and water and blood mixed in a muddy mess as Penny and her companions took on the near-feral humans. Some of them might have been turned, but she couldn't see their eyes. All of them were users, evident from their twitchy and fast movements.

"Keep one alive!" Penny shouted as she picked up a blood bucket and swung it at the cultist closest to her, who screamed and attacked. But as the discarded blood coated the cultist's skin and clothes, they paused to *lick it off.*

This one must be more turned than user.

"Got one!" Tara said, hitting a woman over the head with her baseball bat, knocking her out.

Derek hefted the unconscious woman over his shoulder as the rain came down in droves, the cracks of thunder and lightning almost constant as the storm reached its zenith.

But the more cultists they dispatched, the more trickled in to take their place, and the torrential rain was working overtime to put out the fire from the downed tree.

"Penny!"

Raph yanked on her arm.

Penny's throat felt raw, and she realized she'd been screaming Quentin's name nonstop.

Raph's grip tightened around her wrist. "We need to get back inside the city walls." He was right. They had to go.

With a cry of anguish, she ripped her sickle through a nearby cultist's throat and took off at a run, back toward the Capital.

Away from Quentin.

Away from the only thing left in her life that meant anything to her.

With each step, the anchor of guilt and rage weighed heavier on her soul.

I will get him back. I will find Rodney's sick fucks.

And I will make them bleed.

14

Agnes

"This is all spaghetti," Silas said with a huff, flipping through the files projected in the air from the basement scientist's digital notepad.

Agnes looked up from her share of the files she'd uploaded to a spare laptop. So far, she'd only read some basic notes unrelated to anything they needed. "What?"

"You know, like when you keyboard smash and a bunch of gibberish comes out? That's what they called it in my middle school typing class. Anyway, all of these files are scrambled."

Chuckling, she said, "We should program the FPGA to decrypt your spaghetti first. Then I can switch it up for my machine. Between the two of us, it shouldn't take long." Again, she was grateful for the little miracle of a circuit board they'd found.

"If you're hungry," said Lawrence from Derek's living room, where he worked on preparing jars for preserves, "I could probably make something that at least looks like spaghetti."

Agnes snorted, while Silas let out a dramatic groan. "If you're going to try to pass off *mushrooms* as pasta again, then—fuck. Fuck!" Silas slapped the side of the crappy laptop he was using in lieu of a Patch—the damn things wouldn't even turn on now that the network was fried—and shoved aside the digital notepad.

"What happened?" Agnes asked.

"The Pharmatrox drones I set up with repeaters to extend the range of our comms so we could attempt to radio Chicago? Well, I just lost signal. With all of them. I sent five. *Five.*"

"Hijo de puta," Agnes said. "Losing one could be an accident. But all of them? Something is up." They weren't dinky drones for amateur videography—they were military-grade stealth drones. To take them out—or even detect or hack them—would require some equally robust military equipment.

"This is bad," Silas said, wiping a hand across his face. "If we want to contact Kev, it's looking like we might need to go to Chicago ourselves."

"Sounds like it," agreed Agnes.

"We'll talk to Mal tomorrow," said Lawrence. "No way in hell we'd make it to the stadium through *that*." He hooked a thumb at the window as he raided the cabinets for snacks.

It had been a few hours since returning from the earlier raid, and the storm was raging heavily outside, sheafs of rain and gusts of wind rattling the windows. The storm itself was distracting, but her thoughts were locked on Derek and the others, who were hopefully on their way back. She refused to consider what would happen if they got stranded in the storm overnight.

They're coming back.

Repeating positive thoughts barely managed to take the edge off her anxiety, so she did her best to refocus on her task. "You have the FPGA?" she asked. "We could get a jump on programming it tonight before I go completely cross-eyed from exhaustion."

"Sure," Silas said, plugging a power cable into the FPGA's circuit board—"Goddamn it!" Smoke and sparks shot from it, and Agnes's heart sank. "Must have been wet from that musty basement. We're fucked. We need another one."

"Good thing those are just laying around." Agnes thrust a hand through her hair, squeezing her eyes shut. *Joder. Now we really need to go to Chicago.* Maybe their facilities weren't as picked over as the ones in the Capital.

"Well, I can at least write a program to decrypt the scrambled files," said Silas, "but it will take time. And it won't work on Evie's files—without that Helix Key, we can't access them."

Agnes sighed, twisting her fingers in Evie's gold necklace that she still wore every day. As much as she wanted to know what Evie was keeping locked away so tightly, it wasn't worth the time, not when things were going to shit.

The wind kicked up, knocking debris into the back door, and they both flinched.

"Too bad those scientists didn't want to stick around," Silas said. "But asking for *one thing* to go right would be too much. It's like we're jinxed or something."

"I don't blame them for getting the hell out of here," Agnes said. "I wouldn't put it past Pharmatrox to send snipers to take them out—they've already done the same with other defectors who weren't even scientists."

Lawrence grunted his agreement, placing a plate of hastily made peanut butter sandwiches on the table while Silas grabbed two and took a massive bite. "And with how Zeln was able to break into *Penny's* room," Lawrence said, "I'm not sure the stadium's security could protect anyone with a bounty like that on their head. Mal is doing the best he can, but

I bet it worries him to know how easily his, uh, ex-friend got past his defenses completely undetected."

"Speaking of devastatingly handsome men..." Silas nudged Agnes, waggling his eyebrows. "How are things with you and Derek?" Even Lawrence threw himself into the nearest chair, elbows parked on the table in interest.

She couldn't help the slow smile that spread across her face, but then she let it drop. "I'm happy. Maybe happier than I've ever been. And that feels fucked up to say because look around us. Less than a year ago, I was sitting in my office talking about my next project with Dr. Hansen. Now Evie and Hansen are dead, you've been used as a lab rat, and we're working to take down the company that I dreamed of working for my entire life while we try to keep the country from falling apart around us. We're hacking into satellites, cracking codes. Fighting these fucking insane zombie creatures like some kind of bad horror movie. So how can I say I'm happy with all of this going on? What right do I have to feel anything other than absolutely horrified and heartbroken?" Ending on a gasp, she swiped at her cheeks, wiping away the tears.

Silas scooted around the kitchen table to sit beside her while Lawrence grabbed her hand. "We have to find what pockets of happiness we can, Aggie," said Silas. "And we shouldn't be ashamed. Because without that, what do we have? Nothing but darkness. I hold those specks of light close, letting them warm me up even when I feel like I'll never make it through this dark night we've all been forced to walk through. I think of Ivan and how I'll find him when this is all over. I hope that Derek is that speck of light for you. And you keep him close, dammit. He's a good man and he loves you."

"*Love?*" Agnes choked on the word. "We've only known each other a couple months."

Laughing, Lawrence said, "Can't put a time constraint on your feelings. Doesn't work like that."

Silas nodded his agreement. "I knew that man loved you the second I saw you together. Anyone with *eyeballs* can see that. Actually, anyone who has heard him talk about you can tell. It's disgusting. And anyway, I loved Ivan the moment I saw him. Well, okay. The moment *after* he handed me my discounted coffee and bagel, I was enamored."

Agnes wrapped her arms around him, fending off the wave of guilt. *Here I am, blubbering about my happy fucking life, when Silas lost his sister and his partner. What the hell is wrong with me?* "I'm sorry about Ivan. You haven't heard anything from him yet?"

Silas squeezed her back but stared at the wall with a solemn expression. "Don't know how he would even reach me. Phones, personal CLEOs, and Patches don't work anymore. So unless he somehow has the number to this baby"—he slapped the satellite phone on the table—"then the only way I'll find him is if I run into him on the street. Or maybe I could send out some kind of mass text blast to every phone in the entire world. That could be romantic."

Agnes laughed good-naturedly but hated the sadness that lingered in the corner of his eyes. "I'm happy you're here—both of you."

Lawrence rewarded her with one of his classic sunshine smiles hidden in the thicket of his sandy beard. "Wouldn't want to live through the apocalypse with anyone else."

"Love you, Aggie." After a final squeeze, Silas turned his attention back to their files.

A few minutes later, he said, "Wait, I've got something!" Sitting so close to the laptop screen his nose touched it, he waved her over. "Aggie, c'mere."

Looking over his shoulder, Agnes frowned at the screen. "More spaghetti gibberish?"

"Well, yes, it's completely unintelligible—probably whatever signal scramblers Pharmatrox is using against us—but it's a *transmission*! Which means my uplink is working again, and—woah, shit. Looks like they have the message set on repeat, whatever it is. Do we think it's our messengers? Maybe Kev in Chicago?"

"It could be anything or nothing," Agnes said. "There's no way for us to know."

With an agitated harrumph, Silas went back to his files when a loud rumble of thunder lasting a good ten seconds rattled the house, sending Agnes's heart galloping in her chest.

"They should have been back by now, right?" she asked, gripping the edge of the table with white knuckles.

"They've been scouting later at night like this, but I thought Penny would have ditched early because of the storm..." Lawrence said.

"What if they don't come back? What do we do?" Putting a lid on her panic at this stage was impossible. This storm was one of the worst they'd had in a year of increasingly bad storms. Flash floods, lightning strikes causing random fires, downed trees, wind damage...

"I—"

The front door burst open, banging into the wall with the force of the wind, sheets of water pouring inside. The trio leapt to their feet, staring down the hall as their soaked friends fell inside, slamming the door behind them.

Agnes flew into Derek's arms, lips finding his. He tasted of rain and salt, dirt, and rust, but she didn't care. "I was so worried," she said.

He pressed his forehead to hers, inhaling. "I'm here." But at the hitch in his voice, she pulled back, looking at the group.

Derek, Tara—

They were one member short.

Quentin isn't here.

Her eyes locked on Derek, who rested a bloody hand on the wall, red watery streaks racing to the floor.

"Penny needs you," he said, his expression strained. "Now."

15

"Tell me where he is!" Penny reared back a fist and let it fly, cracking the cultist in the face, her cheekbone splitting under the impact. "What did you do with him?" Another punch, then Penny grabbed the woman, shaking her. "Tell me!"

But the cultist just laughed and laughed.

"Pretty Penny lost her favorite boy, oh ho ho, the woods ate him up, ate him up." The woman's blue eyes were glassy, the sclera shattered with black veins in the telltale sign of a user who was extremely fucking high and about to turn. She threw her head back, cackling into the ceiling and rocking the chair she was tied to from side to side.

With the help of Raph and Sanjali, Penny had dragged the woman into the basement holding cells that Rodney used for his prisoners. She'd considered ordering them not to tell Mal about their guest, but she knew they were ultimately loyal to him.

"Give me ten minutes alone with her," she'd said, and sent them off.

That had been five minutes ago.

Tick tock, Penny girl.

Rodney's voice, rising in times when her inner predator was close to the surface. And this time, she didn't ignore the urge.

Penny grabbed the chair's arms and slammed it flat to the floor. Pulling the black-bladed knife from her belt, she pressed it to the cultist's cheek, the ruthless leader of the Marauders melting over her with such ease that it left her breathless. To the woman, Penny said, "Tell Pretty Penny what she wants to know, or she's taking one of these pretty eyes." She'd taken eyes before. And ears and tongues. There wasn't much she hadn't done in the name of hunting down the Architect or during the early days of the Beginning, when she'd been too high to protest Rodney's orders.

And for Quentin?

She had no limits.

Rather than that fact scaring her, it *invigorated* her. Part of her missed the blood, the ease of using blades to solve all of her problems. Quentin would hate to know what she'd done to get the woman to talk. But as she thought of the tortured man, the bodies swinging in the trees, nailed to trunks, the buckets of blood, that sinister little cave—she did not care.

Nothing else matters, as long as Quentin lives.

The cultist's laughs crescendoed in the empty concrete room, echoing down the hall. Penny backhanded her, but it had no effect. If anything, the woman laughed harder. With a frustrated yell, Penny grabbed the woman's hair, yanking her head back and exposing her neck to the blade, the dark blood nearly black. Penny shook her again, edging into hysterics. "Talk!"

Laughter. Only laughter.

It sent Penny into a frenzy.

She banged the woman's head against the wall, again and again, her screams mixing with the woman's cackling.

In an instant, strong arms wrapped around Penny's waist, hauling her away.

She knew those arms.

"What the fuck is this?"

And that voice.

Mal.

Spinning to face him, she kicked out his knee, bringing him down to her level, and thrust her knife point just below his chin. "I told Raph and Sanjali to give me *ten* minutes," she said, teeth bared. "I still have two left."

"You should have considered that before you decided to torture a banshee in the middle of the fucking night." Mal's eyes blazed as he took in the scene, then assessed her.

Penny had no idea what she looked like, but she felt the mud and blood coating her body, her wet hair sticking to her back. He must have seen something...unhinged in her expression, because in one quick move, he disarmed her and hooked a finger in her weapons belt, pulling her close. He remained kneeling, closer to her eye level so he could drop the full weight of his gaze on her.

"I know you want to kill her," he said in a low voice only for her, his hands on her hips preventing her from leaping at the woman, but his fingertips pressing into her skin anchored her in a way that nothing else could. "But she is the only clue we have to finding Quentin. We need her alive. *He* needs her alive. You get me?"

The ragged hole in Penny's chest burned with Quentin's absence. But she managed to nod, holding out her hand. "Can I have my knife back?"

Mal eyed the black blade, lifting an eyebrow. He knew what it was. But he didn't know what it meant to her. Why she carried it. And why she used it now.

He glanced at the woman again, who still laughed to herself, blood caking her dark blonde hair. He held Rodney's knife out to Penny. "Get her to talk. Then do your worst."

Something about his acceptance of her, of knowing she needed this, made an unknown feeling sing in her veins. A feeling she'd never had before, and certainly not because of Mal.

And she fucking *liked it.*

Penny resumed her position, knife to the woman's throat, Mal's presence providing a strange sense of comfort. *Keep your head, Pen.* "Where is your camp? Where did your people take him?"

"Too many, too many," the woman said, lolling her head from side to side and sawing her neck against Penny's blade as she giggled. "Too many rivers. Too many choices. Oh, what will Pretty Penny do?"

As the woman fell off into hysterics again, Penny regripped her patience with both hands. "Tell me where my brother is."

Choking on laughter, she said, "Your favorite boy tasted so sweet."

"The fuck does that mean?" *Oh god, is he—? Did they already—*

Another laugh escaped the woman, her eyes rolling skyward and pointing to the sick carving in her forehead. "The blood of the unbelievers is salvation for the Chosen. See?" Her tongue lolled out, licking at the blood running down her face. "Some blood is purer than others. Rodney said that. Yes, he said. The Watchers don't like that. Don't like us. But they're wrong. You're all wrong. You will see, you will see."

The Watchers?

"Try this," Mal said, holding out a syringe.

"I thought we were running low on detox serum? Agnes said it might not even work anymore."

"Is it worth Quentin's life to not find out?"

Her claws came out at that. But she swallowed her anger, saved it for the ones who deserved it.

Penny grabbed the syringe, then shoved the needle in the woman's neck. The cultist thrashed beneath her, jaws snapping. It was evident when the detox serum began to take effect, but it was weaker than it should have been. A few minutes later, the woman stilled, a suspicious light entering her eyes.

"You're the red-headed bitch," the cultist said in a steadier voice. "The one who killed Rodney. Our Rodney, our leader." She started to lose it at the end as she realized the truth of her words, and began to cry.

What the fuck did Rodney do to these people?

"Where is your camp?" Penny asked. "And who are the Watchers?"

Recognition lighted in the woman's eyes, and for a moment, Penny thought she'd get her answer.

But then the woman laughed, a high keening sound that rang in her ears.

"Oh, Pretty Penny. I'll never tell."

Penny had almost gone feral when Dr. Hansen had taken Quentin at the Spire. But now? To know that this was Rodney's doing, the scourge she should have wiped from the earth the first moment she met him? To know that it was her fault she'd let him live long enough to spread his insane views and amass followers who were nearly as bad—or worse—than he'd been?

She was positively *ravenous* with rage.

And she would not be contained.

Letting loose a cry of fury, she flew at the woman, latching her hands around her throat, *squeezing*, anything to make that horrendous laughing stop, to make this not real, to end it and let it be over. The cultist gurgled and sputtered, that horrific, empty smile on her face even as she was about to die between Penny's hands—

Arms dragged her back again, her nails scraping gouges in the woman's skin, her insane laughter blending with Penny's screams. Mal encircled her in his arms, pulling her against him, cradling her head. "Enough. That's enough," he said.

It was a minute before she realized she was still screaming, and she fell off into wracking sobs, breaking into a million pieces against Mal's chest as he held her.

"He's gone, he's gone." The only words she could find, and she spoke them into Mal's shirt, wet from her tears and blood, as she pounded her fists against him. "He's gone!"

Mal held her as she raged and withstood all of her abuse. And that made her feel worse. She didn't deserve comfort, didn't deserve him. Everyone who got close to her, everyone she cared about, ended up hurt, or worse off, because of her.

I poison everything I touch.

As that thought hit her, she backed away from Mal, refusing to look at him and see the pity or whatever else was on his face.

She turned, and she ran.

Penny sat on the locker room's communal shower floor, fully clothed, as water poured over her. It was probably freezing cold, but she didn't notice. Didn't know how long she'd been sitting there.

She glanced at the water pooling around her, rushing for the drain in the middle of the shower. It ran brown, so she'd been there long enough for the caked-on blood and dirt to begin to rinse off. Reaching for the knob, her arm shook, the skin pebbled.

Oh. I must be cold.

She let her arm fall, no energy to turn off the water.

Not for the first time, she wished for the dust and the oblivion that came with it. But putting that shit in her body again would be the death of her relationship with Quentin—*what does it fucking matter? He's gone.*

A pounding at the door.

"Penny? Are you all right?"

Mal. He'd come for her. But she couldn't bring herself to stand.

More pounding. Calling her name. A grumble and another pound, as if a heavy fist fell against the door.

"I'm coming in."

Heavy footsteps that slowed as they reached the shower. A beat of silence. Then the water stopped and he was kneeling before her. A fingertip lifted her chin up, and her eyes traced over his beard, across his strong jaw, the hard set of his warrior's brow, finally to his eyes. And she thought she might fall apart at the look she saw there. Fierce but tender, enraged but gentle.

"Stay here," he said, then left.

An amount of time later—Penny couldn't tell how much—footsteps returned.

But it wasn't Mal.

Agnes stood at the edge of the shower clutching a towel, a change of clothes, and some soap. She hung the towel on a hook and slid the bottle of liquid soap across the floor to her. When Penny didn't react, Agnes crouched across from her. "Penny—Penelope," she said in a shaky voice, "I know what you're thinking, but the dust won't help you now, and I know you know that. I crave it all the time too. Like a hunger that never goes away. If you want to use again, that's your choice. But if you want to make a different choice, you have people who will support you. You have me."

Her eyes locked on Penny's with the weight of sincerity, and Penny's throat clicked in a dry swallow. *How could she truly mean that, after everything I've done?*

But Agnes continued. "Quentin is a survivor. You taught him that. *We* taught him that. He was doing just fine before either of us showed up in his life."

Her words stirred something to life within Penny. Agnes was more right than she knew. In many ways, for years, Penny had left Quentin to deal with the family drama and the hardships of life without her. *I left him in a den of vipers. I should have been there.*

But she could be there for him now.

"Wash off, get changed, rest for a few hours," Agnes said. "And once this storm passes, we're going hunting."

When Agnes held out her hand, Penny grasped it.

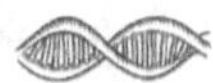

Clean and freshly clothed but shivering, Penny walked out of the locker room, where Mal leaned against the wall, waiting for her. Agnes nodded to him and they parted ways, then Mal ushered Penny down the hall.

"I know where my room is. I don't need a chaperone," she grumbled.

Mal hoisted a brow, daring her to argue.

"What, are you going to toss me over your shoulder like a disobedient toddler?" she asked.

"You *are* throwing a tantrum."

She fell into their bickering with ease and hidden gratitude. It was a nice distraction, and part of her thought he realized that. He always had an uncanny knack for knowing what she needed.

When they reached her room, Penny froze at the door. She couldn't step inside. The cold seeped through the concrete walls, and even the camping lantern on the table couldn't penetrate the darkness gripping her soul. As she stared at her cot, she knew she was in for a sleepless night.

Sensing her hesitation, Mal tugged her inside and grabbed an extra blanket from the shelf, then wrapped her in it and led her to bed. With the extra generators designated to the kitchen and the wing of rooms for the children and elderly, the rest had to make due with flashlights and blankets to keep the cold nights at bay. Her knees finally gave out and she collapsed to the thin cot, knowing no amount of warmth or light would help her tonight.

"Rest," he said, tucking a wet strand of hair behind her ear. "I'll be back in a couple of hours. Then we'll find Quentin."

He turned to go, but she caught his wrist. "Wait—" The words stuck in her throat. She didn't know how to ask for what she needed. Wasn't even sure what it was. She just knew she couldn't face the dark room, the impenetrable night, her empty bed, knowing Quentin was still out there somewhere and she couldn't get to him.

His eyes softened and he said, "I'll stay for a while." Scooping her up, he made room for himself and sat on the bed beside her, back propped against the wall. His massive body took up most of the small cot, and he lifted his arm so she could settle into his side. Curling into a ball against him, she soaked up his warmth until she stopped shivering.

She'd never forget that Agnes was the one to pull her off of that shower floor or that *Mal* was the only one who could calm her racing mind that night. Something in the fibers of those relationships was changing—especially with Mal. She'd considered him an adversary for a long time, based on his history as a troxy general and how he'd treated her like a bomb to be diffused. And she was still that—a dangerous weapon.

But maybe he didn't see her that way anymore...and after everything they'd been through, she might even be starting to see *him* as something different. Someone she could rely on.

As the tendrils of sleep began to pull her under, in the moments before she succumbed to her exhaustion, she could have sworn she heard Mal whisper into her hair, thinking she was already asleep, "I'll always stay."

16

WHEN THE ABSENCE OF warmth registered, Penny's eyes flew open and she threw the blankets off, jerking upright.

Mal sat at her small table, watching her with a hooded expression.

He stayed.

"What time is it?" she asked.

"Early."

"Why didn't you wake me?" she asked, pulling on her boots and grabbing her gear from her locker.

"You looked like you needed the break." Behind her, she heard his boots on the floor as he approached. "You want to tell me what happened last night?"

"Didn't Derek fill you in?" She stuffed weapons in her pack and donned her belt, uninterested in reliving any of it.

"He said you saw someone in the woods. Maybe troxy soldiers. And Quentin chased them."

Penny squeezed her eyes shut, but recounted what she'd seen. "Saw people dressed like troxies, or at least wearing black clothes. Looked tactical. Could have been the Chosen decked out in stolen gear from their victims. Quentin took off. Then the Chosen came." Shoving her sickle in her belt, she turned to face him. Even in her fitful rest, she'd managed to reach a conclusion, and she greeted the day with a hard resolve. "I know you have another raid planned for today. Focus on that." *My brother, my responsibility.*

Pressing his palm flat against the locker, he leaned in, saying, "I'm coming with you."

"You're not." But the conviction in his voice did things to her, and she plowed onward before she could contradict her words. "Our people need you here." His expression softened at that, and she realized it was the first time she'd used that phrase: *our people.*

He looped his fingers in her belt and finished cinching it tight for her, sliding her last knife home in its sheath at her hip. "Bring our boy home."

"I will," she said, letting her fingers trail across his chest as she walked past him and headed for the door.

Time to gather her own troops.

Fifteen minutes later, Penny and her crew crossed McAdams Bridge and trudged to the Wilds. The morning air was cold, but fury burned hot within her.

This time, all of Team Outpost joined her, along with a group of soldiers handpicked by Derek. Sanjali and Raph would accompany Mal on his next sector raid, for which Penny was grateful. Someone needed to have his back.

Silas's presence, though, was surprising, so she asked him about it.

"Gotta find our favorite little twerp," Silas said, tightening his rifle strap across his back. "And, in case I ever have to run for my fucking life again, I want to know what's outside the city walls. Plus, I could use some more target practice. Hopefully on some turned or cultists." Then he paused, paling. "Not that I want to run into either of them."

Penny grunted a laugh. He really could use the extra time with the rifle, although he joined Tara and Lawrence most mornings for shooting practice in the arena.

Out of the corner of her eye, she saw Derek put an arm around Agnes. Penny didn't know why Agnes had come for her in the showers last night. She'd expected Mal to send Ju Lee or someone from the infirmary. But when Agnes had been the one to rally her, she realized something. A thread would always connect the two of them, but maybe it didn't have to be a bloodstained tether weighing them down. Maybe it could be something better, something purer, like their love for Quentin. The two women made eye contact, and Agnes nodded. Penny returned it. *We'll never be friends, but I think we're getting better at being allies.*

With each step into the thick woods, the sky became more blotted out. After a while, they reached the burnt-out clearing. The storm and the fire had destroyed much of the evidence—the bodies and buckets remained, but any clues had been washed away. When they reached the lightning-struck tree, Penny crouched by the spot where she'd seen the booted feet, but didn't find anything.

"You said the cultist mentioned the Watchers," Tara said as she approached. "Maybe that's who the booted feet belonged to. Could be the same crew who saved me." She brushed aside some leaves, searching for a trail in the cold mud. "If they were here, maybe they know where Quentin is. Maybe they saved him too."

Damnable hope flared in Penny's chest, but she quashed it. "You saw the trees swinging with bodies. If the Watchers were here, why didn't they save *them*?"

Tara's hand crunched the pile of leaves she held, forming a fist. "If they've been watching us, they know Quentin is one of ours. And if they want our help weeding out the Chosen, saving Quentin would be a great way to win our favor."

"Or maybe the cult does have Quentin and he's—" Penny didn't dare finish the thought. "Let's keep looking."

"What did the cultist say exactly?" Agnes asked as the rest of the group followed. "Can we ask her again?"

"Don't think she's up for any more questions," Penny said. That morning, she'd checked on the woman, but she sat dead in the chair, the back of her head cracked open. She must have slammed it repeatedly into the wall when they'd left her alone. "Something about some blood being sweeter than others—whatever the fuck that means—and 'too many rivers, too many choices.' Makes sense for a camp out here to be near a source of running water. But she was right—too many rivers to choose from."

At her words, Tara's mouth dropped open, unsteady hands swatting at Lawrence nearest to her. "What is it?" he asked.

"Running water. I remember the sound of running water. I thought it was the wind and it seemed a little distant. But it could've been a waterfall. Not a big one, not big enough for me to fully recognize the sound but...I think it could've been rapids or something."

Penny had never seen the fierce woman look so lost. Losing Quentin wasn't just fucking Penny up, it seemed.

"I think there might be some falls upriver," said Lawrence, pointing in the direction that Quentin had disappeared.

"Let's go," Penny said, forging ahead.

Several miles later, just when she was ready to give up on following that lead, she saw it. Something in the water. Lawrence saw it too.

Wading off the banks, he dipped an arm below the surface and pulled out a fishing net attached to two sticks poking above the waterline, a fresh catch wriggling in the trap. Several similar sticks spread out downstream in a uniform pattern.

Someone lives out here. And I doubt the Chosen are lucid enough to know how to set a fucking fishing trap.

Before she could say so, the sound of several booted feet slapping into the fresh mud came from behind them. Penny whipped around in time to see people dropping out of the trees, brandishing knives, handguns, and all manner of weaponry, all dressed in black.

Just like the people she'd seen hiding in the shadows when Quentin disappeared.

Penny and her group fell into their fighting formation, weapons raised.

One of the newcomers, a solid woman with dark brown skin and a strong face, stepped forward, tossing a pile of cloth sacks and ropes at their feet.

"Put those on," the woman said in a voice rich as honey but hard as steel. "She'll want to see you." Then she glared at Lawrence, pointing with her machete. "And we'll be taking that."

Lawrence offered the fish with a sheepish shrug, and one of the black-clad people took it and went to empty the other traps.

"Who wants to see us?" Penny asked, not relaxing her stance one bit.

"The Watcher of these woods. She sees everything. And she's had her eye on you." The woman's piercing glare shifted from Penny to Tara. "Not sure if she'll be pissed or impressed that you managed to find your way back."

Tara blinked. "I—how—so *you* saved me from the Chosen?"

"You're very smart, Tara, so do not waste my time with pedantic questions," the woman said. "Let's go."

"Hold up," Penny said. "We're not going anywhere with you."

The woman didn't even twitch. "It wasn't a request."

Penny turned to Derek and Tara, the two closest to her, with a questioning look. Tara shrugged. "They would have killed us by now if they were going to."

"The Watcher might have seen Quentin or know where the cult's camp is," Derek added, cutting a glance at the imposing woman. "If she really does see everything."

Then Penny's eyes landed on Agnes, and she found she wanted her opinion more than anyone else's. Agnes had a good stranger-danger alarm, thanks in part to Penny ruthlessly hunting her for months. "This is why we're out here, isn't it?" Agnes said. "We need to know what they know."

"Now that you've all had your fucking continental congress," said the woman in exasperation, slapping the ground with the point of her machete. "Bags on heads. Ropes on wrists. Now. Keep your weapons."

What the hell?

The confusion must have been clear on Penny's face because the woman looked down her nose at her with a sly smile. "We've studied exactly how each of you fight. You are no threat to us."

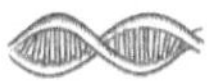

"Ow, Silas, that's my foot," Penny said from the front of the line, narrowly avoiding tripping over a root she couldn't see.

"Sorry," Silas said behind her.

"And watch where you're walking." Tara's voice. "Keep a steady pace or I'll keep bumping into your insanely massive back."

"Little hard for me to watch where I'm walking with a *bag on my head*."

"You know what I mean."

"Sorry that my walking while tied into a rope chain of ten other people after being ambushed by an insanely terrifying Amazonian woman threatening to chop my balls off isn't satisfactory enough for you."

Penny slammed into a body, probably the terrifying Amazonian woman in question, and the rest of their group crashed into her from behind. "Do you always bicker this much?" *Yep, there she is.* "You're giving me a migraine. No talking." The rope attaching all of their hands yanked them forward. Penny could cut her way out if she needed to, but she didn't want to start a fight or murder them all unless it was necessary. She needed to find out if they knew anything about Quentin first. Then she'd decide about murdering them later.

After walking for about an hour, the sounds of water rushing over rocks became a dull roar in the background. *We're close.* The Amazonian pulled them to a halt and pushed them to their butts until they were sitting in a heap. One by one, the Watchers went down the line, removing everyone's bags.

They sat in a clearing in front of a roaring fire. At their approach, people dropped out of the trees—but they weren't just hanging out up there like she and Quentin had when they were kids. Small huts and shacks were built into the trees' strong boughs, disguised by leaves and branches wrapped around the outsides.

The Amazonian watched as her team unloaded their packs of food, and the people who'd come out of the treehouses joined to help. Judging by the homemade wreaths of fall leaves hanging from the trees, the camp looked decked out for a celebration, which was fucking weird.

"When do we get to see the Watcher?" Penny asked.

Clicking her tongue in disapproval, the Amazonian said, "When she's ready."

"Looks like you're setting up for a party," Agnes observed. "Little strange, given the circumstances."

My thoughts exactly.

Crouching in front of Agnes with a mean look, the woman poked her in the forehead. *Kind of ruins the angry warrior vibe.* "Pretty chatty for prisoners, aren't you?"

"Is that what we are?" Penny brought her hands down on her sickle at her hip, slicing through the rope and standing in one smooth motion. "I kept the rope on out of courtesy, but now I'm bored. Get to the fucking point."

The woman drew herself up to her full height, and they stared each other down. She had a good six inches on Penny, and Penny was a little on the taller side too. *She could snap me in half, easy.*

Then the woman barked a laugh. "Ballsy," she said. Taking a basket of supplies from the pile, she continued. "One of our hunting parties came back today. Been gone a while. Brought food and supplies from as far as Lake Erie. So yeah, we're celebrating. Celebrating that all of them made it back alive, no thanks to you Faction scum."

"Making friends already, Jaha?" A pale woman with jet-black hair dropped out of a nearby tree. Her black cargo pants and long-sleeved shirt clung to her slim body as she walked through the dry grass on soundless booted feet. *Not even a slight crunch. How is she so goddamn quiet?*

Ahh.

"You're the Watcher," Penny said, assessing her. She was slightly shorter than Penny and maybe around the same age. Her hands sported the rough calluses of someone who knew how to handle a weapon, and she carried herself like a skilled hunter. "With a mysterious name like that, I was expecting an old woman in a cloak carting around a crystal ball."

"Sorry to disappoint," said the Watcher with a smile that didn't look sorry at all. Then it wiped off her face, replaced by the visage of a hardened warrior. A really fucking pissed warrior. The Watcher walked a slow, assessing circle around Penny as she spoke. "So here she is, the reason I have a deranged new threat on my hands that paints my woods bloody night after night."

"What the fuck is that supposed to mean?" Penny asked.

"When you banished the Chosen from Faction lands, you pushed them into my territory. Some might even say you're the reason they exist at all."

Her words speared straight to the heart of the hard truth that plagued Penny day after day. On the defensive, she snapped, "*I* killed Rodney. If anything, you should be thanking me."

In a flash, the Watcher had a blade at Penny's throat in the same instant that Penny pressed her sickle to the Watcher's ribcage. Everyone in camp tensed, hands on their weapons, and Penny's crew made movements to untie their bindings, but Penny waved them off. The Watcher was testing her, and she intended to stand her ground.

"Looks like you didn't finish the job, did you?" the Watcher hissed. "You left his followers alive, and not only that, by killing him, you gave them a *martyr*. Someone to worship, something to invoke when they drain their victims. And now, their movement will never die. Not unless they all do."

"So why haven't you killed them yet?" Penny asked, nodding to the dozens of people gripping their weapons. "You seem more than capable."

"What do you think we've been doing for the past month, twiddling our fucking thumbs? We *have* been killing them. But their numbers are many, and their territory is rife with wild turned." The Watcher pressed the knife deeper and her eyes darted to Tara. "How did you find your way back to our camp?"

Tara held up her hands, still tied to the rope. "I didn't see shit when I was here," she said, nodding to Penny. "She's a good tracker."

The knife pressure at Penny's throat dissipated slightly as the Watcher studied her. She must have made some kind of decision, because the Watcher pocketed her blade and signaled to her people. "Found something of yours."

The crowd parted around someone being pushed to the front who was saying, "Hey, I haven't finished my sandwich yet—"

Agnes reacted first, her jaw dropping. "Quentin?" In an instant, she sliced through her bindings and ran to his side.

"Oh good, so we're done pretending to be trapped, then?" Derek stood, cutting everyone else's ropes.

Abandoning all pretenses, Penny flew to her brother and pulled him into a hug. "Quentin, goddamn it. I was so fucking worried." *Alive alive alive,* each beat of her pulse sang with the realization.

For a brief, heart-bursting moment, Quentin hugged her back, then crammed the rest of his sandwich in his mouth and patted Agnes as she hugged him next. "Would have come home sooner, but Vick wouldn't let me."

"Vick?"

Behind them, the Watcher groaned. "So much for my veil of secrecy. Little punk eavesdropped on our meeting this morning. Happened to catch my name. But he's too freaking cute to murder, so I let it slide."

"Hey!" Quentin said, pointing a finger at himself. "War-hardened expert sneak over here. I am *not cute.* You're lucky I'm not better at throwing knives or else I'd pitch one at you right now. Actually, if you lie down, I'm pretty good at hitting the ground."

Jaha, one of the scariest women Penny had ever seen, *chuckled*, ruffling Quentin's hair as he ducked away. "Very cute."

Silas snorted, rubbing at the rope burn on his wrists. "Good to see that Quentin's propensity for making friends with literally anyone is still intact."

Penny dug her fingertips into Quentin's shoulder to assure herself that he was there and safe. "You said she wouldn't let you leave? What happened last night? Are you hurt?"

"I saw some of Vick's people and I thought they were the Chosen, so I followed them. Then the fire happened and I got cut off from you guys, and I got turned around in the dark. The Chosen came, and I thought they were going to use me as a pin cushion—one of 'em even bit my arm, the weirdos—but Jaha helped me and brought me back here to wait things out."

The cultist's words filtered back to Penny. *"Your favorite boy tasted so sweet."*

Good fucking riddance.

"I was going to leave as soon as Vick said it was okay," Quentin continued. "And after I had my sandwich."

"Classic Quentin," Lawrence commented with a laugh. "But we need to talk about you running after murderers in the dark. That's really not a good idea."

"I have a lot of not good ideas, Lawrie," he said with a cheeky grin. "Those are the most fun."

"Hold on," said Tara, planting her hands on her hips. "So you've been hanging out here all morning? Why didn't Vick send you home?" She turned an accusatory gaze to Vick, who shrugged.

"I was curious if Penny would be able to find us," Vick said. "I was about to kick him out when you showed up. If he stuck around much longer, we'd have run out of food."

"Yeah, thanks for coming to get me," Quentin said, smiling at Penny, and the broken pieces of her heart zoomed back together. "My beef jerky stash is almost gone and the only 'snacks' they have here are *vegetables*."

"So I passed your test, then?" Penny asked Vick instead of clawing her eyes out. "What do you want?" Her blood boiled at the thought that this woman had kept her brother from her when she'd been mad with grief. She wanted to throttle Vick with her bare hands. But glancing at the Watchers, she wasn't sure it was a fight she'd win. If their two leaders were anything to judge by, these people knew how to handle themselves.

"I *want* you to take your kid brother and stay the fuck out of my woods." *Damn, this woman runs hot and cold. Joking one second, ready to throw blades the next.* "Consider this a warning. Let me clean up your fucking mess that you made of the cult, leave us alone, and stop killing our people."

That slammed on the brakes real quick.

Derek was the first to recover. "Killing your people? We didn't know you existed until Tara told us. Which, you would know if you're really as all-seeing as you claim to be."

For once, Vick remained silent, her mouth pressing into a thin line. After a moment, she said, "It's the wild fucking west out here. Can't say for sure who's killing who anymore. But the Faction and the troxies are the biggest perpetrators. And now the Chosen too, thanks to you."

"Don't know who's killing your people, but it isn't us. You're sure it's not the cult?" Penny asked.

Vick narrowed her eyes, tracing her fingernail across her blade. "I'm not sure of anything."

"Maybe there's something else out here," said Silas, always the analytical mind. "Some other threat we aren't seeing."

Vick regarded Penny and her crew with a skeptical look. "And you want to do something about it?"

"We should work together to take down the Chosen, at least," Penny said. "If you could have taken them out by yourselves, you would have already." Vick's jaw hardened as she jutted out her chin, ready to protest, but Penny cut her off. "But if we help you with the cult, you'll help us reclaim the Capital."

"After I just told you we want to be left alone? Why the fuck would I do that?"

Allowing Penny into her domain had been Vick's way to show her power, her influence, how good she was at being sneaky. But it also gave Penny all the ammo she needed to sway Vick to her side. This oasis she'd created for her people, hidden from the rest of the world—this was Vick's pressure point. This was what she cared about most. What she'd give her life to protect. In bringing Penny here, Vick had overplayed her hand. And Penny had every intention of taking advantage of that.

An easy smile slid across her face. *You're mine, Vick.* "It's in your best interest if the Faction wins the war. Because if the troxies win? They'll come for you, and they'll destroy all of this. But we plan to start things fresh. Give our country back to the people and keep it out of the hands of fascists and corporations. We'll build something new, and you'll help create the country you've always wanted."

"What makes you think I haven't already created the country I've always wanted?" Vick said, gesturing around the clearing. *Oh, trust me, Vick. I see right through you.* But Vick was intelligent, ruthless, and a huge fucking asset. They needed her and her people on their side.

"If this is how you want to live, then *fight for it*," Penny said.

Twirling her knife across her knuckles, Vick stared at her with brown eyes so dark they were nearly black. Without breaking eye contact, she said to her commander, "Well, Jaha. Turns out I can be bought, for the right price. Let's see if Penny here is willing to pay."

Jaha crossed her arms as if she doubted Penny had any negotiating power.

"Name it, and I'll see what we can do."

Vick twirled her blade faster as she circled Penny. "We want unlimited access to your armories, whenever we want. Whatever supplies we want. And we want your farmer man's help," Vick said, cutting a glance at Lawrence, who paled. "He will set us up with our own farms and teach us. He'll help with fishing and hunting traps too. And after the war is over, this land remains ours to live in as we see fit."

Out of the corner of her eye, Penny saw Derek balk, and the Faction soldiers he'd brought shifted uneasily. *He's probably just envisioning the nuclear argument Mal and I are about to have.* Because weeding out the cult was one thing, but offering the Watchers anything they wanted was not something she and Mal had discussed. *Not that I need his permission to do anything.* But after everything, making a decision this drastic without Mal felt...wrong. She'd mentioned her idea about partnering with Tara's rescuers, albeit briefly, but this was the right call. She knew it, and she'd convince Mal and everyone else too. *He's not here, and it needs to be done.*

Penny held out her hand, and Vick grasped it. "You have a deal." She'd worry about the "after the war" part later, but she had no problem with the Watchers living wherever and however they wanted. *Now I just need to get Mal on board.*

For a moment, Vick clutched her hand tighter. "And if you do not make good on your end of the bargain? Well. We know where you lay your heads at night. Go home. We will be in touch soon." Vick released her, turning to continue the preparations for their hunters' homecoming.

When Penny rejoined the group, Derek shook his head. "Mal is going to murder you and then me for letting this happen. You just promised them all of our weapons and farm supplies!"

Agnes elbowed Derek, saying, "Not *all* of them. Just some of them. Sounded reasonable to me."

"Would have been nice to be *asked* if I wanted to participate in your unauthorized transaction," Lawrence said, lifting a sandy brow, but he waved away Penny's attempt at an apology. "It's a good idea and I'm happy to do it."

The support from both Agnes and Lawrence sparked an unfamiliar feeling in her, and she gave them a nod as Tara reached over to muss Quentin's hair. "No more chasing cultists in the woods, eh, tomatito?" Tara said.

Quentin shrugged and pulled a piece of bread out of his jacket pocket, then munched on it. "I didn't see any of you finding any clues. You should be thanking me for finding the Watchers when none of you lazy bums could."

"I don't think 'getting captured' qualifies as finding them. And do you have snacks stuffed in every single crevice?" Derek asked in disbelief.

In response, Quentin pulled out a stick of beef jerky from his other pocket and chucked it at him. Derek caught it and kept it, chuckling.

Suddenly nervous, Penny said to Quentin in a soft voice, "You're okay? Really?" She'd been so worried, and now that he was safe, she'd fallen back into her anxious state of not knowing where she and Quentin stood. She wanted to hug him again but wasn't sure if that would be a welcome interaction. He'd only just started being okay with her touching him again.

He turned sharply intelligent eyes to her and said, "You came back for me. You found me." Almost as if he didn't believe that she would. *But there was a time when I abandoned him, so he has every right to doubt me.*

"Of course I did." She squeezed his shoulder and, unable to help herself, she added, "You are the most important thing in this world to me, and I'm sorry I ever made you feel otherwise."

He frowned at her for a moment, as if weighing her words, and then nodded, and she was able to find her breath again. "Let's get going," she said, tucking her sickle into her belt. "Don't want to give Vick enough time to reconsider."

As the crew readied themselves to leave, a group of people appeared in the far side of the clearing, and a cheer went up from the Watchers.

"Must be their returned hunters," Tara said, standing on tiptoe to catch a glimpse.

But Silas stood rooted to the spot, wide eyes unblinking.

"You okay?" Penny asked.

No response.

Agnes waved a hand in front of his face, and he grabbed her wrist, pointing to the newcomers led by a stocky blond man.

Agnes gasped, tears pooling in her eyes as she looked at the blond dude.

Everyone else looked just as confused as Penny felt. After Penny poked him, Silas finally answered the unspoken question in a shaky voice. "My boyfriend. I thought he was dead, but...well, that's him right over there."

17

Agnes

IVAN IS ALIVE, AFTER all this time. When Silas didn't move, Agnes towed him through the crowd. "Ivan!" she said with a wave, and he glanced up.

The former barista looked harder than she remembered. Scars scraped across his arms and a small one slashed his forehead. Muscles that had been toned Before were more well defined now, honed from whatever he'd been doing to survive for almost a year. Ivan looked at her in disbelief, then his eyes found Silas, and he melted.

"Si?" In a few quick strides, he crossed the clearing and crashed into Silas, tangling him into a kiss.

After a moment, Silas finally found his voice. "I thought you were dead," he choked through his tears, dipping his head to Ivan's shoulder. "Where have you been?"

Gravitating to Derek's side, Agnes hooked her arm through his, fighting back her own tears. She couldn't imagine the multitude of feelings rushing over Silas but was pleased that for once, it wasn't a deluge of awful revelations.

Quentin bumped her shoulder with a grin, and she pulled him into her. *Gracias a dios.* If anything had happened to Quentin, it would have gouged a deep, dark hole in all of their lives. And if it would have been bad for her, she couldn't fathom what it would have done to Penny.

And thank god we don't have to find out.

"I'll give you the full story later," Ivan said, then turned to Vick, who watched the exchange with a veiled expression. The woman was hard to read, but she appeared to hold Ivan in high esteem if she'd thrown an entire party for his hunters' homecoming. "I'll escort them back to their camp and stay a while. My apologies for missing out on the festivities, but I'm sure you understand."

Vick inclined her head, granting permission. To Penny, she said, "We'll send someone tomorrow to work out the details of the deal and come up with a plan of attack for the Chosen." She flicked her fingers in dismissal and climbed into a tree, disappearing.

Sidling up to them, Quentin eyed Ivan's weapons belt. "Is that a grenade?" he asked.

"It's actually a flash-bang."

"Can I have it?"

"Sure, kid." Unhooking the device from his belt, he tossed it to a wide-eyed Quentin, who snatched it up despite everyone's protests.

"Yes! Thanks. I'm telling Raph I have a new friend who's cooler than him. Maybe then he'll give me his grenade and I can have a full set. How'd you get this?" Quentin asked, turning it over.

"Made it myself." Ivan, too, had a knack for inventing—something he and Silas had bonded over when they'd first met. Agnes had seen them many times with their heads together over a new piece of tech.

Quentin's eyes turned into dinner plates. "Will you teach me? Penny, can he teach me?" He turned to his sister with an imploring gaze, and, at a loss for words, Penny's eyes widened.

"Let's just make it home in one piece first, okay?" Agnes said, swooping in to save Penny from the spotlight when she was clearly emotional from her brother's return. "Then we can talk about blowing yourself up with Ivan."

An hour or so later, they made it back to Maple Street with no issue—only because Ivan knew the best ways to skirt the cult's hunting grounds. After showering off the grime of the day, Agnes stepped out of the bathroom, where Derek awaited her, leaning against the wall. "Lurking?" she asked.

"Just waiting my turn," he said. "Gotta get in there before Quentin. He takes forever primping."

Chuckling, Agnes shifted to let him pass. As he stepped into the bathroom, he pulled his dirt-stained shirt over his head, exposing a muscled, tattooed torso, and suddenly, Agnes's mouth went dry. "Is there something you want?" he asked in a rough voice. Her eyes dipped to his lips, and before she knew it, she was in his arms, mouth on his, savoring the feel of his velvet tongue against hers.

Still running high on adrenaline from earlier, their kiss took on a more urgent edge as he backed her against the door, arms caging her in. She'd never been good with talking about her feelings, and kissing Derek like this was the only way she could begin to show him how she felt. What he meant to her. *Do I even* know *how I feel?* In that moment, it didn't matter. She didn't need to quantify her feelings and put them in a perfectly labeled box. Derek was hers and she was his, and that's all she needed to know.

As her hands traced the ridges of his abs, he made a low sound in his throat and she pressed into him, breathing him in, his hands finding her backside—

"Okay, *gross*," Quentin said from the end of the hall. "Now I have to boil my eyeballs."

Agnes sprang away, but Derek hooked an arm around her waist, lips finding her neck. "I still have the bathroom for five more minutes," Derek said. "Check the schedule."

Quentin clapped a hand over his eyes and wandered for the stairs with his other hand out, feeling for the banister. "*Fine.* I'll make sure to bring a barf bag in case you're not done when I come back."

"He's getting a wedgie for that later, and I'm definitely eating all of his beef jerky," Derek said, turning his attention back to Agnes as Quentin disappeared downstairs. The way Derek looked at her, she felt a sense of peace she'd always thought was unreachable, even in her life Before. Silas's words came back to her. *"I knew that man loved you the second I saw you together."* Her hand drifted to his face, tracing the angular line of his jaw. He must have seen something in her expression because he dipped his lips to hers in a soft, sensual kiss, slow and powerful like a wave rolling toward shore. The things he made her feel...it was hard to find the words.

But it was getting easier every day.

Breaking away with a hum of satisfaction, he said, "I really do need to get in there. Quentin is probably sitting downstairs with his stopwatch."

"Would hate for him to catch us twice," she said with a laugh. "See you soon."

Once everyone had taken their turn at cleaning up, they gathered in the living room to hear Ivan's story.

"We have most of the Wilds mapped out and we know generally where the cult's home base is, but we haven't been able to get close enough," Ivan explained, kicking back on the couch. "The area is really foggy this time of year. Nothing like the enemy charging at you out of the mist."

Agnes shuddered at the thought. She'd battled turned in the dark before and imagined it was similarly terrifying.

"How long have you been with Vick's crew?" Penny asked, arms crossed. She'd looked more tense the closer they'd gotten to the Capital and paced a fervent path in the kitchen. *Probably gearing up to go head to head with Mal later.*

At the question, Silas shifted in his seat next to Ivan, interest piqued. It was something Agnes had been wondering too.

"In the Beginning at the height of the Red Riots, I made it out of New York before Containment." He turned to Silas with a stricken look, grabbing his hand. "I tried calling you, Si. I went to your apartment. I looked everywhere. They killed the phone lines before I could reach Agnes, and by that point, the city was about to tear itself apart. So I did the only thing I could think to do—I ran, and I regretted every day not going back to look for you." His voice broke as the tears gathered in his eyes. "I'm sorry I gave up. I'm sorry—"

"Stop." Silas pressed a hand to Ivan's mouth. "You'd never have found me anyway, and you could have died. We're together now, and that's all I care about." He caressed Ivan's face, eyes aglow with admiration.

Penny cleared her throat. "Sorry to interrupt—but Vick?"

"Right," said Ivan, continuing. "I got on a bus heading to the Capital, but it was ambushed by troxies. They pulled everyone out, checked IDs, chucked some people into big trucks. They grabbed a woman, but she fought back. Lodged a knife in the guy's throat and took on five others at once. Another woman and I jumped in to help, and we escaped together." A fond smile flitted across his face. "That's how I met Vick and Jaha."

"Vick and Jaha are together?" Tara asked, feigning disinterest as she tossed another log on the fire. Agnes suppressed a smile. She'd seen the way Tara's eyes had lit up when Vick dropped out of that tree.

Ivan must have noticed it too, because he said with a twinkle in his eye, "Jaha is her second in command. Vick values her solitude."

Tara made a noncommittal sound and stuck a poker in the fire, while Quentin played at lighting little sticks on fire and snuffing them out. "You trying to smoke us out?" she grumbled at him, but Agnes could tell from her slight smirk that Tara was pleased with Ivan's answer.

"And you've been monitoring the Wilds since then?" Penny asked.

"Pretty much," Ivan said. "We've kept to ourselves until the coming winter forced us abroad to look for resources. I'm glad Vick agreed to an alliance. With turned and the Chosen encroaching on our territory, we're getting dragged into more fights. Would be nice to feel secure in our own homes again."

Penny must have gotten whatever information she needed, because she nodded, rapping her knuckles on the countertop. "I'm heading back to let Mal know what's going on."

"Want some backup?" Derek asked.

"Could help soften the blow," Agnes added. Now that Quentin was safe, Penny seemed better, but the woman was still clearly on edge.

Penny rubbed her forehead, sighing. "The deal with the Watchers was my idea, so I should be the one to face his wrath. See you guys tomorrow."

"Bye," Quentin said with a wave. "I'll be there for training, if we're still doing that."

"Sure." Penny gave him a slight smile. "See you."

Mal would likely not take kindly to their allying with someone they didn't know, while offering up their armories on a silver platter. It had been a risky gamble, and Agnes had to admit, Mal had a right to be pissed off. While it would probably work out this time because Vick seemed decent, Penny did have a tendency to go rogue, which could sometimes end in people dying.

Mal's desire to work with Penny and steer her in a less violent direction was admirable, and while today showed Penny was capable of handling situations without resorting to her sickle, one different decision didn't negate her record of violence. But Penny was clearly making progress with Quentin, and the fact she'd been more open to Agnes, Tara, and the other Outposters definitely earned her bonus points. Agnes was more cautious than optimistic, but that feeling of dread that usually accompanied Penny's entrance into a room no longer occurred.

When she'd found Penny in the showers the other night, she'd seen herself sitting there—the woman she'd been after Evie's death. Agnes didn't know why Mal had sent for her, but strangely, she'd been the right person. Because maybe she was the only one who could truly understand and cut through the noise in Penny's head to draw out the strong, fierce woman that lurked beneath the surface of grief.

And maybe Mal knew that too.

18

"**O**H, GENERAL?" PENNY CALLED, leaning over the railing in the stadium's arena as Mal ran drills with his soldiers before the dinner bell. But Will was the first to pause, loping over with that charming smile of his.

"You find Quentin?" Will asked.

Penny couldn't help her answering grin. "You bet your ass."

"Fuck yes!" Will extended his hand, and she slapped it.

"William," barked Mal from a distance. "Back in line."

With a last grin at her, Will jogged back to his group as Mal trudged over. Even in the chilly air, Mal wore a tight tee shirt that clung to him in all the right places, and the man wasn't even shivering. But his jaw ticked as Will passed, a frown creasing his brow.

I need *to stop noticing shit like that.*

Penny jerked her head toward the hallway that led inside. "A word?"

Mal grunted his assent and dismissed his troops for dinner, then headed for the men's locker room exit, indicating with a gesture that he'd meet her inside.

As she waited for him, his soldiers milled about the hallway, laughing and talking. The sector raids must be going well for everyone to be in such good spirits. A few greeted her and she acknowledged them, but her heart rate kicked up a few notches. Maybe she'd made the wrong decision today. But if Ivan was running with Vick, that had to speak to her character somewhat, right? She liked Silas, and his choice in partner seemed like a decent guy. They—

"You're picking at your nails."

Penny jumped, hand flying to her chest, as Mal watched her with a bemused expression. "Jesus Christ, announce yourself next time."

"You asked me to meet you here. Didn't think it would shock you that I showed up two minutes after we discussed it."

"*I* discussed it. You did a series of grunts and gestures. And what do you mean, I was picking at my nails?"

"You only do that when you're nervous." *How the fuck does he know that? I don't even know that.* Mal leaned against the wall, eyes running over her from head to toe in a way that said he saw more than she told him. It felt intimate and...exposed. "So, Penny. Why are you nervous?"

Glancing at the people filling the hallway, Penny made a frustrated sound and backed him into a nearby supply closet, shutting the door and clicking on the camping light. She was already nervous, as he so helpfully pointed out, and she didn't want any eavesdroppers to her demise. "You've never seen me nervous." *Has he? Fuck. I'm losing my damn mind.*

The small room was packed with shelves of cleaning supplies and yard tools crowding against the walls, forcing them to stand chest to chest. She wriggled in an attempt to make some space between them but knocked over some rakes, the door bumping against her back.

Mal anchored her in place with a hand on her hip, hoisting an eyebrow as he looked down at her. "Stuffing me into a closet because you don't want an audience is not helping your case."

"I—don't have a good answer for that," she admitted, trying to concentrate on the cold metal of the door behind her instead of the heat of his hand.

"I'm guessing you got Quentin back, or else we'd be having a very different conversation right now."

"Oh yeah. I did." *Double fuck. He knows something is up. I should have led with that.* "We also found Tara's rescuers. Call themselves the Watchers. They helped Quentin too."

"Sounds like good news." Mal's gaze swept over her again, *scrutinizing* her, and he brought his hand up beside her head, leaning in. "But I'm guessing there's more. What happened?"

Ignoring the fact that she was apparently as transparent to this man as a fucking window, and that him *looking* at her like that made her want to combust, she said, "They agreed to an alliance. We help them take out the cult, they help us here in the Capital."

Frowning, Mal asked, "And that's all they wanted? Our help taking out the cult?"

Penny ran her tongue across the bottom of her teeth. *Here we go.* "They want access to our armories and Lawrence's help setting up farms to get them through the winter. And they want to be left alone after the war is over."

Mal dropped his hand and a blank look flattened his face. "Access to our armories."

"Yes."

"To this crew of unknown people living in the woods."

"Yes."

"Who could also be the ones behind the recent stabbings and stolen supplies."

"Vick—their leader—said that wasn't her, and I thought we agreed it was the cult? You saw that fucked-up tree."

"Doesn't mean the Watchers aren't also picking off our messengers and patrols. And it didn't occur to you that maybe they're looking for a way into our armories to take us over and push *us* out? We're supposed to be uniting the country again, not splintering it further."

Fucking hell. I should have thought of that. Vick and the Watchers hated the Faction and everything they stood for, but she thought they'd found a common enemy in the cult. But part of gambling was reading your opponent, and her gut told her Vick could be trusted.

"I made a judgment call, Mal. And honestly? If the Watchers wanted to take us over, they probably could, just because they're stealthy enough to get in wherever they want. They might not like us, but they're capable fighters and willing to ally on this one issue. If joining forces with them means a stronger presence in the Capital, I thought you'd be all for that. *Especially* since you're so concerned about the troxies now that your boy Zeln is in the picture."

Mal's nostrils flared as he absorbed the information, grinding his teeth.

"Are you pissed? You look pissed."

"Am I—? Yes, I'm pissed. Penny, we don't know anything about these people, and you gave them a blank check, a ticket straight into the center of our power. And now if we deny them access after you've already made a deal, we'll start a whole new war. You're acting like a free agent, but we're supposed to be a *team*, you and I. We make decisions together. This—" He broke off, running both hands through his hair with a frustrated noise, then spun her aside and ripped the door open, stalking down the hallway.

"Where are you going?"

Over his shoulder he said, "War room. Need to think." By his tone, it was clear that he meant *alone*.

After taking a cold shower and grabbing a quick bite to eat, Penny kicked back in her cot, staring at the ceiling. Vick's representatives would be coming tomorrow, so this deal was going through with or without Mal's support. He'd asked her to step up and she did. Sure, *maybe* she should have asked his opinion on the deal first before accepting, but he'd said that she had good ideas, so what was his fucking problem?

He is *the one with the actual war experience…but what's done is done, and he'll have to deal with it.*

A knock at her door interrupted her thoughts. It was late and she wasn't expecting any visitors, so she approached with caution. When she answered it, Mal stood there, bracing an arm against the doorframe. He'd changed into a clean set of tactical pants and a tee shirt, and his fresh scent of something almost minty reached her across the small distance.

"Back for round two?" she asked.

Running a hand through his neatly trimmed beard, he said, "Can I come in?"

Wary, she stepped back to let him pass, their arms brushing as he slid by her. He looked extra huge towering over her meager possessions in her small room. For a moment, he stood there, hands clenching and unclenching at his sides. "I'm sorry, Pen."

Penny blinked. "You're—what?"

He glowered for a moment, but then softened. "I just—" He broke off, scrubbing his hands through his hair. "Earlier, I reacted emotionally because the thought of you—I mean, you and your team—out there, facing Vick's crew, an unknown threat—I should have been there, and I wasn't. You made the best decision you could, given the circumstances. You saw a possible advantage for us, and you took it. I'm sorry I got angry, but making unilateral decisions of that magnitude isn't how we do things. That's how people get killed. Next time, run something like that by me first, okay?"

Mal is apologizing? To me? For the second time ever? That couldn't be right. "You're...sorry."

His lips twitched and he said, "You want me to write it on a greeting card?"

"Would be nice, so I have tangible proof. Nobody will believe me otherwise."

Suppressing a smile, he leaned against the small table, crossing his arms. "So what happens now?" he asked, his gaze landing on her.

Good god, those eyes. Honey brown and glinting in the glow from the camping lamp, they pinned her in place, watching her every move. But instead of feeling hunted or watched, she felt *powerful.*

"I could get used to this. You, sitting there, awaiting my instructions." She'd meant the line to come out in jest, but the roughness of her voice had it sounding...husky. *Am I—did I just* flirt *with him? Jesus fucking Christ, end this conversation.*

At her words, the ring of gold in his eyes thinned as his pupils flared wide, and for a wild second, Penny got lost in those eyes. *Drowning. I would drown here, with him. In him.* And for a second, she actually keyed in to the words he'd said before...how he'd spoken of concern for her, needing her first, then correcting himself. *Maybe...maybe his interest in me isn't purely related to our war efforts.*

And maybe I want more too.

Pushing off from the table, he closed the distance between them with slow, deliberate steps. When he was breaths away, he stopped, close enough to feel his body heat, and her head swam. She didn't know what she wanted to happen, only that having him this near, looking at her with such raw intensity, was the closest she'd ever felt to flying.

"There aren't many people who hold sway over me," he said. "But you? I'd go to hell and back for you." He traced a fingertip from her cheek across her jawline to her chin. *How can one fucking fingertip make me feel this alive?* "The next time there's a battle or any kind of confrontation, we're dealing with it together. Not because you can't handle it on your own—but because *I* can't handle losing you. You get me?"

Penny swallowed, mouth suddenly dry, and looked away. "Right. Because the Faction needs its figurehead."

But Mal pulled her chin, tugging her gaze back up to his. His expression tightened for a moment, as if he wanted to contradict her and say something else. But instead, he said, "The Faction doesn't need a 'figurehead.' It needs *you*. I've always known you could be more than just the rallying cry of the resistance, Pen. I hope you start to see it for yourself."

There he goes again, believing in me when I've done nothing to earn that. She'd fallen into this role with fresh blood on her hands. Hands that would never be clean no matter how much good she did. But that was okay. She didn't need to redeem all of her past wrongs, and she didn't want Mal's *faith* or for him to see the good in her—there was hardly any left anyway. But for once, she didn't feel like fighting with him. So she gave the most diplomatic response she was capable of.

"I'm not someone people should look up to, Mal. I'm just here to finish this war and that's it. Don't make me into more than I am."

Her words doused the heat of whatever had been building between them, and she lamented its loss, but she couldn't let him say those things about her when they just weren't true. He dropped his hand, his expression closing off as he turned for the door. He paused as if he wanted to say something else, but he only said, "See you in the morning," and left.

The urge to call him back, to say something that would wipe that dead look off of his face sparked through her, but instead, she turned off the light and crawled into bed.

And tried not to think about how amazing it felt to have someone see the good in her, even when she barely saw it herself. But not just someone.

Mal.

The most infuriating and inspiring man I've ever met.

19

THE FOG ROLLED IN as Penny and the group approached the edge of the Wilds, settling over them in a thick blanket. "Nothing like swimming through a goddamn cloud," she muttered as their platoon of Faction and Watchers marched onward.

As promised, Mal trudged at her side, volt rifle held at the ready as he scanned the area. He hadn't mentioned their encounter last night, and Penny was grateful. There was something about facing her *feelings*, or whatever, in the light of day that made her feel itchy. But having him there felt good. It had been a while since they'd been in the field together, and she didn't realize she missed having him beside her until that moment.

"Something about the air currents here keep the area in a heavy fog most of the time," Vick said, eyes trained on the forest breathing and sighing around them. "It's why we haven't had much success in finding exactly where the cult makes camp. Can't ever see a fucking thing."

Earlier that morning, Vick and a crew of about twenty or so people, including Jaha, Ivan, and his hunters, awaited them outside the stadium. When asked how they'd gotten past the Faction patrol, Vick had smiled sweetly and said, "What patrol?" *As if we needed a reminder that she can go anywhere and do anything she damn well pleases.* Mal had been grumpy after that, so their new alliance was not off to a great start. After doing introductions and reviewing Vick's maps, Mal had gathered his best people and they'd set out.

"Too bad we didn't bring our resident flying squirrel," remarked Derek, slushing through the wet leaves. "Quentin could jump from tree to tree and be our lookout above the fog."

Bumping Ivan's shoulder, Agnes said, "I'm just hoping Quentin doesn't singe his eyebrows off."

"Hopefully Silas locked up all the dynamite," agreed Tara.

Quentin had protested being left behind, but Ivan tempted him with working on a pyrotechnics project he'd started in Derek's garage. Penny had given Silas strict instructions to not allow Quentin to blow up the entire house, to which Silas had saluted with a giggle that left Penny feeling less than confident. Lawrence, meanwhile, was setting up the Watchers' gardens today—and doing some snooping.

"How is the fog still this fucking thick?" Mal grumbled as he dodged a trunk. "It's damn well past noon and I still can't see a tree at ten paces."

"Vick?" Penny called. "We know where we are?"

"We're past the limits of where we've scouted." Hacking one of her knives against a nearby tree trunk, Vick made a deep gouge in the bark to mark their path. "We're in uncharted territory now."

"That's not unsettling at all," Agnes whispered.

The longer they walked, the more looking into the thick fog felt like staring into the void. Penny's mind began playing tricks on her, showing her shapes and shadows, movements in the mist of things that weren't there. When a thick tree branch cracked underfoot, she latched onto Mal's arm, then felt like a jumpy idiot. He glanced at her, a slight smirk hiding in the corner of his trim beard.

Giving her hand something to do besides grasp at Mal's insanely huge bicep, she took a knife from her belt and held her sickle in the other hand. If more enhanced turned showed up, she wanted to be ready.

Deeper and deeper they headed into the Wilds, the sounds of the forest silenced except for their footsteps.

A flash of movement in her periphery.

"Did you see that?" she asked Mal.

"See what?"

"I saw it," Agnes said, drifting to Penny's side with her machete. "Could be an animal?"

Jaha clicked her tongue. "Animals stay away from here. They know this land is cursed."

Penny didn't subscribe to that kind of belief, but with each step, the ominous feeling grew and an overwhelming urge to run the opposite way swept through her. She'd seen a lot of bad shit in her life and done half of it too, but something about this—the air, the land—didn't feel right.

Okay, maybe she'd begun to believe in curses just a little bit.

"Look." Tara's voice, breaking through the veil of uneasiness. She pointed to a nearby tree as a gust of wind carried the pungent scent of death. Nailed to the trunk was a headless body, its feet several inches from the ground, multiple metal spikes driven through the torso and limbs. Below it sat a rusty metal bucket, now empty.

Penny squinted at the body as she choked back a gag at the smell. "Are those...bite marks?" Several half-moon shapes marred the neck, and a few chunks of flesh were missing from the arms. Some of the bites looked fresh. *This is fucking repulsive.* Whether the bite marks had been from cultists or turned, it didn't matter. Both implications were bad—because it meant they were either dealing with a cannibalistic cult or there were turned out here, and they were close.

A few steps later, a person-sized wooden pike materialized out of the mist, a rotted head pierced atop it, wide blue eyes clouded. With each step, more trees appeared, each with its own body, the head detached onto a pike.

"A sentinel force of the dead, guarding the way to their camp?" Vick murmured to Ivan, who nodded, drawing the hunting bow from his back and nocking an arrow.

"This entire thing is creepy enough without your commentary," said Tara.

Vick bared her teeth in some semblance of a smile, but it looked too feral to be considered anything but a predator showing her fangs.

Clicking her tongue at her soldiers, Vick and her crew branched out, disappearing into the fog. "We'll cover more ground if we spread out," Vick said. "But stay close. If you hear sounds of fighting, maybe run toward that." Shooting a last edgy smile at Tara, Vick took off into the mist.

Mal nodded to their troops, who fanned out through the trees. After passing several more heads, Penny noticed something about the eyes.

"They were all healthy," she said, lifting the eyelid of one with the point of her sickle. "No shattered sclera, no black veins, no full-black eyes. These aren't just random killings—they chose these victims with a purpose." Glancing at Agnes, Penny lifted a brow. "But why?"

Agnes shrugged. "You were closest to Rodney. What would cause his people to do something like this?"

Closing her eyes, Penny recited what the cultist had said when she questioned her. "'Some blood is purer than others. The blood of the unbelievers is our salvation.' Maybe she meant people who aren't users or turned? No idea. Maybe that's why she said Quentin tasted so sweet."

At the mention of Quentin almost getting eaten, Agnes tightened her grip on her machete. "Let's ask them ourselves."

And in that moment, she knew that as long as Quentin was her top priority, she could rely on Agnes to have her back.

As they continued, more bodies appeared, missing limbs or pieces of flesh. As if something had come by, looking for a snack...

A low guttural sound echoed through the mist, impossible to tell from which direction. Penny whipped around, eyes straining. "Did you hear that?" she asked Mal.

"Get behind me."

Her annoyance cut through her fear. "Seriously?" She crept ahead, sickle ready for whatever was coming. To Mal's credit, he let her take the lead. Derek, Agnes, and Tara were close by, along with a few soldiers, but Vick and her crew had completely disappeared. Hopefully they were somewhere nearby and hadn't abandoned them to get eaten by whatever awaited them in the woods.

Mal seemed to be of the same mindset, because he said, "If Vick wanted most of our leadership dead, this is the perfect cover. Lead us into the fog and leave us for dead."

"Vick wouldn't do that," Tara said, a notch forming in her forehead.

"Better hope not," Mal said. "We're on our own."

The smell of death was thick around them, the dense air making it hard to breathe. Penny wasn't afraid of turned or cultists, but she *was* fucking afraid of not knowing if they were slowly being surrounded by the enemy, hidden in the fog.

And she wasn't the only one jumping at every rustle of the branches, every slap of a boot against the wet ground. Everyone was on edge, watching, waiting.

Two seconds later, a harsh snarl ripped through the silence and a staggering shape burst out of the mist, plowing straight for them. Wasting no time, Penny sliced her sickle across its throat, the head tumbling to the damp leaves. *Decapitate first, ask questions later.*

Another guttural growl as a turned dragged itself between the trees, Tara bashing a crater in its head.

Another appeared. And another.

Before long, dozens of bodies careened through the fog in a chorus of moans and wails.

"Remember what we've been drilling," Mal shouted to everyone, his troops rushing into formation. "We don't know what kind of turned these are."

In seconds, they were surrounded as creatures crashed into them from every angle, some darting in and taking chunks of flesh, screams both human and creature filling the air. Back-to-back, Derek and Mal rotated, shooting volts. Some turned fell as expected.

But some didn't.

Enhanced turned, even all the way out here.

It didn't take long for the thrill of battle to pull Penny under, falling to the mechanical work of slashing throats and severing windpipes with ease. But unlike when she'd been with her Marauders, she found herself looking out for those around her. Agnes, Tara, Derek, Mal—even some of the soldiers here who she knew by name—she cared about what happened to them. They were *her* people in a way that the Marauders never had been. She'd trained them, and trained beside them, but they all followed her now willingly, not because of some drug she could give them or the fear she lorded over them.

When a turned lunged out of the mist and dove for Agnes's legs, Penny punted it into the nearest tree, taking her knife to its eyeball, black blood spurting. Panting, Agnes said, "Thanks," as she hacked her machete at a turned until its ribcage came apart under her blade.

"Puñeta, this shit is disgusting," Tara said, swinging home runs left and right, black brain matter flinging everywhere.

Penny almost wanted to laugh at the absurdity of it all. Everything about the world they lived in now was one of Quentin's favorite graphic novels come to life. But the feeling dissipated as several turned circled Mal and Derek, somehow labeling them as the biggest threats, and pounced. A group of three went for Mal, grabbing his arms and dragging him down, while Derek fought a few of his own.

"No!" Penny leaped over some bodies and thrashed through others to reach them. At her shout, Agnes was at her side in seconds.

A few turned latched onto Mal with their black, sharp teeth, his fresh blood running into their mouths and driving their frenzy even higher. Penny sliced at them while Mal ripped one off, its teeth scraping his skin into ribbons. Grunting, he grabbed its jaw and tore it from its head, then threw both away from him. A deep roar erupted from his chest as he dealt with the others surrounding him.

But still more came.

As she cut through the onslaught, Penny said, "Where the fuck is Vick?"

Tara grunted, swinging her bat. "Maybe they got ambushed too."

"What do we do?" Penny asked, turning toward Mal. "Shit!" Shoving him aside, she hooked her sickle across the throat of a turned that had snuck up behind him, severing its head.

"Thanks," he said, his eyes burning into hers for a split second before he spun, firing volts into the mist. But then a shrill voice cut through the din.

"Look who it is! Pretty Penny, come out to play!" A peal of high-pitched laughter seemed to come from all sides.

Penny's blood ran cold at the moniker, and she locked eyes with Mal. "The Chosen. They're here."

"Showtime," Derek said as he took aim with his volt rifle.

"But we still haven't found their camp," Agnes reminded them.

"I say follow the cackling laughter," Tara said.

Mal nodded, wiping the gore from his forehead. "Let's finish this."

Through the mist, Penny zeroed in on a cultist heading toward them, "chosen" carved in scabbed letters on his forehead. But before he could take another step, a turned crashed into him, devouring his screams along with his face.

More cultists appeared, their lips forming words, whispering something. Another charged, and as she drew closer, Penny heard what she was saying. What they were all chanting.

Pretty Penny.

Slicing the woman's throat, Penny said, "Maybe we should let them take me, Mal. That's the only way we're going to find their camp and wipe them out for good."

Mal grabbed her in an iron grip, yanking her into him, teeth bared. "Don't you fucking dare suggest anything like that again. We'll find another way."

Breaking away from him with a frustrated sound, she threw herself back into the fight, even though his reaction struck her like a match flaming to life. But as more cultists and turned appeared, Penny wasn't sure if they'd survive long enough to find another way.

Suddenly, a harsh battle cry went up, and Vick, Ivan, and her hunters blew through the woods, arrows and spears flying.

Tara let out a whoop of triumph. "Ha! Knew she wouldn't abandon us."

"No you fucking didn't," Penny muttered.

But while Vick's appearance brought a moment of relief, the woods that had become a blood bath was attracting more turned. She took quick stock of their people—and it wasn't good. *We can't go on much longer.*

Taking advantage of her distraction, something grabbed Penny's hair from behind and slammed her to the ground, letting out a crazed laugh. The cultist, a bigger guy, straddled her, his meaty hands clutching her throat. After kneeing him in the balls, she wriggled out and scooted away—but cultists and turned swarmed her. Yelling, she slashed and cut, the panic constricting her throat. She'd never been surrounded like this before, never in a place where she couldn't fucking *see*—

"Mal!" she yelled as cultists clawed at her, dragging her across the forest floor. "Help!"

Through the bodies, she saw Mal charge toward her, but a group of cultists swarmed him.

"Derek! Agnes!" she yelled any name that flew through her mind, anyone who might see what was happening and help. Kicking at the hands that held her, a few fell, but more jumped in to take their place.

And when she heard the familiar screams, she knew all would soon be lost.

Frantically trying to catch a glimpse through the mass of bodies dragging her off, she saw Tara and Agnes in a similar situation.

Penny jerked and thrashed, yelling until her throat was raw.

"Quiet now, Pretty Penny."

The last thing she saw before a cultist slammed a rock into her head was Mal, pinned against a tree by cultists and fighting off turned, the tendons popping out of his neck as he screamed her name.

Then everything went black.

20

*S*MACK. MUFFLED SCREAMS. *THUD.*

Pause.

Whimpering. *Smack.* Wailing, unintelligible. *Thud.*

A rusty smell, something metallic, and—*hay?*

Penny blinked back into consciousness with the taste of blood, dirt, and motor oil on her tongue. A filthy cloth was stuffed into her mouth and tied behind her head, gagging her, and she leaned forward over something.

Wrists bound behind me. Ankles and knees too. Feels like rope. Weapons gone.

The world looked fuzzy and her head fucking hurt, but she could see enough to tell she was in a dimly lit barn, kneeling on the packed dirt over a trough.

And she wasn't alone.

Agnes and Tara were to her right, bound and gagged, wide eyes leaking tears. Several dozen or more cultists clung to the shadows, chittering to one another, surrounded by the detritus of a well-used camp. *This is it. They've brought us to their lair.*

To her left, Penny recognized some of their soldiers and Watchers, all restrained in the same way, kneeling in a line. Wooden buckets and metal pails sat in front of them. Old farm equipment packed the remaining space—a dilapidated tractor, hay baler, wheel barrow, pitchforks.

And in the corner sat a pile of bodies. It was too dim to tell, but some could have been the first round of messengers they'd sent to Chicago.

Fuck, this is bad.

At the end of Penny's row, five people away, stood a massive user. Shock jolted through her—she recognized him. The big bald bearded user that had tried to stop her and Silas at the stairwell to the Spire, the one who had been working for Callum, Rodney's protégé. *Is he in charge now?*

He grabbed the man at the end of the line by the hair—a Faction soldier—and punched him in the back of the head. *Smack.* The soldier let out a garbled scream as the cult leader pulled his head back, exposing his throat.

With a horrible, plummeting sensation straight into the pit of her stomach, Penny realized what they were doing.

And she was powerless to stop it.

The leader's assistant slashed a knife across the man's neck and he slumped forward, blood leaking into the bucket. *Thud.*

At the end of the line, a few bodies sagged over another trough, fresh blood flowing freely. The leader moved on to the next in line, one of Vick's hunters, and did the same routine. *Smack.* The woman screamed, attempting to wriggle away. But she met the same fate, her body dropping over the bucket, leaking blood.

Fuck fuck fuck, this can't be happening. Penny struggled against her restraints, but the rope was tight. Sticking a finger down her sock, she cursed. Bastards had taken her boot knife. The familiar shrinking sensation of panic prickled over her, the edges of her vision darkening and making her want to claw out of her skin.

No. I need to keep my head. For Agnes and Tara. For Quentin.

"How many is that for today?" the leader asked.

Another assistant—the one not busy cutting throats—checked a grubby notebook. "Sixteen."

The leader nodded. "Could use a few more."

Smack.

More screams and another body fell.

Thud.

Beside her, Agnes and Tara both yelled around their gags, writhing in vain. But Penny couldn't see a way out of this. Even if they escaped their bindings, they were in the center of the cult's power, outnumbered and unarmed. She didn't know where they were, and neither did anyone else who could rescue them. If she could get free, she could grab the assistant's knife, but with her hands tied behind her back, her mobility was severely limited.

Sobs and whimpers. *Smack. Thud.*

Two people left, and then it's my turn.

The cloying smell of blood filled the air, overwhelming, and the jeers of the Chosen buzzed in her ears.

I'm not going to let these fuckers take me down.

Frantically, she searched the ground for anything that could be used as a weapon. *There.* A rusted nail, one of the ones they used for the bodies in the trees. Agnes saw it too, and with her knee, she nudged it to where Penny could grab it with her hands behind her back, hiding it between her palms. Locking eyes with the two women, Penny poured every remaining ounce of courage into her gaze, hoping to impart some to them.

We still have a chance.

The Faction soldier kneeling beside Penny cried out as the leader grabbed his head, and he looked at her, tears pouring down his face. She wanted to console him, to stab the shit out of the cult leader or do anything to make this stop, but she couldn't talk and the leader was out of reach. So all she could do was watch as one of her soldiers had his throat cut, his blood spraying on her face as he fell forward.

"I love it when they struggle," the leader said as he moved to stand behind her.

I will burn all of this to the fucking ground. As far as she was concerned, anyone witnessing this horror and *cheering it on* was fucking guilty and deserved to die.

"Ah, Pretty Penny. Finally your turn." Crouching, the leader grabbed her chin, pulled her close, then darted his tongue out to lick the side of her face. As she squirmed in his hold, he chuckled. "Fear makes the blood taste so sweet. And yours will be *delicious*." Grabbing a fistful of her hair, he pulled her head back, forcing her to rise up on her knees as his assistant stood ready with the knife.

Now.

Moving the nail so the point extended in both hands, she brought her arms straight up behind her, jamming the nail into the inside of the leader's thigh with all her strength. Crying out, his grip loosened and she threw herself backward, toppling him over. Agnes and Tara sprang into action, flopping themselves at the leader, using elbows and knees to throttle his tender parts.

When his assistant came at Penny with the knife, she kicked out with both feet, sweeping him to the ground and sending the knife clattering out of his hand. She rolled over to it and sawed through her bindings as the cult leader roared, ripping the nail from his leg and grabbing Tara and Agnes by their necks.

Penny stood, finally free, but cultists approached, ready to drag her down. But some went for the buckets and trough of fresh blood, dipping their hands in to get a taste. Her stomach rolled, but she ignored it, taking stock of her limited options.

In the far corner, Penny spied a stall piled with weapons—too many to have come from just their group alone. *I can at least get more than this blade to work with.* But before she could move, cultists swarmed her.

As Penny cut them down with the small knife, she wracked her brain for a plan. *Too many for me to take on without more weapons. Weapons too far away. Big cult leader will kill Agnes and Tara with his bare hands any second. Need to end him and everyone in this fucking place.*

Then she saw the tractor parked on the far side of the barn near the sliding door, hay baler hitched to the back. And she had an idea. *If I can get over there—*

Glancing around, she looked for what she needed. Old farm tools leaned against the stalls—hoof picks, brushes, a hammer—*pliers*. Penny dove to the ground and scooped up the pliers and the hammer for good measure.

Rushing through the crowd, she made her way to Agnes and Tara, sliding the last few feet in the dirt on her knees and ramming the hammer into the leader's kneecap. He dropped the women, who thudded to the ground, and Penny made quick work of slashing their bindings. Tossing them her hammer and knife, she said, "Extra weapons in the far stall if you can make it there."

"What are you doing!" Agnes shouted as Penny ran for the tractor, but she didn't bother replying.

Come on, come on. The tractor was different from the one she was used to on the family farm, but she knew enough about old engines from all the maintenance work she'd done for her father. Ripping off the side panel, she located the battery's positive terminal and stuck the pliers on it, the engine coughing to life. No telling how long the thing had sat or how much fuel was in it, but she was betting not much as she swung up into the driver's seat, kicking off cultists grabbing for her feet, and shifted the tractor into gear.

At the sound of the engine, the leader threw back his head, howling. "Oh, our Pretty Penny! She is so smart! But it will not save her or her friends." He yanked Tara toward him by the hair, and Penny pressed the accelerator, the tractor gaining speed as she aimed toward the leader.

At the last second, Agnes swooped in, kicking the leader in his already destroyed kneecap and pulling Tara to safety as he crumpled to the ground in front of the tractor. Penny let out a yell as the vehicle bumped over him, the hay baler's blades whirring and stuttering as they found purchase against his flesh, his screams joining her own.

Diving from the driver's seat, Penny rolled out of the way as the tractor and hay baler continued wreaking havoc on the cultists, chopping them to pieces if they didn't get out of the way in time. "Come on!" she said, dragging Agnes and Tara to the weapons stall.

Tara yanked on the barn door in vain, a shiny padlock barring their way. "If there's an axe in there, we can chop the lock off." Agnes tore through the stall, finding their own weapons and tossing out others that could help, finally finding a hatchet. As Tara took to the lock with it, a voice came from outside, filtering between the wooden slats.

"Tara! Are you in there?"

A sob tore from Tara's throat as Penny and Agnes fought off the cultists. "Vick! Yes, we're locked in."

"Stand back," came Vick's muffled voice, and after a few booming blows, a huge axe burst through the wooden barn doors, hands reaching through to pry away the splinters.

I'd know those hands anywhere.

"Penny!" Mal shouted as he continued ripping planks away, creating a big enough space for them to crawl out.

A relieved sob tumbled from Penny's chest as she pushed Tara and Agnes through the opening, then followed, falling into Mal's arms.

He's here. He came.

He clutched her to him with bone-crushing intensity for a moment, then moved her aside as cultists attempted to crawl out after them, forcing them back. The remainder of their crew and the Watchers surrounded the barn as Derek pulled Agnes into him, the two colliding in a brief but fierce kiss. Vick helped Tara to her feet with a relieved expression as she took in her disheveled appearance.

Penny shook her head in disbelief, wiping the sweat and dirt from her brow. *How the fuck did we survive that?*

A crashing sound, and the barn shuddered.

In answer to everyone's questioning looks, Penny said, "Hot-wired an old tractor and let it ride. Crashed, probably."

Blinking, Mal said, "I want to know more about that later."

Recinching her weapons belt, Penny found her silver lighter in one of the side pockets. "Guard the doors. No one gets out." Flicking her lighter, she approached a pile of hay, lighting it up. The flames devoured it and crept to the wooden barn. It was damp, but it would burn. "Everyone else, scour the surrounding area for stragglers or see if they have other camps. We're ending this here. Today."

Vick jerked her head at a squadron of Watchers, and they took off. The howls of cultists crescendoed as the fire ate away at the structure, and before long, it was raging like a bonfire. Penny had harbored a thin hope of recuperating some cultists and helping them re-enter normal life. But those people in the barn were too far gone, the dust destroying their minds beyond what the Faction's limited detox serum supply could repair.

Turning her back on the flames, a familiar feeling rose within her of the last time she'd walked away from a fire. But this time was different. This time, she wasn't burning down her whole life, her whole family, because of a horrific hallucination that personified everything she hated about herself.

This time, she was burning out the last dregs of Rodney's evil that still grasped for her from beyond the grave.

He could not haunt her any longer.

21

WALKING ON LEGS HEAVY as cinderblocks, Penny found a chair in one of the stadium's grand entryways they used as the cafeteria and sank into it, followed by the rest of their group. It was late, so it was largely deserted except for a cook who had stayed up to reheat some food for them. Grateful for the lack of an audience, Penny rested her head in her hands. *The Chosen are finished. It's over. Done.* But the only feeling she could muster was exhaustion.

Mal said a few words to his soldiers and delivered claps on backs, making his rounds, but he avoided Penny. Before she could wonder what the fuck that was about, Agnes and Tara took seats on either side of her, and Derek, Ivan, and Vick joined them, the rest filling the other tables. Something lodged in Penny's throat as she noticed their numbers were smaller than what they'd left with that morning.

The cook, a kind woman who lived with her two kids in one of the northern hallways, set up cups of water and hot coffee on the concession stand counter, and Tara brought some to their table. Shoving down the resurfacing memories of the barn and the blood trough, Penny reached for a cup and downed the scalding liquid. *At least I still have a fucking throat.*

Vick turned a sly smile to Tara and lifted her coffee cup. "Ookini," she said in a language Penny didn't understand.

Tara returned the smile. "Dou itashimashite."

Vick's smile widened, snapping her fingers. "Knew I heard you let loose a Japanese curse during the fight. Yes, I think we'll get along just fine."

Even in the blurry comedown from her adrenaline rush, Penny could have sworn she saw Tara blush. *Ha. Never thought I'd see the day when our tough girl met her match.*

Beside her, Agnes shifted in her seat, picking at the chipped handle of her mug. Finally, she turned to Penny and said, "You saved us. You're—that was...I don't even know. I still can't believe what happened." She broke off, raking her fingers through her hair, then locked her piercing blue eyes straight to Penny's. "Tara and I wouldn't have survived if you weren't there."

Overhearing the comment, Tara broke away from her conversation with Vick. "Damn right. You had our backs, Penny. Thank you." After barking a short laugh, she said, "Now there's a sentence I never thought I'd say."

Derek threw an arm around Agnes and pressed a kiss to her temple. "Thanks for bringing our girls back, Penny."

Penny managed a weak smile. "Don't thank me." *Please do not fucking thank me. I might throw up.* Truth be told, she didn't know how she felt about what just happened. *Still in shock.* But the other soldiers had overheard their conversation and quieted, looking to her. Frantically, she glanced around for Mal and saw him walking down the hallway. *Fuck.*

Raising her voice to the group, she said, "Today was...fucked. There's no other way to say it. We lost some of our own. Good people. And we're all still standing here because of every single person in this room." *And one six-and-a-half-foot tall glaring omission who should really be the one giving this motivational speech.* "Rodney's cult is finally finished, and we gained some new allies. We just made winning this war that much easier. We've got a long road to go, but we'll get there if you all keep showing up for each other like you did today."

"Hear, hear," Derek said, thumping a fist on the table, which was quickly taken up by everyone else, then they went back to their meals.

After taking a few bites of soup and rice, Penny quickly abandoned the idea of food. Something about facing down the evil that Rodney had inspired, the evil she had almost been sucked into in the Beginning...it was different than any battle she'd fought before. It left her feeling sick. Shaken.

As soon as she dropped her spoon, a freight train plowed into her from the side. Or that's what it felt like. Gripping the table to keep from toppling over, she clutched at the foreign and yet familiar gangly shape in her arms. When Quentin pulled back from his attack of a hug, he stuffed his hands in his pockets and stared at his feet. Clearing his throat, he said, "Mal said you were pretty badass today." He shifted back and forth, a tiny smile hiding in the corner of his mouth. "So when do I get to learn how to hot-wire a tractor? Don't remember Dad teaching us that one."

Tears pricked at her eyes and she could only laugh at his comment. "I don't know how I did it without electrocuting myself, but I'll teach you on one of the cars in the junk lot," she said. "You saw Mal?"

Quentin bobbed his head. "He was heading to the showers." Then he jumped at Tara, Agnes, and Derek, pulling them into the biggest group hug his spindly arms could manage. "Glad you all still have your noggins." His words were light, but she could see the utter relief that glowed behind his eyes. He'd really been afraid, and rightfully so. *Hopefully Mal didn't tell him the details of what happened today.* A gagging feeling rose in her throat, and she gulped more coffee to keep it down. *I've been close to death before, but never like that.*

A few steps behind Quentin, Silas appeared, swooping in to drop a kiss on Ivan. "You'll all be pleased to know that we only started three small fires today while working on our project."

Ivan chuckled, pulling Silas in for an extra kiss. "It's a new record." To Quentin, he said, "I'll be by tomorrow to take a look."

"We should get back to our camp. See what kind of progress Lawrence has made," said Vick, her gaze lingering on Tara. "But we'll be back in a few days to check in." Then her eyes snapped to Penny. *And to collect on her unfettered access to our armories.*

Something about the bubbly relief and reunion-ing caused Penny's panic to rise, which made no fucking sense. She was alive, and Quentin was happy she was alive. So why did she feel like she was going to fucking explode if she didn't leave immediately?

Pushing away from the table, she said, "I'm going to find Mal—debriefing."

Quentin snickered. "Well, he's showering, so he's already *debriefed.*"

"Boooo. Get off the stage," Tara said, poking him as he laughed.

"I'll see you tomorrow," Penny said to her brother. "Training, bright and early."

"Are you sure?" It was Agnes who spoke, watching her with a wary expression...but maybe it wasn't so much wary as *concerned*. As if she knew the feelings Penny was currently holding at bay by a thin thread of control. "We could take a break for a day."

Penny shook her head, managing half a smile in Quentin's direction. "War waits for no one."

Wringing out the last of the blood and dirt from her hair, Penny shut off the shower. She'd needed a fucking second to lose her shit in privacy before she faced Mal, and she'd rather talk to him without gunk in her hair.

The cold water had brought clarity and quelled the after effects of her panic attack, but her chest felt tight, her head heavy. She'd burned down the heart of Rodney's power, but like the haunting memories of the fire she'd set at her own home, Rodney was another scar she'd always carry with her.

When the cult leader had gone down the line bashing heads, his assistant slicing throats, it felt justified that Penny should be there. In their last moments, had the people she'd killed felt the same fear that she'd felt, leaning over that trough, waiting for a blade to bite into her own throat?

It didn't matter now. She'd learned long ago that regret served no purpose. But that didn't always stop her from thinking about Lexa or wishing she'd done things differently with Agnes. Getting justice for all of the people Pharmatrox poisoned, for all of the lives they ruined—and for the lives she ruined too—maybe *that* would help her heart feel a little less heavy.

After pulling on dark jeans and a black sweater, Penny toweled off her hair, turning her thoughts to Mal. On the way back to the stadium, he hadn't said a word to her, or to anyone, as he'd stalked through the dark woods. Maybe he was pissed off that her decisions had led to his soldiers' deaths. Or maybe he was still upset about the deal she'd made with Vick. Whatever the reason, she intended to face it head-on. She'd already dealt with one of her demons today, might as well take on another.

Gathering up her things, she set off to find Mal. She didn't have to look too hard—opening the door, she bumped into him as he walked out of the next-door men's locker room. He reached out to steady her, and her hand found his chest.

Shirtless. Mal, shirtless. Fuck.

The sight stopped her in her tracks, her brain cells crashing into each other as they scrambled to come up with any thought that wasn't completely idiotic. "It's nearly December and you're walking around half-clothed like it's fucking Miami?"

He glanced at his Army-green tactical pants. "Not nearly enough neon blue and pink for that." His hands were still at her waist from where he'd caught her, and she shifted away. Not because she didn't like the contact, but because she *did*, and that was too fucking confusing. "Forgot a shirt," he added, avoiding her eyes.

Penny narrowed her eyes. "Clearly." He still looked anywhere but at her. "Mal, you haven't so much as glanced in my direction since we got back."

He dragged a hand through his hair, and she tried not to notice how his body flexed in a way that had her wanting to slide her own hands across his skin. *I must be insane. It has to be the adrenaline of everything I just went through. I cannot be attracted to him.*

Crossing her arms in defiance of her own thoughts, she said, "If you're angry, tell me."

Glancing toward the sounds of the troops in the cafeteria, the muscle in Mal's jaw flickered.

"Use your words," she said, prodding him in the ribs.

Making a frustrated sound—*was that a* growl?—he turned on his heel, saying, "Don't push me, Penny," and stalked toward his room.

Taking off after him, she said, "But I'm so good at it."

Mal balled his hands into fists as she followed him. Ripping open the door to his room, he stomped inside and busied himself finding a spare shirt, then pulled it on. She watched from the doorway, hands on her hips. But he still wouldn't fucking look at her. And it was starting to piss her off. Slamming the door shut, she said, *"Look at me,* Mal, for fuck's sake."

Finally, he did. Eyes bright and fierce, he crossed the room in seconds, backing her against the door. "I'm not *angry,*" he said through his teeth, that jaw muscle jumping again just like she knew it would.

Raising an eyebrow, she said, "Could have fooled me."

"I'm not angry," he said again, calmer this time, but his muscles bunched and tensed under his shirt. He was close enough she could see the ring of gold around the center of his irises, and his chest brushed hers as his agitated breaths came faster. Planting a palm on the door to steady himself, he said, "When they took you, I lost my goddamn mind. I was fucking terrified, Penny. I was supposed to be commanding our troops, making sure everyone made it out of there alive, and all I could fucking think about was *you.* Finding you and obliterating whoever had hurt you. I was wild with fear, with rage. That's never happened to me before. And it fucking rattled me." His calloused fingertips found her cheek, featherlight in contrast with their roughness, and her hands drifted to the planes of his chest as if drawn to the beating of his heart, thumping against her palms. "You'll be the death of me, woman," he said, sweeping a thumb across her jaw. "But I'll rip apart anything that tries to take you from me."

For a moment, their breaths were one. A pause, as if everything in the world held its breath for one collective moment. Perched on the edge of a cliff. Waiting to see if she would fall or fly. Barely above a whisper, almost against his lips, she said the only thought in her head, the one truth she could find through the murkiness of everything that had happened in the past twelve hours. "Nobody looks at me the way you do."

A swooping sensation rushed through her as she watched his eyes flare from sunny brown to deep whiskey, that golden ring eaten up by the darkness, and her lips parted as he closed the breaths of space between them—

A knock pounded behind her and she jumped. With a growl, Mal ripped the door open, a look like murder on his face. "What?" he said to whoever stood in the hall.

Penny glanced over her shoulder and saw Tara with a clipboard poised at her hip, checking off a list. "After today, we owe Vick some weapons. I was thinking the armory in Sector 12 could be good. Sanjali said we have a surplus of—" When she looked up, a smug smile slid across her face. "I can come back later." Her eyes ran over Penny, and she had no idea what expression was on her face, but it was something that made Tara add, "*Much* later."

"That won't be necessary." He held out his hand for the clipboard, and Tara passed it to him. After a cursory glance at the list, he handed it back and said, "Sounds fine. Anything else?"

"Sounds *fine*?" Tara tilted her head back to peer at him. "You were up in arms about letting them into our weapons caches just this morning. Changed your mind?" She shot a pointed glance at Penny.

"Changed my mind," he said bluntly, shutting down any further questions.

Tara gave a flippant shrug and a smile that said she knew exactly what they'd been up to. What they'd been about to do. *Christ. What the fuck had we been about to do?*

And, part of her wondered with a hidden thrill, *how far would it have gone?*

"Guess I know who to consult when I need you to 'change your mind' on some of our other policies. I'll tell everyone that you're, ah, *busy* and to hold their questions for the morning." With a wink and a mock salute, Tara headed off.

The two stared after Tara, Mal's hand resting on the doorframe above Penny's head. Suddenly, the desire to bolt down the hallway coursed through her, and she took a step outside. He looked like he wanted to pull her back to him and finish what they'd almost started so many times now. And part of her wanted nothing more than to lose herself in him, in *them*. But they had work to do.

"We can't afford any distractions, Mal. I don't want to be the reason you end up dead on a battlefield. You said it first—we shouldn't be involved with each other." The words burned like acid as she said them. She meant them, but maybe...maybe it wasn't what she wanted. *But what I want doesn't matter.* "There's too much at stake. We can't lose focus. If we don't win this war, we have nothing left—our *people* have nothing left. The cult is gone, but we've still got the troxies to contend with. We need to plan our next move."

The silence hung between them as he tightened his grip on the doorframe to the point where she thought it might break off into his hand. Finally, he looked at her, all trace of the previous heat sapped out of him. "Right. No more distractions." His tone was cold and final, and that secret compartment of her heart ached at the loss. *This is what you said you wanted. You did this.* "See you tomorrow for training," he said, and shut the door on her.

Later that night when Penny finally crawled into bed, she couldn't stop shaking as the trauma of the day rattled through her. Instead of thinking about how she wanted to throw up her entire guts, she thought about Agnes and Tara. It felt almost like they were beginning to trust her. *I wonder if that's as fucking weird for them as it is for me.* But she was making progress, and it felt good.

If she focused on repairing her relationship with Quentin and the others and ending the war, it was easier to ignore whatever was going on between her and Mal. Nothing *could* happen. That happily-ever-after bullshit was for other people, not for her. For Agnes and Derek, for Silas and Ivan, hell, maybe even for Tara and Vick one day. At their core, they were good people unburdened by the kind of bloody past Penny had. No, there'd be no happy endings for her. Not in that way. All she needed was her little brother back, and to win this war for him.

And that meant staying focused and being the weapon she needed to be. The weapon they all needed her to be.

And weapons didn't get happy endings.

22

Agnes

THE LATE-NIGHT AIR SWEPT across Agnes's bare arms and she shivered, hugging her legs into her chest. She should have brought a jacket, but she'd been too preoccupied with getting some *space*. After showering and rinsing away the evidence of the horrific past twelve hours, she'd all but dove out her bedroom window, climbing for the sanctuary of Derek's rooftop. The house's walls felt too close, too confining. Angry red ringlets encircled her wrists, rubbed raw from the rope bindings. Her body ached all over with various cuts and bruises, but nothing too serious. No, the serious stuff was going on inside her head.

I was almost murdered. Slaughtered like an animal.

That reality had finally smacked her in the face the moment she stepped into the shower and felt the sting of hot water on her injuries. And then the sobs came. Big, wracking ones that shook her entire body. And for just a moment, she longed for the dust, to fall into the void if only to stop reliving those seconds of sheer terror.

Living like each breath could be her last—that's what came from almost a year of existing in this fucked-up world. But kneeling in a line, knowing exactly what was coming for her, exactly what sounds she'd make when she got punched in the skull, or how red her blood would be as it spilled into the trough...that was a new kind of horror. And it would haunt her until the end of her days.

With slow, deep breaths, she attempted to calm her racing heart and thoughts, turning her eyes skyward to count the stars. It reminded her of the first serious conversation she'd had with Derek on this very rooftop, marking the moment when she realized that what she felt for Derek was something...more. And now, staring at the same sky, her final thoughts in the barn when it looked like their deaths were imminent bubbled to the surface.

It's too soon, she'd thought. *I haven't told Derek yet.*

"Agnes?"

Startled, she jumped at the sound of Derek's voice, then patted the eave beside her. He crawled over and sat, sprawling out his long legs and resting his thigh against hers. Leaning into him, she laid her head on his shoulder, timing her breaths with his.

After a while, he asked, "I know this is a stupid question, but are you all right?" He swept his hand through her hair, pushing it back so he could get a clearer look at her moonlit face. "When they took you—" He bit off the thought, clenching his jaw. "I was so fucking scared, Aggie. I thought—"

"I know." *Please don't finish that sentence.* She knew what he thought because she'd thought the same. "I'm really fucked up about it. But it's nothing I can't recover from. How's Tara?" Guilt punched her in the gut at the reminder she'd been too wrapped up in her own shit to check on her.

"She still hasn't made it out of the bathroom. Silas and Quentin are trying to coax her out, but she keeps asking for Lawrence."

"They've been through a lot together. He should be back from Vick's camp in a few days." Agnes lapsed into silence, thoughts swirling.

"Do you want to talk about it?" Derek shifted his hand to her thigh, rubbing his thumb in soothing circles. "It's okay if you'd rather not."

It might feel good to purge the poison. And so she told him, sparing no detail. Giving voice to the events reduced their power over her, and although the trauma still had its claws in her and probably always would, she knew she could get through this. She wasn't okay. Not by a long shot. But she would be. As she spoke, his expression grew more enraged, and she could tell he was holding onto his control by a thin wire.

"When I bumped the nail toward Penny," she said, the scene replaying in her head like a movie, "she gave me this look. And I just *knew* without a shadow of a doubt that she would get us out of there, or die trying. And that's not the Penny I thought I knew." Turning her eyes to him, blurry with tears, she said, "Derek, we would have died without Penny. What the fuck am I supposed to do with that?"

"I can't imagine how much of a mind fuck that is," he said, wrapping an arm around her. "I never thought I'd say this, but I owe Penny everything for bringing my woman back to me."

Agnes choked on a laugh-sob, twining her fingers with his. "'My woman.' Never took you for a caveman."

"You're right. That's more Mal's department." Ducking his forehead to hers, he hauled her close. "But it's true, Agnes. You're mine, for as long as you want to be."

Breathing him in, she smiled at his comforting scent. But then her earlier thoughts circled back, banging around in her head and making themselves known. *I can't hold back anymore. I'm all in, and he needs to know.*

"Derek, I—there's something else." She cleared her suddenly dry throat at the look of concern on his face. *Keep going.* "This is the most at peace I've ever felt. Not exactly in this moment because of...yeah. But here, with you—I know everything will be okay, as long as you're beside me." Tracing her fingertips across his tattoos, up his neck, then across the expanse of his cheekbones, she gathered the courage to say the words she'd been feeling for a while. "I love you, Derek. I love who we are together. I love how you are with Quentin and the rest of our family. I love how you just let me be who I am, even when I don't always know who that is." With a shaky breath, she said, "I just really fucking love you a lot, and I thought you should know. You're mine as much as I am yours."

At her words, Derek's eyes blew wide and his posture tensed, muscles coiled. Before she knew it, his lips crashed against hers in a union that sent sparks jolting through her entire body. Lifting her into his lap, he held her tighter as if he were afraid she'd slip through his fingers like sand. Against her lips, he said, "I love you so much, Agnes. You and me, babe. It's you and me."

Home.

A feeling she never had anywhere else, with anyone else—not even Silas and Evie.

Running her fingers through his hair, holding him captive, she vowed that she'd never let him go. "You and me," she agreed.

"Tara?" Agnes knocked on the bathroom door for the fifth time in as many minutes. "T?" Muffled sobs and a string of Spanish curses filtered from under the door.

"Vete, tía. Please." Tara's voice broke on the last word in a sound that she'd never heard from the feisty woman before.

"It's just me. The boys are downstairs."

A few beats of silence. Then the doorknob twisted, the door cracking open.

Tara sat on the floor, her filthy clothes clinging to the grime and blood slicking her skin. With an aggravated sound, she swiped at her puffy eyes, tear tracks cutting through the dirt on her face. Agnes bent to sit beside her, shutting the door.

It was a few long minutes before Tara spoke. "I just—I'm fucking *stuck*, tía. I know I'm not in that barn anymore. But I keep hearing the screams." Clutching her hands over her ears with a distraught expression, she said, "It just won't fucking *stop*. Make it stop, Agnes. Help me make it stop."

Still shaken from the encounter too, Agnes didn't have much to offer. But she loved Tara and hated to see her best friend struggle. "The Watchers and our people made sure the woods are clear of Chosen. They're gone and they can't hurt us anymore. So how about I sit here with you until you feel ready to rinse off? And I'll sit up with you all night tonight until you fall asleep, and then again every night after that until things start to feel right again. I don't know a lot about PTSD, but we'll figure it out." At Tara's wobbling lower lip, Agnes slid her arm across her shoulders. "We'll get through this together, tía. I promise."

23

PENNY TUGGED HER JACKET closed against the cold air. It would be plenty warm in a few hours, but the early mornings before the sun came up held the bite of the coming winter.

The fire pits they'd built sporadically down the stadium halls helped warm certain areas, but with the cavernous ceilings and drafty doors, the heat was difficult to contain. Blankets and layers of clothes were their only options for staying warm—*that and body heat.* Without warning, her thoughts zinged straight to Mal like a goddamn magnet, remembering his breath tingling against her lips, his hands on her waist, and how she wanted them running over every inch of her.

Damn him.

It had been a few days since their...moment in his room, and Mal had gone back to strictly business. No private training sessions or meetings, no lingering looks or touches. He was giving her what she asked for, and even though a tangle of emotions balled up inside her chest, she did her best to get her head on straight too.

They had a war to win.

Rounding the corner, the scent of a cooking fire caught her interest. It was a bit early for camp to be stirring, but with the watch schedule rotation, someone was always up. Unable to sleep, she was heading to check the perimeter just to have something to do. *And maybe get my mind off of unproductive things.*

Lawrence sat at a blazing fire pit, hanging a kettle over the flames, and he looked up at her approach.

"Surprised Vick let you come back so soon," she said, taking a seat in a folding chair across from him. He'd only been gone a week.

"I got them set up with a hydroponic system in no time. Just arrived about an hour ago." A beat of silence, then he said, "So Vick's people said you got rid of the cult." The statement was loaded with everything he didn't say. *I swear to god, if he fucking thanks me too...* He must have sensed her apprehension because he said, "That's good news for our messengers."

"A crew is out sweeping the Wilds now to make sure the cult really is cleared out before we send messengers tomorrow." Lawrence made a sound of agreement, and the awkward seconds ticked by. They hadn't addressed their complicated history, and she didn't feel the need to bring it up now—or ever. While she wouldn't accept his thanks, she had some gratitude of her own to deliver. "Thank you for looking after Quentin. When I couldn't."

Pouring two cups of coffee from the kettle, Lawrence said, "He looked after us more than anything. Your brother is smart." He handed her a mug, adding, "Don't tell him I said this, but that little twerp saved me too. Him and Tara. After—after what happened at Evie's camp, I wasn't sure if I had what it takes to make it in this world. But seeing how Quentin met every hardship with a smile and a joke even after everything he'd been through, I knew I'd be okay too."

The ache in Penny's chest had nothing to do with the scalding-hot coffee she gulped down. *I'm here for Quentin now—but is it enough?*

Turning to other matters that didn't make her heart feel like a bowling ball, she asked, "Any luck at getting a read on Vick?"

Lawrence shook his head. "I poked around her treehouse—booby trapped, by the way, so if you want to start using those kind of guerrilla tactics, I think you've found a new consultant. Anyway, wasn't much to snoop through. She's as much of an enigma as she ever was."

"Think we might have some more insight into that soon," she said, thinking of Tara and the heavy glances she and Vick exchanged. "What's your assessment of the Watchers as a whole?"

"Many of them are staunchly anti-Faction and anti-Pharmatrox, but they're loyal to Vick. So if she says we're in an alliance, they'll fall in line. But that goes the other way too—we cross her, we cross them. And I don't know about you, but I wouldn't want to face any of them in a fight."

She wasn't afraid of the Watchers but also didn't want to have them as an enemy. The Faction couldn't afford to fight any more battles.

"Vick's coming by soon to collect the weapons they want from the armory," Lawrence said, adding a pot to the fire and tossing a handful of carrots into it. "I'll let you know when they get here."

"Tara might be more interested in giving them the grand tour," she said with a loaded glance, and he chuckled.

"You got it."

She stood to go, but something snagged at her conscience as she watched this quiet, pensive man who was one of the only reasons they'd have enough food to make it through the short winter. But he was more than just an asset. He was a good person. *Another example of someone good whose life I ruined because I didn't have all of the information.* She opened her mouth, maybe to apologize, but different words came out.

"Thanks for going to the Watchers' camp. I know I didn't ask and just expected you to do it, but thanks."

Stirring the now boiling pot, he nodded. He didn't smile, but at least he didn't look like he wanted her to collapse and die on the spot, so that was an improvement. Taking her leave, she braced herself for the crisp air and headed outside. Boots crunching in the frosty grass, she went to where the first set of guards was posted at the edge of the lawn.

Or where their first set of guards was *supposed* to be.

Frowning, Penny looked around, hands on her hips. And then she saw them.

The guards had strayed to the small park across the street, crowding around a stubby tree. Striding over, Penny said, "What in the entire fuck is so interesting that you had to abandon your posts to—" She stopped, eyes glued to the scene. "Get Mal. Now."

Ten minutes later, Mal blazed a trail through the frost, looking every bit the bull charging the matador. They hadn't interacted much over the last few days, so when confronted with the full force of *all* of him—his height, his strength, his fierce demeanor that commanded attention—she felt as if someone had folded her into origami, her stomach in the wrong place, her chest compressed, her brain bent in half.

"*Someone* left you a present," she said, regaining her composure. Sanjali, Raph, and Will appeared a few steps behind him, ready to go to battle.

But Mal wasn't listening.

A turned—very big and very dead—was speared to the tree trunk with a knife to the back, black blood staining its Army-green tactical pants and shirt. It even wore the signature red Faction mask they'd all ditched after ousting Rodney. But that wasn't what had her sending for Mal at the ass-crack of dawn. Someone had scrawled a hasty message on the shirt with blood-dipped fingertips.

FOR MAL

"When did you find this? Why didn't you send for me right away?" Mal asked, inspecting the body.

"Just saw it after the overnight watch change," one guard said. "We were about to get you when we saw Penny."

Tapping the knife in the turned's back, she noted the specific placement. Upper right back, where Mal had his own scar. *And now the Army outfit and mask make sense.* With a significant look at him, she yanked the blade out and the body slumped to the ground. "God, why don't you just challenge Zeln to a fucking duel already and leave us all out of it?"

At his sides, his hands balled into fists, the tendons rippling up his arms as he held his fury at bay. "I will handle it."

"No, no. I take it back," she said, planting a hand on his chest to keep him in place. Clearly he was hiding something about his past with Zeln, but she didn't have time to interrogate the bastard. "As much as I'd love to entertain your bromance, we can't have our general running off with his emotional guns blazing and getting himself killed."

A dark glower crossed Mal's face. "I can assure you, I will be the one doing the killing."

"Yes, I understand, you're big and strong. But we've been over this. Zeln wants to get in your head, and until you can prove you're not idiotic enough to fall for his games, you're benched. Go inside and cool off. Lawrence is making coffee. Ask him nicely and maybe you can have some."

Mal opened his mouth to lay down the law, but Sanjali cut him off. "She's right, sir. Er, minus the idiotic part."

The guards snuck glances at Penny, some nodding their agreement, to Mal's annoyance. *Ha. I actually did it. A successful semi-coup.*

"Fine," he said. The vein in his temple looked ready to explode as he doled out instructions for the day's patrols, then trudged back to the stadium, muttering.

"What's all the hubbub?" Vick asked as she approached with Ivan, Jaha, and some Watchers.

"And what the hell is *that*?" asked Jaha, pointing at the zombie Mal.

"A prop in a dick-measuring contest," Penny said. "Don't worry about it. I'll get a crew together and we'll head to the armory."

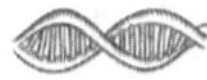

"The way those leaves are bent suggests whoever left that disturbing present came from that way," Vick said, pointing in the direction of the SubTran station as their group passed a small park.

How the hell did she see that? Even though she'd downplayed Zeln's taunt, Penny was on high alert. That asshole was up to something. Walking through the wrecked city streets, Penny was grateful for the present company. Living in the woods and hunting made the Watchers skilled trackers, and they'd be the first to know if they were heading straight for a trap.

"Looks like someone is in the running to take over your title as best tracker," Tara said, shooting a glance at Penny, but the jest was half-hearted. It had only been a few days since the barn, and Tara's eyes held a haunted gleam that mirrored Penny's own soul. But she admired how Tara picked herself up each morning and trudged onward, even though she probably felt like hiding in a hole. Penny sure did.

"I'm no tracker," Quentin said as he bounced on and off the curb, "but if you need someone to get their eyeball taken out from five feet away, I'm your guy. I'm getting pretty good with my slingshot."

Derek snorted. "*That* is good? Five feet is like"—Derek held out an arm and gave Quentin a shove—"that close. Might as well stab them at that point."

"*Derek*," Agnes said, thwacking him on the arm. "We're trying to teach Quentin nonlethal ways to subdue an opponent, not encourage him to go around sticking knives in people."

"Oh, I'm getting better at that too!" Quentin supplied happily, patting his pockets. "See—oh. Forgot my knife. Rats."

"Gracias a dios for that," Tara said.

Once she'd laid eyes on Vick, Tara had been quick to join their trek, and Agnes had been close behind. Derek too, since the smitten bastard never went anywhere without her. Their relationship seemed stronger after things went down at the barn, and Penny was genuinely happy for them. Quentin joined because, well, he'd overheard her talking to Agnes, and she could not deny him another adventure. Besides, they had some of the best warriors in their party.

Didn't stop him from getting taken in the woods that night. But this time was different—the sun shone brightly and they were squarely in their own territory.

After a few blocks, the Sector 12 warehouse came into view, sandwiched between the high rises. With a few words to the guards, the group was ushered inside. But Quentin lingered behind, looking upward.

"What is it?" Penny asked.

He pointed at the twenty-five-story neighboring building. "I want to climb that."

"You...?" Penny had heard of his knack for climbing insanely tall things. He'd always been good at the small-scale stuff as a kid. The look on his face dared her to object, but she said, "Okay. I'll meet you at the top."

Frowning, he said, "You can climb too?"

She laughed. "Hell no. I'll take the stairs. See you in a few." Busting her way inside, she found the stairwell and made a quick ascent. She wondered idly if she was insane for letting Quentin do this, but she wasn't his mom, and he was almost an adult. He could make his own decisions—something she sensed was maybe his point for climbing the building at all. To have some illusion of choice in a world where much of that had been taken from them.

A few minutes later, panting—no matter how much she worked out, going up stairs would always kick her ass—she exited onto the roof, where Quentin sat on the edge, dangling his feet.

"Nice. Can see all the way to the cathedral," she noted.

"There's a building a few streets over that gives you a better view. It's taller."

Penny looked at him sidelong as he swung his feet with a smug look. "How often do you climb buildings tall enough to give me an aneurysm?"

He shrugged, saying, "Few times a week whenever Derek or Tara or someone goes out. I get bored, and it's good practice. Plus, I keep track of troxy patrols." He pulled a pair of binoculars out of his pack and trained them on the horizon. "They don't always have a regular schedule, which is weird. And some different cargo trucks have been popping up recently. Yep, there's a few right now."

Penny shook her head, in awe. "I didn't know you were doing all of this."

Quentin shrugged again, letting the binoculars dangle around his neck. "I like to help."

An overwhelming feeling rushed through Penny, and she wrapped an arm around him, giving him a quick squeeze. "I'm really proud of you. Of who you're becoming."

Quentin leaned into her for a moment, then went back to his binoculars. But she saw the smile tucked into the corner of his mouth.

Then his hand shot out, gripping her wrist. "Penelope?" he said in a strained voice.

Oh god. "What?"

Pointing, he said, "That's not a troxy patrol. That's an *army*. And they're heading right for us. What do we do?" He handed over the binoculars, and she took a look.

Fuck on a stick. A sea of troxies and a few armored vehicles marched down the road. They'd be on them in minutes.

"Go get one of the guard's radios and call Mal for reinforcements. Then tell everyone to get ready for a fight."

"Got it." Quentin slipped over the edge to make a hasty descent while Penny ran for the stairs. Whether or not the body left for Mal had been meant as a provocation or a diversion, it didn't matter now. They had some troops here, but not enough to hold off an entire army. When she reached the ground floor, their people were already posting up in the street behind the concrete barriers.

Derek barked instructions while Tara ran down their measly line of people, making sure everyone had adequate ammo. Even Vick, Jaha, and Ivan took up position in their line of defense.

"You should get out of here while you can," Penny said.

Vick's only response was a piercing glare as she drew both of her knives. "I do not run from a fight." *Damn. I really like her.*

"Penny! I have an idea," Quentin said as he ran up to her. "The flash-bang explosives Ivan and I have been working on—I have some. They're not ready yet, but I think it'll slow them down."

"Great, do it. Ivan?" Penny gestured for him to accompany Quentin, and the two took off to set their trap.

As Penny grabbed a volt rifle from the warehouse, Agnes approached with an update. "Mal is sending troops, but they might not get here in time."

"We can hold them off," Penny said, tossing a rifle to Agnes. "We just—"

Volts sizzled through the air, breaking windows and singeing the pavement as the first of the troxies appeared about a hundred yards away.

"Positions, everyone!" Tara shouted, ducking behind the concrete barrier. "Return fire!"

"Fuck. Quentin and Ivan are still out there." Penny pointed to a building they'd ducked inside.

"They'll be okay," Agnes said as she fired into the approaching troxies. "If anything, they're safer than us."

They'll have to be. They were outnumbered, and it was only a matter of time before the troxies overtook them. "We can't lose this armory," Penny said. "It's the biggest one we have."

"Enough gabbing!" Tara yelled. "Just shoot!"

The armored trucks pulled in front of the troxies, providing cover. A few guards broke free and pushed toward the Faction, but once they passed the doorway where Ivan and Quentin were hunkered down, an explosion ripped through the air, decimating the bottom floors of both buildings on either side of the road, bricks and glass flying. *Must have passed a trip wire. Smart.*

With the concrete barriers and a virtually endless supply of weapons from the armory, the Faction had a slight advantage. But as the troxies' armored trucks inched slowly forward, their troops followed, gaining ground until their shots became more precise—and deadly. A few Faction guards slumped behind the barrier, volts burning through eye sockets, bullets finding their marks.

When the troxies reached the halfway point, she recognized a guy driving one of the armored trucks.

Zeln.

She wasn't surprised to see the troxies' newest guard dog, but seeing him like that, smug and smarmy as he helped the enemy overtake them, had Penny rising to her feet to get a better angle as she let loose a torrent of bullets and volts at the truck's windshield.

Until Derek threw out a hand to stop her. "Penny! *Armored* truck. Don't waste your ammo."

"Oh, it's not a waste," she said, glaring at Zeln, but aimed her weapons elsewhere. She wanted Zeln to know that she saw him and that she knew what he'd done. She was more convinced than ever that he'd been the one to break into her room and leave the body for Mal. He was taunting Mal, rattling his cage, trying to get him to lose his composure and make a mistake.

I will not let that happen. He was Mal's Rodney, and she'd be damned if she let him win.

A few seconds later, the worst sound she could have imagined pierced the air, cutting through the din of battle.

Turned. They were close. And they sounded feral as hell.

"Tara, get us some snipers on the roof," Penny instructed. Tara nodded, signaling Vick and a few others. "Derek, any word on when our backup is getting here?"

"Sector 7 troops are a few blocks away," he said. "Mal's troops, I'm not sure."

"We—"

Growls and shrieks sounded *behind her*, and she whipped around to see gray bodies with black beady eyes racing down the street to sandwich them in.

Great. We couldn't have the ones that are slow and stupid, no, gotta make this difficult as fuck.

Before she knew it, turned crashed into them, crazed and ravenous, fresh blood dripping from pointed teeth. *Hopefully they were snacking on troxies and not our reinforcements.*

"Go for the heads!" she shouted, reminding everyone of their new decapitation policy—she wasn't taking any risks with wasting ammo if they were enhanced turned.

Some turned jumped the barricade and rushed for the troxies, driven by their bloodlust. When they got within grabbing distance, that same wailing microphone feedback noise filled the air. But instead of the frequency calming the turned and enhancing their focus, it only unhinged them further, causing them to swarm the apparatus mounted atop Zeln's armored truck and rip it from the bolts, metal screeching.

One of the troxy commanders fired, saying, "It didn't fucking work! It was supposed to work!"

"Now! While they're distracted," Agnes said, unloading her M4 into the troxies as everyone else followed suit.

Another explosion from the middle of the street filled the air with a fine white smoke, courtesy of Quentin and Ivan, and provided cover as the Faction surged forward.

More shots came from behind the Faction's line—but the Faction wasn't the target. Turning around, relief flooded through Penny as she saw Raph leading their reinforcements from Sector 7.

"The fuck is going on?" Raph asked.

"Shit show, as you can see. Thanks for coming," she said, passing him her volt rifle. "Keep shooting. I'll go in and smash some skulls."

"Mal's almost here," Raph said. "We've got this."

As Penny threw herself into the fight, watching as troxies dropped around her thanks to Vick and her snipers, she thought they just might make it out of this on top, even with the enhanced turned making everything into a blood bath.

But then something happened.

A huge armored truck unlike any she'd ever seen trundled into view at the end of the road. A dozen or so guards decked out in the armor and helmets Pharmatrox reserved for their super soldiers—people on some version of troxapine that made them obedient, elite fighters—filed out of the back, organizing into a tight formation, training their weapons on the Faction. *That's new.* They hadn't seen many super soldiers since the cathedral. *First sound wave–controlled turned, now more super soldiers... Pharmatrox is changing tactics again.*

At the same time, Quentin and Ivan chose to make their escape from their hiding spot, tossing some grenades and dashing for the concrete barriers.

"No, wait!" she shouted in vain.

The super soldiers fired, one of the shots catching Ivan in the back, but he kept running, pushing Quentin ahead of him until they finally reached the armory.

After fighting her way to Ivan, Penny asked, "Are you hurt?" Frankly, she didn't know how he wasn't fucking *dead* after getting shot in the spine.

Wincing, he reached behind him and pulled something out of his back. It was a dart attached to a clear class vial, now empty. "I'm fine," Ivan said, tossing the vial aside.

What the fuck is going on? But no time to dwell on it, as the super soldiers advanced down the street, shooting their weird dart vial things into the Faction troops, some finding their marks, but the ones that didn't shattering or skidding across the pavement.

"Quentin, stay inside," Penny said. "I mean it. I don't know what the fuck is in those things, but I don't want you getting hit."

For once, Quentin didn't argue and stood inside the warehouse door, passing out weapons and ammo as needed. To his credit, the kid didn't even look afraid, just determined.

As Penny and the others kept fighting, she wondered how long their luck would hold out.

"Puñeta!" Tara said as she swung her baseball bat for a turned and missed, a dart lodged in her neck.

"T!" Agnes rushed to her side. "Estás bien?"

Grimacing, Tara ripped the dart out and threw it at the ground. "Fine," she said. But Penny wasn't so sure. She pocketed the vial for inspection later.

With this new threat, Penny's confidence waned. The others hit by darts seemed fine too, but there had to be something more sinister at work. The Faction managed to drop a few super soldiers, but the bastards were just so fucking hard to kill, and with their attentions divided, it wouldn't be long before they fatigued.

Just when she thought they'd have to retreat, Mal showed up, an overwhelming number of soldiers at his back.

And she knew they had this fight in the bag.

"How bad is it?" Mal asked, frowning at the battlefield.

"Better now that you're here," she said. "Super soldiers are shooting some kind of dart thing. It's not harming or killing anyone, but I don't trust it."

Nodding, Mal said, "Let's finish this."

With Mal's reinforcements, the battle quickly turned in the Faction's favor. The super soldiers, rather than stay to fight, shouldered their weapons and piled back into the strange armored truck, driving off. When the other troxies noticed their absence, they fell back too.

All except one.

Zeln leaned out the truck's window, a lazy grin on his face as he gave Mal a mocking salute. From across the battlefield, Penny saw Mal unload a slew of shots at Zeln as he drove away.

In their wake, the streets were bloody and riddled with bodies, most of them turned and troxies, but they'd lost some of their own in the surprise attack. As their troops worked on cleaning up, Quentin zoomed out of the warehouse straight to Penny's side. Wrapping him into a tight hug, she could finally breathe again.

"You're okay?" she asked, looking him over.

"I'm okay." He ducked his head and headed off to help with clean-up duties.

Out of the corner of her eye, she saw Mal frowning at the scene. "They lost," he said. "We obliterated them. But why does it seem like Zeln got exactly what he wanted?"

"Rattling your cage, Mal. We won. The troxies overplayed their hand today and they know it. So enjoy the victory." But an eerie feeling wrapped around her too, tightening its hold. "Ah. There's something else. Agnes? Tara and Ivan too," she called, motioning them over. She took out the dart and handed it to Agnes. "Any idea what this is?"

Agnes examined the empty vial and the needle, cursing in Spanish. "If you find any darts that still have liquid, bring them to me." Ivan nodded and headed off to spread the word, and Agnes turned to Tara. "But you feel okay?"

Tara rubbed the back of her neck with an uncertain look. "I thought I did. But, um…"

"What?" Penny asked.

"Well…I feel a little high, to be honest."

Penny and Agnes exchanged a look. The dust—powdered troxapine in its raw form—affected both of them differently, but they could agree that the feeling included an element of lightheaded euphoria.

"What if this"—Agnes held up the dart—"contained troxapine? It didn't immediately kill anyone, and I don't know what else they'd deem worthy of putting in a vial and shooting at people."

Ivan, Tara, and some other soldiers began swaying on their feet—*they must've gotten hit too.* At that moment, Vick burst out of the warehouse and elbowed her way to Ivan's side. One look at him, and a scowl darkened her face.

"Troxy poison," she said. When she noticed Tara leaning against the wall, her expression shifted to one of cold murder. "These people need treatment—now."

"You've seen this before?" Mal asked.

Vick motioned Mal, Agnes, and Penny to the side, out of earshot of everyone else. "Few weeks ago, saw those elite soldiers patrolling the outer roads, shooting darts at civilians, and they fired on some of our people."

"What happened to them?" Penny asked.

Vick grimaced. "Some reached an extreme state of euphoria and would do whatever anyone told them to. Some got really sick—puking, fever. We had a few vials of detox serum we got from lab raids same as you, but maybe we didn't use enough of it. I'm not sure. Because eventually, all of them turned."

"*Turned?* Fuck," said Mal, running a hand across his face. "Did you—?"

"Headshots," Vick said with a grim look. "Without any more detox serum, it was the only mercy we could give them."

Tara blinked slowly. "I'll take some detox serum when we get back. We still have a bit left."

Agnes turned a panicked look to Mal. "What if we don't have enough to treat everyone? Or what if it doesn't work? I still don't know how to make more."

Mal's gaze hardened, his jaw clenching as he rubbed a hand across his close-shaven beard. "We'll find more," he said.

Toeing at a crushed dart on the pavement, Penny had a thought. A really fucking bad one. "What if this isn't troxapine? What if it's something completely new—like the stuff that creates the enhanced turned? And we don't have a detox serum or a cure for it."

"Shit," Mal said, turning to Vick. "How much time do we have?"

"Few weeks, at most," Vick said.

Jesus fucking Christ. The hits just keep on coming. "We'll figure this out," Penny said.

Vick nodded, but her eyes never left Tara. "Whatever help you need, you've got it."

"I—mierda," Agnes cursed. "Have the infirmary ration out the detox serum. I'll work on fast-tracking a solution." Then she took off without another word.

Penny watched her leave, a dark feeling gathering within her. To Mal, she said, "If there's any more detox serum in this goddamn city, we need to find it. So that lab raid we had planned for tomorrow? It just got moved up to right the fuck now."

24

Agnes

Back at Maple Street, Agnes let loose a yawn, a headache hovering at the edge of her temples. She and Silas sat in their regular seats at the kitchen table, her poring over holofiles and him with the piece-of-crap laptop and notes spread before him in a pile of wreckage. They'd worked all day yesterday and through the night but had made little progress on finding clues to the doomsday bunker. Penny and Mal had taken a crew to raid a nearby lab after the battle, but she hadn't heard if they found any detox serum yet.

"Satellites are supposed to be *easy* to hack," Silas said to seemingly no one. "Everybody fucking knows that."

Tara, Derek, and Lawrence discussed battle strategies in the living room while Quentin and Ivan were working on some project. *Keeping busy and pretending like everything is normal to avoid the sense of impending doom.* She understood but found it hard to join in. *We're running out of time.*

"Problem?" Agnes asked, snagging a bite of his breakfast sandwich.

"Yeah, I guess people finally got smart and put more protections on their satellites. I keep losing the uplink. Or maybe Pharmatrox has hackers thwarting me from the SubTran station or somewhere. And I'm still getting that garbled repeated transmission like before. Don't know who it's from."

"Hmm. And still no luck reconnecting with the lost drones?"

Silas gave an aggravated harrumph. "No. And I can't control any of our few remaining ones if I can't get some goddamn internet access. So Mal's eyes in the sky are benched for now. Man, I hate to disappoint him."

"Stop pouting," Ivan called from the corner.

Silas stuck his tongue out as he continued typing away. "I'll take another crack at it, then I'm borrowing one of Mal's bazookas to shoot the goddamn thing out of the sky."

"Fresh out of bazookas," Ivan said. "Vick took all of those for us."

Silas rolled his eyes, but Agnes had never seen him look happier since they'd found Ivan. As she spun a holofile around, she scrutinized Ivan and Tara. *I have to figure this out.* Because if she didn't, Silas would lose his partner for good this time, and—

"Quit staring at me, tía," Tara said without looking up from the map she was studying. "I'm not going to drop dead."

Agnes swallowed, a lump suddenly forming in her throat. *I will never let that happen. Pharmatrox will not take another best friend from me.* "Are you two feeling okay?" she asked.

"Still feel high," Tara said, circling something on the map.

"I've got the chills," Ivan added.

So the detox serum isn't working. Maybe it really is like Penny said—this is something we've never dealt with before. She rifled through the pile of stuff until she found the few darts they'd collected. Each was about three inches long and had the same series of numbers etched faintly into the glass—nothing else. If her machine was finished, she could take a swab of the needle, pop it into the reader, and it could spit out the chemical make-up of whatever was in these darts. But without that, maybe she could at least figure out *where* these darts were made.

Turning to the digital notepad from the basement raid, she plugged in the sixteen-digit number and ran a search. When the results pinged back, the numbers appeared in a few files and spreadsheets with a bunch of other sixteen-digit numbers—but no indication of what they could mean.

"Why you always gotta go for the sharp, sparky object, huh?" Tara's voice came from the living room as she swatted Quentin's hand away from a fuse.

"I need to learn how to use it sometime if I'm going to be the Faction's bomb-maker extraordinaire," he protested.

Derek slapped a hand to his face with a sigh. "Lord help us all."

"The Faction's *what*?" Agnes asked, pausing in her work.

"We like it better when your projects don't involve a metric shit ton of C4," said Derek.

Eyeing Ivan as he tightened a bolt, Tara asked, "You sure you know what you're doing?"

"He was top of his class at MIT for mechanical engineering, so he's the only one in this room who knows what he's doing," Silas offered, eyes still on his laptop.

"I liked it better when you *weren't* helping," Tara grumbled. "Go back to your binary code or whatever."

Snorting, Ivan said, "Thank god it's *not* binary code. I would pluck out my own eyeballs."

"Won't have to do that when Quentin's invention can take out everyone's eyes for us all at once," Derek said, to an outburst of protests from Quentin that devolved into a wrestling match.

Agnes shook her head. *Our little dysfunctional happy family.* Her insides twisted at the thought of losing any of them. *There has to be something in these files.*

"If you'd all like to pitch in instead of snarking at each other, we might find something faster," Agnes said, waving everyone to the kitchen table. "Derek, you take these holofiles"—she shoved a pile across the table to him, and he grimaced—"and everyone else, come grab a few. Search for anything that looks like a drug formula or clues to where Pharmatrox's doomsday lab might be."

"Don't know what a formula looks like, but I'll assume it's a string of unintelligible stuff," said Quentin, scanning through a holofile. "Oh look, I already found a bunch of formulas."

"Those are employee timesheets from ten years ago," Agnes said.

"Maybe I should stick to pyrotechnics..." he said with a hopeful look, already drifting back to the living room.

"Yeah, let the kid play with fire in an extremely flammable room full of carpet and dry firewood," Derek encouraged.

"See? Derek understands me." Quentin went back to his project, with Ivan offering input from the kitchen.

Sighing, Agnes reached for more of the New York holofiles. But the blank face of Evie's untouched digital notepad stared at her, taunting. The damn thing had been bothering her since she'd found it. Whatever was in there had to be important, or else why keep it under such tight lock and key? *I knew Evie better than anyone, so I should know where the hell to find her Helix Key.* Since Evie kept the notepad in her desk, that meant she accessed it often at work, so the key would have to be within easy reach. But she never carried a set of keys—she was always losing them—and her ID badge lanyard never had any extra things on it. It couldn't be something common like a pen for the same reason it couldn't be on a set of keys—always losing or breaking them. The only thing that she always had on her was—

Hostia, that's it. I don't know how, but that has to be it.

Taking off the gold pendant she always wore—Evie's gold pendant—she slapped it all across the digital notepad's screen, searching—

Clink.

"Yes! Si?" she said, holding out Evie's digital notepad, the necklace stuck to the thumbprint reader. "I don't know what's happening, but I think I unlocked it?"

The notepad's screen blinked to life, the Pharmatrox double helix logo swirling and dissolving into pixels as Evie's home screen appeared.

"Gimme!" Silas snatched the notepad, severing the connection with Evie's necklace, but the screen remained active. "Magnetic connection. It didn't need a Helix Key—that was to throw off any snoopers. *This*"—he waved the necklace—"is the key. Hand me those holofiles!" Upending the backpack, Agnes spread out Evie's array of holofiles. Silas tapped the necklace to each, and they blinked to life, projecting their data in the air. "My sister is a brilliant, beautiful *genius*!" He set to work, organizing the unlocked files by keyword while referencing Evie's digital notepad.

Time became a blur as they all worked to get a grasp on the new onslaught of information. At some point, Silas said, "Look," spinning Evie's notepad toward Agnes, pointing. "This list of numbers? The notepad from the basement lab has the same ones. But Evie wrote some notes of her own. Some of them are starred. And check this out."

At the bottom of Evie's list was a handwritten note, scrawled in haste with the pad's digital pen.

0248—Saratoga? Or Schaghticoke*

0093—Eugene, not Portland*

2289—San Francisco, maybe Oakland

The list continued on for about ten or more numbers and cities, some with Evie's notes and speculations. *What are these? Billing codes? Some kind of numerical catalog?* But when Agnes got to the last number on the list, she froze, then grabbed a dart. Looking back and forth between the screen and the dart, her hands began to shake.

"Si?" she said. "The last four digits on this dart are 3391, right?"

Glancing over, Silas said, "Yes? Did you forget how to read?"

"*No.* Look," she said, flipping the screen toward him and pointing to the last number in Evie's notes. *3391*—*

"Holy shit, we found it," Silas said, pulling Agnes into a hug from across the table.

Could this really be it? Excitement flowed through her like an electric current and sparked a hope she hadn't felt since taking down Pharmatrox's network.

"Could one of you payasos please finish a sentence?" Tara asked. "We want to jump up and down and hug each other too."

"Evie was keeping track of numerical codes and locations of labs she thought they were associated with," Agnes explained, showing the list of numbers and cities. "Some of them are starred, and this one matches the code on the dart. They were produced there. It's Pharmatrox's doomsday bunker, the place we've been looking for. And Evie was looking for it too. We found it," Agnes said, pointing to the end of Evie's list and holding up the dart with matching numbers. "Or, Evie found it."

3391—Chicago*

"Is this for real, tía?" Tara asked.

Agnes could have sworn she saw tears glistening in her stoic friend's eyes, and she grasped her hand. "We go there, we get it all—their servers, detox serum, the cure for whatever's in the darts, everything." Pulling both Tara and Ivan into a hug, she said, "You're going to be okay. I promise."

But after a moment, Ivan pulled away, frowning. "Why would Evie have been looking for their bunker? How could she have known? I thought it was top secret."

"After Dr. Hansen and Dr. Chun stole her original idea for dionazole, I imagine Evie lost faith in Pharmatrox and had her suspicions," Agnes said. "Maybe she came across the codes and started trying to work out what they were for or find what labs were making the corrupted troxapine. Maybe the stars are her suspected locations."

"Evie worked closely with Dr. Chun, so maybe she overheard something she wasn't supposed to, but she didn't—" Silas cut off, his throat working in a swallow. Agnes knew what he'd been about to say. *She didn't live long enough to figure it out.*

"Wait a second," said Derek, holding up a finger. "If they're producing these darts in Chicago, and the darts create enhanced turned, then..."

His words sucked the brief excitement out of the room.

Silas, ever the analytical, was the first to speak. "Then Chicago could be overrun, and Kev could be in deep shit." Then his face went pale, like he'd just come face-to-face with the devil. "And that repeating scrambled message I keep getting? Maybe...maybe that's an SOS."

25

1 YEAR AGO

"Y OU CAME!" QUENTIN BOWLED into Penny as he answered the door.

"I told you I would," she said, returning the hug in earnest. *Let's get this over with.*

She hadn't been home, like into her house, in a few years. Its walls were stained with bad memories. The last time had been when her parents signed the farm over to Uncle Hal and she'd gotten into a knock-down, drag-out verbal sparring match with both him and her father over his scummy business practices that she herself had been investigating at the insurance firm. Her father had thrown her out, followed by the violent confrontation with Hal.

But even so, when Quentin had called to invite her over for dinner, she could not deny him. So here she was, following him into their family's traditional farmhouse. It smelled just as it always had—fresh-baked bread, the wood-burning stove, the sweet notes of the wind from the apple orchards blowing through the open bay windows.

It smelled like home.

A deep sadness swelled through her as she walked past the family photos, the creaky floor board she'd always avoided when sneaking out of the house, the table in the entryway that always held seasonal decorations. It was a beautiful home. A great home. She missed it, and she missed the time in her life when it had felt like home. But now, it only served as a reminder of everything she'd chosen to walk away from.

All because of her fucking Uncle Hal.

Walking into the brightly lit kitchen, her mom stood over the stove fluffing a pot of mashed potatoes as her dad finished setting the table. "Penny! You made it." Her mom beamed, but all Penny could manage was a wooden smile. She loved her parents, but they were naive. Born and raised in their small town, they never imagined life outside of their safe little bubble. It was how Hal had been able to scam his own brother out of the ownership share of the farm. Penny had never forgiven him for that, or her parents for being so trusting and *stupid*.

When she saw who sat at the head of the table, the room spun.

She froze, eyes glued to Satan himself.

"It's been a long time, Penelope." Hal steepled his hands under his chin and watched her like a cat hunting a mouse.

Not wanting to ruin the moment for her mom or Quentin, Penny went to the bar cart to make herself a drink. "Anyone else want one?" she asked, pouring a generous helping of whiskey.

"I'll have a backwards hammer with a sunroof and make it sing," said Quentin.

Penny snorted into her drink, despite her skin crawling under her uncle's scrutiny. Pouring Quentin a glass of seltzer with two lemons, she said, "Only had the ingredients for a fuzzy sunroof with extra sun."

Laughing, Quentin grabbed the drink and snagged a dinner roll before taking his seat. He patted the empty chair next to him, and Penny sat. *Just thirty minutes. Then you can get the hell out of here.*

"Let's all bow our heads," her dad said, closing his eyes. Penny remained silent, opting to give up her own thanks to the earth for the food instead of some dead guy she didn't believe in anyway. Beside her, she noticed Quentin wasn't partaking in the prayer either. She bumped his shoulder with a smile. *I hope he isn't taking after me, but goddammit, I hope he isn't taking after our parents either.* If his sense of humor and interest in inventing things was any indication, he was shaping up to be very different from all of them. Different, and better.

I'll get him out of here if I have to sell my fucking soul. Hal will not get his claws into him.

"Amen. Dig in, everyone," said her father, passing the plates of food.

"So, Quentin," said the slime ball of a human being sitting at the end of the table, helping himself to some baked chicken. "Thoughts about a part-time job? Could really use your help on the farm, smart guy like you."

Penny white-knuckled the mashed potato spoon as she heaped some onto her plate, wishing her glare could burn a hole through Hal. She opened her mouth to tell him to go to hell—probably, she wasn't sure what would come out—but Quentin answered first.

"I took a job at the metal shop on Main. Mr. Winslow will teach me to weld, and I'll clean the shop for him."

"He's not gonna pay you?" Dad asked, frowning around his bite of green beans.

"He can't afford to pay me much, but I want to learn, so I told him it was okay." Quentin bobbed eagerly in his seat, munching on bread.

"That's not right. The man ought to pay you. *I* can pay you," Hal said, watching Penny over the top of his wine glass.

"Few more years and he'll be making his own decisions," Penny said in the most neutral tone she could muster. "Don't see why he can't start now."

"That's for his parents to decide, don't you think?" Hal said, pointing his fork at her, which only made Penny want to shove the fucking thing down his throat. Reaching for the steak knife beside her plate, she envisioned flinging it across the room, lodging it in his pudgy neck—

"Quentin already cleared it with me," her mom said. "I told him to do whatever makes him happy."

Penny hadn't ever loved her mother more than she did in that moment as she watched the rage flicker in Hal's eyes. Wanting to antagonize him further, Penny turned the conversation to her father. "Heard in the news last week about that ground water pollution they found downriver," she said. "Terrible stuff. You know they found high levels of organochlorines? Causes cancer, not to mention it's a banned substance."

"Everything causes cancer," Hal said, unconcerned.

"Good thing we're all organic here at Pine Creek Orchard," her father said. "Can't handle the thought of that kind of poison going on the food we eat."

Oh, Pops. If only you knew.

"They think runoff got into the rivers from a farm's irrigation system. Which farm, you think?" The question was directed at her dad, but her eyes never left Hal, and she took pleasure in his twitching eye.

Her mom chimed in. "Could be Sunny Acres. They've got a big operation and don't seem to be too careful about following regulations, from what I hear from Kathy at the corner store."

Eyes still on her uncle, Penny said, "Whoever it is, I'm sure they'll get found out eventually." *Yeah, I see you, motherfucker.*

Penny's phone buzzed in her pocket, interrupting the stare-down, and Satan took that moment to excuse himself from the table, heading down the hall. "Yeah, Lexa?" she said into her phone.

"Our suspected arsonist is scheduling a meet with a recruiter for the Salvadors. Get your stakeout equipment and meet me at Wagon Wheel."

"Holy shit." Penny nearly choked on her food. If he was meeting with the Salvadors, an infamous crime family, this case just got a whole lot bigger. "Thought you were too busy to work this case with me?" she asked.

Lexa snorted. "As if I could ever say no to you. See you soon."

Hanging up, Penny pushed back from the table, dropping a hand on her brother's head. "Sorry. Work."

Wrapping an arm around her waist for a side hug, he said, "It's okay. I know you have stuff to do."

"I'll see you soon though, okay? Maybe I'll come by Winslow's shop."

His hopeful smile almost had her glueing her butt back to the chair. "I'd like that."

"Thanks for dinner, Mom. Dad." After doling out awkward hugs to her parents, Penny made her escape.

When she stepped onto the wraparound porch, a hand closed around her throat, slamming her into the siding, the cold, familiar feeling of a gun barrel pressing into her forehead.

"What the fuck you doing here, Penny? Thought I made myself clear last time." Hal's onion breath puffed in her face, making her want to gag. She wasn't afraid of him. But she *was* afraid of what he'd do to her family. To Quentin.

"It's my fucking house. My fucking family. I'll show up when I want to."

"If you breathe another word about that news story in this house, I'll make that baby brother of yours work the field until his fingers rot."

"As if our parents would ever allow that to happen."

"There's a lot my brother will allow, if given the right incentive."

"You mean, if you outright lie to him and swindle him out of his own business."

"You got no proof of that."

"No, but I am pretty fucking close to proving you're the one dumping pesticides into the river, using it on the 'organic' crops, and lying to the regulators. How'd you like to do some federal time? I can arrange that."

His hand tightened around her throat, and the gun clicked as he pressed the hammer, a kernel of fear flashing deep in his soulless eyes. "Watch your fucking step, Penelope. If I go down, your whole family goes down with me. Even your precious little Quentin."

The overwhelming urge to head-butt the smug fucker in the face, to feel the bone crunch and his blood explode, surged through her. But he was an idiot and terrible with a gun, so he'd probably accidentally shoot her in the head.

The asshole had a point and he knew it. She could nail him to the fucking wall right now with the evidence she had of his crimes, of all the environmental laws and FDA regulations he was breaking. But if she took him down, her parents would lose everything, and there was no guarantee that they would get off scot-free. She didn't trust any justice system except her own.

"I know what you are. I know what you're doing. And I'm coming for you." Breaking his grip on her neck with ease, she kneed him in the balls and headed for her car, smiling at the sound of his sputtering.

Hopping into Lexa's car, Penny tossed a fast food bag across the seat. "Grabbed your favorite."

"Ah, Big Burger. Yes!" Lexa unwrapped the double cheeseburger and took a bite. "You are the best. Have I told you that lately?"

"Never tire of hearing it, babe. So what's going on? Any news?" They were parked a few blocks away from a nondescript brick building on the outskirts of town. It was late on a weeknight, but a few people milled about Wagon Wheel, the local watering hole, or settled for the liquor store on the corner.

"Been tailing our guy all day," she said around a mouthful of burger. "Managed to slip a bug in his back pocket when I 'copped a feel' at a bar earlier. Gross, I know. Anyway, they've been shooting the shit for a while, but the recruiter should be here any second. Oh yeah, look." Pointing across the street, a sleek Lincoln town car pulled up to the curb, and Lexa nearly swallowed her burger whole when Mr. Salvador himself stepped out, straightening his dark velvet suit jacket. Rarely did the big man in charge take small interviews for lackeys, so whatever was afoot must be important enough to get him to meet in person.

Penny clapped Lexa on the back as she coughed, then adjusted the knobs on their surveillance equipment.

After some shuffling around and the typical boastful dude conversations about the ponies and the strip club next door, Salvador said, "Got another job for you, Terry. If you think you're up for it."

"Ain't much I'll say no to, boss," came the voice of their arsonist through the radio.

"Riverside Lofts. If you take care of this one as well as the others, there's another bigger job in it for you—Pine Creek Orchard."

Lexa choked on her drink, and Penny froze. This could only mean one thing—her uncle was in it with the Salvadors, and he was in it fucking deep. If they were destroying the farm for the insurance money, afterward they could resell the land to launder money for his crime ring.

The fire would be the perfect cover too, destroying any evidence of a fake organic farm using illegal pesticides. She was sure the fire would conveniently take the farmhouse and the barn too, for the extra payout. And she knew her parents would never see a dime of that insurance money. They'd have nothing. Which meant Quentin would have nothing too.

"We've gotta stop this guy, Lexa. Do we have enough to bust in there and get him?"

"Not without a warrant. Only way we'll get him is if we catch him in the act."

"So we keep tailing the arsonist. We have to nail this guy." But it wasn't just about getting the arsonist. They had to take down Salvador and her uncle. All of it. Because if she didn't, Hal would just keep coming for her and her family. The only way this would end is if she landed both of their asses in jail. Lexa knew that as well as she did. She reached across the center console and gripped Penny's hand.

"We'll get him, Penny. I promise."

26

Early the next morning, Penny sat in the war room and propped her boots on the table, tossing a moldy tennis ball in the air and catching it over and over. She needed to *think*.

The lab raid after yesterday's battle had been less than fruitful—not even a scared troxy in sight. Just a building full of garbage. Agnes and Silas were hard at work on finding an answer to their big fucking problem, but without any concrete leads, Penny didn't have much confidence. While detox serum might buy them some time, without a true cure for the darts, Tara, Ivan, everyone who got hit were going to turn—and maybe into something even worse than they could imagine.

The door creaked open, puncturing her thoughts, and she gripped the tennis ball, primed to throw it—

"Oh. It's you," she said, tossing the ball into a bucket in the corner instead. "Didn't expect anyone else to be up so early."

Mal hoisted an eyebrow, pausing in the doorway. "Sorry to interrupt. I can see you're exceptionally busy."

"Very." Penny leaned back in her chair, peering at him. "Glad to see you decided to forgo hunting down Zeln in the night. I half expected you to run off after him yesterday to avenge Zombie Mal."

The only outward sign of his agitation was his hand tightening around the doorknob.

"Don't break that," she said. "It upsets Raph when he has to do so many repairs." Before she could say anything else, a ruckus sounded in the hallway. Exchanging confused looks, she and Mal went to investigate and—

"Raph?" she called as he sprinted past her, skidded to a stop, then turned around and ran back.

Bending over to catch his breath, Raph wheezed, "Messengers...here." He pointed toward the atrium, where Will, Vick, Jaha, and a group of new people came bursting inside. A youngish guy with jet-black hair was at their helm, conversing with Vick in what sounded like Japanese.

"Tanaka?" Mal said as he caught sight of the guy. To Penny's questioning glance, he explained, "They're from Chicago. My old division."

"Found them in the Wilds when we were heading back to our camp," Jaha said. "Thought they'd like an escort."

A look of relief washed over Tanaka's face as he shook Mal's hand, his fellow soldiers gathering around him. "General Olesa, I'm glad as fuck to see you. The troxies breached Chicago's wall."

"What?" Mal growled.

Tanaka grunted—Penny wondered if Mal taught all of his troops to communicate like that. "Yeah, shit's bad. We were holding the perimeter, but when the network went down and comms went dark, they snuck in some forces to breach our outer wall. Last week, they finally succeeded. We'd been trying to get messengers out before then but never heard back."

"Just like we thought," Penny said to Mal. "The cult offing anyone who wandered through the woods. But with them gone and the troxies licking their wounds today, there was even more of an opening for people to finally get through."

"Uh, a cult?" Tanaka asked.

"We had a...situation, but it's been dealt with," Mal said.

"I only ask because on our way here, one of the splinters mentioned seeing other groups run through this corridor. It didn't sound like a cult, but they're not just civilians trying to survive—they're a bit more organized. Anti-troxy, but anti-Faction too. Shot up some of our groups about an hour's drive outside the city."

"What did they want?" Penny asked.

"Don't know. They just don't want anyone telling them what to do."

Penny glanced at Vick, who shook her head slightly. *So it's not the Watchers.*

Before they could unpack that any further, a commotion sounded from the stadium's main entrance, and Agnes and the rest of Team Outpost barged inside.

"Pharmatrox's doomsday lab is in Chicago!" Agnes shouted without preamble. "We need to leave right—uh, who's this?"

"We're from Chicago," Tanaka said. "And I don't know anything about a doomsday lab—that's above my pay grade—but we've definitely got a situation there. Like, an all-hands-on-fucking-deck situation."

"What's the plan?" Derek asked, looking to Mal and—surprisingly—Penny too. *Don't know what to make of that.*

"I'll ask my suburban contacts if they know anything about these other crews you mentioned," Vick offered. Ever since Tara got hit with a dart yesterday, she'd been more willing than usual to pitch in. "We have a sort of dirt bike Pony Express system for delivering messages. It's not that fast or foolproof, but if we push it, we might be able to send word to assist in Chicago. Jaha?"

"On it," Jaha said. "Derek, if I can borrow your motorcycle, I'll head out now."

Derek tossed her the keys. "Have at it. But don't wreck her."

Jaha's fierce look shut up any other snarky comments he might have made, and she jogged off.

"She is *so* cool," Quentin said. Even Derek stared after Jaha's retreating form with a look of begrudging admiration.

"You just like that she rides motorcycles," Lawrence said with a knowing smile.

"That's not—okay, maybe," Derek conceded.

Mal gave Vick a nod of respect, then raised his voice to the larger group. "Look, there's never going to be a perfect time to go to Chicago. We crushed the troxies yesterday and it will take a while for them to regroup, so we have a brief window where we can make a fast trip. We'll take a small strike team to help out as we can, coordinating with Vick's contacts when they arrive. If the lab is in Chicago, Kev or his man on the inside might know about it."

"And," chimed in Agnes, "destroying Pharmatrox's one remaining functional lab and server farm—it could mean the end of everything. They'll have nothing to fall back on. The darts will disappear, the enhanced turned will die out as we continue battling them, and we'll be slightly better off."

"Right," agreed Mal. "Raph, Will, and Sanjali—you're in charge here, along with Vick and her Watchers, if they're willing. Tanaka, your guys too. Knowing you're shoring things up makes me feel slightly better about leaving." Then a shadow passed across his face, and for a moment, Mal looked absolutely gutted as he locked eyes with his Chicago soldiers. "I'm sorry I wasn't there. You're my troops, and if you were going through hell, I should've been with you."

"All due respect, sir, but this isn't your fault. And you're helping us now. That's what matters. So let's do this," said Tanaka, and Vick nodded her agreement.

But even as he continued doling out instructions, Mal still seemed shaken. "Agnes and Silas, I'll need you with me in Chicago. Derek too. Tara and Ivan, I know you want to come, but—"

"We're weak as shit right now and would be a liability," said Tara, a fine sweat dappling her forehead. "I get it."

"I'll stay behind too," offered Lawrence with a concerned glance at Tara. "Take on some extra patrols."

But Penny knew he wanted to remain at his friend's side if anything should...happen.

Mal spared a sympathetic look before continuing. "Which means we'll need someone who's good at pyrotechnics and booby traps, so Quentin, you're in too."

"Oh, *hell yes*," Quentin said, punching the air in triumph. Penny wasn't a fan of Quentin being involved, but she'd rather have him along where she could keep an eye on him.

But then Mal turned to her—*what's that fucking guilty look for?* And then she knew. "No, Mal. *No.* I know what you're going to say and I'm not doing it."

Bracing himself, he said the words. The fucking words. "Penny, I need you to stay here."

Already shaking her head, she said, "You're taking my brother on one of the most important stealth missions of this entire war and you want me to *stay here?* Are you out of your goddamn mind?"

"How's it going to look to the rest of our troops if both of their leaders take off, especially after Kev left them? I trust Vick and the Watchers and my Chicago troops, but our people don't know them—they know *you.* We'll only be gone four days, max. I need you to hold down the fort."

"You need me with you," she said, seething. "When you find that lab, Agnes and Silas will be preoccupied with getting the cure and taking out the servers. So, what, it's going to be you and Derek against the fucking world, fighting for your lives and getting everyone out of there in one piece? I have experience breaking into black ops Pharmatrox facilities and making it out alive. Can you say the same about yourself? And if Zeln is really as big of a threat as you say, then why don't *you* stay here and keep things stable? Or has he already gotten so inside your head that you can't even see straight?"

At her last words, a frown darkened his brow and she felt a pang of regret. She hadn't meant to throw his personal shit in his face, but goddamn it, she would not be left behind, and he needed to get it through his thick fucking skull.

"I'd love to consider sending you on your own to handle things with Kev," he said, drawing himself up to his full height. "But you've already demonstrated that you are willing to make bad choices if it gets you what you want."

"What are you talking about?"

"Your negotiation with Vick and the Watchers."

"Still harping on that? Seems like it worked out pretty well for us."

"It worked out because Vick is Vick, not because you made the right choice. Anyone else might have used our own weapons against us, and you didn't consider that possibility. You don't have the experience to handle whatever we'll face in Chicago."

"I know you did not just say I can't fucking handle it."

Pinching the bridge of his nose, he took a deep inhale. When he opened his eyes, they were bright with fury. "I know you'll go rogue and do whatever the hell you want anyway, so fine, Penny. Have it your way." Before she could say anything else, he stalked off, calling over his shoulder, "Tanaka, with me."

As the group dispersed to prepare for the trip, Agnes hung back, looking uncertain. "For what it's worth," she said finally, "I think you're right. We need you with us."

Stunned into silence, Penny could only nod. *At least one person agrees with me.* She just never expected it to be Agnes.

27

"OF ALL THE TIMES for us to get a cold snap, it *had* to be when we decided to go roving around in a tin can?" Silas grumbled from the EV's cargo space, swaddling himself in a blanket.

Penny had to agree. Terrible fucking timing. Temperatures had dipped low enough for them to see their breaths—which was bad news for the EV's battery life. Even with a mat of solar panels on the roof continuously recharging the battery, the colder night temperatures might force them to make an overnight stop until the sun could warm up the battery enough to continue.

"We should still make it to Chicago by late tonight, barring any other issues," Agnes said.

Their crew cozied up together in the back of the van to keep warm while Derek drove and Agnes navigated, Quentin wedged between them. He stared at Derek, inches away from his face, then delivered a solid poke to his ribs.

"Ow! What the hell?"

"I need to make sure you stay *alert* and ready for anything," Quentin said with a self-satisfied smile.

"Does 'ready for anything' include booting an irritating teenager out of my car?" Derek grumbled.

"We can always strap him to the roof if he gets to be too annoying," Agnes said, giving a significant look to the annoying teenager in question.

"You'll thank me later when we aren't careening into a ravine because *someone* fell asleep at the wheel," Quentin said.

"I nodded off *once* for *two seconds*, and he brings it up every chance he gets. It was a month ago!" Derek said, clutching the steering wheel in a death grip, eyes comically wide to prove he wasn't drowsy.

Agnes looked at Derek, considering. "You know, Quentin, it's probably best to keep you on poking duty."

Quentin cackled, delivering a deluge of prods into Derek's side as he swatted him away. "If we wreck, it'll be because of *him*," Derek said.

Penny shook her head, stifling a smile. She was glad for Quentin's presence, and Agnes had been right. Including him was doing wonders for repairing their relationship, but she still had work to do.

In the back, Penny sat on a metal bench seat next to Mal, Silas across from them. She could practically feel the irritation coming off of Mal in waves—apparently he wasn't over their argument. After Tanaka had shown up, they'd left within the hour, Mal stonewalling her the entire time, and she'd endured a few hours of his surly silence in the car already. But as she thought about everything they'd learned that morning, she wondered if his frustration wasn't entirely directed at her. Maybe the thought of Kev struggling without him was fucking with his head. And with Zeln already doing a great job of that on his own, Mal was probably having a hard time.

While she understood, he had no right to demand she stay behind, nor be pissed off that she refused. If Quentin was going, she was going, and that was that. *But...*

She didn't want to admit it to herself, but she had another motive for wanting to go. A small, scared part of her worried that if Mal went to Chicago without her and saw how bad things had gotten for his troops in his absence, he might decide to stay there. Indefinitely.

And where would that leave them?

With the status of the war in the Capital, I mean. Not with our relationship. Which we don't have.

If she was there, she could convince him to come back to the Capital. Because they needed him there too.

Mal's hand rested on her knee briefly, yanking her out of her thoughts. Clearing his throat, he said, "You were bouncing your leg and moving the whole seat. Everything good?"

"Just pent-up energy," Penny said, then blanched when Quentin snorted, covering it with a cough. *Jesus Christ.* "Ah, I mean—haven't been this far outside the city in a while. Not sure what we'll find."

And she was apprehensive about seeing Kev again. The Penny that Kev remembered was very different from the person she was now. But after her brush with death in the barn, she'd been feeling more on edge as remembrances of who she'd been simmered to the surface. Not to mention, hell yes, she still had some *pent-up energy* when it came to being in close proximity to Mal, but she shoved those sticky feelings aside. There was too much at stake.

An unreadable expression crossed Mal's face, then he said to Derek, "Keep a lookout for anything strange."

"Thanks," Derek said. "Wouldn't have known to do that without your astute guidance."

Thankfully for Derek, he was out of Mal's reach or else he probably would have received a hearty shove to the shoulder. Another hour passed in a blur of desolate land and ruined cities. But then something hit the back of the van, rattling the cargo space.

"What the fuck was that?" Penny asked, hand flying to her sickle.

"Hit another pot hole?" Quentin accused Derek.

"Pot holes don't leave dents like that," Silas said, pointing to a sizable indentation in the back door.

The group exchanged a tense look, hands drifting to weapons. *There's only one thing I know of that's capable of that kind of damage.*

"What do we do?" Derek asked, looking at them in the rearview mirror.

Slam. Something plowed into the side of the van.

Then Agnes screamed.

Many gray hands with nails covered in dry blood reached for the driver and passenger side windows, cracks forming as they beat against the glass.

"Might want to pick up the pace, Derek," Quentin said, digging in his pack for—*a dead raccoon?* With one of the knives at his belt, he slit the furry body up the middle, then opened the back door as the van picked up speed. A herd of turned chased them, their obsidian eyes weeping black tears. He tossed the still-bleeding raccoon into the crowd, and they ripped into it with fervor, abandoning their pursuit.

"You always have a backpack full of dead things?" Agnes asked, clutching the dashboard as Derek sped away.

"Ivan's idea," Quentin said, wiping his hands on his pants. "He says it pays to have a blood bag you can throw at turned if you need to get away."

"That's my man," Silas said. "Full of crafty, yet disgusting, ideas."

Quentin chuckled, then stared at Penny with a funny look. She glanced down and paled—she hadn't realized that in the chaos, she'd clutched onto Mal's forearm. As she jerked her hand back to her side,

Quentin gave her a goofy smile. Mal's eyes slid over her in an expression she couldn't interpret as the van tore down the road. *Still pissed at me, probably.*

An hour or so passed without event, and Penny watched the barren landscape pass by, Silas keeping a lookout for trouble with Quentin's binoculars. Bare trees like skeletons lined the road surrounded by grass faded to a dismal yellow. By the time they crossed the state line into Ohio, about halfway through the trip, the sky began to grow dark as evening approached. Her eyelids grew heavy, her breath fogging the frigid window, and she was seconds from sleep when an interruption jarred her into alertness.

"Stop the fucking car," Silas said, nearly falling out of his seat.

"I didn't take the salmon, Your Honor, I swear!" Quentin shouted as he burst out of a dream.

Derek screeched to a halt. "What is it?"

But Silas was already moving out the back door, grabbing a volt rifle. "Something heading right for us. Fast."

"What?" Derek said, squinting out the windshield.

Then it came into view.

An armored troxy truck, speeding down the highway, dead ahead, a machine gun mounted on its roof.

"Shit," Penny said, passing out weapons to everyone. "Quentin, stay in the van. I mean it."

He opened his mouth to protest as she jumped out the back, but Mal backed her up. "We don't know what this is, so hang back."

"Okay," Quentin agreed, hunkering down in the front seat. He only looked slightly disappointed, but she knew he'd listen to his hero.

"Thanks," Penny said to Mal as they took position on both sides of the highway.

"I care about him too, you know," Mal said, glowering at her.

"I didn't mean—"

The sound of the truck's engine revving tore through the air as it ate up the distance in no time, skidding to a stop beside them. Troxies poured out, weapons firing, bullets and volts chewing up the pavement, as Penny threw herself into the ditch in the highway median, returning fire.

"Not super soldiers," Derek shouted from somewhere to her right.

A hand grabbed Penny by the jacket, pulling her back as bullets sprayed through where she'd just been. Gasping, she turned to see Agnes in the dirt beside her. "Thanks," she said.

"Don't mention it," Agnes replied as one of her shots kneecapped a troxy. "We'll never make it out of this if that gun is still operational."

The machine gun rattled through another belt of bullets, punching holes in the side of their EV. *Fuck. Quentin.* Penny scrambled to her feet, but Agnes yanked her down.

"He's not in there," Agnes said. "You ever known Quentin to listen to instructions—even Mal's?"

"Then where the fuck is he?"

"He'll turn up. Probably has some wild idea."

Penny didn't like leaving it up to chance, but there was no time. Suddenly, one of the abandoned cars beside the armored truck exploded, melding with the fiery sunset.

"See? There he is," Agnes smirked. Sure enough, Quentin scuttled away from the car and rolled into the ditch beside them.

"You see that?" he asked, grinning around his chattering teeth, breath puffing in the cold. "Awesome, right?"

"It would be more *awesome* if you'd listen to directions for once in your stubborn life," Agnes said.

"Yeah, but if I'd listened to you—what is Tara always calling me now? Bobo?—you bobos, I'd be looking like Swiss cheese right about now."

Penny grumbled but tossed Quentin her handgun. "Just stay put, okay?"

"*Fine.*"

"I'll handle the machine gun," Penny said. "The rest of you, try not to die."

With the troxies distracted, Penny sprinted for the truck, climbing up the back and almost slipping as her hands, clumsy with the cold, lost their grip. But even so, she managed to surprise the gunner, stabbing him in the neck, and took control of the gun. "Stand the fuck down!" she shouted to the ten or so remaining troxies, who shot volts of blue electricity at her. "Your choice," she said, squeezing the trigger until the belt was spent.

Finally, everything was silent. Everyone sported nasty cuts and minor injuries but appeared largely okay. Their EV, on the other hand, was not.

"Well this is craptastic," Silas said, kicking the flat tires. "I have a patch kit and a portable air compressor, among other repair equipment, because I'm always prepared for things to go catastrophically wrong, so Penny, do your mechanic thing and get to fixing."

"Would love to, but I can't feel my fingers," she said. "Patching a tire in the cold like this is a fucking nightmare."

"Aaaand the battery is drained anyway," said Derek, shaking his head at the gauges on the dash.

"We'll have to make camp somewhere and wait until morning, then," Silas said. "Hopefully Jack Fucking Frost decides to skedaddle in the meantime so the battery will actually hold a charge."

"Looks like there's a state park a short walk that way," Agnes said, pointing to a brown sign on the side of the road. "Forest is thick there. Should provide some good cover."

Mal looked murderous at the prospect of being delayed overnight, but he rubbed a hand over his beard, nodding his agreement. "Grab the gear and let's go."

28

T HE GROUP TRUDGED DOWN a narrow gravel road to the state park, arriving in a small lot bordered by dark woods. As the sun dipped below the horizon, the temperature plummeted even further, and Penny was grateful for her leather jacket, although a big puffy coat would have been better for the night they had ahead of them.

A quick walk down an overgrown path led to a small clearing in the pine trees, and Derek wasted no time in building a fire while everyone unpacked.

Shit. Penny dug around elbow-deep in her bag, searching in vain for the tent that she was rapidly realizing wasn't there. "Forgot my fucking tent." *I could have sworn...* A movement in her periphery caught her eye. Agnes, elbowing a way-too-innocent looking Quentin, both stifling laughter.

"Guess you'll have to share with someone." Quentin cut a pointed glance at Mal, and Penny's frown deepened. Mal froze, hand halfway to his bag, eyes locked on hers.

"It's fine," Penny said. "I can keep watch."

It was Mal's turn to frown. "You can have my tent. *I'll* keep watch."

"Does that mean I can take Mal's tent and don't have to share with Silas?" Quentin asked.

"No," Penny and Mal said in unison.

"Both of you can keep watch, for all I care," said Silas. "Between the light from the fire and the screeching quality to your arguing, you'll attract every turned in the goddamn area, so you can fight them off while I get some sleep." He plopped some potatoes into a pot, muttering as he divvied out rations of dried meat.

Penny peered at Quentin, shaking her head in a way that promised they'd have words about his meddling later. For now, she took a seat as close to the fire as she could get without singeing her eyebrows off and relished the warmth.

Soon after finishing their hot meals, everyone drifted off to their tents. Agnes and Quentin were the last to leave, Agnes saying, "I better not find slugs in my sleeping bag again, bobo."

"Too cold out here for slugs," Quentin said as he ducked into his tent. "Could probably find some beetles though."

The tent zipper closed around Agnes's laugh and then Mal and Penny were alone. He threw another few logs on the fire, sparks flying. Recent events finally caught up with her, and the cold air seeped into her bones. She watched as Mal stoked the flames higher, his strong hands flexing, and her thoughts flashed to how it felt to have those hands flexing against her skin.

Fucking hell. Think about literally anything else.

The silence between them weighed heavy in the aftermath of their argument that morning. She sure as shit wasn't going to apologize for speaking the truth, but she didn't have to be such a dick about it. "Look, Mal, what I said about Zeln earlier, I—"

"Don't worry about it."

"If you're pissed at me, just tell me."

"I'm not pissed at you for that."

"Oh, so you are pissed at me?"

"No, I—I'm mad at *myself*," he said, hands curling into fists. "You're right—Zeln is getting to me. If I'd had my head on straight, I might have seen that body he left for what it was—a distraction. Maybe I could have prevented the ambush, saved some of our people from getting darted."

Penny blinked, taken aback.

"What?" asked Mal.

"I'm still reeling from the fact you said I'm right."

Mal snorted. "Don't be an asshole."

"Wouldn't dream of it. So...we're good?"

"We're good."

"And you're not pissed that I'm here instead of back in the Capital?"

"You did save our asses taking out that machine gun earlier, so I'm warming up to the idea." But the way his voice rumbled at the end of the sentence had a whole new kind of heat going through her.

Keep it in your pants, Pen. In an attempt at distraction, she asked, "You think we'll run into more troxies tomorrow?"

"Probably. It's what Zeln would advise them to do—small but frequent patrols." Mal's hands tightened around his kneecaps.

Penny studied him for a moment, inching closer to the fire. "You ever gonna tell me what happened between you two?"

She thought he'd brush her off like always, but instead he blew out a breath, running his hands through his hair. *Holy shit, he's really going to spill it.*

"I ever tell you why I defected from Pharmatrox?" he asked.

She shook her head, saying, "You mentioned something about having to abandon your culture and your name." Even though he was the person she spent the most time with these days, the man was still a mystery. But with everything that had passed between them recently, she was getting a taste for Mal, and she wanted *more* of him beyond the surface level.

When he spoke, his forearm tendons rolled as he clenched his hands. "I met Zeln in boot camp fourteen years ago when we were a couple of twenty-two-year-old idiots. We were in the same platoon and rose through the ranks together, thick as thieves. Until six years ago, when one of our missions in the Middle East went bad—one Zeln was leading. On the way to rendezvous with another command, a skirmish in town had bombs and shit going off, so we had to detour. Because we were on unfamiliar terrain and it was dark, we didn't see it—an IED took out our Humvee, and Zeln and I were the only survivors. Because Zeln was in charge, our superiors deemed he was at fault. That we weren't supposed to be on that road. That he blatantly disobeyed an order by straying from our designated route. But he claims *he* got last-minute radio orders from his commander to change course.

"I believed him, but it didn't matter and they stripped Zeln of his rank. It was bullshit, but if your superiors don't want to take the hit for something, they pass the blame on to someone else. It wasn't long before something in him...broke. He refused to reenlist and wanted me to leave with him. Kept saying that Pharmatrox had taken our best friends from us, treated us like we were expendable. That the system was broken and unfixable, and we should get out while we could.

"I was angry as fuck about it too, but I'd worked my ass off to get my position, and I wasn't about to throw it away. I couldn't abandon my men like that either. I still believed in Pharmatrox and I told him so. And then he just disappeared. I'd heard he went freelance. I tried to reach out to him but never heard back.

"Then one day, he pops back up. Rival royal family challenging the Samari's power in Eastern Europe. All of them, assassinated. The photos leaked on the newsfeed, and when I saw them, I knew it was him. A neat pairing of shots in a diamond shape, center mass. The same on every body. His signature—it was how he'd always shot when we practiced together.

"But even then, knowing he'd done something like that, I missed him. He was the only reason I survived those early days of training, where the troxies tried their hardest to break us. So I threw myself back into work, determined to do right by all of my troops and fix the broken system from within."

So fighting for a cause, burying himself in the mission, is how he masks the pain too. Maybe she had more in common with the noble soldier than she'd thought.

"I thought I was fighting to protect a country that had given me and my family so much," he continued. "For years, Pharmatrox convinced me that's what I was doing. And then they became more overt about their agenda. It started small. Asking me to cover my tattoos." He brushed his hand over his bicep, where the traditional Polynesian patterns swirled beneath his jacket. "Then it was, I needed to get them removed if I wanted to be considered for a higher rank. Suggested changing my name to something less 'exotic.'" He made a sound of disgust. "I refused, of course, and nothing came of it. But microaggressions from the other officers made it clear they thought I'd made the wrong choice. Then as the Faction gained more respect among the people, the troxies ordered me to discipline recruits who spoke out against Pharmatrox."

"'Discipline,' meaning...?"

"Meaning, beat the hell out of them."

"Did you?"

Mal's mouth flattened into a grim line. "At first, yeah, I did. But I knew it was wrong, and I didn't want to do it. They'd trained me to obey orders, and so I obeyed. But I knew something bigger was coming. Something worse. So I sent my family back to Samoa before everything went down.

"And then the day came when the troxies asked me to do something I couldn't—something really fucking *wrong*. When the Red Riots spread to Chicago, one of my men helped the Faction evade arrest. An officer caught him, and my CO threw him in front of me, handed me a gun, and told me to deliver justice. At that moment, I knew everything I'd been working for my whole life was one big lie. I refused to execute my own soldier, and that's when they brought out Zeln. They hired the one person they knew it would break me to see. They wanted me to know *they* controlled everything. That I had to submit or watch everyone I cared for turned against me, one by one. He should never have even wanted the fucking job—he hated Pharmatrox. But I think in that moment, he hated me more. I hadn't abandoned my men, but I'd abandoned *him*.

"I knew if I stayed, it was only a matter of time before they asked me to do something even worse, and they'd kill me if I refused again. My whole life, I'd trusted the wrong people—Pharmatrox, even my best friend. So I defected that very moment. I fought back. It was the only way to end the vicious cycle and reclaim some sense of control.

"Zeln and I fought, nearly killed each other. Even though the man who'd been my boot camp friend was dead, replaced with a gun for hire, a mercenary without morals, I couldn't kill him. So I escaped, but not before he managed to stab me in the fucking back and shoot my soldier in the head."

His voice remained strong as he spoke, but Penny knew how that choice had ripped him in half, this man who cared so deeply for his soldiers and would never willingly abandon them. While she admired him, that small seed of fear she'd been harboring since the morning began to take root. *What if he stays in Chicago?*

"I met up with Kev later that day. And—and that's how I got here," he finished abruptly. He'd stared at the fire during his entire recounting, but now, he finally looked at Penny. Her breath hitched at the raw emotion etched into his normally stoic face. A tiny sliver of her heart cracked just for him, for all the pain and hardship he'd endured, just because he came from a culture that their government deemed as "other." Outsider. Undesirable. Which was bullshit. Reaching for his hand, she slipped her fingers through his.

"I know what you're thinking," she said. "Don't."

He looked askance at her. "How could you know what I'm thinking?"

"Because, at least in this one thing, we think alike. You feel like a failure for abandoning your men. For 'taking the easy way out.' For letting your friend down. For putting your trust in people who didn't deserve it. But that's all bullshit. You made the best choice you could with the information you had. You fought for what you believe in. You fought *back*." She was saying the words to him as much as she was saying them to herself, and as she heard them aloud, an unnamed feeling rushed through her, tears pricking at her eyes. *For fuck's sake. Keep it together.* "You're a good man, Mal. Don't fucking forget that."

He gripped her hand, both of them enraptured by the moment. Time pulled and stretched between them, the cold forgotten except for the smoky puffs of their breaths as the sparks of the fire danced in the background. *He looks so fierce like that, with fire in his eyes. A warrior.*

My warrior.

The last thought caught her by surprise, and she pulled away, shattering them back into reality.

His eyes drifted to her hand at her belt and he lifted a brow—she'd started fiddling with the black-bladed knife to give her fingers something to do besides twine with his.

"I know that blade is Rodney's," he said carefully. "Will you tell me why you carry it?"

Uncomfortable with the sudden shift in spotlight, Penny studied the knife to avoid looking at him. But because he'd let her peek behind his mask tonight, maybe she should do the same. Before she could think better of it, she started talking.

"This knife has a lot of blood in its history," she said. "It was his favorite. Watched him cut out tongues, carve out teeth, stab and flay. Guy was a fucking monster. In the Beginning, his group of raiders found me after—" *Shit.* Looking down, her hands shook and she slid the knife back in her belt. "Sorry. I've never talked about this before."

At that, Mal leaned closer with an earnest expression, dropping his large palm on her kneecap. "You don't have to."

But she wanted to let him in, just a little. Plowing onward, she said, "After I set that fire at my parents' house, I was adrift, and then the ferry happened. I was using all the time and my stash had run out, so I broke into a pharmacy outside of New York. But I wasn't the only user looking for a fix. Rodney and his goons were there, and they had all the troxapine in the place. So I joined them and did Rodney's dirty work because I was high, depressed, and so fucking lost. Simple as that."

The look in his eyes said he suspected there was more. "But you quit. Without detox serum."

"Yeah. I faked using for a while because Rodney didn't like it when his minions didn't obey. But Kev saw something in me, and he showed me another direction—leading my own raiding crew. I took him up on it, and soon, Rodney and I became rivals. But I'll always owe Kev for helping me get out from under Rodney's thumb."

"But *you quit. Without detox serum.* How did you do it?"

"I don't know, Mal. I just stopped taking it. Thought I was going to fucking die from the withdrawal. I had fever, shakes, vomiting, sweating, all of it. I didn't know it wasn't possible to stop using, but the more users I met, the more I realized my experience was unique. Didn't know what to make of it. Still don't. But I'll never touch the stuff again, even though I miss it. God, I miss it all the fucking time. But I know who I was when I was a user, and I don't want to be that lost, *obedient* woman ever again. It's maybe why I went a little overboard with the blood and the savagery when I got free of Rodney. Because I was trying to prove that I was strong, even though a black hole was eating away at me every day."

Taking the knife out again, she smoothed her thumb across the metal. "We all have a black-bladed knife—a sharp darkness, whether it's a painful memory, a twisted past, poor decisions that cut deep. I carry Rodney's knife so I remember exactly who I don't want to be. And I was so close to being him, Mal. If Quentin hadn't shown up...well. I would've killed Agnes, and I'd still be painting the country bloody in the search for absolution that I'd never find.

"This knife is a reminder that I don't have to be the Penny of the past anymore. And that it's okay if I still hold onto that darkness, that sharp sliver of myself that cuts and bleeds. Because without that Penny, I wouldn't be where I am at this exact moment. And there's nowhere else I'd rather be, as fucked up as that sounds. Of course I wish that my parents were still alive, that—" *Lexa.* But that wasn't a story she was ready to tell—maybe not ever. "That Quentin and I didn't have this awkward boulder of guilt between us. But this knife tells me that I've been through hell before and I'm right in the middle of it now, but I'll pull through because, somehow, I always do."

By the end of her story, Mal's thighs bracketed her own and his hands enveloped hers, the warmth of his body warding off the cold night. "You don't need bloodshed or a knife—or a sickle—to prove you're strong," he said in a soft voice. "'Weak' is never a word I would use to describe a woman with a story like that."

As he held her gaze and his words burned through her, she didn't feel vulnerable or exposed, even after everything she'd revealed. Instead, Mal met her with the one thing he'd always given her—acceptance. For exactly who, and what, she was.

But what I said to him tonight barely scratches the surface.

And before she could stop herself, the question that had been plaguing her ever since that shared moment in the woods those few months ago broke past her lips. "What do you even see in me?" She'd meant it to sound harsh, maybe even accusatory, but it came out in a whisper she hardly recognized as her own.

His golden eyes bore into hers, and the intensity of having his *full* attention cut through the dim chambers of her heart. Tilting her chin up with his rough fingers, he said, "Don't ask me questions you can't handle the answer to."

He's right. I can't even handle thinking that I might want him, *let alone hearing what he truly thinks of me.*

"You should get some rest," he said, breaking the trance. "Sunrise is in a few hours, and the battery should be warmed up enough for us to make repairs and take off."

"What about you?"

"Someone should keep watch."

"Agnes is an early riser. Let's both catch some sleep. We'll be useless tomorrow otherwise."

"I don't need sleep."

"As much as you do a great impression of an impenetrable boulder, you're only a man, Mal. Come on."

Penny prodded him toward his one-person tent, and they both clambered inside, but she quickly realized the problem—Mal seemed extra fucking huge in the tiny space. Wriggling as far to one side as she could, Penny tried to hide the fact that she was making a barrier of blankets and spare clothes between them.

Unsurprisingly, the thin tent did little to protect them from the cold. Their body heat would warm the space marginally in a little while, but at that moment, she couldn't feel her hands or feet. *Fat chance of getting any sleep when it's this fucking cold.* Stuffing her hands in her armpits and curling away from Mal, she settled in for a long night of freezing her ass off.

"Come here." Mal's voice reached her through the darkness, close to her ear.

She almost snapped her neck from looking at him so fast. "What?"

He opened his arm, breaching the wall of blankets. "You're shivering. It's fucking freezing. Come. Here."

She jutted out her chin in stubborn refusal. Or she would have, if her teeth would stop chattering.

"Pen." His tone brokered no argument.

"Fine." She scooted into his side and had to admit, it was a bit warmer next to him than plastering herself to the tent's wall. But even after a few minutes, her chattering had not abated. Making a sound that rumbled low in his chest, Mal sat up and began removing his layers.

"What are you doing?" she asked, but it hurt as her teeth slammed into each other.

"Take off your clothes."

Dear god. She was grateful for the dark to hide her undoubtedly flaming face. Sensing her hesitation, he clarified, "Just your outer layers. We'll use them as blankets, but it will make it easier to share body heat."

With shaking hands that weren't entirely related to the cold, she did as he said until she was in only a thin tee shirt and he was down to the same. When he opened his arm to her, she crawled under the pile of blankets and clothes to reach his side, immediately enveloped in his furnace-like warmth. Sighing, she slid her hand across his chest and down, pretending she wasn't feeling the ridges of his abs through the softness of his shirt, and he hissed out a breath.

"Goddamn it, woman. Your hands are icicles." He pulled her closer and wrapped the blankets tighter around them, a hand gripping her hip in a way that felt...possessive. As if he were claiming her.

"I'm only doing this because it's cold," she said, but she found her fingers pausing at the bottom of his shirt, wishing beyond reason to delve underneath and feel his hot skin against hers.

The exhale of his soft laughter tickled the hair by her ear. "Me too," he said, tucking her head under his chin.

As the warmth began to spread, her thoughts turned to what had just transpired. Tonight, she and Mal had taken a chisel to the wall between them. But to dismantle that wall completely, she'd have to be able to stand in front of it, trusting that Mal would be there on the other side, no matter what she did or what he might learn about her. The thought of being that reliant upon someone scared the shit out of her, and he probably felt the same, after everything he'd been through.

Beneath her, Mal's chest rose and fell, a steady metronome to calm her racing thoughts. His story tonight showed her they both shared coping mechanisms, but they were still so opposite. Mal was their leader, the one who would save the day. But her? She got her hands dirty and bloody. She made the hard choices that no one else could stomach. And she was *good* at it. But Mal had made some hard choices too, choices that left him with scars. He'd been betrayed by his best friend and the government he'd sworn an oath to, yet instead of hiding away, drowning in his vices, he chose to fight for the world he wanted. And despite giving him every reason to hate her when they'd first met, he extended a level of trust to her that maybe he hadn't done with anyone since Zeln.

What does he see in me, that he's willing to trust me even though he doesn't know the half of the horrible things I've done?

True, he hadn't run away at her story, but Mal deserved someone whose moral compass wasn't constantly spinning around. No, whatever was growing between them, she couldn't indulge it. After hearing more about Zeln, Penny thought she had more in common with him than with Mal. Working outside of the law, pursuing their own goals through questionable means, dipping out when life or their choices got to be too inconvenient, committing heinous acts in the name of "just doing a job." Rodney had bought her loyalty with dust and an outlet for her rage—the two things she'd craved. And she wondered if, maybe, Zeln could be bought too.

They just had to find the right price.

As she settled into the warmth of Mal's body, her thoughts became fuzzy with sleep. She ran through her usual sleepy-time list of reciting everything she planned to do once the world was back to normal. *Drink a good whiskey, take Quentin to Alaska, go surfing in Tahiti...learn how to surf.* But her last thought before drifting off wasn't envisioning herself riding waves in the Pacific. Instead, it was her and Mal, huddled together beside a fire, watching the stars in a pine-scented forest.

29

AS THE FIRST RAYS of sunshine hit the tent, Penny blinked awake. Awareness crept upon her, the steady *thump-thump* of Mal's heart beating beneath her cheek where she splayed across his chest. Her legs were tangled with his, melting into him as if it was the most natural thing in the world. In his sleep, Mal's shirt had rucked up, exposing his chiseled torso. She watched his face, calm and serene as he slept, and she itched to run her fingers through his soft beard or feel the stubble of his fresh haircut rasp across her fingertips.

She must have shifted slightly, because Mal's arm tightened around her and he slowly opened his eyes, looking down at her. And he smiled. For a split second, she forgot everything she was, everything she'd been. She was just...content. At peace. Here, with him.

And then the sound of something banging into a metal pot had both of them catapulting into wakefulness.

"Rise and shine, people!" Quentin shouted. "No time for canoodling when we've got places to be!"

Propped on an elbow, Mal ran a hand through his beard, but she saw the smile hiding underneath. "Kid has terrible timing," he said, donning his layers.

At his comment, that secret feeling she rarely indulged unfurled deep within her, and she avoided looking at him as she pulled on her boots.

Then they clambered out of the tent, where everyone paused in their packing, staring at them. Derek and Quentin had particularly smug looks on their faces, while Silas and Agnes exchanged a knowing glance.

"What?" she demanded as she removed the tent stakes and began deconstructing it.

"How'd you sleep?" asked Quentin, bouncing over to help.

"I'm not answering that."

"Okay. Mal, how'd *you* sleep?" Quentin tried again.

"Just fine," he said neutrally, but again, she saw his small smile.

"*Interesting,*" Quentin said, making quick work of packing up their tent. "Almost like you guys rehearsed that."

Penny rolled her eyes, accepting the bread and dried meat Silas passed around for a quick meal. While everyone else finished packing, Agnes sidled up to Penny with a cup of coffee, which she quickly gulped down as Agnes watched her with a keen gaze.

"Do I have something on my face?" Penny asked, wiping her mouth.

"If you're talking about the *smile* I saw when you walked out of your tent, then yes. You never smile."

"Not *never*," she protested, but she got the point, rearranging her face into a scowl.

Agnes just shook her head and went to the van. "Looks like the grumpy one is soft for the grumpy one," she threw over her shoulder.

Thankfully, nobody else heard that.

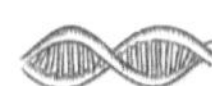

CHICAGO, 5 MILES. Peeling white letters reflected in the sunlight as they blew past the faded green sign. They'd made it before midday, Derek pushing the limits of the EV's battery and patched tires.

Out of the corner of her eye, Penny studied Mal, his gaze trained out the windshield. Quentin was on lookout duty with the binoculars, and it was clear from the set of Mal's brow that he expected things to go to shit—and soon. But a look of...regret pinched the sides of his eyes.

Tugging on his elbow, she pulled his ear down to her level and said, "Chicago's wall getting breached isn't your fault. Tanaka would punch you in the dick for thinking what you're thinking and you know it."

He hoisted an eyebrow, a slight smirk playing at his mouth. "You reading my mind again?"

"What mind?" she quipped.

He surprised her by *chuckling*. It wasn't even one of her better lines. *What the fuck is wrong with us? I'm fucking smiling, apparently, he's chuckling, and we're a few hours away from the biggest battle of our lives.*

But as he looked down at her with a secret smile, all of that faded away, and she wished for nothing more than to be back in that sunny tent, wrapped up with him. Even though she'd sworn to ditch her feelings, that smile shot straight to her center in a way she couldn't ignore.

And maybe she didn't want to ignore it anymore.

As they trundled onward, the atmosphere in the car grew tense and loaded, everyone on edge, but the miles ticked down without event. *We just might make it.* Looking out the window, she noticed an abandoned car with the passenger window shot out.

And then she saw the black-uniformed guard sitting in the front seat, speaking into a satellite phone. *Oh shit.*

"Derek—"

As they passed, an explosion blew them sky-high and they flew through the air. Mal grabbed for Penny and pulled her into him as the van flipped over, tossing them into the ceiling, everyone tumbling around like clothes in a dryer until the van came to a stop on its side.

Disoriented, bleeding from her head, and definitely concussed, Penny crawled to the back door and kicked it open. "Next time, we are getting a van with seat belts for everyone," she said.

Then the rain of ammo came down on them.

Ducking behind the overturned van, Penny spared a cursory glance to make sure everyone was unharmed—covered in cuts and bruises, and she wouldn't be surprised if someone had broken bones, but no one complained as they readied for battle.

"What's the plan?" Derek asked Mal as he powered up his volt rifle.

"We're two miles out." He slid a mag into his M4 and cinched a volt rifle across his back.

"Everyone ready to run like your fucking lives depend on it?" Penny asked. Everyone nodded, but Silas looked scared shitless. Giving his shoulder a squeeze, she said in a low voice, "We've been through worse together. You've got this."

Silas swallowed and nodded, choking up his grip on his rifle like she'd taught him, Quentin slapping him on the back.

Mal peeked around the side of the van, then ducked back as bullets pinged against the metal. "Incoming troops, about twenty or so."

A low rumble vibrated through the pavement behind them, a few black dots appearing in the distance.

"Quentin?" Penny asked. With his binoculars, he looked in the direction of the noise, and his face plummeted.

"Two armored trucks and a Humvee," Quentin said as bullets and volts dinged the van. "We're about to be caught in a troxy sandwich."

"The abandoned cars will provide cover until we get to the wall's fences and sandbags," Mal said. "Partner up and stay low."

As she ran, Penny kept one eye on Quentin and one on Mal, who took up the rear, firing into their pursuers. The vehicles rumbled closer and

Penny sprinted until she saw stars, but the sight of Quentin racing ahead kept her focused, and she fired into the troxies ahead of them, slashing their throats for good measure as she passed.

Ducking behind a car, Penny paused for a second to catch her breath, Silas stopping with her. "You okay?" he shouted over the gunfire.

That's when she saw the woman in the back seat of the sedan, bleeding from her side and shooting a small handgun at the troxies. But then her gun clicked—out of bullets.

Fuck, I do not have time for this.

Penny tapped on the dirty glass, and the dark-haired woman glanced over, blue eyes wide. Before Penny could say anything, the woman kicked the passenger door open, knocking her backwards into Silas's arms.

Fuck this.

The woman landed on top of her, attempting to wrap her neck into a choke hold, but before she or Penny could do any damage, Silas hauled the woman off. Between coughs, Penny managed to splutter, "With Kev. Here to help."

Glass shattered as a bullet caught the car's back window, and the woman threw herself at the ground, taking cover.

"You wanna fucking die?" Penny shouted. "Let's go."

"Can you run?" Silas asked, eyeing the woman's wound.

The woman narrowed her eyes but nodded, and they headed toward the first line of fences.

Almost there. Just a one-hundred-meter dash.

Making it to the fence, the woman climbed over it with skill that implied she had combat training. Silas blinked after her and then followed suit, albeit much less gracefully.

Few more steps—

Something tackled Penny from the side. Skidding across the pavement, a troxy guard rolled atop her. But instead of freezing, the hours of drills she ran with Mal in the arena came back to her. She framed up and kneed him in the balls, ripping off his helmet and dragging her sickle across his exposed face as she scrambled away—directly into Mal's arms.

Helping her up, Mal shoved her ahead of him. "Go!" he said, unloading the rest of his mag into the approaching vehicles.

Finally, they all climbed over the fence and zigzagged their way through the barriers, sprinting for the city's gate less than a mile ahead.

"I hate running!" gasped Quentin as he pushed his gangly legs faster. "I hope they have snacks in Chicago!"

To their left, Penny saw the rest of their group charging down the other side of the highway. But the armored trucks plowed through the fences and barriers. And whoever awaited them at Chicago's gates had weapons raised, ready to fire.

"Don't shoot!" Mal bellowed. "It's General Olesa with reinforcements from the Capital."

Suddenly, a high-pitched whine of a motorcycle engine ripped the air in two, and before Penny knew it, a fleet of dirt bikes peeled into view, weaving through the highway debris straight for the convoy chasing them down.

And the bikers weren't alone.

A large crowd of people armed with an assortment of guns, machetes, bows, and other rudimentary weapons swarmed out of the trees and jumped the guardrail, taking on the remaining troxies and overpowering them.

One woman with wild blonde hair ran over to Penny, shouting, "Jaha sent us!"

I'll be damned. Vick's contacts came through for us.

At the new crew's arrival, the Faction guards at the gate stood down, waving the friendlies through. Once they were behind the safety of the cinder block wall, Penny said to Quentin, "Stay here." She tossed him a knife, and he caught it with a grin. "But listen to the nice man," she said, pointing to one of Mal's former soldiers. Quentin rolled his eyes, and she rolled hers right back as she re-entered the battle.

Vick's people had everything well in hand, crawling over the vehicles like ants. Penny ran to the blonde woman's side, slicing through troxies as she went. "Good timing," Penny said.

"Yeah, you're welcome." The woman grinned through the gore on her face, some of the blood black.

"Turned?" Penny asked.

"They weren't a problem," she replied as she slammed a knife into a throat. "Let's finish this."

The woman was an excellent fighting partner, and between all of them, they decimated every troxy in their path.

"Thanks for the assist. You planning to stick around?" Penny asked, gesturing to the other dirt bikers.

But the woman shook her head, already rounding up her people. "You can take it from here. But we'll be close by keeping watch."

True to the Watchers' namesake.

Chest heaving and slicked with sweat and blood, Penny leaned against the hood of a nearby car as Mal approached, his eyes scanning her for injury. She waved him off, although she had no idea if she was hurt or not, with the gallons of adrenaline pumping through her veins.

"Think we earned our ticket into the city?" Penny asked.

"Without a doubt," he said. "Come on. Kev will want to know about this."

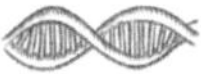

Walking into the ornate lobby of a once fancy hotel, Penny felt wildly out of place in her dirty clothes and combat boots. Not that she gave a fuck. She was just happy to be alive and finally in Chicago. The city looked much like the Capital, with the streets transformed into battlefields and the buildings showing the scars of war.

"You okay?" Mal asked her.

"Body feels like one giant bruise," Penny said, rubbing the back of her neck. She eyed the injured brunette woman they'd rescued, who had remained in a stoic silence as they'd traversed the city, leaning on Derek as she walked. "You good?" she asked her.

"Yes. Sorry for giving you trouble earlier. I'm Naomi. Thanks for bringing me."

"I think the van wreck broke some of my ribs," Silas wheezed. "Running earlier almost killed me."

"General Olesa! You're back," interrupted one of the approaching Faction guards—a pretty young woman with dark brown skin and a gorgeous smile. "Thank fuck for that. We need you."

"Kya. So I've heard," Mal said, sticking out a hand, and she shook it. "But I'm not here to stay. We're in a bit of a hurry, actually. Kev in the war room?"

"Yep." Kya pointed to a lounge located off the lobby. To Silas, she said, "Infirmary on the third floor, if you'd like someone to take a look at your ribs." Shooting Mal another dazzling smile, she waved them along.

"Friend of yours?" Penny whispered as they followed Kya to the war room, something unknown churning within her.

Mal cleared his throat. "Kya is—was my second in command here. I personally recruited and trained her. Guess she's in charge of Kev's troops now."

"Don't think I've ever seen you blush before, Olesa," she said.

Grumbling, Mal pushed open the door into a surprisingly comfortable lounge, decked out with couches, bookshelves, and a large walnut table where a stocky middle-aged Mexican man conversed with several troops. When they entered, he looked up, his eyes crinkling in a smile.

And the anchor of responsibility that had been weighing on Penny for months finally began to feel a bit lighter. She smiled back and said, "Kev Hernandez, as I live and breathe."

"Penny," he said, pulling her into a hug—maybe one of the only people she'd allow to do that. She hugged him back, then stepped away, clapping him on the shoulder. "Wish we were seeing each other under different circumstances," he said, greeting the rest of their people as Penny ran through quick introductions. "General Olesa." He held out a hand, and Mal shook it. "Glad to have you back. We could use your help."

"And we could use yours," Mal said as they took seats around the table.

"Ah, Naomi," Kev said. "I'm sorry they ambushed your departure. It won't happen again. I'll personally escort you this time."

Waving away his concern, Naomi said, "It's okay—Penny helped me." She turned a warm smile to Penny, who wasn't used to people looking at her like that.

"Where were you headed?" Agnes asked, tugging Quentin back into his seat, as he looked ready to wander around the room and play with the various trinkets on the bookshelves.

"I had just finished assessing the situation here in Chicago and was headed to the Capital to get eyes on the ground and report back to Canada," Naomi said.

"Canada?" Mal asked. "Thought we didn't have any options there," he said to Kev.

"Naomi thinks she can persuade them. She's a friend from my private security firm days and has contacts in Canadian special operations. They're not unwilling to hear us out, but we need to show them compelling evidence that this is a war we can win, if we have a little outside help."

Well, shit. Guess it's a good thing I didn't leave her for dead. Having Canada on their side would be a huge asset. But it sounded like it would take an act of god to convince them to intervene. While Vick's civilian contacts and the Watchers were helpful, throwing bodies at the problem wouldn't work forever—especially if they ran out of food, weapons, and supplies. If they couldn't get Canada, Penny had an idea of where they might find some help—but it would send Mal into orbit. *After the meeting, I'll talk to Kev. Alone.*

"I got your SOS transmission that you've been sending on repeat, but it was all garbled and unintelligible," Silas said to Kev.

Kev frowned. "That wasn't from us. We only have short-range radio comms, but our receivers are decent and we picked up something similar. We thought it was from *you*."

"Then who the hell is it from?" Agnes chimed in.

Kev exchanged a glance with Mal, saying, "I haven't heard from my contact on the inside at Pharmatrox since you took out the Spire. If they're in trouble, it could be from them." He gripped the edge of the table, closing his eyes briefly in a rare show of emotion. "And without knowing where they are, we can't help them."

So his contact isn't just a random person. He knows *them.* Penny filed that tidbit away for later.

"So that answers my next question about if your contact has any intel to share," Mal said, shaking his head.

Damn. "How bad is it here?" Penny asked.

"The southeastern section of the city is compromised," Kev said. "We have the troxies contained, but we need more troops and supplies."

"How did the troxies breach the wall in the first place?" Penny asked. "I thought the Faction had Chicago locked down."

"It was—and still is, to a degree," Kev replied. "But the troxies are getting supplies and reinforcements from somewhere. I sent messengers right away to splinter groups without radio comms, calling for aid, but never heard back. I can only assume the messengers are dead, whether by troxy hands or the turned, or whatever other militant groups are out there now. I couldn't afford to lose any more people, so we hunkered down and fought back as best we could. We're at a stalemate now."

"Uh, yeah, about the messengers..." Penny said, and caught him up on everything that happened with Rodney's assassination and the cult. "We made some new civilian allies who are pretty damn good, but our biggest issue is these sound wave–controlled turned." She nodded to Agnes to take over.

"Do you have any enhanced turned here? We think they come from these darts." Agnes rolled one of the dart vials across the table. Kev caught it with his palm and examined it with a grim expression.

"Started seeing these maybe a month ago," Kev said. "Some of our guards were hit. Detox serum didn't work. Those 'enhanced' turned, as you say? The city is crawling with them."

"The darts were manufactured at a lab here in Chicago," Silas said, "so makes sense the troxies are popping these things out like gangbusters."

"That's another reason we came here," said Mal. "Agnes says this lab is their last remaining outpost with all of their servers and everything. We're going to find it, get a cure for the darts, then take it off the map. This could be the killing blow—or at least the start of it, especially if we get help from Canada."

Kev rubbed his short goatee and glanced at his troops. "Pharmatrox has been converging on the city and concentrating their power here recently, so I agree, it sounds like the lab is here. And I'm willing to bet my contact is there too. They're..." He trailed off, clutching the chair's arms in a death grip. *What the hell is going on with him?* "I'm sorry. I can't blow their cover. They're too important."

Important to the war or important to Kev personally? Penny thought it might be both.

"Have you seen any sign of this lab?" Agnes asked. "It would need to be near a power source, so maybe somewhere on the lake's shore? Probably not too large and accessible enough to get their shipments in and out."

"When I first established our presence here," said Kev, "we scouted and mapped the whole city, including the shore, either on foot or with drones. There's a hydroelectric power plant on the lake that keeps some of the buildings supplied with electricity, but we haven't found anything like what you describe."

Kya interjected, saying, "Some guards on night patrol swear they've seen small boats without lights speeding across the lake with their night vision goggles, but it was too fleeting to know for sure. We sent a boat to check it out, but there was nothing there. Not sure what we expected to find in the middle of the lake anyway. That's one angry body of water."

But Silas and Agnes exchanged wide-eyed looks. "Perfect place for a doomsday bunker—where no one would expect to find it."

"Kya is right. The lake is volatile on a good day," Kev said. "Surely it's unlikely they'd put their last-stand final outpost there?"

"'Unlikely' is Pharmatrox's specialty," Agnes said. "I know how Dr. Hansen thinks—thought." After a brief shake of her head, she continued, "It's exactly what they'd do."

"If I could borrow one of your drones, I'll start looking," Silas said. "I'm sure I can find it—I'm pretty good with drones, when they aren't getting shot out of the sky, that is—then we'll plan a stakeout."

"Of course," Kev said. "Kya, can you take him to the hangar?"

The two of them left, Silas rubbing his hands together in excitement. *Nerd.* But where would they be without him?

When Kev spoke again, he looked more tired than Penny had ever seen him. "We're holding strong, but we need to finish this war—soon. If this lab is truly what you say it is and we destroy it, the Canadian emissary will see this as evidence that Pharmatrox is crippled enough that their assistance will bring this violence to an end."

"Spoken like a true diplomat," Naomi teased, but her smile was good-natured.

Kev sighed but returned the smile. "I could never have imagined that my small group of protestors would grow into...this."

"If by 'this' you mean 'this amazing group of good-looking people who absolutely kick butt,' then I'm with you," said Quentin.

"Of course. That is definitely what I meant." Kev gave him a bland smile, and everyone chuckled. "We'll take the rest of the day to scout out the lab's location and come up with a plan of attack. I'm sure General Olesa is eager to return to the Capital."

Out of the corner of her eye, Penny saw Mal flinch. *Shit. Is he worried about leaving Vick and the Watchers in charge at home? Or is he feeling guilty about how things went to hell here in Chicago?*

"There are extra rooms upstairs," Kev continued. "Someone will show you." With that, everyone was dismissed.

Penny hung back. "Kev? A word, if you don't mind." She dropped her voice. "Ah, alone."

Kev quirked a brow but nodded as everyone filed outside. Mal waited by the door, and Kev motioned him out. With a concerned look at Penny, Mal left and shut the double doors behind him. "What's on your mind?" Kev asked.

"I have another idea for how we can get some assistance. We won't need to directly establish contact with other nations or worry about being overly reliant on our new civilian allies," she said, tapping her fingernail against the table.

"I sense there's a 'but.'"

"But Mal won't like it."

Kev chuckled. "Mal doesn't like most things. Except for..." He trailed off, giving Penny a look. "Well. Anyway. You were saying?"

Ignoring that. "When you ran your own security firm, did you ever come across a mercenary named Zeln?"

Kev's expression wiped blank as he steepled his fingers under his chin. "I have not seen him in many years."

"So you know him."

"I hired him for many jobs. Bodyguard, extraction, courier. He is excellent and—ah. I see where this is going. And I see why Malosi failed to bring it up in the meeting."

So he knows about their history too. "Is he excellent enough to help us win this war?"

"He is one of the most connected mercenaries in the field, and he would be an asset. My contacts are doing what they can, but they're nowhere near as plugged in as he is. Getting Zeln on our side would open up a lot of doors, especially in other nations if things with Canada fall through. I know he gets on well with the Samaris. They could be a major supplier of ammunition, fuel, food—everything we need to win. It's an appealing idea. But I'm sensing there's a problem beyond Mal's objections, or else you would have already done something about this."

He always was able to see right through me. "He's fighting for Pharma-trox."

Kev shrugged. "He is a mercenary. He's on the side of the highest bid-der. Trust me on this. I have worked with many just like him. I *was* one for many years." Kev tapped his fingers against his thigh, contemplating. Finally, he said, "I don't have high hopes for Canada, if I'm being honest. And I am sure Zeln has some way to contact his allies. He'd be useless to the troxies otherwise. Find out what he wants, and give it to him—if it's within reason."

"I'll take care of it as soon as we get back," she said.

"Gracias, mija, for bringing this to me," he said, patting her arm. "I am grateful to have you on my side."

Kev's compliment was nice, but it did little to thaw the orb of ice forming in her belly. As she walked out of the lounge to find her room, she couldn't help but feel like she'd just hammered the first nail into the coffin of her relationship with Mal if she chose to continue on this path.

30

WHEN PENNY ARRIVED AT her assigned room on the third floor, Agnes awaited her. "You have a plan, don't you?" Agnes asked.

"I have a plan," Penny admitted.

"Will it work?"

"It might."

Agnes stared her down for a moment, then nodded, twisting the door handle and pushing it open. A sound like a chainsaw came from within. "What the hell is that?" Penny asked, peeking inside. And then her heart melted. Quentin, splayed across the spare twin bed, snoring.

"He wanted to bunk with you," Agnes said, her mouth turning up as she watched him.

"He did?" she asked in disbelief.

Agnes nodded. "You know, he wouldn't be prepared for any of this if it weren't for you." She paused, chewing her lip. "And I wouldn't be either. Your training in the early days, teaching me how to use this"—she tapped the machete in her belt—"it saved my life."

Penny blinked. "I tried to kill you. Multiple times."

"And yet you're the reason Tara and I walked out of that barn, and that Derek came back from the Wilds, and Silas at the Spire. All of that adds up. Look, Penny. I've seen a change in Quentin since you've been trying with him—a good one. He's happier, even when he's still finding it hard to forgive you for what you did. But there's no doubt in my mind—that kid loves you. And he wants you around. That's good enough for me. It should be good enough for you too."

Something caught in Penny's throat. *Fucking hell, not in front of her.*

"Anyway. Check this out," Agnes said, reaching behind Penny and flicking the light switch a few times. To her surprise, it turned on and off. "I know, right?" Agnes said to Penny's wide-eyed expression. "Hydroelectric power plant Kev mentioned. You know what that means—*hot water.*"

"Oh fuck yes," Penny said, nearly collapsing on the spot.

"Enjoy," Agnes said. "We're reconvening with Silas soon to see how his drone search is going."

With that, Agnes left Penny to her religious experience of a shower.

As the hot water scalded her skin, Penny was at war with herself. Part of her felt guilty for going behind Mal's back and suggesting an alliance with his sworn enemy. But the practical part of her said that wars were messy and they couldn't be picky about their allies, especially if those allies could help them win. She wanted there to be another option besides buying off Zeln, and she would do her damnedest to find one. But if they were backed into a corner and things got even worse, she'd make Zeln an offer. She had to.

That flimsy justification was enough for her to put the thoughts behind her and shut off the water, donning her black tactical outfit. Quentin was still snoozing when she stepped out into the hallway in search of Kev's armory to gear up.

Bumping directly into the one person she'd just banished from her mind.

"Mal," she said as he exited from his own room. Right next to hers. *Of course.*

"Hey," he said, pulling his door shut and nodding to her wet hair. "Enjoy the hot water?"

From his freshly trimmed beard and hair, she could tell he had enjoyed the hot water too. And *those* kinds of thoughts made her insides warm in a way that had her skin prickling underneath of her layers. "Um, yep," she said, hoping to fuck that she was *not* blushing.

"What did you talk to Kev about?" he asked.

Cutting right to the chase, I see. "Just war plans—er, Rodney stuff. I mean, nothing important." *Very convincing. Jesus Christ, change the fucking subject.* "How's it feel to be back in Chicago?"

Mal's expression tightened as he ran a hand through his beard. "Really fucking bad, to be honest." *Well shit.* "It feels like I abandoned my troops again and left them to their fate while I ran toward better things."

Fuck me, I am so bad at talking. But she tried again. "This isn't the same as when you defected from Pharmatrox. And when you left Chicago for the Capital and stayed, it was because Kev ordered you to, not because you were running from something."

"Doesn't matter the reason though, does it? I left, and Pharmatrox breached the wall. My soldiers died. I should have been here for them. And now, I've left my soldiers behind in the Capital. I know the Watchers can hold us for a few days and everything is fine. But I can't help but think...what if it's not?"

"Things won't fall apart in a few days, Mal."

"That's all it took for things to fall apart here."

"Things aren't 'falling apart.' They're getting back on track."

But Mal rebuffed her. "I'm needed here." He blew out a breath, looking abashed. "But I'm needed in the Capital too."

"Fair enough." Having dated a few military guys, she knew how their training affected them, so she could understand why he felt torn. But the thought of him staying behind in Chicago and leaving her to lead things in the Capital on her own had her wanting to dig herself into a deep, dark hole. "So what are you saying? You want to go back to the Capital right now? Or are you trying to relocate here permanently?" She wasn't sure what answer she expected, but it wasn't the one she got.

"I don't know," he admitted, thrusting a hand through his hair, conflict warring across his face. "I—it's fucking *hard*."

A frosty feeling of fear flooded through her veins, straight to her heart. *I can't lead the Capital by myself.* Her chest tightened, and a riptide of panic threatened to pull her under. And just like that, the walls that he'd begun to break through were back up again, and she crossed her arms in an attempt to hold herself together. Blitzed by the sudden torrent of emotion, she lashed out.

"Maybe you should stay here, if you feel like you're *needed*." The lie tasted bitter on her tongue, but she couldn't ask him to stay with her. Wouldn't. Not this time. Because after the way his face lit up at being reunited with Kya and his troops, seeing how well he fit in here, how conflicted he was about leaving, she didn't know if he'd say yes.

And somehow, that was more terrifying than leading a war by herself.

She moved to shove past him, but he snagged her arm, spinning her into him and catching her by the waist. Her hands fell to his chest, and she wasn't sure if it was to push him away or pull him closer. Her heart throbbed in her throat, and those golden eyes held her captive as he said, "Pen, I—"

"You guys ready to head out soon?" Derek said from the end of the hall, holding a small arsenal of weapons. Penny stepped away from Mal, but she didn't miss the smug look on Derek's face as she did so.

"Yeah," Penny said. "We're coming." She turned to say something to Mal, but he was already disappearing down the hall.

"I won't make it to the stakeout with Silas. I need to speak with Kev," he said over his shoulder, offering no other explanation.

Derek frowned. "I've never seen Mal look so constipated before."

Penny lifted a brow. "Traveling will do that to you, I guess."

"No, not *literally* constipated, Penny. Jesus. *Emotionally* constipated."

"The fuck are you getting at?"

Derek narrowed his eyes at her. "What were you talking about before I walked up?"

"About his role in the war."

"And what did you tell him?"

"I didn't tell him anything."

He laughed, saying, "I find it hard to believe that you, one of the most outspoken women I have ever met, did not have an opinion to share."

Scoffing, she said, "I told him things aren't as bad here as they seem."

"Hmm, no. Things *are* pretty bad here, but that's not it."

"What's not it?"

"Something else has him pissed off. Besides me interrupting him flirting with you, I mean."

"What—I—he was *not*—"

"Oh, Penny, he was. He's *always* flirting with you, in his big, brutish way. But no, something else you said set him off."

"I told him that he should stay here."

"Yep. There it is."

"He's being a bone head."

"So are you. You don't want him to stay, so ask him to go back with us. He will. He listens to you."

"This is a pointless conversation," she said, shoving him down the hallway. "We're wasting time. This stake won't out itself."

"Taking notes from Quentin's book of quips, I see," Derek said. "But like it or not, you've gotten your way under Mal's skin. Hope you're ready to deal with the consequences."

That strange yet familiar feeling stirred deep within her, rising closer to the surface with each moment she spent with Mal.

I am well and truly fucked.

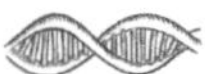

Mal didn't show up for the stakeout.

Penny tried not to care, but inside, she was boiling. No one had seen him since he'd left earlier to talk to Kev. They were still in their secret meeting, discussing whatever Mal had deemed so important that he needed to bail on their mission. She tried to be understanding, but part of her wondered if maybe he was finalizing his plans to remain in Chicago.

"It seems I'm cursed to always have my drones shot out of the sky," Silas lamented as she, Agnes, Derek, and Quentin piled into an EV with Kya and headed toward Navy Pier.

"We went from 'it's somewhere on this state-sized lake' to a much smaller search radius, so I'd call that a success," Agnes said, patting him on the shoulder.

"And Kev will forgive you for losing the drone," Kya said. "No biggie."

"If he's just giving drones away, do you think he'd let me crash one too?" Quentin asked, and Kya chuckled.

"I did not *crash* it, you punk," Silas grumbled.

Silas had spent all day flying the drone around the lake, searching areas that his GIS analysis indicated had the right water depth and current to accommodate a structure or floating vessel.

Until the drone had been shot down four or five miles offshore—confirming their suspicions.

Someone was up to something out there, and they didn't want anyone else to know about it.

"You okay?" Derek asked her ten minutes later when they reached the waterfront and piled out of the car.

"Fine," Penny said. But she felt anything but fine. Ready to bash some fucking heads in is what she felt like.

Kya led them to the pier, where a small deck boat with an open bow and a few seats in the back awaited them. They climbed aboard and took off. At the late hour, the wind whipping off the lake was frigid, and Penny pulled her coat tighter around her. "How long of a ride is it?" she asked. A storm was brewing, and she didn't want to be caught in the lake on rough waters.

"About twenty minutes," Kya said.

"Colder than a witch's britches," Quentin said as he fiddled with the new toy Kya had given him—night vision goggles. They all had a pair. "I'm keeping these. They're awesome," he added to Kya, who laughed.

The boat's motor was silent because of some new technology Penny didn't understand as they sped toward the location where the drone had been shot down. Finally, Kya cut the motor. In a low voice, she said, "This is the spot."

They settled in to wait. During their journey, the wind had kicked up and the boat rocked a bit more than Penny was comfortable with, making it hard to keep a steady eye out for the ghost boats Kya's guards had seen.

After a while, Kya joined her in the bow. She was silent for a few minutes before she said what was on her mind. "General Olesa would never abandon you," she said as she looked through her goggles.

The abrupt statement caught Penny off guard. "What are you talking about?"

Still looking through her goggles, she said, "You're his people, his troops. He'll be there for you when it counts. Don't be so quick to believe the worst about people."

Penny ground her teeth as she scanned the water, making a noncommittal sound. They fell into silence after that.

Kya had a point, but Penny had seen the very worst in people, the very worst in *herself*. Both since the Beginning and well before it. But hardships could bring out the best in people too. Maybe she did need to have a little more faith in Mal. *But this is different.* She'd begun to open herself up to him in ways she'd never even thought could crack before. The thought of him leaving her behind, even after all of that, injected her heart with a bone-chilling ice, hardening her against him. She needed to abandon whatever feelings she thought she had for Mal. They were nothing more than a distraction, and in battle, she couldn't afford that. Especially if she had to lead the Faction in the Capital alone.

"A boat," Quentin said. "Heading that way."

Suddenly, a shape flashed across her goggles. "Another one. Going the same way. Follow it," Penny instructed Kya. "We're taking those boats."

Kya cranked the key, and the boat jetted forward on its silent motor as thunder rumbled in the distance. The storm would be the perfect cover for a couple of troxy boats gone missing—their tickets into the lab.

Quentin settled next to Penny to keep an eye out. "This is so cool. I feel like I'm in Call of Duty."

Penny tugged him back as he leaned too far over the side. "Butt on seat," she said. "Unless you want to fall overboard and become a human popsicle."

"Depends on what flavor," he said. "I like the red, white, and blue ones."

"Firecrackers?" Silas said, joining them. "Fitting for our little pyromaniac."

As the boat gained, the shapes in Penny's goggles drew closer. They looked like the smaller boats she'd seen in military commercials, built for speed rather than hauling supplies.

Agnes must have noticed the same thing. "Maybe that's what they use to get their darts and troxapine to shore."

"What's our play?" Kya asked.

"I think we're at the point of 'shoot first, ask questions later,'" Penny said. "We don't know for sure it's the troxies, but they can't be the good guys. Pull up between them. Shoot the drivers first. Should slow them down enough for us to jump over and take the boats. Kya? Seems like something you'd be good at."

"Absolutely," said Kya, already checking the charge on her volt rifle. "Quentin, you get to drive. No crashing."

"Oh *yes*," he said, jumping for the steering wheel.

In less than a minute, the two boats came into view with the naked eye.

Then the volts started flying.

Kya shot the drivers, taking them out in one go, while the others shot the boat's occupants and Quentin pulled between them. Silas and Penny jumped across to one boat while Derek and Agnes took the other, with Kya laying down cover fire.

Penny's boat had four guards and she made fast work of them, knives lodging home, while Silas covered her. In the moonlight, she could make out their uniforms. *Double helix insignias.*

When the sounds of struggle from the other boat ceased, Penny called across in a soft voice, "They're troxies."

"Ours too," Derek replied. "Tracking device under the steering column. I already tossed ours in the lake."

Silas heard the instructions and got to work, removing the device and smashing it with the butt of his gun, then lobbing it as far as he could. Checking under the seats, Penny came across a square black bag that looked like a cooler. When she unzipped the lid, a rush of vindication surged through her.

Agnes had been right.

"We've got darts over here," Penny said.

"Us too," Agnes called back. "Save those! I want to study them later."

Holy shit. This is it. We found it.

Well—they'd at least found a way to sneak into the lab and check it out. The hard part was yet to come.

"Let's get back and regroup," Derek said. "We'll use these boats to come back tomorrow night and head farther into the search area. Silas, maybe you could fly another drone and scope it out. If there are any left, anyway, after you broke them all." Derek's chuckle was cut off by Silas's elbow to the ribs.

After they finished shoving the bodies overboard, they lashed the boats together to tow them back to shore.

"I can't believe you were right about all of it," Penny said to Agnes as the wind whipped around them.

"Yeah. I expected something to go horribly wrong."

"Don't worry. There's still plenty of chances for things to go horribly wrong," Quentin supplied cheerfully as he scanned the shoreline with his goggles. Kya was back at the helm.

His comment had been in jest, but Penny felt unsettled. A lot of things needed to go right tomorrow for this infiltration to be a success. They had capable people on their side. They could do it.

But that dark, secret part of her wondered if Mal would be there when it counted.

31

T HE FOLLOWING EVENING, DRESSED in her stolen troxy uniform, Penny slid the last knife into her belt as she prepared for the evening's infiltration in the hotel's armory.

They'd planned as much as they could. Silas had caught sight of "some kind of dark, suspicious blob" with the drone's camera earlier, providing a clearer direction of where they needed to go. Kya and another group would accompany them with other boats, hanging back in case they ran into trouble. But Penny was nervous as fuck going into this mission tonight. Because if shit went too sideways? Well. They were stuck in the middle of a fucking lake.

All day, there'd been no sign of Mal, or Kev, for that matter. But Kev had a lot on his plate, stuck in a long meeting with the Canadian emissary offsite somewhere. Mal, however? She had no fucking idea what he was up to, and that...*shit.* That scared her. If Mal chose to stay behind, it would mark the end of whatever was going on between them—and she wasn't sure if she was ready to close the door on that, even though she'd told herself many times to ignore it and stay focused. *Yeah, I did a great job of that.*

Behind her, the armory door opened and closed. *Probably Derek.* Without looking back, she said, "Where are the LED flashlights? I can't find them."

"Locker to the left."

Penny froze as the timbre of his voice washed over her, her brain stumbling. Slowly, she turned.

And there he was.

Mal, dressed in stolen troxy gear, strapped and ready. And the way he looked at her...*Jesus.* Something ignited within him—his carefully curated facade opened up into something...hungry. Something wild. Eyes latched to hers, she saw a peek beneath the surface into the raw emotion roiling underneath, and damn if she didn't want him to unleash it.

"Nice of you to make time for us in your busy schedule of secret meetings," she said, and a thunderous expression rolled across his face. She was being petty, but she didn't care, and he continued staring at her with that intense expression that had her on edge—in a good or bad way, she wasn't sure.

"What did you speak to Kev about yesterday after we first got here?" The...irascible look on his face told her that maybe he already knew.

Her stomach plummeted into her toes, but she had some fucking questions of her own. "I have one five-minute conversation with the guy, and I'm the one on trial? *You* disappeared as soon as we got here. Where the hell have you been?"

He allowed her deflection, but his sharp look said they'd be circling back to it later. "I was meeting with Kev all night and the emissary for part of today. I just got back, but Kev is still with them."

Parking her hands on her hips, she said, "If things are bad enough here to warrant an all-day, all-night meeting, maybe you should stay. We can handle the infiltration ourselves." Flinching at how snarky she sounded, she lowered her hands. She'd genuinely meant it, but with every breath, the fragments of fear pierced her lungs like shards of glass.

In a few deliberate strides, he crossed the room and slid a finger into her belt loop, tugging her into him. "You really think it would be so easy for me to drop everything and leave you—leave *all* of you—to fight one of our biggest battles alone? Is that what you truly think of me?" Her heart galloped, and she was certain he could hear it as his golden eyes burned into her, spearing her to the spot. "I'm not fucking going anywhere—not without you."

Before she could even process his words, he fisted the hair at the nape of her neck and crushed his mouth to hers.

The touch of his lips sent electricity pumping through her veins, surging within her in a way unlike anything she'd ever experienced. She'd kissed her fair share of men, but she'd never been kissed by a man like Malosi Olesa. A man who was her equal and her opposite. A man who *saw her* for exactly who she was and didn't shy away from it. A man who held her like she wouldn't break, who kissed her like he'd been holding himself back for months.

And she had to admit, she'd been holding herself back too. But in that moment, all of her inhibitions evaporated with the explosive force of their union. Everything else faded away until the only thing she thought or felt or smelled or touched was *him*.

Grabbing the front of his shirt, she hauled him closer as he backed her into the wall. She reveled in the feeling of every part of him molding against her, of his strong hands gripping her tighter, *tighter*. The kiss took on an edge of desperation—after fighting this thing between them for so long, it felt so good to finally give in and let go, to feel his silken tongue against hers, the surprising softness of his lips punctuated by the sharpness of his teeth as he nipped at her lower lip.

The heat from his skin burned through his shirt as she traced her fingers along the dips of his muscled torso, enjoying when she heard his breath hitch. As he made a deep sound of satisfaction against her mouth, something within her pulsed, calling out for him, for *more*.

But as soon as she had the thought, awareness crept back in, and she realized what she was doing. Who she was doing it with.

She broke away with a gasp, the cold stone of the wall behind her anchoring her back to reality. Touching a hand to her damp and swollen lips, she looked up at Mal.

And she'd never seen anything more beautiful in her life. He looked at her like he was seeing sunshine for the first time. Reaching out, she ran her fingertips across his beard as she'd thought of doing so many times, and he smiled. Like *really* smiled. Full pearly whites and everything. *He has dimples. I never knew.* It broke her heart just a little to see the effect she had on him as she remembered every harsh thought she'd ever had about him. A man who looked at her like that was not someone who would ever abandon her, no matter what happened. *And that's the scariest fucking thing I could ever conceive of.*

I don't deserve someone like that. I would ruin them.

I will ruin him.

Then the door banged open, interrupting them, and her fist tightened in his shirt. "Penny, do you—oh. Mal. Penny and Mal." Derek blinked as he processed the sight of them entangled together, and Penny shoved Mal away. She didn't miss the frown that darkened Mal's brow as she did so. "Right. Well it's about fucking time. Congrats and all that. Mal, need your big muscley muscles to load up the gear. Time to go."

"Right," Mal said, following Derek outside.

As she trailed her fingers across her lips, processing what the fuck had just happened, Mal caught her eye, his expression fierce and unreadable, before turning away.

Unworthy, said the dark voice in her mind. *You will ruin him.*

She shoved the thought aside, locking it up tightly, all the while knowing it would return to slice her up.

As their boats sped across the water toward the lab's suspected location, Penny fidgeted with her sickle, squirming under the magnitude of what they were about to do. Winning this war hinged on how tonight's infiltration went. If they failed, Pharmatrox would only continue to grow more powerful.

So no pressure whatsoever.

It didn't help that her earlier...encounter with Mal had rattled her to her core—and she slammed the brakes on that train of thought before it could plunge off a cliff. The team needed her focused, *not* worrying about whatever was going on between her and Mal. Her gaze slid over the distraction in question as the moonlight reflected on the planes of his face. Mal caught her staring and lifted a brow, but she looked away. *Focus.*

Quentin scooted closer to Penny on the bench seat, interrupting her thoughts. "So. Did you swoon and fall into the loving embrace of his big, meaty arms? Did his brooding gaze penetrate you into the depths of your very soul?"

Penny choked back begrudging laughter. "Derek is such a gossip queen."

"Agnes told me, actually."

Nudging his shoulder, she said, "Mind your own business."

He shrugged, then meandered over to pester Derek.

They'd nearly arrived in the approximate location of Silas's designated search zone, the adrenaline pumping through her in overdrive. From his position at the steering wheel, Mal said, "Everyone ready?"

"'Kill everyone and burn the place to the ground' is a pretty simple plan, so I'd say yes," said Derek, shouldering his volt rifle. At Mal's deadpan expression, Derek heaved a sigh. "*Okay.* I'll stay with Quentin and help him rig up his fireworks display to blow when we're ready. Silas will search their system for the server farm and take it out while the rest of you look for the cure. Guards and soldiers are fair game, and if anyone else shoots at us, we shoot back. With the lab being so hard to reach, anyone in it went to great lengths to get there and stay there. So probably no amnesty for anyone on this trip."

"But they could be trapped like the scientists Silas and I found in the basement," Agnes reminded them. "So see if they're willing to help us before, uh, taking drastic measures. Even better if we can find Kev's contact—if keeping their identity secret is so important, they're probably higher up the chain of command, and maybe they can point us straight to the cure."

"And if not, we can improvise. Penny is great at that," Derek said.

She appreciated the vote of confidence, but something about this whole situation felt not quite right. But she chalked it up to nerves and the fact that Mal had *kissed her* earlier.

"We're in the search zone," Silas said, signaling to Kya's boat. "Look out for our spooky, mysterious blob."

Everyone grabbed a pair of night vision goggles and scanned the darkness. The water was rough tonight and made maintaining a solid grip on the goggles a challenge. Luckily she didn't get sea sick or else she'd be barfing over the side right about now.

A half hour passed as they plunged through the waves, desperately searching the area. When a wave crashed over the bow, she was ready to call it off and try again tomorrow, but then she saw it. "Silas! The spooky blob," she said, pointing in the distance. Looking through his own binoculars, he grinned. He saw it too.

Mal steered toward it, Kya's boat following. A few minutes later, the moonlight caught the shape of a big black building on platform situated ten feet above the water. As they approached, a ramp lowered beneath the structure, the deep red light within bathing the water's surface, and Kya's boat fell back into the shadows.

Penny and Mal exchanged a glance. "Automatic sensors somewhere on the boat?" he suggested. As he maneuvered them up the ramp, Penny couldn't help but feel like they were entering the belly of an unknown beast.

The boat stopped in a hangar and the ramp lifted behind them, water pouring off the sides, enclosing them within. Several guards waited on the platform as the red lights switched to bright fluorescent ones, illuminating the double helix insignia on their lapels. Troxy guards. *This is it. Their doomsday bunker.*

"Your tracking beacons are busted," one of the guards said to Mal. "What the hell happened last night? Get caught in that storm?"

"Something like that," Mal said. But his smile held an edge. Faster than a blink, he sliced his knife across the man's throat, blood spurting and steaming in the cold air.

Penny and the rest sprang into action. She went for the guard closest to the door, slashing his throat open before he could raise the alarm. In less than thirty seconds, they'd dispatched all of the guards.

Once Agnes and Silas hacked into the facility's security system, Silas pulled up a 3D model of the building while Agnes disabled the cameras.

Silas expanded the glowing blue web so they could all see, and Derek leaned in, pointing at a large space in the center surrounded by dozens of other rooms. "That looks like their lab. They'd want to keep it protected, make it harder to reach."

"What about their servers?" asked Agnes.

Silas typed a few quick commands on the holographic keyboard floating before him. "Huge power draw in the northwest quadrant. Has to be there. I'll scan the servers for anything relevant to troxapine or detox serum, put it on my holofiles, then destroy the bastards. Get going," he said, shooing them away.

"Be careful," Penny added in a whisper to Quentin.

He rolled his eyes. "I'm not trying to blow my face off. Derek will make sure I don't."

"If you're made, get back to the boat and signal Kya," said Mal. "Let's make this quick."

Even at the late hour, troxy scientists in white lab coats orbited the halls, absorbed in their digital clipboards. As they passed, Penny held her breath, but the scientists passed without comment.

But their luck didn't hold out.

At the end of the hall, a group of guards turned the corner, and Penny stiffened. *Must have noticed we cut the camera feeds.* Before they got too close, Agnes swiped a card at one of the doors and pulled them inside.

"My old Pharmatrox ID," she said. "Silas gave my credentials access to the security system earlier."

"Who are you?" said someone behind them.

Penny turned to a room filled with dozens of people in thin medical robes. Their bones protruded at sharp angles, their faces gaunt with malnourishment. The frail man who'd spoken looked half dead, his deep purple veins showing through translucent skin.

More human lab rats for the troxies to poke and prod.

Penny's rage roared to life at the reminder that Dr. Hansen had done the same to Quentin. "We have to help them," she said to Mal.

"We will. But if we let them out now, it'll blow our cover. We'll get them on our way out."

Knowing he was right, she could only concede. Agnes peeked out the door and said, "All clear."

"We'll be back for you," Penny said to the man, who watched them with a suspicious gaze as they filed outside.

"Double doors to the left. That's the lab," Agnes said. Sliding her card through the reader, they burst inside, weapons drawn.

"Hands up, everyone!" Penny said.

But these ten or so scientists weren't as compliant—or as un-armed—as she'd anticipated. Pulling out weapons, they fired without hesitation.

Penny dove behind a lab table, returning fire as Mal slid beside her. "Cover me!" she said, then rushed the nearest troxy, slicing his windpipe as Agnes joined her. Any empathy she might have held for these people evaporated the moment she saw the room of prisoners. This lab had one purpose and one purpose only—to create and perfect their poison. And none of these people were innocent.

They'd almost cut down the last scientist when someone entered the lab from the other side.

"Dr. Chun!" the last remaining scientist said, limping over to the slim, dark-haired middle-aged woman. "Thank god you're here. They—"

The newcomer—Dr. Chun—pulled a handgun from her lab coat and shot the scientist in the head, point blank. He fell to the ground, blood spraying. "Fuck," Dr. Chun said as she surveyed Penny and the rest, arms crossed. "I was hoping it wasn't true. You idiots. You left the Capital unattended?"

What the...?

Beside Penny, Agnes's jaw hit the floor.

"Dr. Chun?" Agnes said in disbelief. "How—what the *fuck* is going on?"

"You know her?" Penny asked.

The woman pocketed her weapon and smoothed her lab coat lapels. "Dr. Wanda Chun, Head of Experimental Pharmaceuticals at Pharmatrox. And you people are about to have a serious fucking problem on your hands."

32

Agnes

B LOOD DRIPPED DOWN AGNES's blade, *pat-patting* on the floor as she blinked at Dr. Chun. Evie's boss. The woman at the forefront of troxapine's development. Having only met her a few times, the only impression Agnes had was what she'd heard from Dr. Hansen and Evie—that of a dedicated and hard-working woman who would stop at nothing to further her own agenda, much like Dr. Hansen.

But Dr. Chun had just shot her own employee in the head.

And with it, Agnes's preconceived notions about the woman.

"What are you talking about?" Agnes said, her voice sounding as if it was squeezing through a tunnel.

"Ah, excellent. I'm as good of an actress as I think I am," Dr. Chun said. "I'm not surprised Ingrid poisoned you against me. Can't say I was sorry to hear about her death. I wish it made a difference in all of this mess, but at least she's gone. Oh. Sorry. Probably shouldn't speak ill of your mentor, but since you shot her in the head, I imagine you came to realize how abhorrent she was."

Agnes could only blink, uncomprehending.

"What's this about us leaving the Capital 'unattended'? What do you know?" Mal asked as he watched the exchange through narrowed eyes.

"Pharmatrox troops armed with a new set of darts will be converging on the Capital any day now," Dr. Chun replied. "They sent the orders a few days ago. I was unable to prevent it or get word out to Kev in time, what with being trapped on this godforsaken lily pad."

"To *Kev*?" Penny said, then blinked. "You're Kev's top-secret contact."

"Yes. Kev is my husband."

Husband?

"Your—? Kev's not married," Mal said with a suspicious look.

"Of course we couldn't be married on paper. We're not morons—Pharmatrox tracks things like that. We've been together for fifteen years. I met him when he was on one of his reconnaissance missions and I was a lab tech. I knew Pharmatrox would fire me if they found out my affiliation with someone like him—they choose their employees very carefully and would not want someone who could be compromised.

"At first, I was like you, Agnes. I thought I was working toward a better future. But when I rose to the head of EP, I found out what Pharmatrox was really doing. I wanted to rejoin Kev, but then I realized I had more ability to aid the war by being his woman on the inside.

"The troxies think I am their prisoner, their loyal lackey, but I've been slowing them down, sabotaging them, feeding Kev information. Although since I've been relocated here, the only thing I've managed to send is scrambled up nonsense." *The garbled transmission Silas intercepted—it was from Chun?* "I have a trusted guard who assists me, but activities here are closely monitored. Also, where the fuck am I?"

"About seven miles into Lake Michigan," Penny answered. "Close to Chicago."

Dr. Chun said something else, but Agnes didn't hear, her head spinning from the sheer amount of questions filling it. The more she thought about it, the more sense it made. Of course the true head of Pharmatrox, the Leader, would mislead Agnes into thinking that someone else—Dr. Chun, in this case—was the one behind Pharmatrox's deranged agenda. Dr. Hansen had done nothing but spout lies and twist the truth. So why would she have been telling the truth about Dr. Chun's role? *Plain and simple—maybe she hadn't been. And maybe Dr. Chun really is on our side.*

"What is this place?" Agnes asked as she surveyed the room that looked exactly like their New York lab.

"Pharmatrox's last chance to complete their fucked-up plans to turn the population into mindless, obedient weapons."

I was right. This is everything we need to save Tara and Ivan. "So you have the troxapine formulas here? Detox serum too?" Agnes didn't even try to hide the desperation in her voice. "And a cure for whatever is in the darts?"

"There are a few vials of detox serum in there." Dr. Chun pointed to a cabinet, and hope swelled within Agnes as she pocketed them. "But it will only work against specific strains of troxapine. The darts...that's what's fucking odd," she said, and Agnes didn't like the troubled expression on her face. "There's no cure for the darts. Not that I know of."

A rushing sound filled Agnes's ears as she failed to compute what Dr. Chun had said.

"What?" Mal snapped.

"No," Agnes said as the wheels of her mind began turning. "That's not possible. Evie told me Pharmatrox procedures always called for some kind of antidote to whatever they were working on, for testing and safety purposes, or in case of emergencies—right?"

"You're correct, that is standard policy," Chun said. "But nothing about the darts is standard. I'm telling you, *there is no antidote for this,* and it's had me slamming the panic button. Pharmatrox is all about order. But they broke protocol. I don't know who's in charge anymore since I've been trapped here, but something strange is going on, and I think it's centered on the Capital."

"So, what—our people who got darted are just going to turn, and that's it? There's nothing we can do?" Agnes's voice rose as the panic ignited within her, thoughts of Tara and Ivan sprinting through her mind.

"I haven't just been sitting here worrying myself into a stomach ulcer," Chun said. "I've been working on a cure under the radar since Pharmatrox clearly isn't interested in creating one and I don't want to out myself. Here are my notes." She tossed her a holofile, and Agnes almost collapsed from relief, catching the black chip that would be their savior. She'd been carrying this burden alone for so long, but now, she had help. "Don't get too excited," Chun said. "It's basically a nothing burger, but it's better than a nothing nothing. This was always Evie's area of expertise, but I built off of what she started with her original idea for dionazole. But this is where I need you—your DNA editing machine. Do you think it can help us find a cure?"

"Way ahead of you," Agnes said. "I'm almost finished with the modifications, but I need an FPGA to program it. Do you have anything like that here?"

"The server room. Rip one out before you torch the place."

De puta madre, this is great. A dim ray of hope flickered within her as she grabbed the radio at her hip, giving quick instructions for Silas to do just that.

"But as I was saying earlier," Dr. Chun continued, "we have much bigger problems. Pharmatrox has been able to hold New York because it's getting supplied by foreign countries."

"Like that tanker we saw docked on our way out of the city," Agnes noted. "How the hell were they able to get other nations' support?"

A grim expression darkened Dr. Chun's face. "Like this."

Pulling a holofile from her pocket, she clicked it on and a video archive of the international newsfeed projected in the air. As the various footage of bombings, battles, explosions, *murder* flashed before their eyes, Agnes's anger at the injustice of it all burned deep within her. Because it wasn't a true depiction of the events as they had occurred—it was Pharmatrox's propaganda painting the Faction as domestic terrorists.

"You may have killed the network and the life force of Pharmatrox's internal functions, but they found a way to continue broadcasting their bullshit to the rest of the world—one of their outside allies, I imagine, aided them in getting this doctored footage out."

"Explains why Kev is having such a hard time getting Canada's help," Mal said, eyes glued to the projected atrocities. "Nobody wants to side with people who they think kill kids and bomb hospitals. This has to be a result of Zeln's consulting."

Out of the corner of her eye, Agnes caught Penny watching the scene with a strange expression, like she'd known something like this could happen. *I'll need to ask about that later.*

"Don't know who the hell that is, but none of that is the most impending issue," Dr. Chun said. For the first time in the course of the conversation, she looked apprehensive. Maybe even afraid.

"You mean, there's something *worse* than everything you just told us?" Penny asked, hands on her hips. Agnes hoped she didn't reach for her sickle, but she seemed in control.

"Pharmatrox's foreign allies are looking to expand—in a big way," said Dr. Chun. "In addition to the new shipment of darts, there's also a resupply cargo ship coming to the Capital—troops, weapons, supplies, everything needed for an extended siege. Troxies will come from New York to defend it, and if that ship lands, it will be just like New York. The Capital will fall. If Pharmatrox controls the seas and the ports, there's nothing to stop them from expanding westward, and I don't think I need to tell you how fucked we are then."

Agnes's hand tightened around her weapon as the gravity of the situation collapsed all around them. But Chun wasn't finished.

"That resupply ship is already on the way," continued Dr. Chun. "At this point, we can't stop it. We can only intercept it. We have at most two weeks before it's here. I can delay them from making progress with troxapine and the darts, but I can't stall forever." Her dark brown eyes bored into Agnes, and she felt the weight of responsibility fall heavily onto her shoulders once again. "You need to get back to the Capital now with reinforcements. And get *me* the hell out of here. You're going to blow the place sky-high, I presume? I'll escape in the confusion. But make sure it's a really *good* explosion, like I'm definitely dead. I don't want anyone looking for me."

"Hold it." Mal held up a hand. "If we get you out of here, where will you go?"

"To the Capital to infiltrate the facility there and see if I can figure out who's calling the shots and why they created these darts without a goddamn cure first. My trusted guard here can get me in an EV built for speed. Any idea where their headquarters in the Capital might be?"

After a brief pause, Mal said, "We pushed the bulk of their forces back to the SubTran station in the north."

"Excellent. When I get in, I'll find a way to signal you and make contact," Dr. Chun said. "If you don't hear from me within a week, get in there on your own."

Penny eyed the shorter woman with suspicion. "You've got this all figured out."

"I've had a lot of fucking free time on my hands, unable to leave this floating prison. I've also plotted each and every way I planned on killing my colleagues, although you've already taken care of many of them."

"Why should we trust you?" Penny pressed.

"Did you not just see me shoot that guy?" Dr. Chun asked, pointing to the body at her feet.

"I've killed my own men before," Penny said. "It isn't hard."

Agnes didn't miss the way Mal frowned at her words, but he remained silent.

"If she's lying," said Agnes, "it doesn't matter. We got what we needed and we're destroying the place. There isn't much she or any of the troxies can do now. We're blowing up their knowledge. This is where the orders to the other labs were coming from. If the orders stop, everything becomes even more decentralized. But if we kill her and she's really Kev's wife, I think he might take issue with that. And if she's telling the truth about this oncoming shitstorm, we're going to need her help further down the line."

"Thank you, Agnes," Dr. Chun said. "I appreciate your commendation. But you all have been here entirely too long already. Whatever plan you have, it's time to put it into fucking action. Your permission to escape in one of the lifeboats?" she asked Penny with a sardonic lift of her brow.

"Plenty of opportunity to kill you later, should the need arise," Penny said.

Agnes guessed that was as close to a concession as they were going to get. Into her radio, Agnes said, "Silas? Time to go."

"Got it. I'll head back to the boats. But I hear something—"

The building groaned as it began sagging to the left.

"Quentin and Derek must have run into trouble if they're doing their demolition plan already," Mal said, running for the door.

"The prisoners," Penny said. "They shouldn't have to die here too."

"I'll take care of it," Dr. Chun said. "Just go, and make sure this lab sinks to the bottom of the lake. And stay away from cells 18 to 25. Let those go down with the ship." She grasped Agnes's hand for a moment, then said, "Give Kev my love. Tell him I'll see him soon."

With that, Dr. Chun raced for the lab's back door and disappeared as the building creaked around them, teetering on the edge of destruction.

33

"QUENTIN!" Penny barked into her radio as she ran after Agnes and Mal, the building tilting so much they were almost running on the wall. "Quit it with the bombs for a minute. Wait until we get there."

Guards chased hot on their heels while scientists scattered everywhere, searching for escape as another explosion rocked the other side of the building, the cracks of splitting concrete echoing around them.

It was a full thirty seconds before Quentin replied. "Bit of a problem here. Guards everywhere and—oh crap, there's tu—" The transmission cut off and her stomach guttered.

"We need to get to them," Penny said. "Now."

But they were about to run into a problem of their own.

Blocking their route back to the boats, a few doors hung by their hinges. Gray bodies with eyes black as night poured out, snarling and grabbing at the unwitting troxies.

Turned. Here.

Troxy screams filled the air as turned ripped into them, blood spraying the walls.

Penny glanced and saw the numbers on the doors. *Eighteen, nineteen, twenty.* Dr. Chun's earlier warning sped through her mind, interrupted by a shrill sound from behind them.

At the noise, the turned stopped attacking and faced the direction of the signal, tilting their heads, hands forming into black-nailed claws.

Awaiting instructions.

Enhanced turned. Patient zeroes.

Without hesitation, Penny and the group took to the monsters with their blades. Another high-pitched signal had the turned focusing their attacks on the intruders, ignoring the other perfectly tasty morsels in white lab coats and troxy uniforms.

Slicing their way to the door, Penny kicked it open into a red-lit room boiling with activity. Troxies and turned fought as Silas and Derek held them off—but Quentin was missing.

"What happened? Where is he?" Penny asked, shooting a guard, then slamming a turned with her rifle.

"Took a troxy boat to set the rest of the charges on the support beams," Derek said. "We're just waiting on you."

"Then let's get the hell out of here," Mal said, jumping into their original boat and starting the engine.

Silas slapped the button to lower the ramp, shaking off a turned that tried to bite his arm, then hopped aboard as the frigid outside air blasted them. Everyone followed, and in seconds, they were in the water.

Derek took up position in the stern with Agnes, firing volts above them. With her night vision goggles, Penny saw a boat underneath the structure, but they'd have to speed around the outside to reach it, as the building was already collapsing.

"Done." Quentin's voice came from the radio at Agnes's hip. "I'll ditch this boat and get Kya to pick me up, then meet you back at shore."

A minute later, Penny watched Quentin's boat speed toward Navy Pier, Mal following at break-neck pace. Less than thirty seconds passed, then an earth-shattering *boom* echoed through the night. Penny turned to see the remnants of the explosion take out the lab, crumbling into the lake.

"You really know how to put on a show," Agnes said into her radio.

A surge of pride went through Penny. Quentin was proving himself a valuable member of this team—one who didn't need so much shielding from the harsh realities of this world.

Behind them, in the light of the burning lab, Penny saw an orange inflatable boat take off in the opposite direction. *Dr. Chun lives to fight another day.* Agnes noticed too and watched it depart in silence, a notch forming in her brow.

They'd done it. The servers, the lab—gone, and whatever horrible experiments with them. But with Dr. Chun's revelation—if she'd been telling the truth—their problems were only just beginning. And for the first time since they'd started this trip, Penny wondered if she'd made a mistake in coming with them.

Because if the Capital fell now, it would be her fault for not staying behind where she was needed.

"We need to speak to Kev. Immediately." Mal's voice boomed through the lobby as he stepped up to the guards posted at the hotel headquarters' main entrance, Penny hot on his heels. The rest of their group was in the armory, stowing their supplies and gearing up for the trip back to the Capital.

One guy hustled forward, forehead pinched. "You can't, he's—"

"The hell I can't. Take me to him now, and that's an order."

"*Sir,* you can't speak to him. He's gone."

All sounds faded until they were a high-pitched whine inside her head. *No. This can't be happening.* "What?"

"His meeting with the Canadian emissary was ambushed," the guy said. "Emissary's dead, his escorts too. But we didn't find Kev. He's not answering his satellite phone or radio, and the signals from both are lost. Naomi's contacts aren't answering either. Canada must have cut her off, and whoever else she was working with. Whoever took him is in the wind. Or—" The soldier cut off, eyes wide.

No. Kev couldn't be gone—dead. *Impossible.* The man was larger than life, the glue holding everything together. The one with the diplomatic relations and the contacts, the one who'd led them through hell and kept on marching. Without him...who did they have?

"You're telling me the commander of our entire revolution is gone. You have no idea where, or who took him, or if he's alive." Mal's voice was soft and deadly calm. "So *why are you still standing here and not out searching for him?*" he thundered, grabbing the guard by the front of his shirt and lifting him off his feet.

"Enough, Mal," Penny warned, gripping his shoulder, more grateful than ever that he was beside her and *alive. Because he could've been at that meeting too.* "Murdering him won't solve anything." Seething, Mal set the poor guy down.

"We *are* looking for him, sir. But—"

"War room. Now," Kya barked as she stalked down the hallway. "General Olesa, you too."

The guard looked like he had more to say, but one harsh look from Kya shut him up. "Understood, sirs." He hurried off before Mal decided to hoist him up by his underpants.

"Kev made a contingency plan for if he...for if we ever lost him," Kya explained to her. "It's not ideal, but it's what we've got." To Mal, she said, "Would appreciate some assistance getting things organized before you take off."

Mal agreed, and with a nod to Penny, Kya took her leave.

Leaving her alone with Mal for the first time since—*since our kiss earlier, dear god.* Under the constant onslaught of new information, Penny barely had time to process any of it. When Derek had interrupted them, she'd physically and emotionally shoved Mal away. And looking up at him now, his eyes blazing, she knew she was about to pay for that.

Taking a step closer, he dragged a thumb across her lower lip, and she thought she'd burst into flames right then. "You and I have unfinished business," he said, his low voice rumbling through her.

Christ, that voice.

"I—"

Footsteps sounded down the hallway as the rest of their crew and a couple guards for the watch shift change approached, Quentin leading the way.

"I don't know about you guys, but blowing stuff up really makes me hungry," Quentin said, eyeballing the soldier beside him who was eating a bag of chips. The guy rolled his eyes and handed it over. Quentin took a handful with a grin.

Agnes snorted. "You're always hungry, you bottomless pit."

"How else would he have the energy to irritate me twenty-four-seven?" Derek said, pulling Quentin into a headlock while Silas tickled his armpits.

But Quentin surprised all of them by stepping back and hip tossing Derek to the floor. A swell of pride went through Penny—she'd taught him that. He punched at the air in triumph, then looked at his hand in dismay, saying, "Aw man. Crushed my chips." But he shoved the crumbs in his mouth anyway and gave Derek a hand up, saying, "See? Not so gangly and awkward anymore, am I?"

"I wouldn't go that far," Derek said as he punched him lightly in the shoulder.

"What are you guys doing?" Quentin asked Penny, narrowing his eyes at how close she and Mal stood.

"Discussing—war things," she said, practically feeling that Mal wanted to sigh in exasperation.

"Kev is missing," Mal said, to a resounding chorus of "what the hells" from the newcomers. "You"—he gestured to the guards—"man your posts and we'll fill you in later." As they saluted and left, Mal turned to Silas, saying, "Keep trying to get us into satellite comms to send a warning to the Capital about the incoming cargo ship and an SOS to whoever is listening internationally." Silas nodded and took off.

To the rest of them, Mal said, "Finish packing and then catch some sleep. We'll take a replacement EV and head back to the Capital in three hours. We might make it there before the troxies arrive with their new set of darts, but we should be prepared for a fight."

As he spoke, Penny felt about as big as a grain of sand. *I should have listened to Mal and stayed behind in the Capital. If I'd had my ear to the ground, maybe I could have better prepared everyone for this incoming Armageddon.*

"So we believe Chun, then?" Derek asked. "Would've been nice to at least confirm with Kev that she's his inside contact before we rush back to the Capital based on her intel."

"We're low on options," Mal said. "We can only hold the Capital for so long. Same for Chicago and our other Faction outposts. Looking for Kev would take time and resources we don't have, and if Canada won't help us, we need to find another ally."

Penny's stomach guttered as she realized the unavoidable truth staring her in the face. *I have to make that alliance with Zeln. It's our only option. I have to fix this.*

But Mal forged onward, ever the commanding officer even in the face of impossible odds. "Our immediate priority is securing the Capital and getting Agnes whatever she needs to make a cure. Penny?" Her eyes jumped to his and the...searing look on his face had her feeling every single bit of their unfinished business right down to the tips of her toes. "I'll find you soon."

Before Penny could reply, he followed his soldiers filing into the war room. The group dispersed to their own devices, Agnes and Derek murmuring about Kev's disappearance as they went to the armory to pack, their faces pinched with worry.

As Penny headed to her room to take a shower and freak out about whatever Mal wanted to discuss with her later, Quentin fell into step beside her. "Good work today," she said. The words felt inadequate for all of the emotions swirling inside her. "I can't believe the things you can do."

He smiled, bouncing beside her. No matter how bad things got, he was always in a good mood—something she admired. "I'm just glad you're letting me help instead of barricading me in my room like Tara and Agnes threaten to do all the time. Mal even used my special throwing knife I made today," he said with a bright smile.

Penny suppressed a laugh. "See? Even your superhero needs his trusty sidekick."

But instead of joining in her joke, Quentin scrunched his nose as he paused at their room. "You keep saying that."

"Saying what?"

"That Mal's my hero. But he's not—I mean, he's very cool and I like him a lot. But he's not my hero, Penelope. You are."

A profound pang of regret went through her as his words speared her in the heart. "What?" she breathed.

"You saved me from Dr. Hansen. You came for me when you thought the Chosen had me. But it's not just because of that stuff. You're so strong. You always have been."

"I've done some fucked-up things, Quentin. Things you don't even know about."

"I might not have believed this before meeting Agnes, but I bet you had your reasons for everything you did."

"But the fire—"

"I know the dust makes people...do things. See things that aren't there. It happened to Agnes too. Using the dust was your choice—a bad one—but I forgive you for what happened with our parents"—her knees knocked together and she almost collapsed—"and I want to move past it. And I *don't* want you beating yourself up about it anymore. I miss my sister and I want her back. Can you do that for me? Can you be my Penelope again?"

Penny gripped the doorframe for support. *I do not deserve him.* "I'm sorry, Quentin. I know nothing I say can erase what I've done to you. To...our family. I'm just—fuck." She broke off, running a hand through her hair. "I never say or do the right things. But I want to do right by you, kid. You're the best thing in my life, and I love you more than anything."

Quentin eyed her, hand stuck to the doorknob. "Right back at you." Then he ducked inside their room, leaving her alone with her thoughts. *He...forgives me?* She hadn't thought it possible, but it was a testament to how *good* of a person he was that he was willing to work on it. For them. For her. *I really don't deserve him.*

And that had her thoughts shooting straight to someone else. Moments of her kiss with Mal came flying back to her with all the speed and heat of a meteorite. She didn't know what to make of it. All she knew was that she *liked it*, and that was very fucking bad. Because any future for them would be doomed if she went through with her plan to recruit Zeln and his network of allies, which was looking more like a necessity now that Kev was in the wind.

After a scalding-hot shower and a change of clothes, the thoughts still plagued her. When she left the bathroom, Quentin was already snoring up a storm, and she was about to crawl into bed herself when a soft knock sounded at her door. Her heart ricocheted in her chest, because she knew who it was.

Wiping her palms on her jeans—*since when do I get sweaty hands anyway?*—she opened the door.

Mal stood there, freshly showered, wearing a clean black tee and tactical pants that made him look every part the powerful general. But the way he looked at her hinted at something softer, yet no less fierce. It was a look only for her, lighting a long-dormant fire deep within her.

He traced a fingertip across her collarbone, up her neck, and to her chin. "Come to my room."

His room? Oh hell.

But she nodded and followed, entirely unprepared for whatever she was about to face.

"Are you all right?" he asked as he sat at the foot of his bed, the door shutting behind them. "You look like you're about to throw up or bolt for the nearest window."

Recovering, Penny huffed a laugh, parking herself atop the desk across from him. "Could you blame me, after everything we learned today?" Between Kev missing, Chun's revelations, the shit they were about to go into in the Capital, her conversation with Quentin—all of it churned her into a storm of anxiety and guilt.

"Yeah. What a shit show." Mal blew out a breath, rubbing his beard.

Before they got into…whatever they were about to get into, Penny had some things to get off her chest. "I talked to Kev last night. About Zeln."

Mal's posture straightened, his eyebrows lowering.

"Before you get pissed off, just listen to me for a second. We need help—that much is clear. And after today, I think it's safe to assume Canada is out. Without any strong ties to other nations, we have to take reinforcements where we can get them. We're in disaster mode here. And that means considering any and all options—including Zeln and guys like him. Kev said it would be the right move, but he knew you wouldn't like it. That doesn't mean we're wrong, Mal. Getting Zeln on our side could mean a whole slew of other allies with deep pockets."

"And questionable fucking morals," Mal groused.

"Do you want a fucking gold star for being 'honorable' or do you want to win this war?"

"We can win without having to work with the likes of him. You don't understand what he's into, Penny. You don't want to side with a guy like that."

Suddenly, the embers of her temper flared to life. "With a guy like what, Mal? Someone who would say or do anything if it meant getting what they wanted? Someone who would kill anyone without a second thought if it was to satisfy their own ends? Someone who'd abandon their family and friends, not caring who they hurt, just to take any action that felt good and numbed the pain enough so they could fall asleep at night? Someone who'd sell their soul for their favorite vice? *I'm* like that."

"You're different now," he said in a soft voice that rumbled with an undercurrent of something she didn't want to acknowledge.

"I'm not that different, Mal. Don't make me out to be a hero." But she was saying the words to Quentin as much as she was saying them to Mal now. "You'll be sorely disappointed when you see that I'm just like Zeln and those other shadows that live their lives in the gray. And because I'm like that, I understand Zeln in a way you don't. I know we can buy him off."

"Do *not* compare yourself to him. We'll find another way," he said in a hard and final tone.

Penny shook her head, sighing. "That's the difference between you and I. I'll do whatever it takes to win. *Whatever it takes.* And there's a line you won't cross. Doesn't mean you're wrong, doesn't mean I'm right. But you might want to take a hard fucking look at your *morals* and think about what you're willing to compromise on. We've all gotten our hands dirty in this war. You're no different."

But he *was* different. He was everything good and noble and *right*. And she was not. And after her conversation with Quentin and the realization that she'd fucked up by not staying behind in the Capital, maybe that was why she had this gnawing feeling in her chest that made her want to cut him with her words, to drag the ugly truths out into the light and throw them at his feet and say, *See? See how different we are? See why we can never work? Why there can never be an "us"?*

Even as her words pushed him away, this time, Mal didn't let her. Slowly, he closed the small distance between them until he stood between her legs where she sat on the desk. As she looked up at him, the rest of the world fell away, sealing her in a trance as her heart thudded against her rib cage. His gaze did not waver as he fastened a hand behind her neck, holding her captive, and she felt at once protected and dangerous at this thing brewing between them. "The lies that hide within—the ones we tell ourselves—are the most pervasive and insidious of all. I tell myself a lot of lies, Pen," he said, sweeping a thumb across her jawline. "About who I am, what I want. But the ones about you? Those are the biggest."

As she gathered the courage to speak, she placed a steadying hand on his massive shoulder, searching for strength. "What lies do you tell yourself about me?" she whispered, scared to breathe the words into existence.

"Remember what I said about asking me questions you can't handle the answer to?" He was so close she could count the flecks of gold and amber in his eyes, like spots of sunshine dancing in a sea of whiskey. Time narrowed until there was only this single moment of existence, their mingled breaths, so many words unspoken between them.

"I can handle it," she said, even though she wasn't sure she could. But she had to know. *Craved* it.

Another hand slid up her thigh, widening her legs to make room as he pulled her even closer. As he spoke, every word brushed against her lips. "I tell myself every day that I don't want you. That I don't want your hands all over me, that I don't want to fall asleep tangled up together. That I don't want to be the reason you smile, or the person who makes you feel like this," he said, tracing a finger across the delicate skin just below her ear and making her pulse jump in response. "Or that you're not the most aggravating yet amazing woman I've ever met. I've tried to stay away. Tried to ignore whatever the fuck this is between us. But I fucking can't, and I'm done trying. Now that I've had a taste of you, I need *more*."

But instead of kissing her like every cell in her body screamed for him to, he pulled back to look at her face. "Can you handle that, Pen?"

Her mind was a maelstrom of questions and emotions. Everything was going to hell, they might lose this war, but the only truth that shone through all of that was—

His hands tightened their hold, forcing her head back. "Tell. Me."

He's going to make me fucking say it. Fine. Fisting the front of his shirt, she hauled him down to her level and said the words. "I want you, you bastard. Whatever this is—I want it. With you. Now fucking kiss me before I—"

He silenced her with his mouth.

Their lips battled for dominance as they unleashed *everything*. All the tension that had been building since he'd first kissed her hours ago snapped between them, blazing through her like a wildfire. Her hands found the hem of his shirt and she dug her fingertips into his hard torso, enjoying the feel of his muscles like she'd imagined doing so many times. A growl rumbled in his chest as he ripped the shirt over his head, tossing it away. She'd seen him shirtless before, but now...now, she could do whatever she wanted with him.

And that had a sly smile curving her lips as she did away with her own shirt, baring herself to him for the first time.

"Fuck, Pen," he said, the heat in his eyes burning her alive as he drank her in. But she'd gone long enough wondering what it would be like—what *they* would be like—if they ever gave in to temptation. She was ready to fucking *know*.

"Put your hands on me. Now."

And he did, pulling their bodies flush and capturing her mouth, teeth grazing her lips, leaving no part of her untouched. When his lips found her neck, she dropped her head back with a sigh, nails rasping over the sides of his buzzed hair. In one swift move, he lifted her from the desk, taking them to his bed, and a swell of desire surged through her.

But as his hands continued exploring her while she straddled him, a dark seed spread its tendrils within her heart. She wanted him—god, did she fucking want him—but even so, part of her rejected every beautiful thing he'd just said to her. Here now, in this room, she could be his and he could be hers. But out there? In their world rife with war, where Mal stood squarely in the light and where she traipsed the line, courting the darkness?

Their relationship could never survive in that world.

But goddamn it, she wanted them to try.

When his fingers brushed over a sensitive spot, all other thoughts of protest, of *anything*, abandoned her, and she fully gave in, losing herself in Mal.

They could afford just this one fucking second of peace.

The problems of their world could wait.

34

*F*IFTEEN MORE MINUTES. PENNY dug her fingers into the cracked leather of the van's bench seat and forced herself to remain calm even though she felt amped enough to sprint the rest of the way back to the Capital. A small convoy of reinforcements from Faction splinter groups and Vick's civilian contacts rumbled behind them in scavenged vehicles. *But it's still not enough.*

Across from her, Naomi sat wedged between Silas and their gear. In the wake of getting cut off from Canada, she'd latched herself onto their cause, determined to reconnect with Canada and convince them to intervene. Penny wasn't complaining—they needed all the help they could get.

Beside her, Mal sat with crossed arms, tension lining every muscle. But as he caught her watching him, he gave her a look colored with every delicious thing he wanted to do to her. Waking up with him that morning, tangled in the sheets, was a far cry from what they were headed into now. She wished they'd had more time to remain in their little bubble, exploring each other, but duty called—abruptly, with a very exuberantly knocking Quentin at their door, who'd about hit the ceiling when he saw them in bed together.

As Quentin made googly eyes at her from the front seat, she shook her head. She'd never live that one down.

Glancing at Derek and Agnes, she wondered how those two had managed to find love, or whatever, even as the world fell apart around them. The thought of getting that close to someone made Penny feel itchy, and when Mal's leg brushed against hers, she got even *more* itchy. Even though she and Mal were together now, the doubts still plagued her. After the war, if—*when*—life went back to normal, would Mal still want her? Would he still feel the same way he did now? When there was no war to hide behind and she stood before him, battered and broken, would they still want each other?

Too existential for right now. So she did what she did best and shoved the things she didn't want to confront under the very crowded rug in her mind.

But below the seat where no one could see, Mal linked their pinkies with a secret smile.

And she didn't let go.

As they reached the city limits, the radio at Silas's hip crackled with Sanjali's voice. "We're about to be overrun here. Turned incoming, troxies with those fucking dart things. We need—"

Silas fumbled for the radio, clicking the receiver. "Sanj, we're almost there. And we have help—well, kind of. It's better than nothing. Where are you?"

"Silas? Oh thank fuck. Stadium. We need you."

"On it," he said. "Floor it, Derek."

Derek rubbed his palms together, grinning. "My pleasure." The van surged forward, blowing through the rest of its battery charge to race toward the stadium. Once they crossed McAdams Bridge, Penny saw smoke billowing into the sky from the direction of their home base.

"Shit," said Mal, gripping Derek's headrest as he leaned forward to get a better look. "Silas, radio our hangar and tell them to send in the drones—the solar powered ones, if we have any left. No jets yet. We need to conserve fuel to fight off the cargo ship later. Derek, swing by the armory, then we'll take the fight to them. We'll—"

BOOM. BOOM.

A deafening explosion rocked the middle of the street, concrete and asphalt spraying and clouds of dust clogging the air. Derek swerved, bringing the convoy to a screeching halt. Something screamed overhead as more booms echoed in the distance.

"*Raid,*" Agnes wheezed from the front seat. "It's a fucking *raid.*"

*There hasn't been a raid in months, not since—*That could only mean one thing. Penny's frantic gaze found Mal's. He looked grim.

Another screaming jet shot overhead as they abandoned the van, Penny barking orders to the civilians and Faction members piling out of their own vehicles. Clinging to the buildings, they moved as a group to the armory, feeling their way through the smoke cloud. From behind, Penny felt a finger slide through her belt loop and Mal's gruff voice spoke in her ear. "Not gonna lose you again."

Penny raced for the armory, Mal's touch a reassuring tether to reality. Another explosion from the end of the street, concrete flying, the rumble of armored trucks heading their way an ominous undertone. But a roar came from behind, cutting through the noise...

Glancing over her shoulder, Penny saw a motorcycle burst out of the dust cloud, a few EVs in its wake. *Vick.* Laying the bike down on its side, Vick skidded across the pavement, rapid-fire shooting at the oncoming troxy vehicles, her black hair flying behind her.

"Hey, that's *mine!*" Derek shouted, looking at his bike in devastation.

"Inside!" Vick shouted. "Now!"

When they finally reached the warehouse, Mal kicked the door in, and they all fell inside, sweaty and covered in dust.

"*Fuck,*" Mal said, scrubbing both hands through his hair with a growl.

"This is bad," Derek said. "This means—"

"I know what it fucking means," Mal snarled.

At that moment, a few Faction guards streamed down the aisles, Ivan at their helm, Lawrence right behind them. "Care to share with the rest of the class?" Ivan asked while the troops looked to Mal for orders, and he redirected them to get more weapons, explaining the situation as he walked.

Filling everyone else in, Penny said, "The armory in Sector 3 is our aircraft hangar with a few fighter jets and drones. We use them sparingly because of the lack of fuel. But if they're currently flying around bombing *us,* that means Pharmatrox has retaken the armory, and they don't care about wasting fuel because they know they're getting resupplied by that incoming ship."

"Incoming ship?" Lawrence asked, eying Naomi. She gave him a subtle smile, which he returned. With interest. *Jesus, now is not the time for love in the fucking air.*

"What happened in Chicago?" Ivan asked, looking paler than usual and sweaty, but his voice was strong. "Did you find a cure?"

Vick zeroed in on Penny with a sharp gaze as she awaited her answer, and her heart sank as she realized the only thing she had to share was bad news, so she said, "Later. After we deal with this."

"Where's Tara?" Agnes asked, casting a concerned glance at Ivan. *Probably wondering if Tara looks as bad.*

"At the stadium with Jaha and Tanaka," Vick said. "Troxies launched multiple attacks. We're holding them off, but barely."

"You have tanks with anti-aircraft weaponry, don't you?" Ivan asked. "Those can take the jets down easy."

"The troxies know about that," Derek answered. "But they *are* mounted on vehicles. We can get them on the move."

"Too slow," Vick said, walking down the aisles of weapons, searching. Then she pulled what looked like an oversized volt rifle out of the pile, hoisting it onto her shoulder with a determined look. "Get me to the roof. I'll handle the planes and drones. You guys deal with the rest of this shit. Ivan, make sure they don't kill all of our people."

As Penny pointed Vick to the stairs, she had to admit she was impressed. Taking out a plane with a weapon like that was pretty fucking difficult, but if anyone could do it, it was Vick.

"Quentin, you're with me," Ivan said, then glanced at Penny. "If your sister says it's okay."

Penny nodded her approval. Ivan would make sure he stayed out of harm's way. Quentin beamed at her, pleased to be included. She never took any of his smiles for granted. Not anymore.

The rest suited up, and as Penny slung a volt rifle around to her back, Mal made his reappearance.

"How bad is it?" she asked.

"Troxies retook the aircraft hangar and are attacking the stadium," he said, sliding a vest over his head and cinching the sides tight. "We're pushing them back to the SubTran station and Sector 14 in the north." Then he looked to Agnes. "But they have those fucking poison darts like Dr. Chun warned us. We need a cure, yesterday."

"On it," Agnes said. Derek and Silas followed her outside—but they ducked back in as a high-pitched wail keened through the air.

Fuck, not now.

"What is it? What's wrong?" asked one of the civilian newcomers, the others shifting uneasily.

"You don't wanna know," Penny said as she headed for the door. "Half of you, go with Mal to the stadium." She could feel his glare burning through the side of her face at the idea of being separated, but she ignored it. "The rest of you, we're about to face some turned. Blades only. Hold them off so Agnes can get to Maple Street."

Without another word, Penny stepped outside into the swarm of gray bodies, a Humvee with a sound system on the roof rolling slowly behind the sea of destruction.

As she fell into the familiar motions of battle, she considered their options. Slicing heads with her sickle, the rhythm of fighting coursed through her, the sounds of war a low hum in the background.

Until an explosion ripped through the air overhead, one of the fighter jets spewing smoke from an engine as it plowed into a stack of buildings a few streets over. Penny followed the line of smoke back to the armory's roof.

I'll be damned. Vick is a killer shot.

But even though the Watchers were helping, it wasn't enough. *This attack changes everything.* Slowly retaking the city sector by sector and squeezing out Pharmatrox's presence until there was nothing left was no longer an option. The troxies could not be allowed to hole up in the SubTran station anymore. They had to do something to get them *out*. And they had less than two weeks to come up with a new plan.

And they needed to take Zeln off the board.

By the time they'd smashed their way through the turned, Penny's resolve had hardened.

She had an idea.

35

Agnes

"Feels wrong to be typing away safely inside while shit blows up around us," Silas said as his fingers flew across a portable keyboard mat on the work bench in Derek's garage, his eyes focused on the unseen. Instead of relying on the crappy laptop, he'd engineered a Patch for use as a personal computer, and he was currently helping Agnes finish up some last strings of code while she outfitted the FPGA into the new and more portable version of her machine.

Behind them, Derek paced in front of the closed garage door, clutching his volt rifle and jerking his head toward every noise.

"If you want to rejoin the battle, you should," she said. "We'll be fine."

Derek stuttered to a halt, fixing her with a harsh look. "I'm not leaving you unattended in the middle of an ambush."

"You forget I was on my own for almost six months before I met you," she said, but a small smile played at her lips at the protective current in his voice.

"I know you can take care of yourself," he said, resuming his patrol. "Doesn't change the fact that I still want to be here. I'd be useless to Mal in this state anyway."

"The state of perpetual idiocy?" Silas smirked as he continued typing.

"Don't you start. I get enough of that from Quentin," Derek said with a grin. The two had quickly fallen into the habit of bickering like brothers too, and Agnes found it oddly charming. "But seriously. How are things going?" he asked.

"Almost there," she said. "I just hope the detox serum we got from Chun works on our people who need it, even though we can't do anything yet for those who were darted. Are we in close enough range that you can radio someone to find out?" She'd given Ju Lee all but one of the detox serum vials before they'd left for Maple Street.

"I'll see what I can do," Derek said.

"He's a good one, Aggie," Silas said to her in a low voice without looking away from his work.

Agnes suppressed a smile and went back to her machine. "I know." As she watched Derek making calls, a stoic slant to his brow, she realized that even after everything she'd been through, everything they'd *all* been through, she wouldn't trade it for anything. They'd all lost so much, but if none of this had ever happened, she wouldn't have found the people she now considered family. They were all dealt a shitty hand, but it was up to them to decide what to do with it.

And Agnes would make sure that Pharmatrox could never harm anyone again.

When she resurfaced from her work an indeterminate amount of time later, she sat back, shaking, and not from the chilly air that leaked under the door cracks. *I did it. Finally. It's done.* Wiping the sweat from her brow, she surveyed her machine. A shiny metal cylinder no bigger than a microwave with a compartment for inserting substances and a port for uploading information from holofiles. Something so small and yet so vital for their success over Pharmatrox. And it was finally complete.

Oblivious to her moment of creation, Derek fiddled with his radio while Silas's fingers flew across the keyboard.

"I'm done," she said, her voice croaking from disuse.

Derek paused, looking up with wide eyes. "You're...?"

"I think it's ready to test," she said. "Si?"

"Me too," he said, sliding a holofile across the table. "I modified your original program using Chun's notes and Pharmatrox's drug database I downloaded from their servers before I blew them up. Everything they have related to troxapine—the formulas they've tried, other ingredients they're considering, what Chun was working on—it's all in there."

"If you found all of that in their servers, why not just download the detox serum formula too?" Derek asked.

"Trust me, I would have. But there's no record of it anywhere. If I had to guess, anything to counteract their poison isn't recorded for security reasons. They wouldn't want the detox serum formula to get out—it's the one thing that can ruin their plans."

"And now we wait," Agnes said, plugging the holofile into her machine's port and starting it up. "It'll take a couple hours to catalog all of Silas's data. Then we'll add in one of the darts and start running simulations. What about the detox serum Chun gave us?"

"It seems to be working on the users we're rehabilitating, but we won't know for sure for a few more days," Derek said.

Apprehension swirled in the air, and the unspoken words floated through her mind. *We won't know if they're going to turn until they turn.* So far, there hadn't been any reports of blackened sclera or inky tears, but that could change at any moment.

"So we find out what's in these darts and how to cure it, but how do we make it?" Silas asked. "We still need the supplies. And a scientist."

"If the troxies are consolidating their power in the SubTran and looking to expand like Dr. Chun said, then we need to get in there," Agnes said. "They might have what we need."

Maybe that was why all of the labs they'd come across in the Capital were bare bones or picked over. She'd thought it was from looters or troxies destroying everything before fleeing. But what if the SubTran was a cache of supplies just sitting there?

"If Chun infiltrates them successfully, we might have an in," Derek noted.

"So we wait around until we hear from her? Tara and Ivan don't have that kind of time," Agnes said. "We need to get in there before the resupply cargo ship arrives. Maybe even leave right now while they're distracted with their ambush."

"I know you're worried about them," Derek said, wrapping an arm around her, "but we can't run in there without a plan."

Agnes wanted to brush him off, but he was right. Scooping up her empty coffee cup and heading for the kitchen door, she asked, "Anyone else need a recharge?"

"I'll take one," Silas said.

As she stoked the fire in the hearth and set the kettle above it, her mind cranked through the possibilities. Chun could be arriving in the city any day—might already be there, if she'd gotten a helicopter or something—but if the SubTran had scientists, she didn't necessarily need to wait for Chun. Surely she could convince one of them to—

A sound pierced her thoughts and immediately she was on high alert.

Because she knew that sound.

The creaky floorboard in the hallway. The one she'd stepped on all those months ago when she'd intruded into Derek's house, catching him mid-conversation with Mal and discovering he was in the Faction.

Someone was trying to sneak up on her.

Machete too far. Knife under the coffee table.

Diving for the weapon, she grabbed it and whipped around in time to kick out the intruder's knees, slicing at his face as he pitched forward—into a forward roll?—regaining his footing with ease.

Sweat poured off of her at the heat of the fire at her back as she gripped the knife tighter.

And then she recognized the face of the man grinning at her.

"You're him—Zeln. What do you want?"

"Your machine. Where is it?"

How the hell does he know about that?

But instead of waiting for an answer, he lunged, faster than any opponent she'd ever faced. Screaming, she swiped for his throat while reaching behind her, yelping as the fire burned her, but she knew it was somewhere—*there.*

Grabbing the kettle, she swung it for his head, scalding-hot water splashing over him as he roared. She scrambled away, shouting for help, but Zeln caught her by the ankle and yanked her back, raking his knife across her leg. Twisting at the last second, she avoided getting an artery sliced, but blood poured from the wound, hot and slick. That didn't stop her from slashing with her own knife for any part of him she could reach. From the series of grunts, she knew her strikes were getting through.

"Agnes, are you—what the fuck!" Derek fired off some volts, one of them shattering the living room window, but Zeln was too quick, dashing for the opening.

But before he could dive outside, Agnes threw her knife and it clipped him on the arm. Not enough to stop him.

Derek moved to jump out after him, but Agnes held him back. "You won't survive a fight with him," she said. "I almost didn't."

"Excellent job at guard duty, Derek," quipped Silas as he bustled inside and took in the wrecked living room. He got snippy when he was scared. "What happened?" he asked, his face creased in worry.

Derek muttered something about a "faulty latch," but Agnes wasn't listening, because at that moment, Penny banged through the front door and stomped into the living room. Black blood sluiced her arms and face, and she looked like she'd stepped straight out of a monster battle. *She probably had.*

"What happened to *you*?" Silas asked, that same concern transferring to Penny. Agnes wasn't sure she'd ever get used to people *liking* Penny, or the fact that she might even be warming up to the woman herself.

"Enhanced turned at the armory," Penny explained. "We took care of it. Mal and the rest are at the stadium now and sending reinforcements. Got Derek's SOS and I was nearby. What happened here?"

"Zeln," Agnes said, wrapping an old tee shirt around her leg and tying it tight to stanch the blood until she could properly clean it. But something about the entire encounter bothered her... "He knew about my machine. He was there that day Silas and I broke into the facility with the scientists imprisoned in the basement. Maybe he snuck in and overheard something. I don't know, but he knows enough about our operations to know I'm working on a cure, and he knew where to find me. But..."

"But what?" Derek asked, smoothing a hand across her back.

"If he wanted me dead, I would be. Same as when he broke into Penny's room. So what if he wanted to *recruit* me? What if Pharmatrox wants me back on their side? Maybe they realized their mistake of creating something without an 'undo' button and sent their guard dog to fetch them someone who could help?"

"Jesus," said Penny, but a shadow of...something unreadable passed across her face, gone in an instant. "From now on, all of your sciencey stuff is to be kept at the stadium until we secure the SubTran back under our control."

"Those concrete walls didn't stop Zeln before," Derek remarked.

"No," agreed Silas, "but at least there, we're in a place full of soldiers and weapons and one really massive, deliciously temperamental Samoan general who can rip the guy in half with his bare hands."

"Set up there and we'll regroup about our next moves," Penny said, sliding her sickle into her belt.

Then her earlier words caught up to Agnes. "You answered Derek's SOS," she said, unsure of how it made her feel that *Penny* had been so willing to come to her rescue.

"You needed help, so I came," she said easily. As if the statement wasn't loaded with the weight of the past that sank heavily between them. But maybe after everything they'd gone through recently, with the training sessions, the cult, the lab infiltration...maybe some of that weight was getting easier to carry.

For both of them.

36

1 YEAR AGO

"ARE YOU SURE THIS is it?" Penny eyed the brick building that looked like it couldn't decide if it was a townhouse or a fire station, with its big bay doors and clouded windows.

Lexa checked her notepad from the driver's seat in the murky streetlight. "Yep. This is the address Salvador gave him. Wait, is that him?" She pointed to a shadowy figure that ducked into the alleyway.

"Showtime," Penny said as she checked the gun in her waistband.

"I didn't see that," Lexa said, sliding her own gun into her holster.

"I've got a permit," Penny said. "And I have a friend in the department." She smiled at said friend, who rolled her eyes.

"I can only pull that trick so many times before the chief catches onto me. Come on."

Dressed in bulletproof vests, they piled out of the car. She wasn't sure how Lexa had managed to get a warrant, but she had her ways. It was why Penny loved partnering with her.

Inside the dark building, construction materials for renovations covered every surface like the most annoying obstacle course in history. Treading lightly, Penny headed toward the scuffling sounds of Terry hard at work prepping to burn down the building. On the opposite side,

Lexa ducked behind a saw horse. Before they could interrupt, someone entered from a side door.

Shit. No one else is supposed to be here.

"Terry. You made it."

Uncle fucking Hal?

"The fuck you doing here?" Terry sneered. "Don't need no supervisor."

"Quality assurance," said Hal.

"Salvador thinks I can't get the job done?"

"Nothing of the sort. In fact, I'd like to hire you for another job. I want to see how you work first. Make sure I'm getting my money's worth."

Another job? Something Hal didn't want Salvador finding out about.

Ignoring Lexa's "stand the fuck down" signal, Penny made her appearance. "Hal," she said, gun aimed at his balloon of a head. She took pleasure in the shock that flashed across his flabby face before his signature greasy smile slid back into place.

"Penelope. Should have guessed you'd stick your nose where it doesn't belong." Unsurprisingly, he pulled a revolver out of his jacket pocket.

"Hey, woah!" Terry took out his own gun, unsure of who to point it at.

"Gun down." Lexa emerged from the shadows, aiming at Terry.

"I'll put it down when you all put *yours* down," Terry said.

Lexa pointed to the badge on her vest. "Cop. I win. Put it down. You too, Hal."

"Not a chance," Hal said. "You—"

"Oh, Terry!" *Shit, that's Salvador.* His voice came from outside the front door. "Thought you might have run into some trouble."

"Damn it." Hal looked around in a panic as the footsteps pounded up the rickety front stairs. In a move swifter than she'd expected of the old man, he grabbed Penny by the hair and dragged her behind a construction drop cloth separating the main room from the workshop.

"Let me go, asshole," she said, pressing her gun in his ribs as he shoved the barrel of his into her mouth.

"Shut up," he hissed. To Lexa, he said, "Stay hidden or I'll kill her."

Eyes bright with fury, Lexa hid behind some boxes—hopefully calling for backup—just as Salvador walked inside.

All the fuckers we want to take down in one place. Normally, Penny would be thrilled. But with a gun in her mouth and now Hal's knife at her neck, she wasn't in the optimal position to take advantage of the situation. She could still get out of it, but she wanted to see what Salvador had to say first.

"Where is he, Terry?" Salvador asked, smoothing the lapels of his velvet suit jacket, his two beefy bodyguards looming behind him.

"Where's who?" Terry said, blinking entirely too much. *Idiot.*

"Hal Cromwell. I know he's here."

"Don't know who that is."

Heaving a put-upon sigh, Salvador pulled out a gun and shot Terry in the kneecap, who collapsed, screaming, "What the *fuck*, man?"

"Perhaps that will jog your memory."

"He's over there," wailed Terry.

Footsteps sounded across the floor planks, but before they drew too close, Hal swore and ducked out, holding the knife to Penny's throat with his gun trained on Salvador.

"How original," Salvador said. "One of my employees thinks he can hire my staff out from under me, use them to get a better payout. You are not the first one to try it, but this will be the last thing you ever do."

Hal scoffed. "Talk about originality, with a line like that."

"I am not amused. But I am curious. Who's the lady?" Salvador's eyes slid over Penny, and she took both of their momentary distractions to stomp Hal's foot and disarm him of his weapons, spinning to pin both to his kidney.

"I'm the one who's putting you both behind bars," she said.

Salvador's eyes sparkled with delight. "My, my. Could use someone like you on my payroll. Isn't hard to get the drop on a flea bag like Hal, but I'm *insatiably* curious to know how you managed to find out about this little operation."

"We're good at our jobs," Lexa said, stepping out from her hiding place. "Lower your weapons. That means you too, Penny. We're doing this one by the book."

But Penny didn't move, the knife wedged into her uncle's back. Just a little slip and he'd be bleeding out on the floor, and her family would be better off. Lexa would overlook a lot of things for her, but blatant murder probably wasn't one of them. But she couldn't put the knife down. Jail was too good for Hal—he'd post bail and hire the best lawyers. He'd be back to using her family's farm for his own depraved ends, back to skulking around Quentin.

The only thing that would stop him was death. The only way Quentin would truly be safe from his clutches is if those clutches turned to ash and disappeared.

And for Quentin, she'd do anything—*anything*—to keep him safe.

"I'm fucking *bleeding* and you're all just having a nice chat like a chunk of my leg isn't laying on the floor," cried Terry.

"Shut up," Salvador said. "You're as whiny as you are useless. You're fired, obviously."

"Hands up, Salvador," Lexa said. "I mean it."

"And you"—Salvador turned to Hal and, before anyone could move, shot him in the forehead—"your services are no longer required."

The world snapped into fast forward, everything happening too quickly to process. Hal's body collapsed while Lexa fired at Salvador. But he must have been wearing a vest too, because he remained standing, unharmed, and returned fire at Lexa, while Terry took the opportunity to toss his lighter into the accelerant.

A burst of heat and light momentarily blinded Penny as she groped for her gun. Finding it on the floor, she aimed at Salvador—but Terry tackled him by the legs and her shots went over his head, taking out one of Salvador's minions.

Penny was dimly aware of Lexa shouting, but the roaring fire and cloying smoke drowned out anything else. With her uncle now dead, Salvador and Terry were the last loose ends to assure her family's safety. Lexa would prefer them alive and in jail, and Penny didn't care either way, so long as the farm was saved.

As Salvador ran for the exit, Penny pursued, coughing through the smoke. Lexa must have subdued the other minion because no more shots were flying—

Glass shattered overhead as Terry grabbed Hal's fallen gun, shooting wildly. Salvador turned and aimed, but Penny knocked the gun out of his hand, shoving him against the wall with all her strength. He hit a work bench, tools and nails spewing. Grabbing for the nearest thing—a circular saw attached to an extension cord—he turned it on, swinging for Penny's head, but she ducked and rolled away.

But he came after her, swinging again, the blade whirring millimeters from her face. Finally, she circled behind him and kicked his knees out. He fell forward, the still spinning saw flying out of his hand as another gunshot sounded—

A high-pitched whir, a deep *crunch*. A sickening thud.

No.

Penny turned—

Lexa in a pool of blood. The saw gouging into the floor where her neck—

Penny wrenched her eyes away.

This cannot be happening. Please, no.

Her foot slipped in something and she looked down, Salvador bleeding from a headshot, his blood mingling with Lexa's—

She was dimly aware of the red and blue lights flashing outside of the building. Of Terry shouting obscenities. Of the sea of carnage that surrounded her, soon to be lost to the rapidly spreading fire.

But the only thing she saw was Lexa, the only person she'd ever called a friend, bleeding onto the plank-wood floor, the spinning circular saw lodged in her neck, her light blue eyes glassy as she stared right through Penny's soul.

A sob lodged in her throat as she yanked the saw's cord, tossed it away, and pulled her friend into her arms. Stumbling outside into the cops gathered on the sidewalk, she tried to explain what happened, but all that came out was a keening wail as someone took Lexa from her and steered her toward an ambulance.

Some time later, Penny came back to herself, wrapped in a shiny, crunchy shock blanket, the remains of the warehouse smoldering across the street. She couldn't bring herself to care that most of the evidence had been destroyed, nor the fact that the biggest crime boss on the East Coast was now dead along with her manipulative piece-of-shit uncle. As she watched the cops zip the black body bag closed over Lexa's face, something in her shifted.

Part of Penny died that day too. A vital piece she'd never reclaim, no matter how many bad guys she put away. Nothing would ever be enough to make up for putting Lexa in that position, for disobeying her orders, for pulling her into the investigation. For being the reason Salvador lost his grip on that saw.

Lexa was dead, and Penny was the only one to blame.

As she tried and failed to fall asleep night after night, she lay awake in bed, the haunting sound of a whirring saw blade tolling its death knell in her ears.

Your fault. Your fault.

37

Trudging down the hallway, Penny steeled herself for what she was about to do. *It's the only way. The only hope we have.* Yesterday, they'd pushed the troxies back to the SubTran station, but they'd lost the armory and aircraft hangar in Sector 3. Although, since Vick had taken out the jets and drones, the aircraft hangar would be useless to the troxies now. But they'd be back, maybe even before their resupply ship came in. Or they'd just wait them out and obliterate the Faction once the ship arrived.

And Penny would do anything in her power to ensure that didn't happen.

Silas, along with Lawrence and Naomi, were working on reestablishing comms with Canada through some sort of back-alley technology, but pinning all their hopes on that was a long shot, as was finding Kev.

All of this—the battle, losing the armories, Zeln attacking Agnes, the new round of darts converging on the unsuspecting city—she was partially to blame for it. She should have been there to coordinate and keep things from falling apart when the team went to Chicago. But instead, she'd shoved her responsibilities onto others so she could go off and, what? Be the Faction's enforcer? Bash in some skulls like she always did? She should have done better, and she needed to fix this. And knowing Pharmatrox had their sights set on Agnes again spurred her into action sooner.

She was breaking into the SubTran station—alone—and she was going to cut a deal with Zeln. And she wasn't taking no for an answer.

According to Sanjali's intel, a core group of troxies remained behind at the SubTran during incursions, headed up by a guy who matched Zeln's description—the attack on Agnes yesterday being a rare exception. Tomorrow, Mal planned to launch an assault on a Pharmatrox armory, so if she happened to be inside the SubTran at the time, she might get her chance to talk to Zeln. Problem was, she had no concept of what price he would name to switch sides. She just hoped she could give it to him. And if she couldn't...well, she was prepared to fight her way out.

Mal would never go for the idea, and usually, she'd just do whatever she wanted, consequences and other people's opinions be damned. But after the night they shared, taking off on her own, even if it was the right choice, felt...wrong. So, in a move that was completely unlike her, she was going to talk to Mal about it first. She owed him that.

Normally, at the late hour, she'd expect to find Mal in his room. But she knew that in the aftermath of battles, he liked to hole up in the war room, updating maps and making plans.

Sure enough, when she entered the large conference room, he loomed at the head of the table, papers strewn before him. He hadn't noticed her yet, and she took a moment to observe him. The way his brows knitted together as he strategized, strong fingers brushing his lips. The hard line of his jaw flickering as he concentrated.

Then she noticed other more intimate tics she'd come to know about him—the way he capped and uncapped his pen when he was mentally cataloguing how many volt rifles they had left. How he scratched his beard with both hands when he arrived at a conclusion he didn't like.

The way he flipped through the maps when he was thinking, always double-checking they were in order by sector from east to west. One look at him, and she could know exactly what was going through his mind. Like reading her favorite book.

As she inhaled a shaky breath, Mal looked up, his eyes softening in recognition. "Penny," he said, gifting her one of those rare smiles that was only for her.

"Hey," she replied, propping a hip on the edge of the table. "How bad is it?" She pointed her chin at the now organized pile of maps and papers.

"It's...not great. But it's manageable."

She knew he was lying from the way his lips twisted. "How bad is it really?"

He blew out a breath, lacing both hands behind his head, and fixed her with an earnest gaze. "It's pretty bad. I don't know how we'll survive the next two weeks, let alone fight off that resupply ship. We're spread pretty thin. Vick is out now recruiting in the suburbs, but who knows if it will be enough."

"I have a plan for how to help with some of that," she said. *Here goes.* "I'll sneak into the SubTran station alone. I can get eyes on their comms capabilities, maybe find out their troop movements, weapons cache locations, details about this resupply shipment—like when exactly it's coming, where it's docking, what's on it. If Chun hasn't infiltrated already, I can steal whatever Agnes needs to make a cure and swipe some of their comms equipment so we can get a message out to Canada or Faction splinter groups on the West Coast." As she reached the end of her spiel, she took a deep breath, plowing on with the grand finale. "And I'm going to find Zeln and cut a deal with him."

He sat back in his chair, arms crossed. "I already told you, Zeln won't make a deal with us. You don't know him like I do." But as Penny took in the sight of this man—her man—and all the goodness he brought with him, she knew that *Mal* was the one who didn't realize who he was dealing with—with her or with Zeln. "But as for the rest, it's a good idea. I'll go with you," he added.

She wasn't surprised, but a warm feeling glowed within her anyway. "I can wear a troxy uniform and helmet and blend in—not you though. If Zeln doesn't recognize you, any of the soldiers could. You've made a name for yourself. And," she said, tracing a fingertip across the tattoo swirling on his bicep, "you're a pretty memorable man."

With his big hand, he tucked a tuft of red hair behind her ear, rubbing the strands between his fingers. "You think they won't recognize the face of the Faction?"

She turned away from the intensity of his gaze, unable to look at him with the guilt roiling inside her, knowing full well what she planned to do. "You make me out to be more than I am."

At her words, his brows knitted together and he fastened a hand around her thigh, pulling her closer. The heat he ignited within her seeped into her bones, warming her in a way nothing else could, and his bright eyes seared through her. In a low, rumbling voice, he said, "You're everything."

The overwhelming desire to wrap her arms around him, to sink her fingers in his hair and feel the rasp of his beard against her lips shot through her like a bolt of lightning. The way he was looking at her had her heart beating a thunderous tattoo against her ribcage. And it had her second-guessing everything she was about to do, everything she'd ever thought about him or herself.

Malosi Olesa had tilted her world on its axis with just the power of his belief in her. She wished she could have that much faith in anything, let alone in herself.

Instead of saying any of that, she said, "I'm just a cog in the machine."

"No." He tilted her chin up until their eyes met. "You're everything to me, Pen," he said. "That's my truth."

How could she be everything to this man? *I don't know how to be that for him.* She had nothing to offer but her lifetime of scars and poor decisions. But as he tucked his hands into her back pockets and hauled her close in a deliciously possessive way, the weight of his words rushed over her, washing away all of her protests, if just for a moment. Before she was aware of what she was doing, she kissed him, even as part of her brain screamed at her for being such an idiot.

This would make it so much harder when he learned of her betrayal and inevitably left her—because she was going through with her plan, whether she had his support or not. And it was vital she carry it out alone. Because if it failed, she'd be the only one in harm's way. No reason to take a whole team down with her. And if Mal went too, he'd try to stop her.

It has to be like this. I'm the weapon of the revolution and I make the hard choices. All of the shit yesterday happened because she didn't do the hard thing—stay behind in the Capital where she was needed. But now, she'd do the hard thing that no one else wanted to do. The one thing that might be their only hope in winning this war and ending the troxies for good. The one thing that Mal should never have to do—make a deal with the devil.

But that idea didn't scare her—because she was a devil too.

The pain in Mal's past would never allow him to see his enemy as an asset. But Penny had no such qualms. It was *because* of who she was that she saw Zeln for the invaluable weapon he could be for them. She didn't have much to offer Mal, but she could do this for him. Remove the burden, the blame, the guilt, and take it upon her own shoulders. With Zeln on their side, she'd be protecting all of them, because he'd only continue picking them off, going after anyone who was close to Mal one by one—unless they killed him or converted him.

Whatever happened when she finally came face-to-face with Zeln, those were the only two outcomes she was willing to accept.

But to Penny, he was worth more alive than dead.

Any other thoughts were obliterated when Mal's tongue parted her lips, and she gave into him, just for this one moment before everything between them changed. Because if she went through with this? Allying with his sworn enemy?

There'd be no coming back from that.

Breaking away, she placed a hand on his chest, and he pressed his forehead to hers, breathing her in.

Even as she primed herself to nail the coffin of their relationship shut, a pang of...something blistered through her as Mal looked at her in that way no one else did. She wasn't sure if the feeling was joy and relief at being accepted as she was, bloodied past and scars and all, or...

"We'll hammer them tomorrow at the armory when they aren't expecting it," Mal said. "That will lay the groundwork for us to plan an incursion into the SubTran. We'll discuss your ideas in the war room debriefing afterwards."

...or is this how it feels to break your own heart?

Because the words that came out of her mouth next were nothing but lies.

"You're right. We'll come up with a plan together."

38

THE ARCHED METAL ROOF of the SubTran station glowed in the afternoon sunshine as Penny shivered from her lookout spot atop a nondescript office. Wind snarled through her hair, but the chill in her bones had little to do with the weather.

After lying to Mal last night, she'd laid awake for hours, every unspoken thought burning in her veins. She felt the same about everything he'd said and more, but she couldn't tell him. Not when, after what she was about to do, it would destroy them both.

"You okay?" Quentin asked, pulling away from his binoculars to frown at her. "I'm feeling a little funky myself. Naomi was distracting Lawrence in the kitchen last night, and the soup tasted like soapy boot water."

Penny snorted despite the bowling ball in her stomach. "I don't even know what that means."

"Gross is what it means."

"Keep a lookout," she said as she headed for the rooftop exit. "We don't want anything sneaking up on us. See you soon."

Quentin grumbled his agreement, disgruntled at being sidelined instead of blowing stuff up with Ivan, but continued his surveillance.

On the street below, Mal and his troops prepared for battle. Towering over everyone else, he caught her eye and headed over. "You ready for this?" he asked.

Not in the slightest. But she nodded. "Ready."

Mal flashed a brief, bright smile. *He's doing that way more often.* But then he grew serious, tracing a finger along her jaw before Will approached with a question, and he turned back to his troops, shooting another glance at Penny. She gave him a wooden smile, the only reaction she was capable of without feeling like a complete fuck bucket.

Before anyone else could show up and say something to make her feel squishy, she got into position. Agnes, Derek, and Vick nodded to her as she looked down the line at the rest of the regular crew—even Tara and Ivan were in on the fight, although both were sweaty and shaky. She cast a questioning glance at Vick beside her. As she spoke, the fierce woman's eyes never left Tara. "I don't know how much time they have left."

All the more reason to get into the SubTran today.

One street away from the armory, a blockade spilled across the road, armored trucks and troxy guards marching on patrol.

About five minutes later, the first of the bombs went off at the end of the street.

Thank you, Ivan and Quentin.

Shouts and engines roared to life as the troxy patrol came to investigate the disturbance, heading straight for the Faction's choke point.

"Now!" Mal shouted, and their blockade rushed straight for the incoming troops.

With a yell, Penny launched into the battle. Before long, she slipped into the sea of troxies without notice. She'd left her sickle behind today, opting for less noteworthy weapons. Zeroing in on the nearest troxy, she engaged him in a quick skirmish, backing away and luring him to a nearby alley. When she was out of sight of the Outposters—and Mal—she slammed her knife into the guard's throat. *Gotta hurry.* Ripping off his vest and helmet, she donned both, shoving her hair up inside the helmet.

Slinging the guard's volt rifle, she fired toward the Faction as she backed down the street, making sure her shots went high. But as she snuck farther behind enemy lines, she caught a quick glimpse of Mal, and a spike of doubt speared through her. When the battle was over, how long would it take for him to realize she was gone? Would he...would he think she was dead? Like when the Chosen took her?

Something visceral writhed within her at the thought of how Mal might react. Of what he might do. But she buried it deep, keeping her eyes peeled for trouble as she merged with the troxies. *No sign of Zeln.* Which meant he should be back in the SubTran station.

She approached an armored van where troxies were making quick work of loading crates into the back. Jumping in to help, she snuck a peek as she stacked one.

Darts. Fuck. A huge supply of them.

"Get this back to the station," barked a troxy officer. *That's my cue.*

"Yes, sir," she said and climbed in. As the van bounced over rubble, she sat on her hands to keep from fussing with her visor. Nobody spoke, for which Penny was grateful and also disappointed. She wouldn't gain any information from eavesdropping, but she also wouldn't get caught for a wrong answer if asked a direct question. Her disguise worked better if it wasn't pressure tested too much.

Finally, the van arrived at the SubTran and they got out. The troxy's stronghold was a bustle of activity, with vehicles crowding the street and troops coming up and down the stairs to the underground station, rushing off to the defend the armory. Feeling every minute of her clock ticking, Penny said in a gruff voice to a soldier beside her, "Boss wants to see me. You can take it from here?" *Whoever the fuck their boss is.*

The man grunted, waving her off, and she joined the small trickle of soldiers heading downstairs. Deep underground, the SubTran station opened into a cavernous two-story mall. The shops had long since been looted, and the dingy air smelled heavy with moisture and too many close bodies. Most of the troops were heading up to join the fight, but some remained behind to defend the stronghold. Trying not to look too lost, Penny walked the halls, searching for their war room or anything useful while keeping an eye out for Zeln or Dr. Chun.

Toward the end of the hall, someone exited a door marked "employees only," and Penny made a beeline for that. Peeking through the small window, she saw a long hallway stretching beyond, lit with naked incandescent bulbs. *Must be connected to a backup power source. Good chance their comms setup is back there too.* She hurried along, glancing through the windows in the doors as she passed. Some were offices, but she found nothing of interest. One room, their armory, was packed to the gills with weapons, and she snagged a handgun and a few extra knives.

But one of the rooms was a lab.

Eyes bulging, she stepped inside. No sign of Dr. Chun—or anyone, for that matter. *Maybe they're taking a break?* Beakers, tubes, huge machines with blinking LED displays, shelves filled with all manner of vials, pills, and other substances. *I don't know what any of this bullshit is.* But the whole room looked like a relatively capable setup, all of the machines new and shiny. A few vials were labeled as dionazole—detox serum—and she took those.

Once the coast was clear, she stepped outside, wishing she could have brought more things to Agnes and Silas. But maybe she could find a way to get them in here... As she continued searching, she made a mental note to be on the lookout for alternative routes that could be used for a sneaky re-entry—or a hasty escape, should she need it.

Then she arrived at a room with maps on the walls—*their war room?* A map of the Chesapeake Bay dominated the far wall, and one of the United States from the Midwest to the East Coast hung on the adjoining wall. A red pin stuck in the second map just shy of Manhattan. *Looks like Port Newark, maybe?* On the Chesapeake map, another red pin was in Baltimore. Several yellow pins dotted up and down the Eastern Seaboard. *What the...?*

Footsteps sounded in the hall, fast approaching. Without another thought, she hid inside the closet just as the door opened behind her, five troxy guards in the midst of a heated discussion. Through the slats in the door, she caught a glimpse. *Not Zeln.* But he had to be in this compound somewhere. Otherwise, she wasn't sure her plan was worth the risk.

"Look, not too much longer and then we're done with this shit," one of them, a short, stocky man, said.

"You think it'll be over after that?" A woman with dark curly hair. "No fucking way. Big plans like his mean a longer war. There's no way he'll just sit back and be satisfied after the resupply ship gets here."

Another man sat on the table, propping a leg on a chair. "He's out of his fucking mind."

The two troxies who hadn't spoken yet shrugged, one saying, "That's why we like him though, innit?"

"Yeah, 'cept for when he makes us stay here during fights."

"If you weren't so goddamn useless, maybe he'd let you help."

"Hey, you're here too. What's that make you?"

Then the group descended into arguing. *Can't they do this shit somewhere else?* The Faction's assault could be over at any time, and there was much of the compound left to explore.

As she waited for the group to disperse, she thought more about what they'd said. *Hmm..."big plans." So whatever general is in charge here has orders to expand beyond the Capital.* But who was the one calling the shots? Was it each general in each city making the decisions for their own battles? Or was there still some central Pharmatrox leader strategizing across the country? Maybe Agnes would know more about it—Penny wouldn't learn anything else from these bickering bimbos.

Finally, they took off. Penny waited five minutes before she abandoned her hiding place and searched the room more thoroughly, but she came up blank. After swiping a few holofiles for Agnes, she went to check the armory again. Maybe their comms didn't look like standard radios or walkie-talkies.

Spying a desk wedged between overflowing shelves against the armory's far wall, Penny started there, shoving items that looked like contraptions she'd seen Silas use for radio repairs into her pack. Engrossed as she was in her search, she didn't notice the door open silently behind her.

"He doesn't like it when people go in his desk."

Penny whipped around, a *huge* dude who rivaled Mal's size blocking the exit. "Sorry, I—"

"Where's Winslow? You're not the one s'posed to be on watch." The man narrowed his eyes.

"He's—"

"She."

Fuck. Before the man could reach for his weapon, she flung one of her knives, slicing him across the hand. He cried out, and Penny slammed into him with all of her weight. *Gotta shut him up real fast.* He fell back and cracked his head, in a daze, as she ripped the strap off of her rifle, wrapping it around his neck and yanking. His face turned from red to purple as he struggled.

Unable to let go unless she wanted to get annihilated, Penny head-butted him in the face with her helmet, knocking him out and cracking her visor. As he slumped forward, Penny dragged his body under the desk, then went the fuck outside, putting as much distance between them as possible. If she got caught, if they took off her helmet and saw who she was, she was never getting out alive.

A few steps from the exit into the main station, someone said from behind her, "Hey, you there! What happened to Big Roy?"

Goddamn it. Thought I had more time.

Running through their HQ would definitely draw attention, so she kept walking, and once she was through the door, she broke into a fast walk, doing her best to blend into the troxy troops milling about. But a few seconds later, she heard the door bang open behind her, followed by disgruntled voices.

Shit. As she glanced around the station, she had an idea. Jumping to the tracks below, she headed for the opposite platform to a parked SubTran train disappearing into the depths of the tunnel. She climbed up and slipped into the first car through the back door, ducking below the plexiglass to wait until her pursuers gave up.

As her breaths slowed, something felt...off.

Why does it smell like bleach?

Unnerved, Penny tiptoed to the door leading to the connecting car, the window shade drawn so she couldn't see into it. *Even better for a hiding spot.* She ducked inside, closing the door behind her—

And was met with a rotten smell of death so strong she nearly gagged. Dried blood slathered the windows, seats, every surface, but that wasn't the worst of it.

On the floor, a body sat propped against the wall, its skin covered in bite marks and missing chunks of flesh, its detached jaw sitting on the ground beside it. Two more bodies occupied the train car in similar states of decay.

What the fuck happened here?

Before Penny could investigate, the doors at the opposite end of the car opened, revealing the connecting train cars shrouded in the darkness of the tunnel.

Feral growls seeped through the space, followed by gray hands with cracked nails gripping onto the door.

A soft *snick* behind her—

Then the bodies came, mouths parted around blackened teeth, eyes weeping obsidian tears.

Fuck on a stick.

A swarm of turned plugged the door, fighting to get into the bloody train car, their growls crescendoing in the small space.

Penny scrambled backward for the safety of the bleached train car, but the latch wouldn't budge. "No, no, *fuck*," she muttered, yanking in vain. *That sound...someone locked me in.*

Reaching for the emergency window, she pulled the lever—and it came off in her hand. Cursing, she threw it aside and took her rifle, smashing it into the plexiglass. But it wouldn't break. Panic seized her in its unforgiving grip, her breath wheezing.

There has to be a way out.

She tried every window, every door. Nothing. A few seconds later, a turned burst through the bodies clogging the doorway, and the rest followed in an unending stream, heading straight for her.

Her eyes ping-ponged between the dead bodies, and for a brief moment, time slowed to a halt.

No one is coming for me. No one knows where I am.

I'm trapped. Just like them.

A pang of regret spiraled through her at the thought of Mal realizing her betrayal and charging in to find her body in this fucking tomb. Of Quentin on the lookout for her, waiting and waiting for her to return.

There is no way I survive this.

But fuck it, I have to try.

With an unearthly yell, she fired volts into the oncoming turned, who screeched and hissed, leaping over seats. Some shots found their marks, but it didn't matter.

Enhanced turned. Ditching her rifle, she grabbed her knives, wishing for her sickle. As she sliced through gray flesh, black blood sprayed the floor into an oil slick. A few turned fell, but not enough.

A screech, then one leapt onto her back, ripping off her helmet and sinking its teeth into her neck. Screaming, she reached behind her and slammed her blade until the creature fell off.

But at the smell of her blood, the train car churned into a feeding frenzy.

A turned charged her, and when she held out her knife to ward it off, it bit into her forearm, rotten teeth sinking deep into her flesh until her guttural cries matched that of the surrounding chaos.

But as it tasted her blood, something happened.

Instead of ripping her apart, a river of black ichor poured from its eyes and down its face until...the whites of its eyes returned.

No way, that's—

Another grabbed her other arm, biting it. And the same thing happened—black ichor pouring from its eyes and then—

A turned plowed into her, shoving her against the metal wall, her helmet-less head banging against it with a painful crack.

Dizzy from blood loss, she wasn't sure if she was seeing things or not, but two of the turned—the ones that had bitten her—no longer had orbs of onyx for eyes. They looked almost...human again, eyes with white sclera shattered with black veins. Like users not yet turned.

I must be hallucinating.

Another bite, this time on her thigh, and the thing had jaws like a fucking snapping turtle. Slamming her knife into its skull, feeling the scrape against bone, her grip weakened as turned swarmed around her.

Tired. So tired.

The last thing Penny saw before she plunged into unconsciousness was a shadow passing across the window, followed by the screeching metal of a door being pried open.

A brief flash of someone...familiar...

Then the darkness greeted her, and she remembered nothing else.

39

ELEVEN MONTHS AGO

*Y*OUR FAULT. *YOUR FAULT.*

"Shut up," Penny muttered, sniffing more white powder from the back of her hand as she sat inside her piece-of-shit car. She'd been there for hours, hidden in the brush that her dad refused to trim, much to her mother's chagrin. Quentin would be home from his welding internship soon, and she wanted to catch a glimpse of him before she went home for the night.

A month had passed since the...arson incident. And in that month, she'd stayed far as fuck away from her family. From anyone. She didn't want their sympathy or their pitying gazes. A charged hush always fell across the office any time she walked in, so she'd taken to working from home and pulling overnight shifts.

But the thoughts, the memories, the *voices* kept intruding. *More. Need more.* Another hit of dust had her coming more alive by the second. Using was the only time she didn't feel like a walking corpse, but it looked like today, she'd be testing the limits of her tolerance. She'd thought dust was supposed to be some kind of vitamin supplement bullshit—the government was always giving that shit away for free—but it did something different to her. Made her mind sharper, her reflexes better.

Yeah, sometimes it gave her wild-ass hallucinations and she heard different voices than usual, but if the tradeoff was not having to stew in her own misery for a few hours? To lose herself in the feeling of raw power that surged through her? She'd take that over debilitating guilt any day. Relief was relief, and she didn't question it. If she wasn't using dust, it would be booze or drugs or something else.

Blissed out and feeling great, time jumped. Before Penny knew it, it was night and the cloudy lights of their old pickup truck trundled down the driveway. Quentin, returned home. Sitting up, she pressed her palm to the windshield, wishing she could get closer. But no. She couldn't let him see her like this. Of all people, his was the pity she couldn't handle.

The rap of a crowbar against her window had her jumping out of her skin, and she reeled at the sight of Uncle Hal, grinning like a devil. "Your fault, Penny. You brought this on him." In a blink, her dead uncle was across the lawn, following Quentin into the dark house.

Dead. He's dead. But was he? His voice had sounded so real, the heat of his foul breath puffing in her face through the cracked window. Was she really going to sit there and wait to find out if he had been a hallucination more vivid than any of the others? That thought had her feet hitting the pavement.

Visions of *that night* could sometimes break out into living nightmares that seemed real but fuzzy with a dreamlike quality. This time was different though. Something about it felt more *alive*. Maybe a byproduct of using more dust than she ever had, but maybe not. Every detail from *that night* lived in her brain, and she didn't remember seeing her uncle get carted away in a body bag like—*like Lexa*. She forced herself to think the name. So maybe he'd made it out alive, somehow, and now he was here for Quentin and her family.

She had to stop him.

Her feet hit the wooden steps of the porch, and then time jumped again.

Flames. Smoke.

Standing in the middle of her burning childhood home as smoke seared her lungs, her uncle's laughs cackled in her ears, the whir of a circular saw cutting through the roar of the flames. She held her hands to her ears, screaming, sobbing.

"You did this, Penny." Hal's harsh voice. "You did this."

Then everything went black.

When Penny came to, moist leaves stuck to her cheek. Spitting out dirt, she groaned, pulling herself to her feet. She was in the forest near where she'd parked—she recognized the trees from countless times exploring with Quentin when they were kids.

Another night, another bender. Another waking nightmare. Dust didn't always do that to her, but when it did, it could be fucking brutal. Luckily, she often didn't remember much of it.

But this time was different. A feeling of dread weighed in her stomach, the smell of old smoke wafting in the air. The knees of her jeans were muddy like she'd tripped, and her silver lighter lay on the forest floor in front of her. Picking it up, the horrible feeling grew heavier as she flicked it, and the flame ignited.

With a painful gasp, she remembered.

She remembered everything.

You did this, Penny. You did this.

40

B RIGHT FLUORESCENT LIGHTS LANCED through Penny's eyelids as she blinked back into awareness. Raw crescents of pain burned across her body, accentuated by the cold metal of the chair.

Hands zip-tied behind me. Legs duct taped together. Armor is gone. No weapons. Wait—

Wiggling her right foot in her boot, she smiled.

Boot knife still there. I'll have to thank Agnes for that idea later.

She shifted in her seat, turning her neck. *Everything fucking hurts, but nothing is broken.* Dried blood coated her body, and she was sure she looked like a feral beast.

Feral beast.

The memories jolted through her and she felt the pain and shock anew. Teeth sinking into her flesh. Black eyes turning white. Human again.

There's a way to cure the turned? And it's something in my blood? Or I imagined it...

But she couldn't think about that now.

First, if it was true, she had to survive long enough to get the fuck out and get word to Agnes, who could actually do something about it. She had no idea how long she'd been unconscious or if Mal had realized she was gone, but she couldn't sit around and wait for rescue.

Because no one's coming.

But someone had been watching her. *Probably not Dr. Chun, judging by the zip ties and duct tape.* The bustle of the troxies' underground HQ buzzed as a low hum in the background, so she wasn't far from where she'd been attacked, maybe at the next station.

But who had it been? And why?

Footsteps echoed down the tunnel. She thought about feigning unconsciousness until the person left and she could escape, but she was here for recon, so she might as well try and question them and find out what they wanted with her. And if she'd hallucinated the black eyes returning to normal or not.

A few seconds later, a lithe figure vaulted onto the platform. Flexing her hands against her bindings, she wished she could sink her nails into the smug fucker's face.

Zeln.

Brown skin, close-cropped dark hair, and sharply intelligent eyes greeted her. The man carried himself with the ease of a honed weapon who had nothing to fear even in a world wrought with danger. He watched her impassively for a moment, then a chilling Cheshire cat grin melted across his face.

"Pretty Penny," he said. "A pleasure."

The cult's moniker grated against her ears, and the puzzle pieces jolted into place. He'd been in cahoots with the Chosen, probably affording them protection and all that troxy gear in exchange for wreaking havoc and making sure none of their messengers made it to or from Chicago.

A perfect distraction. *A smoke screen to keep us chasing our fucking tails while the troxies plotted resupply shipments.* A brilliant, mercenary thing to do.

This guy's good.

But the only thing she said was, "You."

The grin now replaced with a face that was all business, he said, "Me."

"Pharmatrox is lucky to have a weapon like you in their arsenal," she said, reeling. *This is what I wanted—the chance to make a deal. So I'd better get talking.* And flattery could buy her enough time to get a fucking grip.

"Ah. So Mal has filled you in, then."

Frowning, she jerked in her restraints. "Care to explain why I'm tied to a fucking chair?"

"Purely precautionary," he said as he helped her drink from the canteen he'd brought. "Don't want you running off."

"How'd you get to be the one to draw prisoner watering duty?"

"I volunteered." Something danced in his dark eyes that she couldn't read.

"Were you the one who found me in the train car? How the fuck did those turned get in there?"

"We use those cars for prisoner interrogations, torture, things like that."

"Charming," she said, noting how he didn't directly answer her questions.

He shrugged, capping the canteen and setting it aside. "You asked."

Now that she'd regained her composure, she said, "What are you doing here, Zeln? Guy like you could be doing anything, anywhere and still make your money without having to deal with shit like this."

Leaning against the wall, he slid his hands in his pockets. The picture of ease. "The pay is good. And Pharmatrox has something I want."

Now's my chance. "For a while, I was a mercenary like you. I know you're not interested in who wins this war. I also know you have contacts in other countries with no allegiance to anyone who can be bought, same

as you. If you help us win, Kev can set you up with whatever you want."
At the glint in Zeln's eyes, she could tell her words found their mark. "So
name your price, and we'll pay it. Mal won't like it—which is probably
why you'll go for it. So, what do you really want?"

A slow smile spread across his face, but it was tinged with a hint
of something...twisted. Nothing could have prepared her for what he'd
request.

"You."

Penny's mind wiped blank. "What?"

Without warning, he slammed something into the side of her neck, a
silent scream lodging in her throat. She thrashed, but he didn't relent.
"Specifically, your blood," he said, stepping back and twirling a now
bright red syringe. "I've got big plans, Pretty Penny."

"My...?" Her mind whirred into overdrive as she tried to comprehend
what the fuck was happening. *So it was real, the black eyes returning to
white. And he saw it happen...* The words from the conversation she'd
overheard from the bozos in the map room came creeping back to her.

"Big plans like his mean a longer war."

"He's out of his fucking mind..."

And then the cold truth coiled around her.

Zeln was not Pharmatrox. He was something else entirely. Something
far worse.

Because if he was truly with the troxies, he'd be working to end this
war as soon as possible and subjugate the people. But he wasn't. He'd
want to drain her of her blood, leave her for dead, remove her as a threat
so there'd be no hope to save the turned. But she was still alive.

So if he wasn't working for Pharmatrox, who was he working for?

"You're not trying to end the war at all," she said. "You're feeding it."

With a dispassionate smile, he moved to shove another needle into her neck, but she jerked away, lunging to bite his fucking nose off his smarmy fucking face. Stopping her with a knife at her throat, he said, "Play nice or one of my knives will find its way into Mal's heart. And this time, I won't miss." As she stiffened at his words, he ran the flat of his blade across her cheek in a deadly caress, a knowing look flaring in his eyes. "But perhaps I already have his heart."

"Give me that knife and I'll show you how to fucking use it."

Zeln only laughed at her threat. She wished she could make good on her promise, but her options were limited. She could escape zip ties—she'd practiced many times. Never knew what would happen if a volatile client caught her doing slightly less than legal surveillance. But with her arms behind her, it would be a bit more difficult.

Especially with a knife at her neck.

So she did what she came here to do—she made a deal with the devil. "I'll play nice if you answer my questions. One syringe for one question."

"I could beat you unconscious and take as much of your blood as I want."

"You could. But it would be a shame to risk spilling any of this precious blood that you need so much—which leads to my first question. What do you want it for?"

Zeln studied her as he twirled a syringe. Like a cat toying with its prey. She took the opportunity to surreptitiously test her restraints again. Her calves were duct taped together, but if she could swing forward and stand up, she could break the zip ties behind her back. But now that Zeln might be willing to talk, she could play captive a bit longer.

"I need it so we can continue making a cure for the darts and the turned," he replied, then stuck the syringe in her neck. She flinched and thought, *Continue? So Pharmatrox has a cure for the darts now?* "But there's something about your blood…" His dark eyes roamed over her, observing her like a specimen in a petri dish. "The dust affected you differently, didn't it? You're one of those special ones Pharmatrox likes to study."

Admitting that she'd quit the dust cold turkey and lived to tell the tale didn't seem like a good idea—he'd never let her go. Not that she expected him to let her go at all—she was plotting various escape routes as he talked. One of them involved beating him to hell with the remnants of this chair once she got out of it. So she said, "Never used before."

His expression didn't waver, but the silence that stretched between them said he didn't believe her. But he didn't press her on it, so she asked another question. "Why does Pharmatrox want a cure for the turned?"

"I didn't say Pharmatrox wanted it," he said, sticking another needle in her neck.

"That didn't answer the question."

"*I* want it. My allies would pay billions for a mind-control weapon like troxapine and the enhanced version that's in the darts. But buyers want assurances that if someone tried to use it against them, they'd have a cure if their people turned."

"So you're looking to sell both the hurricane and the insurance."

His reptilian smile didn't touch his eyes. "Something like that."

"Pharmatrox will find out what you're doing, and they'll do worse than kill you."

"They've already tried. But it's too late for them."

"What?"

"That sounds like a question," he said, drawing another vial of blood. It took everything in her not to growl. "*I* have the people, the supplies, the connections to win this war," he said. "They have the ultimate weapons—troxapine and the darts—and now, I have those too."

But win the war for who? "Who are you working for?"

Chuckling, he filled another syringe. "I don't work for anyone."

Oh god. This man is far more dangerous than even Mal realizes. "So you're doing all of this for, what, a personal payday?"

Taking his due, he said, "I've had my eye on Pharmatrox for many years. I'm sure Mal filled you in on our...colorful history. Pharmatrox had no qualms about my past record. In fact, *they* sought *me* out. After leaving their army, I rebuilt my reputation from a demoted failure to a flawless freelancer. I made myself too good to ignore, and Pharmatrox was quick to offer me a restoration of my rank, an official pardon, and a constant flow of contracts. And when they offered me a job only I could do, a job that would bring me face-to-face with Malosi Olesa again to personally stab a knife in his fucking heart? I accepted immediately."

So Zeln knew exactly what he signed up for. She'd known the guy was an evil bastard, but that comment alone had earned him a personal introduction to her sickle.

"I'd been working a few contracts for Pharmatrox in the lead-up to the ferry incident, so I was already plugged in to what they were doing with troxapine. With a product like that in my back pocket, I could make some very powerful friends. Pharmatrox had everything I needed to manufacture and sell troxapine at scale already in place, it just wasn't *mine* yet. Nor was the formula stable. So I bided my time, further integrating myself into their operations, quietly sowing the seeds of doubt among the employees and civilians, waiting for the right moment while they perfected their poison.

"As everything with the dust unfolded, I saw what Pharmatrox didn't. That their own employees were willing to turn against them, if given proper compensation and assurances. That the civilians are not as weak and stupid as Pharmatrox wants to think. That they, too, wanted to join the fight, but not on the Faction's side. So I wove a nice story of a country without Pharmatrox and these creatures running around. They took to the idea like flies to honey, all too eager to pitch in.

"Then when you took out the Spire and Dr. Hansen, you gave me the perfect opportunity to step up and take her place. At that point, they were changing the troxapine formula too fast for the detox serum to keep up, but they thought it was the only way to regain control over a rapidly deteriorating situation. Blinded by their desperation, they pushed ahead and created the ultimate weapon—the enhanced troxapine in the darts—without a fail-safe in place. Their last-ditch effort to salvage everything—something I advised them to do. My buyers would be very interested in something like that."

As the magnitude of his plan swelled around her, Penny couldn't breathe. *He's been planning this takeover for years—and we fucking helped him.* "Ever since the Spire, we haven't been fighting Pharmatrox. We've been fighting *you.*"

"Correct. But you, Penny," he said with that chilling smile, wagging a finger at her. "You and Mal really pulled through for me. When you blew up Pharmatrox's last holdout lab in Chicago, you crushed their chances of ever being able to rebuild or push me out. By then, I already had my scientists here producing a cure for the darts and the turned. Now, with the help of your blood, I'll not only be the hero who cleaned up the mess Pharmatrox made, I'll be getting fucking rich while I quietly sell the sickness and the cure to my very...generous contacts.

"So yes, the payday is part of it. But if I depose both the Faction and Pharmatrox—organizations the world sees as terrorists, depending on what side of the argument you're on—I'll be the one who saved the country from itself. When the resupply ship arrives, I'll have enough reinforcements to seize the Capital and march on New York."

Fuck, the tanker is for him, *it was never for the troxies. We've miscalculated everything.*

"I have other shipments planned, and soon the East Coast will be under my control," he continued. "After the war is over, I can remain in power and keep manufacturing troxapine and darts or sell off my seat to the highest bidder."

Jesus god. "So it's not just about a business opportunity or a personal vendetta. This is a coup."

A vacant smile was his only reply as he took another vial of blood. Something scuffled on the opposite platform from the top of the escalator, but Penny ignored it, reeling from Zeln's revelations. *This is way fucking worse than anything we could have imagined. I have to warn Mal.* But she wasn't naive enough to think Zeln would let her go after admitting all of this. He intended to keep her captive until he no longer had use for her, then he'd kill her. It's what she'd do.

So she did the only thing she could—kept him talking until she could figure out how the fuck to get out of there. "All of this—everything we've been doing in the Capital for the past few months—it's all been a ruse," she said as she stumbled through her thoughts. "You killed our messengers and drones to prevent us from hearing how bad things were in Chicago. And when the messengers finally got through...shit." She broke off at the smug look on his face. "They got through, not because we eradicated the cult, but because you *let them through* to draw us out of the city. I'm guessing that 'troxy' incursion on Chicago's wall and the 'unaffiliated' civilian groups patrolling the roads were your doing? The ambush on Kev and the Canadian emissary too?"

His only response was a smile and to take another vial of blood. *And painting us as terrorists on the international feed, it had to be him if the troxies are really as weak as he says.*

Fuming at the realization of just how deep this went, she continued. "Any progress we made in the Capital was you giving up the battles to win the war, knowing you'd obliterate everything once you had your resupply shipment. No, that wasn't a question," she said, arching away from him.

She'd be impressed if she wasn't fucking pissed they'd fallen for his tactics. They'd been wrong, so wrong. They'd underestimated Zeln, too distracted by all the moving parts he'd been throwing at them while he flew under the radar. This guy was a master manipulator—*and I should have listened to Mal.*

"When I started putting all of this in motion," Zeln said, "I only had one goal in mind—destroying Pharmatrox and Malosi Olesa. The rest is just extra. He and I could've done this together. But all those years ago, he refused me. He chose them, the company that crushed us under its boot, that killed our friends and *blamed me* for it. They took everything from me. But now? I've taken over Pharmatrox from the inside out, forced the snake to eat its own tail, and seized all of their resources, everything they built, for *myself.* They are *mine.* Mine to use and mine to destroy as I see fit. And as for General Olesa? His bill is due next."

And then Zeln put voice to the daunting realization she'd just had.

"You can't buy me off, Penny. What I seek is worth far more than money. And you're the only one who can give it to me. It's been fun playing your little game, but I'm done now. Hold still."

Wait a second... As she replayed his fucking James Bond villain speech at hyper-speed, something else clicked into place. Something vital.

"...and now, with the help of your blood..."

"...you're the only one who can give it to me..."

We might still have a chance.

"When you attacked Agnes," she said, "you knew what she was doing, somehow. You keep saying you're working on a cure, but you need her and her machine. You need *me*. That's why I'm still alive. Because your scientists haven't figured out the cure yet. You have *nothing*."

The slight pursing of his lips was the only indication that he was displeased at her connecting the dots. "I bugged the house on Maple Street, so I've known what she was working on for quite some time." He flicked a syringe full of her blood with a satisfied smile. "But now, my scientists will have everything they need to develop the cure."

As she struggled, another sound came from the opposite platform, a little louder this time, but she only had eyes for the fucking menace in front of her. "You'd better hope you kill me after this, Zeln. Because when I get out of here, I will come for you."

"Not if I keep you locked up here."

"You think I haven't broken out of zip ties before? With me alive, you still have a chance to make your cure. An infinite blood bank—but not if I'm dead."

"You look pretty alive to me."

Sounds like a fucking challenge if I ever heard one. I've got one shot at this, I—

All of the emergency lights blinked out, plunging them into darkness.

What the fuck? Faulty wiring? Or is someone else here?

Doesn't matter.

Leaning back in the chair, she threw all of her body weight forward, kicking for Zeln's approximate location. Her boots made contact, and she landed on her feet as she heard him cursing in the dark. Bent over with the chair behind her back, she brought her bound arms down, using the chair as a wedge to snap the zip ties. Putting her hands together, she forced them between her duct-taped legs and split the tape like an online video taught her all those years ago.

Then the lights flickered back on, illuminating Zeln rubbing a bruise forming on his jaw. Pulling out her boot knife, she held it to her own throat. "I'm pretty quick with a knife."

A brief flash of surprise crossed his face at her admittedly impressive escape—she hadn't been sure it would work—before he smoothed his expression. "You won't do it."

Something shuffled below on the tracks as she pressed the knife harder until blood ran down her neck. "You're willing to bet my life on it? Willing to bet your *cure* on it?"

"There's too much fire in you to go down without a fight."

He was right, and he knew it. If she killed herself right now, it wouldn't matter. Zeln had her blood, and it might be enough to make a cure that he'd hoard for himself and his *customers*. And if any of Zeln's contacts found out about her blood, they'd want it for themselves. Maybe even kill her to prevent anyone else from getting it. She could save more people than she ever thought possible, end the war—as long as she got her blood into the right hands.

Her only option was to steal her blood and get the fuck back to the stadium to warn everyone about the goddamn tsunami that was headed straight for them.

So she had to do something that would make Zeln panic.

"You have no idea what I'm capable of," she said, and drew the knife across her throat.

Zeln shouted, lunging for her, and she stumbled away—but then something plowed into him from the side. Bleeding from the shallow cut on her throat and dizzy from earlier blood loss, Penny almost didn't believe what she was seeing.

Mal, hands wrapped around Zeln's throat, fury gleaming in his eyes.

41

MAL'S HERE. HE CAME for me. Did he hear everything? How did he know where to find me?

No time for that now.

Spying her pack nearby, she scooped it up while Zeln and Mal tore into each other. Reaffixing her weapons to her belt, she took aim at the duo with her handgun.

"Stay out of this, Penny!" Mal roared as he launched a meaty punch into Zeln's side. She couldn't tell if his rage was at facing his enemy or at her. *Maybe both.*

"His pockets! I need the vials in his pockets!" she said, aiming for Zeln's kneecap, but he wouldn't stand still long enough for her to take the shot.

"Wha—?"

Zeln dove into Mal, landing atop him and drawing a knife. He stabbed, but Mal dodged while Penny fired at Zeln's back. But the fucker was wearing specialized armor, so it absorbed the shots and he barely even flinched. As the two struggled, shouts sounded down the tunnel, followed by the sizzle of volt rifles powering up.

They were about to be outnumbered.

"Please tell me you did not come here alone," Penny shouted.

"What, like you did?" he yelled back. "They're coming—"

Right on cue, an explosion ripped through the tunnel, the ceiling raining rubble onto the incoming troxy troops—or, well, Zeln's troops—but enough made it through that they'd still have a problem fighting them off. Keeping the high ground, Penny fired her volt rifle to keep them from climbing up while she scrambled to think of a plan.

A flash of bronze from the opposite platform—Quentin, punching the air in triumph. Instead of being upset he'd disobeyed instructions to stay put, Penny was elated. Because not only had Mal come for her, her little brother had too.

Then another welcome sight—Agnes, Derek, and Tara descending the mile-long escalators.

They came for me. They all did.

Some weird fucking feeling filled Penny's chest, but she refocused on the fight. "Pockets, Mal!" she reminded him as Agnes and the others aided her from the opposite platform. A few soldiers clambered up, heading for Mal, but Penny headed them off.

"How'd you guys get in here?" Penny shouted to Agnes, cross-checking a guard in the chest. "I thought all the smaller stations were sealed off?"

"They were," Agnes said, rapid-fire shooting and hacking with her machete.

"Nothing a crowbar and some determination couldn't solve," Derek replied.

"Took a page out of Quentin's little breaking-and-entering handbook," said Tara. Even with hollow eyes and shaky hands, she was a formidable opponent, thwacking guards with her baseball bat. *But we still don't have a cure. Shit.*

With his knife outstretched, Mal lunged for Zeln's pocket, ripping it open and dragging the blade along his thigh. Zeln yelled but still managed to scramble for the vials. Penny was having none of that though. Planting a firm boot in his back, she kicked him, and he went sprawling. As the vials flew across the platform, she hurried to collect them, then stowed them in her pack with the stolen tech.

"Let's go!" Derek shouted.

But Mal didn't acknowledge him, locked in on Zeln, face twisted in a ferocious expression that craved bloodshed. The two swirled in a deadly dance, both battered and bloodied but more determined than she'd ever seen them. And Mal was favoring his right side, bleeding from his ribs, while Zeln looked ready for another round.

We have to end this now.

Before they could reengage, Penny grabbed Mal's arm, dragging him toward the escalators. He moved to shake her off, but she held fast. "You will die if you keep fighting him," she said. "And I'm not going to lose you." Even though she'd wrecked whatever chance at a future they had, it didn't matter. He would not die in this hell hole because of her.

Teeth bared, Mal looked ready to argue. But across the platform, the shouts of their crew seemed to pull him from his bloody rage. With a growl, he jumped down and raced across the tracks, Penny following.

But Zeln wouldn't give up so easily.

"Stop them!" Zeln's voice boomed through the station as his troops pursued them up the longest escalator Penny had ever seen. Mal brought up the rear, laying down cover fire, as they all surged for the spot of daylight.

"Lawrence and Naomi have an EV parked a few blocks over," Agnes said over her shoulder, feet pounding on the metal stairs.

Finally, they burst outside, and Penny glanced over her shoulder, reaching for Mal's hand—

With a grunt, Mal's face contorted as he fell to his knees. Penny caught him and staggered under his weight, a knife thrown by Zeln lodged in his upper back.

"Derek, Agnes!" Penny whipped around as the troops bared down on them, Zeln in the lead, grinning like a fiend. "Tara!"

But Quentin was the one who grabbed an extra rifle from Derek, holding one in each hand and shooting into their pursuers. "Back off!" he shouted.

Between all of them, with Quentin covering, they carried Mal's massive weight to the EV. Once they were inside, Lawrence peeled away, heading for the stadium.

"What the hell happened?" Derek asked.

Sagging forward with the knife hilt sticking out of his back, Mal draped an arm across Penny's shoulders, bleeding onto her clothes. "I got stabbed," he wheezed, wiping blood from his mouth. "Multiple times."

Fucking hell. Don't die on me, Mal. Please. She'd never seen him look so unsteady before.

"Evidently." Derek frowned. "How bad?"

"Probably have a few more seconds before I pass out," he said, taking a drink from the bottle Quentin offered. "He got me in my old scar. Hurts like a motherfucker. Deep cuts on my ribs, some of 'em bruised or sprained." He descended into wracking coughs and then cursed. "Don't think he caught my lung, but I'm not sure. Don't touch the knife. Take me to Ju Lee. She'll know what to do." Ju Lee had medic field training and experience with battlefield triage, but if his injuries were too severe...

No. He's going to be fine. Because if he wasn't—Penny refused to even complete the thought.

In his last moments of lucidity, Mal focused his full attention on her, golden eyes burning. "I told you—you didn't know who you were dealing with." His words hit her like individual bullets straight through the weak spots in her armor. The scuffling sounds and disturbances she'd heard while interrogating Zeln...it had been him, getting into position to rescue her, even as she betrayed him.

And he'd heard everything.

"I—"

But Mal slumped forward, plunging into unconsciousness.

"Right on schedule," muttered Derek, but Penny could tell from his pinched forehead and the way he clutched Agnes's hand that he was scared too.

Everything is fucked.

Mal's life hung in the balance, and all Penny could do was lie on the floor, anchored to the cold concrete. She couldn't leave her room. Didn't ask anyone how he was. Didn't go check on him.

Because while she feared losing him, the thought of facing him carved a dark pit inside her. To see him clinging to life because she'd gone rogue again—that was more than she could take.

She'd been stupid, careless—and arrogant, thinking that she alone could fix their problems and win the war. She thought she knew best—again—so she hadn't trusted Mal's judgment, had thought he was too biased to see that Zeln was just another pawn to be used.

But Zeln had outplayed them all.

And now Mal was paying the price. Because of her.

It was just like what happened with Lexa. Pain, destruction—death—because she'd taken a stupid risk, made a poor decision, put other people in danger. Lexa should never have been in that warehouse, just like Mal should never have been in the SubTran. And if she'd pumped the brakes and made a plan with everyone like he'd wanted, maybe he wouldn't be bleeding out in the infirmary right now.

I'm so afraid of depending on others, of being part of a team, that I'm willing to get myself and everyone around me killed. Where does it fucking end? When everyone I care about is dead?

She truly did not deserve a man like Mal. Or a friend like Lexa. Or a brother like Quentin. Or the support of any of the Outposters. She'd failed them all, and she'd fail them again.

When their group had arrived back at the stadium, Penny turned over her pack of stolen gear and made a beeline for her room. The feeling of Mal's lifeless body collapsing into her arms played on repeat in her mind, but that was nowhere near as heavy as the weight of guilt that now clung to her like a second skin. Another layer of darkness added to her already black-as-night shroud.

And now, on top of everything else, they were going to lose the war.

If they didn't stop Zeln in two weeks, they'd never stop him at all. He'd grown too powerful, right under their noses. Her rage burned bright, ready to explode. He'd almost taken Mal away from her—still might. And he'd kill anyone close to her to get her to give up her blood. Quentin, Agnes, all of them—they all had bigger targets on their backs now thanks to her.

None of this was worth it. Not if Mal dies.

A banging on her door yanked her out of her dark thoughts. When it flew open, Vick stood on the other side covered in dirt and sweat. Agnes was right behind her, expression grim.

"We've got a problem," Agnes said while Vick caught her breath, as if she'd just run all the way there. "Sorry to barge in, but I was the first one to see her when she came back from the suburbs and—"

"The resupply ship will be here tomorrow," Vick interrupted. "By the evening, probably. Maybe sooner."

This cannot fucking be happening.

Two weeks to prepare for a big battle was a long shot but at least within the realm of possibility. But *tomorrow*?

We are so fucked.

But it fit with Zeln's actions—earlier, he hadn't followed them back to the stadium to hit them with everything he had, because he knew he could wait twenty-four hours for his shipment and take them out easily.

"Are you sure?" Penny asked.

"My contacts are tapped into troxy troop movements and have their own people on the inside," Vick explained. "Some coastal towns are prepping for something big and heard of a shipment coming in. Say it'll be docking ten miles from here."

"There is no way we can prepare in time," Penny said.

"We don't have much choice," Agnes said. "If Zeln gets that resupply, he'll be unstoppable. We have to try."

"It's not enough time," Penny repeated. "We've never attempted an operation of this magnitude, and on unfamiliar terrain with untrained people, with our general benched—" She cut off, wincing. *It's my fault he can't lead his own troops.*

Agnes placed a hand on her shoulder, stopping her in her tracks. "We have *you*, Penny."

It took everything in her not to cower in the corner. Shaking her head and glancing between the two, she said, "I am wildly out of my depth here. Mal should be doing this. We need him. I need him—" As the words flew out of her mouth, the power of them smacked into her like a bulldozer.

I need him. But not as a general. I need him.

And I need him to know it.

"I've gotta go." Running for the door, she left Vick and Agnes staring after her in stunned silence. "Ah, wait!" she said, doubling back. "Need to fill everyone in on a fuck ton of things. Find the crew—you know who I mean—and meet back here." Then she took off again, heading to the infirmary.

To Mal's side, where she should've been this entire fucking time.

42

"WHAT DO YOU MEAN you lost him? How would he get any-where when he can barely stand?" Penny felt marginally bad for railing at the poor infirmary assistant, but all she could think about was finding Mal and telling him how fucking sorry she was, and a shit ton of other things that would probably come spilling out.

"Easy, Penny," Ju Lee said as she approached. After the back-to-back battles, the infirmary was packed. "He can't have gotten far."

Glancing at the assistant with a sheepish look, Penny said, "Sorry for being a dick. I'll send some more people to help," she added to Ju Lee over her shoulder as she hustled away.

Wandering the halls in a frantic state, she willed the darkness gathering around her heart to hold off. She couldn't afford to panic and lose her shit right now. *Just let me find him. Please.*

But where the fuck would he go? Why would he—

And then she realized exactly where he'd go—because it's where she'd gone.

To his side.

Rushing back to her room, her spirits sank when she saw that it was empty. No sign of Mal. Flopping onto her cot, she threw an arm over her eyes and tried to slow her breathing. She'd never find him if she passed out from hyperventilation.

"Pen."

The one voice that could drag her from the brink.

Her body reacted before her mind could catch up, feet carrying her to Mal in an instant. "Are you okay?" she asked, hand frozen on the doorframe as she drank him in, the tattered edges of her heart aching with regret. Because at that moment, the reality of what she felt for him breached the surface for the first time.

Even leaning against the door, bare torso wrapped in bandages, sweating from exertion, Mal gave her a stern look. "Imagine my dismay when I wake up from my short coma to find Derek's ugly mug hovering over me instead of my woman."

My woman. She'd been preparing for the fallout of her actions, readying herself to rip him from her life. Expecting him to rage at her, to cast her aside for going against him, for screwing up and getting him hurt, but nothing could have prepared her for this. She'd been ready to fight for him, but maybe she didn't have to. "You're not pissed at me?"

"Oh, believe me, I am," he said, using the wall for support as he shuffled into her room, collapsing his bulk into one of the chairs at her small table. "But not for abandoning me in the infirmary. For *not fucking listening to me.*" Finally settled, he opened his arm and beckoned her closer, but she hesitated.

"You're right, I shouldn't have tried to persuade Zeln—"

"That's not what I'm talking about," he said, leaning forward to drop the full weight of his gaze on her. "And I didn't drag my ass down here to sit on the opposite side of the room from you." He placed a firm hand on the tabletop. "Come. Here."

Toes curling in her boots as she walked over, she sat on the edge of the table and he fastened an arm around her hips. She craved the closeness as much as she feared it.

"When are you going to get it through your head that we are a *team*?" His voice growled as his grip tightened. "I told you we'd come up with a plan, but you went off on your own. Again. After the battle, when I didn't see you, I searched everywhere, looking for that red hair." Reaching out, he rubbed a few strands between his fingers, then tucked it behind her ear. *Oh god.* The thought of Mal turning over dead bodies looking for her...*fuck*. It gutted her. "But then Will told me he saw you get in a troxy truck, and I knew what you were up to.

"So yes, Penny, I'm so fucking mad at you, but I will always come for you. And Derek, Agnes—all of them—will too because that's what being a fucking team is. And *you* are part of this team. You always have been, even when you didn't want to be, even in the early days when *I* didn't want you to be. You think I'm going to leave you if you mess up or if I see something I don't like. But I'm not going anywhere. We are in this *together*. Now can you please stop fucking running away?"

Together.

It had been so long since she'd allowed herself to rely on anyone. The thought that *he* saw them as a team, as equals, this man who was so different from her, nearly broke her, and something foreign and painful lodged in her chest. He slid her closer, bringing her into the circle of his arms and resting his other hand on her thigh. Everything about his touch said *mine*, and every cell in her body reached for him, pulsed for him, and answered his call.

Mine, mine, mine.

At a loss for words, she brushed her fingers across his beard. He'd hobbled down here, bleeding and in pain, because he'd wanted to be by her side too. Even after everything she'd done—not just with her botched plan to recruit Zeln, but *everything else*.

"I'm sorry, Mal. For so long—even in my life Before—I've been the enforcer. The loner who does the dirty work. I thought by going alone and cutting a deal with Zeln, I was protecting you from getting your hands dirty. When really, I didn't believe I had the clout to call on a team or ask anyone to put their lives on the line for *my* idea, especially after I risked us losing the Capital by not staying behind when you went to Chicago. I should've listened to you so many times." *He could have died—still might die—because of me.* "There's so much blood on my hands, Mal. I never wanted it to be yours." What if his wounds got infected? What if he was bleeding internally? What if—

He caught her fingers as she trailed them across his bandages. "I chose to go in there after you. My injuries are my own and you will not take responsibility for them. And if you hadn't done what you did, we'd never know what we were truly up against with Zeln. Because of you, we know what's coming and we can get ahead of it."

His tone was firm and she watched herself nod, as if in a dream, and then the dam she'd been holding all of her feelings behind broke. She wrapped her arms around him and tucked her face into his neck, taking in a shaky breath filled with his scent.

"I thought I lost you." She spoke the words against his skin, afraid to face him.

His strong arms enveloped her as he said, "I'm here." Then he pulled back and tipped her chin up until she met his eyes. Her own stung at the emotion she didn't dare name staring back at her. "I see you, Penny. I don't need to know every dark thing in your past in order to *know you*, to know that I want the person you are today and the person you're becoming." Sweeping a hand across her cheek and through her hair, he claimed the nape of her neck. His rough voice brushed against her in a velvet caress as he said, "I would walk through fire for you, woman. You will never lose me. I love you."

His words blistered over her, leaving her raw. Exposed. *There is nothing I can do—or have done—that will turn Mal away. Not the people I've killed, the mistakes I've made, the fires I've set.*

He knows my darkness and he wants me anyway.

She wanted to live up to the woman he saw when he looked at her, to be *that* Penny. His Pen. And isn't that what she'd been searching for all this time? Not just someone to see her for who she truly was, but someone who could push her in all the right ways to become the best version of herself.

The words she longed to say swelled inside her but caught behind her lips. As if he understood her inner battle, he pulled her to him, capturing her mouth with his, and she poured all of herself, everything she felt but couldn't yet say, into that kiss, into him. When they broke apart, chests heaving, it was as if something vital had finally shifted into place within her.

This—here, with Mal—was as right as she'd ever felt in her life.

This was how she wanted to feel, always.

A pounding at the door interrupted them. "Open up." Agnes. The crew had arrived.

Time to get this shit show on the road.

Disentangling herself from Mal, Penny opened the door. With Agnes's hand frozen mid-knock, Quentin fell inside from where he crouched against it trying to stick his fingers underneath. Penny pushed the door wider to show Mal sitting at the table, and she cocked an eyebrow. "Should probably talk to Will about better security if the big guy was able to walk out of the infirmary without anyone noticing," Penny said.

"It's possible I threatened his life if he told anyone I left," Mal said. She shot him a look, and he gave her a rakish grin.

"Is this what I have to look forward to now?" Penny asked. "You threatening bodily harm to every man who's ever looked at me?"

Mal's grin took on a sharper edge, and that was answer enough.

"You're lucky you didn't rip open your stitches," Agnes scolded as she came inside with Quentin bouncing to sit on the tabletop. Her eyes slid over Penny, then shot to Mal and the uncharacteristic smile still playing at his lips. "Hope we weren't interrupting..."

Penny cleared her throat and sat across from Mal, saying, "Nope. Where's everyone else?"

"On their way," Agnes said.

"Tía!" Suddenly, Tara's small frame dominated the doorway as she fastened her hands on her hips, appearing out of nowhere. Agnes raised her eyebrows, but Tara wasn't looking at her. *Me? Am I tía now too?* Usually that was a term reserved for Agnes. Marching up to Penny, Tara continued her tirade. "We need to have words about you almost getting our asses handed to us at the SubTran."

Penny had to stop herself from flinching. Tara was right—anger was what she'd expected from everyone, and she welcomed it.

"That's not how this team works," Tara said. "If we're going rogue, you fucking *tell me* first—or Agnes or someone—so we can help. Puñeta, girl. Would've been a lot easier if we knew what we were getting into. Piénsalo next time, okay?"

Penny blinked, stunned. "That's not—I thought—so everyone's fine with the fact that I tried to make a deal with a criminal mastermind behind Mal's—*all*—of your backs, and it completely backfired?"

Tara rolled her eyes, taking the empty chair next to Mal. "Wasn't your first time going rogue and doing something stupid, and it certainly wasn't anyone *else's* first time either. Right, tía?" She cast a meaningful look at Agnes, who pointedly stared at the ceiling. "Anyway. You've got a lot to fill us in on."

"Right, about that—" Penny started.

"Might as well wait until everyone else gets here, unless you like repeating yourself," Tara said, kicking her booted feet up on the table as the sound of bickering came from the hallway.

"No, I'm telling you, a sorlock is superior to a wizard," Derek said, flapping his hands in emphasis. "It just makes sense, Si. Why would you not multiclass? You're being ridiculous."

"*I'm* being ridiculous?" Silas said. "Wizards dominate, hands down. They have *spell books*, which means more spells. Duh."

"This again?" Agnes said as she grabbed Derek by the shirtfront, interrupting him mid-sentence with a lingering kiss while Vick rolled her eyes at the entire display.

"Finally," Ivan said, posting up against the wall. "Those two haven't stopped talking for hours."

Derek brushed a hand through Agnes's hair with a sugary sweet smile on his face. "Fine, Si. You win this one."

Quentin seemed to be of the same mind as Penny, making barfing motions behind his hand and shooting her a grin, which she returned.

"I actually agree with Silas," Lawrence said.

"Thank—!"

"Nope!" said Agnes, forcing Derek to sit in her chair, holding him in the seat. "Pot-stirrer," she shot at Lawrence, who shrugged.

As the group settled in around her, Penny couldn't help the daze that clouded over her. *All of them, here. In my room.* People who had been her enemies, who had hated and feared her mere months ago. And now they were here. With her. Counting her as part of their team. It was a complete mind fuck, to say the least.

"When did this become a goddamn conference room?" Mal asked, chuckling.

"Pretty lame one if you ask me," Quentin said. "No wheelie chairs, no snacks or terrible coffee. How am I supposed to entertain myself?"

"I have some of your tennis balls over there," Penny offered. "You can throw them at Derek, if you want."

"Oh *yes*, let me at 'em." Quentin moved to leap off the table, but Derek grabbed him by the back of the shirt.

"Park it," Derek said as Quentin grumbled, crossing his arms.

"*Anyway,*" Silas said, but then Ivan broke into a coughing fit. Silas gripped his hand in a panic, and a somber mood washed over the room. Tara and Ivan, even though they were in good spirits, were beginning to show signs of prolonged troxapine exposure. Sunken eyes, constant sweating, shakes. Now, coughing.

"We've got time," Tara said, stifling her own coughing fit while looking to Vick. "Right?"

"Right." But Vick didn't look too confident.

Penny wrung her hands, unsure of where to start. "Zeln is our true enemy," she said and filled them in on the resupply ship arriving tomorrow and everything Zeln had said to her in the SubTran station. When she got to the part about getting attacked by turned, Agnes's jaw dropped.

"Your blood cures the turned?" she asked. "How does that work?"

"I was hoping you could tell me," Penny said.

Agnes frowned, picking at a loose splinter in the table. "Must be some kind of natural immunity. I can run your blood through my machine and see what we get, but we have the same problem as before. And while Chun's notes were helpful, I'm still not a scientist." As she broke off with a frantic glance at Tara and Ivan, who coughed again, Penny wished she had better news.

Looking at all of them, a swell of emotion came over her. "Thank you for coming after me," Penny said. "You should've hung me out to dry after I fucked up so badly again. But I'm really grateful you didn't. Nice timing with cutting the lights too. Made it easier to get the jump on Zeln. Quentin's idea?"

"Lights?" Mal asked with a frown. "That wasn't us."

"Don't look at me," Quentin said, shrugging.

"But..." The timing had been too perfect for it to be a random fluke. "So if it wasn't you, who was it?"

As if on cue, the room reached a collective realization. "Dr. Chun," Agnes said in awe. "It had to be her. She said she'd signal us if she got inside—maybe *that* was her signal."

"Hell yes!" Derek said, nudging Ivan and Tara. "If Chun's in there, we still have a shot."

"If I get inside the SubTran lab, she and I can work together on a cure—for the darts, for the turned. For all of it," Agnes said, already pulling a digital notepad out of her coat pocket. "Can hijack Zeln's team of scientists too."

"We've already broken in once," Derek said. "We can definitely do it again."

"Won't be so easy the second time," Mal countered. "Zeln's security will be even tighter. Wouldn't be surprised if he moves locations."

"Nah, too much of a tactical nightmare," Tara said. "Lots of people, lots of stuff."

"Couldn't they relocate to the armory they took from us?" Ivan asked. *Even he's part of the "us" now.*

"They could, but they wouldn't be able to do it quickly," Lawrence said with a sheepish smile. "Especially not after I slashed all of their tires and gas cans."

"Ha!" Tara reached across the table and punched his arm. "That's my boy."

"Nice one," Vick said with an impressed look.

"But back to the, ah, impending doom," Derek said, pulling on the back of his neck. "What's our plan for dealing with the resupply shipments? And fucking *tomorrow*?"

"It'll be all hands on deck—" Penny said, but she cut off, looking at Mal and the bandages wrapping his bare torso, unable to find her voice again.

"If you think I'm sitting this one out because of a little scratch, you have another thing coming," Mal said, crossing his arms.

"You were *stabbed*, Mal," Penny said. "Your ribs are millimeters from puncturing a lung or something. You are *going to sit down*."

Mal paused halfway out of his seat, grimacing and holding his side, but sank to his chair with a thunderous expression. Penny would have felt the same way, had their roles been reversed. But tides of panic ebbed over her and she gripped his hand, everything else melting away until it was just the two of them. *My warrior.*

"I can't do this without you," she whispered.

Squeezing her hand, he pinned her with a serious look. "You have so much more to offer than your bullets and your sickle. You can get people to fight, to hope, even when it seems like all is lost. The Faction still has a chance because you've shown us that we do—because you keep coming back, even from the worst situations imaginable." He tapped the black-bladed knife in her belt. "We will survive this because *you* will survive this. So what's our plan?"

She'd never imagined she could live up to ideals even close to what he'd said. But it wasn't just Mal looking at her with such conviction. They all were. After everything that had happened the past few months, she was finally starting to catch a glimpse of the woman they all saw now. *And I think I'm starting to like her too.*

How the hell did I get here?

Six months ago, she'd been bitter, enraged, broken. Alone. Hated. Feared. No family, no friends. Just her vengeance to keep her warm at night. But now? Her eyes landed on each person in the room, finally finding Quentin, who gave her the toothy smile she adored so much. Now she had something to live for, something to *fight* for, besides revenge.

If these people—*good* people—could find it in themselves to accept her as one of their own, to follow her and trust her with their lives, then maybe she'd become someone who was worthy of their forgiveness. Someone who could become the kind of leader Mal described.

As her eyes landed on him, she made a decision.

Maybe it was time to forgive and accept herself too. Because this endless cycle of self-punishment was only hurting everyone she cared about. And it had to stop.

But under the surface, her rage burned bright. *Zeln tried to take Mal, all of this, from me. He threatened the very reasons I live and breathe.* And she wanted to kill him for it. She'd never be a noble leader like Mal, whose moral compass always pointed north. But she didn't have to be. And no one was asking her to. They wanted *her*—Mal wanted her. And they believed in the person she was becoming enough to follow her now.

First, they had to survive past tomorrow.

Clearing the emotion from her throat, she said, "We're taking that ship. We've fought too long and too hard to allow Zeln to swoop in and wreck everything we've worked for. That shipment is ours—or we're sinking it to the bottom of the ocean."

"Scorched earth," Derek said, nodding. "Brutal, but I like it."

"And it might be our only choice," Vick said. "Destroying a ship is easier than diverting it or taking it for ourselves."

"Between Ivan and I, we can blow anything sky-high," Quentin supplied helpfully, looking entirely too excited at the prospect of mass-scale pyrotechnics.

Ivan gave his partner in crime a little hair ruffle, saying, "We can definitely rig something up."

"If it's docking here instead of downriver, that's logistically easier for us," Mal said. "Less distance for our troops to cover."

"Holy shit," Silas said, eyes flicking through the air at light speed as he read something from his modified Patch.

Ivan placed a hand on his shoulder and tugged him back to reality. "What happened?"

"That satellite I've been trying to hack for the past two months? Zeln had the codes. It's how he's contacting his foreign allies. And now I'm in too. Access codes were buried in the metadata of a holofile Penny brought us." He tapped something in the air and waved a hand. "Chun gave us the right intel. Problem was, she was going off of these dummy shipping logs meant to throw us off the scent. According to this satellite imagery, Vick is right. That cargo ship will be here by tomorrow night, easy. I'll monitor its progress."

"But if you're in the satellite, can't we just use it to contact other countries like Zeln and get some help?" Derek asked.

"Getting a message out is one thing," Silas said, "but convincing other countries to help us, especially after the terrorism propaganda Pharmatrox—or Zeln, I guess—has been blasting out, is another beast entirely.

I'll send as many SOSs as you want, but I don't think anyone is going to pick up."

Everyone's expressions became a mirror of despair.

"Send the messages," Penny instructed. "But we have to assume we're on our own."

"And no one in your network has seen any sign of Kev?" Agnes asked Vick, who shook her head.

Perfect. Keeping with the theme of impossible odds. But as Penny surveyed everyone, her original sense of doom and gloom abated. They had a strong team of capable people. Between all of them, plus the Faction and Vick's reinforcements, they just might stand a fighting chance.

Or they'd at least make it really fucking hard for Zeln to get what he wanted.

"Wake everyone up and get them in the arena," Penny said. "Don't care that it's the middle of the night. Then we'll come up with our plan of attack."

As Penny grabbed her weapons and everyone filtered outside, she swore she saw a look of pride cross Mal's face before he pushed to his feet.

His belief in her glowed bright, a kernel of hope budding in her chest. When she marched to the arena, she held her head high, ready to face whatever Zeln threw at them.

43

"I ALWAYS WANTED TO be a pirate," Quentin said from the bow of the stolen tugboat as they pulled away from the harbor. "I found a tricorn hat in a museum last week when I was snooping around. Should've brought it."

From behind the steering wheel, Ivan snorted. "Missed opportunity." But as the man broke off into wracking coughs, Penny frowned. Silas had wanted him to stay behind and rest, but he'd heartily refused.

"When do I get to blow stuff up?" Quentin asked, turning to Penny.

"Only under Ivan's supervision. It's like you're trying to give me gray hairs," she said, tapping some sort of contraption strapped into his belt that she had no idea what it was.

"Easy with that! Might go off," he said as he dodged away.

Lifting her brow, she said, "Is it wise to have something that could explode at any second so close to your...?"

Eyes wide, Quentin pulled the thing out of his belt and gingerly held it between his two fingers. "Uh, Ivan? Maybe you should take this."

Penny just shook her head, both impressed and horrified at his inventing abilities. Back to the task, she surveyed their small trio of tugboats. They'd snuck to the docks downriver and commandeered the vessels from Zeln's troops, with the help of Mal, Jaha, and their soldiers who were now keeping watch from shore. With a small strike team, Penny and her crew were hiding in plain sight on the tugboat and meeting the cargo ship to sneak aboard. Tanaka and his guys, the Watchers, and Vick's contacts were splitting their support between the stadium and the shoreline. Meanwhile, Agnes and her team were infiltrating the SubTran.

If she thought too much about what they were about to do, about how absolutely insane of a long shot it was, she'd crumble. But these people were experts at long shots. If anyone had a chance of diverting this tanker, it was Agnes's friends. Who were maybe Penny's friends now too.

As if I don't already have too many incomprehensible things to deal with, she thought with a laugh.

Looming on the horizon, the cargo ship approached, multicolored containers stacked high. The tugboats sped toward it through the choppy water, keeping a wide berth. Penny nodded to Ivan, and he picked up the radio to contact the cargo ship and said, "Back off your engines, we're ready to bring you in."

"Roger," crackled a voice through the speaker.

Quentin watched through his binoculars, then whisper-shouted to be heard over the tug's rumbling motor, "Sniper! On that walkway."

Beside him, Vick shouldered her rifle and fired a silenced shot, dropping the guy. "Another one," she said and fired again, a guard falling at the boat's stern.

Swerving, the two tugboats punched the speed to cut through the ship's massive wake, one staying toward the bow. When Penny's boat reached the stern, Quentin grabbed a crossbow that he'd modified into a grappling hook launcher and loaded the clawed hook and rope. Then he handed it to Vick, who aimed at the openings in the aft deck about a hundred feet above. In one shot, she landed the hook over the railing and pulled the rope tight.

"Nice shot," Penny said.

Vick grinned as she handed the rope to Quentin. He made quick work of climbing up and onto the deck nestled between the towers of shipping containers. The seconds ticked by as Penny waited for him to toss the rope ladders from his pack over the side.

Thirty more seconds, and still no ladders.

Should I go after him? She wasn't as good at climbing, but if he needed help—

A body pitched over the railing, limp as it hit the water with a *smack*. Peering over the side, Penny readied herself to dive overboard—

From above, Quentin poked his head out, giving a thumbs-up, then secured the rope ladders to the railing and tossed them below.

And now all of their soldiers had a way up to the boat.

Everyone except for the boat drivers clambered up the ladders. The first tugboat positioned itself to ride the wake of the ship and conserve fuel, while the other maintained its position at the bow, ostensibly to help the cargo ship dock. When Penny reached the top, she said to Quentin, "What happened?"

"One of their guards caught me and I tased him," he said, zapping his taser in demonstration as the rest of their troops joined them on the platform with big-ass spools of rope and cables Penny assumed were for mooring the ship. An elevated walkway bracketed the area—the perfect place for guards to patrol—along with a bunch of other pulleys.

Of the same mind, Vick asked, "Any other guards?"

"Not that I saw," Quentin answered.

"Hmm." Vick slid out her dual knives and took off down the lower walkway.

"Everyone else, spread out," Penny said. "Take out any guards and secure the main deck. Ivan, Quentin, and you all"—she pointed to some troops—"come with me to the bridge. We'll convince the captain to see our side of things. Team leaders, use the radios only in emergencies. If you see anything weird, let us know."

Penny waved her hand in dismissal, and everyone branched out. It was a huge vessel, but the crew would likely only be twenty to thirty people—if this was a normal cargo ship. But Penny suspected Zeln had some tricks up his sleeves.

Taking the stairs to the upper walkway, Penny drew her sickle, palms sweating even as the chilly sea wind rattled the chains and cables around them. The sound of booted feet plunking across the metal gangway came from above, and Penny whispered to the handful of troops behind her, "Blades only. Keep it quiet."

Wasting no time, she leapt up the stairs, slashing her sickle across the guard's throat. He fell, spluttering blood, but another was right behind him.

A crossbow bolt lashed through his windpipe, courtesy of Ivan, and he fell forward atop his companion.

Up another flight of metal stairs, past the lifeboats, then a final set of stairs and they were at the bridge. Penny's heart pounded as she reached for the door, all trepidation flooding out of her, replaced with pure adrenaline.

This ship is mine. And I'm taking it.

Busting inside, Penny brandished her gun. Five crew members swiveled away from their monitors, jaws dropping. One reached for a button—

A knife lodged in the back of the woman's hand and she screamed, a soldier rushing forward to cover her mouth. Penny looked for who'd thrown the knife and saw Quentin with a satisfied smile on his face. "You've been practicing," she noted.

"Learned from the best," he said, grabbing a spare knife from his belt.

Returning her attention to the crew, Penny cocked her gun and aimed at the closest one's head. "Stop the ship," she said, but the watch officer, a black-haired woman, laughed.

"Can't just stop a ship as big as this."

"Either drop the anchor or turn this fucking thing around. Your choice." Then Penny pressed the barrel of the gun into the woman's forehead. "Or there's always the third option." The old Penny would have relished the bead of fear in the woman's eyes, but now, she just hoped she wouldn't actually have to shoot her.

"I'm telling you, we *can't*. The engines won't fire up fast enough to change course, and it takes a few miles to drift to a stop. And the only thing dropping the anchor will do is dig an underwater trench while we cruise along at fifteen knots."

Damn. So we can only take over the ship or blow it up. Just like pirates, indeed.

Licking her lips, the woman reached for the radio—

But Penny's radio went off instead.

"Get down here." It was Vick. "There's something you should see."

That can't be good. "Where are you?"

"Central containers near the bow."

"Coming." To Ivan and Quentin, she said, "You're with me. The rest of you, stay here and make sure they don't try anything."

Ducking back into the cold wind, the trio made haste toward the bow. As they went, they stepped over Vick's trail of felled guards. Traversing a narrow hallway with shipping containers stacked three high towering on either side, they delved into a small courtyard-like opening where Vick and a few soldiers awaited them.

All of the containers on the bottom were open.

And they were full of sand.

"What the fuck?" Penny asked. "Are they all like this?"

"On this level, yeah," Vick said, then tossed Quentin a small pair of bolt cutters. "Can you climb to the second level and get those open?"

He caught them, twirling them like a baton. "Sure thing."

While Quentin fought with the locks, Penny asked Vick, "Any trouble?"

"Nah. Got all the guards I could see, then came straight here." Vick chewed her lip as she watched Quentin. "Something is weird."

A chill swept through Penny that had nothing to do with the cold wind as Quentin finally flipped the latches and pulled the container door open.

"Oh, thank god!"

A hysterical woman's voice speared Penny to the spot as the door swung wide, revealing the contents within.

People.

The container was full of people.

44

Agnes

"**G**OOD TO KNOW THE rats and roaches are thriving," Agnes muttered, shuffling through the detritus of the abandoned SubTran station, surrounded by the tittering sounds of tiny feet.

"Must mean there's still something to eat down here," Lawrence noted, shining his flashlight into the tunnel entrance. Naomi stuck close to his side. Ever since returning from Chicago, Naomi had fully integrated herself into their war efforts. Agnes suspected it had more to do with the dashing lumberjack-gardener beside her than anything else.

Tara made a sound of disgust as she hopped down onto the tracks. "Why did you have to bring *that* up?"

Agnes hit the ground beside her, followed by Derek and the others, plus a handful of Watchers. Readjusting the straps of her bulky rucksack containing her portable machine, she headed into the dark SubTran tunnel, the orbs of light from their flashlights bobbing along the walls. Derek's presence was the only thing that kept her from jumping at every sound. Noticing her edginess, he clasped her hand with a reassuring squeeze. She'd never have made it this far in this world without him—without all of them—and her heart glowed with gratitude, keeping the growing darkness at bay.

But catching a quick glance at Tara had the dread creeping back in. She held her baseball bat in a steady grip, but sweat slicked her face and her rattling breaths echoed in the cavernous station. *I really hope Dr. Chun's in here.*

While Mal had been spitting mad about Penny's disappearance yesterday, Agnes understood why she did it. In her early days of living at the Outpost, she'd been one to ask forgiveness instead of permission too. And without Penny, they wouldn't be where they were right now, marching toward the lab, a cure, and hopefully Dr. Chun.

"How many stations away—yargh!" Silas cut off with a high-pitched squeal, kicking a rat off his foot. "This is my worst nightmare."

"Just three," Derek replied. "Was as close as I could get us without alerting Zeln's perimeter guards."

"This is crazy, right? We have to be insane to attempt this," Silas said.

"You're a genius, Si," Agnes replied. "You'll crack Zeln's comms setup in no time and hijack his airwaves, and you'll be the savior of the world. Parades will be thrown in your name, buildings dedicated in your honor."

Silas narrowed his eyes. "You're stroking my ego, but I'll allow it. Because you're right. I am a genius. And I do love parades."

"Should I break out the confetti cannons?" she asked.

"I never joke about confetti cannons, Aggie," Silas said, affronted. "I bet Quentin could whip me up something like that. Little prankster would probably fill it with deer turds though."

"Don't let Quentin anywhere near it," Derek said. "Took me weeks to get the stench out of my boots after he hid his signature stink bombs in them."

They reached the next station without issue, the sound of water dripping from the ceiling and chittering critters dappling the silence. A rotten smell filled her nose, and her flashlight beam caught something leaning against the wall—

Bodies.

A family, it looked like, huddled close together, faces lost to decay, hunks of flesh missing and rotted off the corpses.

Holding Derek's hand a little tighter, she continued to the next tunnel, but the scuffling grew louder. Thirty paces later, a splash of water dripped on her face, and she reached up to wipe it away with an irritated shake of her head. *No telling what gross shit has leaked into the ground water.* Another drip-drip landed on her face and rolled down her cheek, and she swiped it. But when her flashlight illuminated her hands, they weren't covered in water.

It was a bloody-black grime.

Yelping, Agnes jerked her light toward the ceiling, and a chorus of ear-splitting shrieks echoed through the tunnel.

Turned. Too many to count. Clinging to the ceiling like spiders, crawling after the flashlight beams in the darkness like a beacon leading straight to their next meal, mouths and hands dripping with the gore of their previous feasts. The decaying family flashed in her mind, and her stomach roiled.

"Run."

The group took off, firing at the ceiling, some shots finding their marks. But some turned scuttled along with superhuman speed. *Were these part of Zeln's experiments to find a cure? Or have they been trapped down here since the Beginning?*

Tripping over the tracks, Agnes clutched onto Derek as they ran toward the next station dimly lit with emergency lights. Holding her machete like a lifeline, she slashed at the shapes leaping off the ceiling, snarls and howls bouncing around the cavernous space.

"Get to the lab with Derek and Silas," Tara shouted at Agnes, swinging her bat into a skull as Lawrence and Naomi covered her. "We'll follow."

Rebelling at the idea of leaving them to fight alone in the dark, Agnes slashed her machete through a slew of torsos.

But Derek tugged her sleeve, urging her onward. "They can handle it."

With a cry of frustration, Agnes raced toward the final station—Zeln's headquarters. The platform was in sight when something dropped onto Agnes's back, grabbing onto her pack and slinging her aside.

A crunch sounded as she slammed into the wall, the turned's claws sinking into her skin, but the only thought she had was *Mierda, my machine.*

Wrapping her hands around its throat to hold its snapping jowls away from her, she fended off its attacks until Derek fired a slew of volts, its head exploding in black goop. "Qué asco," Agnes said, sloughing off the yuck and scrambling to her feet. She'd inspect the damage to her machine later—right now, they needed to get the hell out of the dark.

Finally inside Zeln's station, the guards holding the perimeter approached them in alarm as Derek continued unloading the remainder of his volt charges into the turned, while Agnes decapitated the ones unaffected by ammo.

"Could use a little help," Silas shouted at the guards, playing the part of a loyal Zeln soldier.

The guards exchanged a look before jumping in to assist. "Took you long enough," Derek grumbled. A few minutes later, the turned were dispensed with and Tara, Lawrence, Naomi, and the rest emerged from the tunnel, covered in blood.

"What the fuck happened?" a beefy-looking guard asked.

"Boss said there was some kind of disturbance," Derek said, falling into the role of a disgruntled soldier. "Pretty fucking deadly disturbance, if you ask me."

Beefy Guy peered at their motley crew. "You don't look familiar. What're your names again?"

"Look, we can stand here all day jawing or you can let us get back to work," Tara said, stepping up.

Shrugging, Beefy Guy said, "As you were."

Hurrying across to the massive underground shopping mall, Agnes found the employee area that Penny had described.

Guards rushed around prepping for the incoming shipment and ensuing battle, and Agnes kept her eyes peeled for Chun—and Zeln. If he was here and recognized any of them, they were screwed.

Finally, they reached the lab and piled inside, armed and ready to face whatever awaited them. *I just hope my machine still works after slamming it into a goddamn wall.*

"Hands where we can see them, chicos," Tara said to the room full of lab-coated scientists, who raised their palms.

To their credit, only half the scientists looked petrified. *Maybe they're here against their will.* The others appeared unfazed, like they dealt with this every day. No sign of Dr. Chun. *Maybe we were wrong and she never made it here.* "We won't harm anyone," Agnes said, swallowing the lump forming in her throat. "We need your help." Scanning the faces, she honed in on one—the young woman with the glasses from the basement raid. The woman's eyes went wide when she recognized Agnes too. Beckoning her forward out of earshot of the others, Agnes said, "I thought we sent you to Canada?"

"I changed my mind. I ditched the convoy and came back to the city to help," she said in a low voice. "But I got caught by that Zeln douchebag and conscripted into his service instead."

This woman has guts. "What's your name?"

"Chandra."

"Agnes. How much progress have they made on a cure?"

Her throat bobbing, Chandra said, "We've been stalled for weeks. Heard chatter about someone's blood being the answer?"

Agnes nodded, patting her backpack. "I've got you covered."

Blowing out a relieved breath, Chandra said, "Excellent. But there's something you should know. Zeln has us working on something new. Creating a water-soluble serum. Tasteless, odorless, colorless."

"What the hell is he planning to do with that?" Derek asked.

"Everyone thinks it's just another product to sell, but I don't agree," Chandra said. "I think Zeln plans to infect the water supply with troxapine—his escape hatch if things go wrong for him."

A rushing sound filled Agnes's ears as she failed to comprehend Chandra's words, and Silas swooped into the conversation. "Sink the ship and burn it down on his way out, so to speak, with a weapon even more destructive than darts or super soldiers. Jesus."

Madre mía. Zeln really is an evil genius. Because of the insidious way he took over Pharmatrox, successfully keeping his face off the international feeds and flying under the radar, nobody would ever know he was involved. If his coup failed, he could nuke the country and scram, placing the blame on Pharmatrox. *And they'd never object because they're already dead.*

"How much time do we have?" Agnes asked, wishing she could radio the team on the cargo ship with the news. But without a secure channel, the transmission could be intercepted, and she didn't want to blow their cover. Radios between teams were only for dire emergencies—they had to deal with this on their own.

"I don't know," Chandra said, clutching a pen in a death grip. "Now that you're here, you can keep Zeln's scientists from sabotaging me. But you'll have to take care of her too." She pointed to a door that led to a separate wing of the lab. "A woman got here a few days ago. Said she was part of a new research branch. She's a hardass, and a little, uh, unhinged."

The group exchanged concerned looks, and Agnes approached the door, machete held high. Twisting the knob, she primed to attack, but then froze as the woman turned in her chair.

"Took you long enough. Come here, I need a goddamn assistant who isn't terrified of me."

Agnes gripped the door for support, relief flooding through her. "Hostia, Dr. Chun. Are we fucking glad to see you."

45

What the fuck is happening?

Across the second level of shipping containers, every new door Quentin unlocked revealed more and more people. Vick's soldiers tossed up rope ladders to help them descend, and one of them, an older woman with dark gray hair, approached Penny.

"Have we arrived already?" the woman asked, wringing her hands. "Feels like we were in there for days, but couldn't have been more than one at most."

"You're all here voluntarily?" Penny asked.

The woman gave her a puzzled look. "Of course. We were told we'd get safe passage to Mexico, but we'd have to make a few stops along the way." When Penny just blinked at her, the woman continued more slowly, as if Penny were an idiot. "We're refugees? From New York? Shouldn't you know that if you work on the ship?"

Refugees. But something about her words set off alarms in her head. "Who organized this for you?" It certainly wouldn't be Pharmatrox helping its own citizens escape, and she knew the Faction wasn't behind it.

"A few weeks ago, a man approached me and offered to help me and my family get out of the country—for free, even."

"What did he look like?"

"Oh sweetie, I don't remember. We didn't talk long. I think he was maybe average height? Dark hair?"

That could be anyone. But with Zeln's use of and access to cargo ships, he was at the top of her list. Maybe Mexico was offering humanitarian aid totally independent of Zeln, but something else was afoot. "Are you all civilians?" Penny asked.

"I'm not sure, but I think so. There might be some ex-Pharmatrox employees."

"Thanks," Penny said. "Just wait over here and we'll...give you instructions soon." *Once we figure out what the fuck is going on.*

"Got some dudes in armor up here," Quentin shouted from the next shipping container. "Are you Faction? Pharmatrox?" he asked them. Penny didn't hear the reply, but Quentin translated. "Uh, that's a yes. Some of both. Whoa!" He swung the door shut against angry shouts. "Sounds like some of them aren't here by choice and are itching for a fight."

Civilians, troxies, and Faction, all aboard a refugee ship? Some here willingly, some forced...

There was some larger plan at work, but Penny didn't have enough pieces of the puzzle to figure it out yet. From the look on Vick and Ivan's faces, they were just as baffled.

Suddenly, there was a yell from above, then Quentin was dangling from the shipping container by the handle. But this container didn't house refugees.

Guttural groans and growls echoed in the enclosed space, and a bevy of gray bodies with clawed hands poured out of the container, leaping to the ground.

Ripping the radio from her belt, Penny spat orders into it, broadcasting to the squadron leaders on board. "We have a fucking situation. Get to the center of the ship. Now. One of you stay in the bridge. Everyone else, to me." To her soldiers around her, she said, "Kill the bastards and try not to let them eat anyone." Then she charged to Quentin, sweeping her sickle through the crowd churning ten feet below him.

"Making a nice cushion of bodies for me to fall onto?" he asked, kicking his feet in an attempt to swing the door shut so he could climb inside.

"Something like that," Penny shouted back, blood spraying as she took another head. Screams behind her, and she whipped around to see turned diving into the civilians, biting arms and necks. "Goddamn it! I said don't let them eat anyone."

Heads rolled and blood sluiced the deck, turning the metal into treacherous terrain, but even though they'd cut down many, the sea of gray bodies stretched endlessly.

"Penny! Gotta see this." Quentin waved to her from the mouth of the now empty shipping container. He tossed a rope to her, and she pulled herself out of the chaos.

"What is it?" she asked, joining him, but then she saw it.

In the back of the container sat a metal folding chair with a radio on it and a handwritten paper sign.

FOR PENNY

Her stomach bottomed out as she recognized the handwriting. The same penmanship as the sign left for Mal on the turned's body.

On shaky legs, she retrieved the radio and clicked the button. "Zeln," she said. "Got your present."

The seconds ticked by, punctuated by the sounds of battle from below, as Quentin watched her with wide eyes.

Finally, a crackle came from the radio. "Penny. Nice to hear from you." The smooth timbre of Zeln's voice was undeniable, even through the tinny speaker.

"Cut the shit. What's your play?"

"Go to the starboard side."

"Why?"

Silence.

Grumbling, Penny climbed down the rope, radio in tow. "Stay here," she said to Quentin and tossed him her volt rifle. "Shoot from above. Safer for you." For once, he didn't argue. Cutting her way through the battle, she followed a narrow hallway to the right side of the ship.

"Here," she said into the radio.

"See that ship on the horizon at your two o'clock?"

Fucking hell, she did. Another cargo ship.

"*That's* my resupply ship," he said without waiting for her reply. "Look down."

Leaning over the railing, she saw a huge-ass yacht that looked like it belonged to an asshole billionaire. On the back of the uppermost deck stood a figure dressed in black. It raised a hand and waved. *Zeln.* As the yacht pulled ahead, she got a better look.

An unmistakable massive figure knelt before him, a gun pressed to the back of his neck.

Fuck. He has Mal. Which means he found our forces on the shoreline.

"Are you listening, Penny?"

Mouth dry, Penny said, "What do you want?"

"In fifteen minutes, the ship you're on is rigged to explode. As I'm sure you've noticed, it's full of refugees. And if you'll look just slightly to your right—"

A small winged drone swooped by, circling the ship.

"—say hello. I'm recording the entire thing to broadcast to the rest of the world, to show them how the Faction took over a foreign aid vessel full of innocent civilians and defectors bound for the safety of Mexico and blew it up. In that amount of time, my resupply ship will have made landfall. And Mal will have a bullet in his head."

Penny gripped the railing with white knuckles. *This motherfucker is diabolical. I should have killed him when I had the chance. Like Rodney.*

"But if you give yourself up to me," Zeln continued, "Mal will live and I'll edit the footage to pin the refugee ship explosion on Pharmatrox instead. I'll allow the ship to get close to shore so people have a chance to escape before blowing it up. Some of them will live, most will die, it will be tragic, et cetera. But Pharmatrox will be the ones to blame, not the Faction—and we both win. So you have a choice to make, Pretty Penny. Fifteen minutes. I suggest you decide quickly."

The transmission cut off, ending in static, as the drone flew by.

Thrusting a hand through her hair, Penny let out a cry of frustration. *Fucking fuck.*

But instead of losing herself to the rage, she refocused on the mission with a new surge of vigor. She'd find a way out of this.

The only thing Zeln was getting from her was a pair of concrete boots and a one-way ticket to the bottom of the ocean.

46

Agnes

"How did you get here?" Agnes asked. *We have Chun. We're still in this fight.* The room was a small office set up with a holofile projector, digital notepads, and a slew of lab equipment.

"Swiped an EV after ditching the lily pad lab and booked it here," Chun said. "When we got pulled over by one of Zeln's checkpoints, I talked myself into a new job. Nobody outside of the New York office would recognize me, so it wasn't hard to convince his brutes we were contractors he'd hired for his deranged plan. They brought us straight here and the crew out there"—she gestured to the room full of scientists—"filled me in. The guy's a nutbar. Luckily Zeln's not around or else this wouldn't have worked. Probably off wreaking havoc somewhere."

Must be defending his incoming shipment, then. Derek and Tara elbowed their way into the room, Silas, Lawrence, and Naomi right behind. "So you don't know about Kev, then," Tara said.

Chun's forehead puckered as she said, "What about him?"

"He's gone," Agnes admitted. "Disappeared after we raided the Chicago lab."

At the news, Chun sat back, tapping her fingers on the desk. "If Kev were dead, we'd all know it. Especially if Pharmatrox did it. They'd blast his death all over the feeds and declare victory. No, he has something up his sleeve." But beneath the veneer of confidence, Agnes saw the icy terror she was attempting to hide. "I have to believe that."

"I'm with Dr. Chun on this one," Derek said. "If Kev is off the radar, it's because he planned it that way."

But like Agnes, Lawrence was more skeptical. "Or things went wrong at the emissary meeting and he didn't get a chance to tell anyone before he—never mind." He cut off with a quick glance at Chun, who waved away the comment.

"In any case, he's not here and he can't help us now. It's up to us."

Nodding, Agnes removed her pack and set her banged-up machine on the desk. "It's damaged, but still salvageable. And I have these." She removed the vials of Penny's blood wrapped up in a sweater for padding. "Something in it cures the turned. I've run a few simulations and have a few formulas to try."

"Evie was the best of us, but between you and I—and that room of scared-shitless scientists out there—we can make it work," Chun said.

"But won't they figure out we're working against Zeln when we tell them to stop with Project Infected Zombie Water?" Derek said, surveying the room of closely-watched scientists.

"Some might want the chance to fuck the guy over," said Chun. "Sounds like the only friends he made here are the ones who like money. And if they don't want to help, we'll keep them confined until we can undo all of this bullshit and get some international aid."

"Why would Canada or anyone else help now?" chimed in Naomi.

"If we show them we can get the situation under control without obliterating the entire population in a mushroom cloud, I think we have a better chance. But we need time to work if we're going to make that happen," Dr. Chun explained. Then her eyes darted to the other room and she was on her feet, bellowing, "And that means *everyone keeping their hands where we can see them.*"

Too late, their troops saw what Chun had seen—one of Zeln's scientists diving under a desk, lunging for something—

An alarm blared through the underground mall, red lights flashing.

Launching into soldier mode, Derek said, "Get a team in the hallway. The rest of you, barricade the door, and for fuck's sake, *watch them* so they don't try and pull anything else."

"Silas," Agnes said, "see if you can hack into their security system and turn off that alarm. Find out how Zeln plans to access the water supply, how they're communicating, any satellites he controls. You know the drill."

"With pleasure," he said and followed the Watchers outside.

"Chandra?" Agnes asked, waving her into the separate office, where she shut the door and filled her in on everything Chun had said.

After hearing the explanation, Chandra said, "Let's get to work."

But soon, they had a problem.

Derek burst into the office, covered in sweat, chest heaving. "Full-blown battle going on in the hallway. Zeln's people haven't breached the lab yet, but it's only a matter of time. How much time do you need?"

"It's only been five fucking minutes!" said Chun, hands whirring over the holographic keypad of Agnes's machine while Agnes made hardware repairs. "We need more than five fucking minutes. So think of something."

Derek turned to Agnes, desperation evident in his panicked gaze. But she was drawing a blank too. Trapped in enemy territory, they only had the nearby resources at their disposal. Not only did they have to fend off

Zeln's guards, but then they had to fight their way out and stay alive long enough to get help and distribute the cure.

Our backs are against the wall here. Lab rats trapped in a cage.

Lab rats trapped in a cage.

"I have an idea," Agnes said. "It's a bad one."

Derek gave her a knowing grin. "Those are my favorite."

47

"V ICK, IVAN!" PENNY YELLED as she ran to the center of the ship. "With me! Quentin, you too."

"What is it?" Vick asked when they'd all crammed into a small walkway between containers, sheltered from the battle.

Rubbing the knots in her forehead, Penny recounted Zeln's ultimatum to an audience of wide eyes and dropped jaws.

Vick was the first to speak. "We can't let this guy win."

"I don't know how to stop him," Penny admitted.

Zeln had manipulated them into the perfect fucking position where no option was good and any option led to people dying. If she went to Mal, Zeln would blow up the refugee ship. And if they refused to play his game and did nothing, the refugee ship would blow up anyway and the Faction would be blamed. Even if they could stop his incoming resupply, their war efforts were fucked if his doctored drone footage got out.

They were out of time and out of options.

A hand clutching hers pulled her out of her stream of consciousness, and eyes that mirrored her own anchored her to the present. "Yes, you do, Penelope," Quentin said. "We can do this. Just tell us what to do."

The desire to go after Zeln herself burned strong, to make him bleed for everything he'd done, to mete out the justice he deserved. But as much as she wanted to rescue Mal and cut Zeln's fucking head off, she had to keep her own firmly in place.

Even so, everything in her shied away from being the one to make this choice. She'd never been a leader of a worthy cause before, but this—right here and now—was her mission. Her responsibility. Not just the lives of her troops, but now these innocent people forced here against their will. Maybe she wasn't the leader they deserved, and maybe she never would be. But there wasn't anyone else. And if she didn't make a decision, they'd all die.

So she channeled the best leader she knew—Mal. If their positions were reversed and she were captive on Zeln's yacht, he'd find a way to save everyone and save her too—and she'd find a way to do the same.

I can beat Zeln. But it wouldn't be by running off to shoot him in the head. No, she'd win because the Faction had one thing that Zeln didn't, the one thing that he desperately needed in order to complete his plans.

Me.

"We're going to save everyone, stop the resupply ship, and Zeln is getting a knife in the fucking eyeball," Penny said.

Vick smiled, showing all of her teeth. "I like it already. How do we do that?"

"I'm calling Zeln's bluff," Penny explained. "He's banking on me giving myself up to save Mal and allow the Faction a chance to fight another day. But I'm not doing that. I'm the only one Zeln won't kill. He needs my blood for his cure, so I'm our insurance policy. Wherever I am, those people will be safe. But there's a chance he could still blow up this ship rather than let us win, so we need to destroy that fucking bomb. We have fifteen minutes—less, now. Ivan, we'll find the bomb and I'll buy you as much time as I can to dismantle it. We'll keep the ship heading toward shore to make it easier for people to swim and give them a fighting chance."

"Bomb is probably in the engine room," Ivan said. "I can jam the detonator's signal, but my guess is Zeln has some fanatic followers ready to blow the thing manually."

"Then we'll get out as many people as we can before the timer goes off and swim like hell. Quentin"—Penny turned to him, heart in her throat—"I can't believe I'm doing this, but I need you and Vick to take one of the tugboats to the other resupply ship. We might have enough time and distance for it to change course. But if not, sink it. You're the only one besides Ivan who knows how to do that. Better for no one to have the supplies than for Zeln to get them. Take some troops with you."

"Zeln will just send more resupply shipments later," Vick said.

"Not if we end this here," Penny said. "Zeln isn't getting out of this, and his hostile takeover ends today. If he wants to record the entire thing, then we'll give him a fucking show." This constituted as one hell of an emergency, so she clicked on her radio and contacted the SubTran team. "Silas?"

"Are you dead or dying?" came his reply.

"Not yet. There's this drone flying around us, recording everything we do. Can you hack it?"

His laughter crackled through the speaker. "Can I hack it? Who do you think you're—"

"Great. Do it. Change it to livestream and blast the video all over the global feed. This is our chance to get the truth out." At this point, she didn't fucking care if Zeln overheard. Silas could out-hack him before he could do anything about it.

"I'm on it," said Silas.

"Thanks." Penny clicked off the radio.

"What about Mal?" Quentin asked in a small voice.

His name was a lance to the chest, and it killed her to say her next words, but she forged onward. It wasn't the choice her heart was screaming at her to make, but it was the right call that would save the most lives. "If I let Zeln blow up this ship, Mal will never forgive any of us. He'll have to hold his own for now. Once Ivan secures the bomb, I'll go for Mal."

The confidence in her decision was solidified when Vick gave her a nod of approval. There weren't many people she trusted with her brother's life, but Vick was one of them.

Quentin dove into Penny's side, squeezing her in a quick hug. "Please save Mal," he said, his pleading tone absolutely crushing her.

"I will."

Cutting a path through the fight, Penny ushered Vick and Quentin to the stern, where they descended to an awaiting tugboat. She gave Quentin one last hair ruffle before he disappeared over the side. A fist of fear tightened around her throat, but this was the right choice. Vick would take care of him, but he could take care of himself too. He'd more than proven that.

Taking the second radio from her belt, Penny clicked the receiver. "Zeln." One look over the railing confirmed that his yacht was holding steady just ahead of them.

"I'm listening," crackled his reply.

"You've put me in a real catch-22. And I don't like being backed into a corner. I'm staying on the refugee ship. Blow it up, if you must. But if you do, you're sending your only chance at making a cure up in flames. So listen up, motherfucker. Now *you* need to make a decision. What's more important to you? Destroying Pharmatrox, the Faction, and getting your revenge on Mal? Or getting your precious cure and securing your scumbag business dealings?"

Several beats of silence. Then, "Well played, Penny." The transmission cut off into static, and Penny didn't wait for a reply. She'd done what she needed—let Zeln know she was on the ship.

Switching to the Faction's channel, she spoke into the radio again. "Start evacuating people into lifeboats. Less than fifteen minutes before a bomb goes off and sinks this whole thing. Don't ask questions, just fucking do it." The radio squawked with her soldier's garbled answer, but she ignored it, flipping to Silas's channel. "How's it going?"

"Good news is, I've found your drone and am working on its firewall," said Silas.

"The bad news?"

"I need you to put a transistor on it to amplify its signal to broadcast worldwide. Which means you need to catch it. Get one from someone's radio. It's a metallic circular chip. Take it out and stick it to the wing."

Jesus Christ on a cracker.

"Great. Sounds really easy."

"It's making a loop around the ship and will pass the tall tower thingy in the middle in another minute."

"On it," Penny said as Ivan tossed her his radio and she disemboweled it, digging for the chip Silas needed. "Follow the fuel intake lines to find the engine room. I'll meet you there." Taking off toward the ship's bridge, she scaled the stairs, ever aware of the ticking clock counting down to their doom.

Close by, she spotted the drone as it made its rounds. *Fuck me. This was a bad idea, we're all going to die, and now Zeln is probably pissed at me for ruining his game.* Wishing she could turn off her amygdala, she did her best to override the spike of fear that went through her as she latched onto the rivets of the bridge's windows and climbed atop the slippery metal surface. Ignoring the fact that she was more than a hundred feet in the air, she zeroed in on the drone.

I've got one shot at this. One chance to show the world who the real terrorist is.

The drone swooped closer, and Penny took a few steps of a running start, then leapt off the metal platform, aiming for its wing. *I can't believe I just essentially jumped off a building* was the only thought in her head as she cut through the air and grabbed its wing, fingers slipping for purchase. With her other hand, she slapped the magnetic chip on the drone's body as her weight pulled the drone off course, sending it lower toward the deck.

And for the stacks of shipping containers.

Shit. She wanted to hijack the drone, not destroy it and herself in the process.

Hanging by one hand, she aimed herself for the narrow gangway just ahead of her—and let go.

A moment of free fall, then she crashed into the deck, tumbling in a heap as she attempted a roll. Her head slammed into a metal rung and her elbow felt like it was on fire, and then she came to a stop. Looking up, the drone continued on its circling course.

"I'm in, Penny. Good work. We're now broadcasting live." Silas's voice through the radio was a salve to the flaming pain licking her body. *Worth it.*

A door stood open to the ship's interior and she took it, following the stairs down and squeezing through the narrow hallway in search of Ivan and the bomb. As she ran, limping slightly, someone stepped out of a small doorway—Ivan.

"This way," he said, leading her deeper into the belly of the ship.

Penny grew more frantic by the second as their limited time ticked away.

Until a guard crossed an intersecting hallway, straight into them.

Penny reacted first, hooking her sickle around the man's throat in a tight but nonlethal hold.

"Hey, sailor," she said, tugging on her blade and drawing blood. "Just got our free ticket into the engine room."

The man moved to disarm her, but Ivan jabbed a volt rifle into his back from behind. "Best to just do as she says."

Grumbling around his blade collar, the man pivoted, and Ivan marched him down the maze of corridors. Less than a minute later, they passed a sign warning about engineering personnel only and donned the protective earmuffs hanging outside.

Ivan shoved the man in first, saying, "Tell them we're engineers from port."

"Brought some engineers from port, Dr. Brown," the man shouted to the room's unseen occupants.

"Oh shit. Duck!" Ivan shouted, shoving Penny behind the nearest engine cylinder and diving for cover just as volts charred the metal hull of the ship above their heads. Grabbing her boot knife, Penny flung it at a guard. It lodged in his neck, dropping him, as Ivan shot volts into the advancing enemy of half a dozen troops.

"How'd you know he was tipping them off?" she asked.

"Dr. Brown—old emergency code trick I learned from watching too many TV hospital dramas. Fuel tanks there"—he pointed on the opposite side of the room—"and there's our bomb."

"Ready to make a break for it?" she asked, cocking her handgun and volt rifle.

Side by side, they charged and broke in opposite directions, peppering their attackers with shots. As Ivan ran to the bomb, Penny took on the bulk of the soldiers alone, firing until her gun clicked, then ditching it for her volt rifle. But these soldiers were more challenging than the ones above. They fought like special ops guys—mercenaries with nothing to lose.

Glancing over her shoulder, Penny got a look at the bomb. She didn't know much about them, but this one looked fucking huge. A mountain of brown paper-wrapped bricks stacked in a thick bundle around a snarl of wires with a blinking red light and a clock counting down.

7:59, 7:58, 7:57

A bullet whizzing past her ear pulled her back into the fight, and she struck out with her sickle, hooking the soldier's wrist and sending his gun flying.

But there was no respite for her. A bulky dude sliced for her ribcage with a jagged knife while shooting volts at her head. She swerved, but one of them sizzled across her arm, catching her coat on fire. Yelling, she shucked it off and whirled it over her head.

"How's it going, Ivan?" she shouted, whipping her flaming coat at the nearest soldier, who rolled out of the way.

5:31, 5:30, 5:29

"Ivan!"

Bent over the contraption, he tugged at his blond locks in a look she'd seen Silas do more than a few times. "I need more time," he said.

"Goddamn it." Penny tossed her coat that was now a full-on fire ball at an advancing soldier. "There's no time!" Kicking the soldier in the chest, she let out a cry of frustration, stomping until she felt his ribs crack.

"Penny," came the tinny voice from the radio at her hip.

What the fuck does he want now? Shooting volts, Penny ripped the radio from her belt and barked into the receiver. "What?"

"I commend your efforts," said Zeln. "You are a formidable opponent."

"Quit flattering me and tell me your fucking decision," she said.

"I won't stop the bomb from detonating. Because I don't need you anymore. Not if I have your little brother."

Shit, he's going for Quentin.

Or he already has him.

48

Agnes

"You want to *what*?" Derek gaped at Agnes as the lab descended into disarray behind him, with scientists attempting to flee and Watchers keeping them in check.

"I told you it was a bad idea," Agnes said. "But I can't think of anything better. Can you?"

Working his jaw, Derek finally said, "No. You're right. It's our only way out of this. Let's do it."

"Less talking, more doing!" Chun said as she poured liquid into a beaker, assisted by Chandra.

With her radio, Agnes called Silas. "Are you in the tech room?"

"Yeah," came his reply. "Currently trying to turn off that godforsaken alarm. What's up?"

"Do you see sound devices they use to control enhanced turned?"

Static for several seconds. Then, "What the hell do you have in mind, Aggie?"

"Just answer the question."

"Yeah, there's equipment here that could make adjustable high-frequency sound waves."

"Great. We're coming to you." Agnes shut off the transmission, silencing his protests, and turned to Chandra. "Where's the troxapine? Not the darts. I want the super soldier stuff."

"In there." She pointed, indicating an upper cabinet. "But I really don't think—"

"We're outnumbered and we don't have time for anything else. Troxapine affects Derek and I differently, and if this latest version gives us extra abilities and heightened reflexes too, we can win this fight. It's either that or we die here."

With a resigned expression, Dr. Chun nodded. "I was wrong."

"About what?" asked Agnes.

Smiling, Dr. Chun clicked a button on Agnes's machine and it whirred to life, the repairs complete. "Evie wasn't the best of us. You are."

Agnes couldn't agree—she wasn't a hero or a genius. She just happened to be in a position where she could make a difference. But no time to argue the point.

"Come on," Agnes said to Derek, leaving Dr. Chun and Chandra to their work.

Prying open the cabinet, Agnes's hands shook as she removed the vials of troxapine. *I'm about to put poison into my body.* And if the latest version of super soldiers were anything to judge by, this new stuff was way more potent than the dust she'd used before. And if Chun and Chandra didn't come up with a cure or detox serum, she and Derek would turn. And there'd be no coming back. *No. They'll do it. I know they will.* Putting her trust in them, Agnes filled up a syringe, needle poised above the vein in her forearm.

The door to the lab shook as something fell into it, shouts sounding from the hallway. More guards had arrived. Pausing to look at Derek, she said, "You don't have to do this."

Derek rolled up his sleeve. "If you're doing this, I'm doing this. Together. Always."

His words gave her the extra spur of courage to push down the plunger, fire and ice flooding through her veins as the troxapine spread. The familiar feeling of the world coming into sharper focus and her nerve endings snapping to attention buzzed through her, but the new formula amplified it exponentially. As Derek injected his own dose, Lawrence and Tara glanced over from where they guarded the scientists lining the wall.

"What the hell are you doing!" Tara shouted. "Están locos?"

"Derek and I are the only ones who have been on it before and know we can take it without turning right away," Agnes explained, bouncing from foot to foot. "Stay here. Protect Dr. Chun and Chandra. We're going for Silas and getting us out of here."

A conflicted expression dashed across Lawrence's face, but he locked eyes with Agnes and nodded. That small acknowledgment of approval meant everything to her. She was doing this for him, for Tara and Ivan, for Evie. For all of them.

"Puñeta," Tara cursed. "I hope you know what you're doing."

The door shook in its frame again, concealing the battle raging on the other side. "Not really," Agnes said, "but it's all we have." Glancing at Derek, who surged with adrenaline too, she said, "Ready?"

Gripping his gun, he said, "Ready."

The Watchers moved away from the door, and Agnes and Derek dove into Zeln's awaiting forces.

49

2:31, 2:30, 2:29

The red numbers on the bomb's countdown clock blinked in an unforgiving cadence as another soldier charged Penny. Sidestepping, she threw him into the nearest set of pipes hard enough that one dislodged, spewing steam. Then she grabbed the wrist of another soldier and flung him into the burning hot steam, his shouts ringing in her ears.

But even with broken ribs and covered in burns, the soldiers didn't relent, focused on their directive of protecting the bomb.

1:10, 1:09, 1:08

"One fucking minute, Ivan!" she shouted, kicking another soldier into the steam.

"Working on it!" he said.

Ten seconds later, their fates were sealed when he said, "I disconnected half of the bomb, but not the other half."

"Sounds like we're still fifty percent fucked," Penny said, ramming her fist into a soldier's face.

"Even at half capacity, the bomb will likely sink the ship. We need to evacuate right the fuck now."

0:45, 0:44, 0:43

Wasting no time, Penny and Ivan dashed for the exit. Feet slapping against the metal stairs, they burst outside just as the right side of the ship erupted into flames and an impenetrable cloud of smoke.

Groaning, the ship listed to the side, but they still had time before things got dire. Pushing Ivan ahead of her, they ran toward the lifeboats on the left side where Faction soldiers were helping civilians.

"There are only two lifeboats," the soldier said. "We already sent one off and got some people on tugboats, but there are a ton left to evacuate."

Penny braced a hand against the wall as the deck angled to the right. *Soon we'll be walking on the fucking walls.* "Get the non-swimmers on a lifeboat. Everyone else will have to jump. Have the tugboats on standby to pick them up."

Zeln's limited crew fought back, as did the troxies there against their will, but as the deck tilted and the ship took on water, some abandoned the fight and jumped overboard. Scrambling across the deck, Penny grabbed for the railing as she reached the bow. The deck shifted dangerously under her feet, a groan and screech of metal clawing through the air as the water rushed to fill the ship. Just ahead, people screamed, clutching the railing above them as everything on the deck that wasn't bolted down careened into the ocean.

"Anyone who can't swim, get to the back and into a tugboat," Penny ordered. "The rest of you"—she grabbed spools of spare rope and old cords from a pile on the deck before they could slip out of reach—"tie these to the railing and use them to safely descend. Once you hit the water, swim like hell."

Most weren't listening, but the closest few blinked with wide eyes. A young-ish dude took a hesitant step forward and grabbed the rope, doing as she instructed.

"Come on," Penny said, helping each civilian descend. It was a close margin and they had to hurry. Because from this angle, she could see the crater in the side of the ship. And the damage was catastrophic. *Not much time before the ship is completely vertical.* Which would make a descent that much more precarious, especially for anyone older or injured.

The buzzing of the drone flying overhead and broadcasting the entire shit show to the international newsfeed pulled her attention, and she looked up. Beyond the sinking ship, Zeln's yacht prowled across the waves, heading for the other approaching resupply ship. Quentin and Vick's tugboat was nowhere to be seen. *Maybe they already reached the other ship and circled behind it.*

Which meant maybe Zeln didn't have Quentin yet.

And now that the refugee ship was actively sinking, Zeln would think she was trapped here or that she'd died in the explosion.

He wouldn't be expecting her.

But I'm coming for him.

Most civilians were already in the water, so with the casualties minimized as much as possible, there was nothing else to do. It was time to abandon ship—and get Mal.

"Ivan, help get the rest off the boat. Or tell them to do what I do, if they want to get down faster. Then you get the hell off of this thing too." Ignoring his shouts of protest, Penny let go of the railing and slid down the deck on her butt, picking up speed as she aimed herself away from the debris in the water. At the last second before she hit the railing, she launched herself toward the water feet first. With the ship tilted to the side, the fall wasn't as far as it would've been, but her stomach bottomed out as she fell toward the water.

Her feet slammed through the surface and the frigid water enveloped her, fighting its way up her nose. Coughing and spluttering, she surfaced as the sinking ship churned the water into a whirlpool. Breaking into a freestyle stroke, she swam for the nearest tugboat and was hauled aboard.

"Penny?" said Ju Lee, eyes wide as she helped her up.

"Small diversion, then you can get back to saving the swimmers," Penny said. "I need that yacht closer so I can sneak aboard, but they can't know I'm alive. You've been training with Vick, right?" Grabbing a sniper rifle from one of the nearby Faction soldiers in the sea of refugees, she thrust it at Ju Lee. "Fire on the yacht, get it to turn around and head for us. Take out any guards on board. I'll cut the engines. Think you can do that?"

"You bet your ass," Ju Lee said, taking the rifle.

It wasn't a great plan, as it would have Zeln and his bodyguards heading straight for their evacuation, but the tugboat was staffed by soldiers trained by Mal and Vick. *And by me.* They could handle it. And it was the only way she'd get close enough to get on that yacht without anyone noticing.

Ju Lee took aim at a sniper on the uppermost of the yacht's three decks, dropping him in two shots. Not as good as Vick, but not bad. The sniper's partner on the lower deck sent up the alarm and began firing on their tugboat. Penny ducked behind the bridge, yelling "Hit the deck!" at the civilians on board, who cowered below the gunnel.

"It's changing course," Ju Lee said, cocking the rifle, then fired again.

Bullets shattered the tugboat's windows, shards spraying, as the yacht crept closer, slowly turning around. *Just a short swim away.* Penny slipped off the back and into the water. Swimming beneath the surface to minimize splashing, she held her breath for as long as possible before rising to take another. The yacht was beside her now, slowing down to avoid ramming the tugboat, and she ducked under water again, trailing her fingers across the hull to guide her through the dark, frigid water to the stern.

When she resurfaced, the back platform was within reach. A single guard was firing volts while Zeln's other bodyguards cloistered on the upper decks, penned in by Ju Lee's shots. Approaching from the side to avoid the propellers, Penny hauled herself aboard and dove for the man's legs, slashing her knife across the back of his knees. Hamstringed, he cried out and dropped, whirling to shoot. But she was ready and hooked her sickle across his throat, silencing him for good.

"I'll take that," she murmured as she grabbed the volt rifle from his dead hands. Two jet skis were parked on the lower deck, and she stabbed her knife into their fuel tanks, draining them before ducking inside a door beside the staircase. A blast of heat greeted her as she entered the engine room packed with humming machinery. Locating the fuel shutoff valve easily thanks to all those childhood summers repairing tractors on the family farm, she twisted it, cutting the fuel supply. In a few minutes, the yacht would be dead in the water.

She exited and took a set of narrow stairs up. Dead guards littered the sundeck, and a crashing sound like somebody hurling glass against the wall came from inside, followed by a shout—*Zeln throwing a tantrum?*

Penny smiled, slipping her black-bladed knife from its sheath as she crept down the outdoor hallway bracketing either side of the stateroom. Through the tinted windows, she saw him.

Mal, magnificent in his fury as he stumbled onto a pure white couch, bleeding from his back wound with a hand plastered to his side, face sporting bruises and cuts as if Zeln had taken out his frustration on him. Her heart clenched, followed by a rush of rage.

On the other side of the luxurious lounge stood Zeln, hefting a vase in one hand and lobbing it at Mal, who ducked with a snarl. Mal was fending him off, but he was in bad shape. No Quentin in sight, but that didn't mean Zeln hadn't already gotten him when she'd been dealing with the sinking refugee ship.

Behind her, the hijacked drone zoomed past. *Hopefully Silas is getting some good footage.* If nothing else, it would show the rest of the world how destructive Zeln could be as the refugee ship burned in the background.

Mal reached for a decorative bust, about to chuck it at Zeln, when he spied Penny through the window. Like the skilled soldier he was, he gave no indication that he'd seen her, but he shifted, drawing Zeln's attention away from her so she could sneak in through the sliding glass door.

Wielding her sickle and her knife, Penny crept inside behind Zeln, footsteps whispering across the plush carpet, intent on her prey.

Time to feed this fucker to the fishes.

50

Agnes

"**O**NLY YOU COULD THINK it's a good idea to go back into that creepy tunnel when we barely escaped with our lives the first time," Derek yelled as he and Agnes shot and slashed their way through Zeln's guards.

Agnes's grin took on a manic edge as the troxapine zipped through her. Invincible. Powerful. Whatever modifications Zeln's scientists had made to the formula were working damn well. She tried not to think about how difficult that might make it for Chun to find a cure. "Gotta get their sound wave tech first, or else it *will* be a death wish."

With the troxapine super soldier serum, Agnes and Derek outmatched Zeln's mercenary cronies. Between the two of them and the Watchers, they left a trail of bodies as they fought toward the tech room. Some soldiers, though, didn't go down so easily. Taking up a tight formation, they advanced on Agnes and Derek, dodging everything they threw at them.

Elite super soldiers. They must be on the same thing we took.

One soldier grabbed a Watcher and lifted him overhead, chucking him against the wall.

But on a fuck ton more of it.

Hacking her machete, Agnes cut a path through the soldiers filling the hallway. *Almost there, but...*

"Won't we be leading the soldiers straight to Silas?" Derek asked, echoing her thoughts.

"Yes, but when we have our own army of enhanced turned obeying our every command, it won't matter. They'll be scared shitless." At least she hoped it worked out that way. *This plan is sounding worse and worse. But it's all we have.*

When they reached the tech room, Agnes pounded on the door. "Si! We're here." Silas opened it, and they fell inside, slamming the door behind them. Wasting no time, he dragged a heavy shelf in front of it.

"What're you thinking, you insane, psychotic—why are your eyes black?" Silas asked. "Are you fucking high?"

Clapping a hand to her face, Agnes said, "Shit. Just my pupils though, right? No black veins in the whites?" She got in Silas's space, prying her eyes wide, and he batted her away.

"Just the pupils. What did you...you took troxapine, didn't you? God-damn it, Agnes. What the fuck is wrong with you? Who knows what kinds of contaminants Zeln added to it, and you just willy-nilly injected it into your bloodstream?"

"Um, I did too," Derek said, raising a sheepish hand. "Seemed like a good idea at the time."

"You—!" Silas cut off, giving him a death glare. "Whatever. What's done is done. Here's the sound wave equipment. It's battery operated for your convenience." He scoffed, shoving a speaker box with a set of knobs at Agnes. "I can already tell what you have planned, and I hate it. But I hope it works. Now get out of my sight, you absolute fucking morons. I have a utility system to hack and a power-hungry egomaniac to stop."

The door rattled behind their makeshift barricade, and Agnes flinched. "Preferably before we get ripped to shreds by his super soldiers."

"Oh, is that all?" Silas shooed them toward the door, nostrils flaring. "What would you all do without me?"

"Die a terrible death," Derek said with a snort.

"I don't appreciate the sarcasm, but you are correct," Silas said. "Now, go. And make sure I have some Watchers out there to guard the door, please! The lock will only keep them out for so long. Can't do all of this shit if I'm fighting for my life."

"He'll be fine," Agnes murmured at Derek's concerned look. Tucking the sound wave device under her arm, they re-entered the raging battle, intent on reaching the tunnel. Bursting into the underground mall, everything had descended into chaos. In the mix, Agnes recognized Sanjali and Raph. Running over, she yelled, "What are you doing here?"

"We got overtaken at the shore," Sanjali said. "Jaha, Will, and Tanaka are there with some reinforcements from the stadium. We got a distress call from Tara and we came here." With a vicious holler, she unloaded her rifle into a guard, sending him flying. "Zeln has Mal."

"Fuck," Derek said. "He'll kill him."

"Which he do you mean?" Agnes asked.

"Either. Both," he said. "This is going to get ugly."

As Agnes and Derek dropped opponents left and right, Sanjali shouted over the din of battle, "Are you guys on steroids or something?"

"Or something," Agnes said. "Can you handle it from here? I'm getting us some more help."

"We've got it," said Raph, stepping in beside Sanjali. "Do what you gotta do."

Taking off down the tracks and into the tunnel, Derek ran ahead while Agnes fiddled with the sound machine, twisting the knobs until the familiar microphone feedback blared from the speakers.

From the tunnel's cave darkness, screeches echoed as turned scuttled toward them, some on all fours like animals, some sprinting with inhuman speed, locked in on their closest prey—Derek and Agnes.

"Aggie? Maybe turn the knob again?" Derek said as he backed away from the incoming flood. "Don't think they like that one."

Twisting the dial and using a tuner knob this time, the sound pitched lower, and the turned slowed, heads tilting as they waited.

"That's new," Agnes muttered.

"And damn useful," Derek said, peering at a turned that had frozen a mere six inches away from him, black drool dripping from its jowls.

Lower frequency gets them to stop, higher frequency stirs them into a frenzy. But how to keep them from attacking our people? Studying the device, she noticed two other knobs beside the largest one and turned one of them. Nothing happened that she could hear, but apparently the turned could. With ferocious speed, they launched at Agnes and Derek, others racing off to attack anyone and everyone.

"Nope, wrong way!" Derek shouted, using his own troxapine-induced strength to grab a turned by the wrist and whip it into the concrete platform.

Agnes twisted the knob in the opposite direction, and the turned switched their trajectories, only going for Zeln's people. When they realized, they tossed their weapons away from them and ran in the opposite direction, the turned grabbing the rifles and smashing them to bits.

"What the fuck was that?" asked Derek.

"Must be some kind of RFID tech in the weapons that gives off a frequency that lines up with the sound waves. But since I altered the frequency, it made the chips a target instead of a repellent."

With the underground mall in disarray, Zeln's soldiers retreated and the Faction had a slight reprieve as the turned chased down and destroyed the offending weapons—and their owners.

As Agnes threw a piece of rebar at a retreating guard like a javelin, her radio buzzed at her hip. "Agnes?"

Tara's voice.

"What's wrong?" she asked.

"Chun and Chandra made a detox serum they think will work for the darts," Tara said. "I already took some. Should work for you too, so get your asses back here. I don't want my best friend and her bozo boyfriend turning into flesh-eating creatures of the night."

They did it. We *did it.*

"Still working on a cure to bring the turned back to themselves though," Tara said. "Penny's blood is being difficult, just like her."

They weren't out of the woods yet, but at least they weren't going to turn. *As long as Chun's detox serum works.* "See you soon, tía." Throwing herself back into the fight beside Derek, she updated him on Tara's news as they tore through Zeln's guards, aided by Sanjali's reinforcements and the enhanced turned.

The battle became a blur until only she, Derek, and their troops remained, standing over a bloody train platform riddled with bodies, their army of obedient creatures awaiting their commands as the sound machine hummed a dull whine in the background.

"That is creepy as fuck," Derek said, inching away from the turned nearest him, its crimson, clawed hands primed for ripping. The black-eyed, gray bodies formed a festering mass on the platform, swaying in time with the frequency's pitch.

"Make sure the sound machine doesn't run out of battery," Agnes instructed Raph and Sanjali. "Once we get a cure from Penny's blood, they can be our first test subjects."

The duo nodded but looked askance at the creatures—creatures who might soon become people again. *What a weird world we live in.*

"Your gamble paid off," Derek said, wrapping an arm around her. "As much as I love feeling like Hercules, let's get to the lab and take that detox serum."

Before she could reply, her radio chattered again. "—got a message out and—"

"Woah, slow down, Silas," Agnes said into the speaker. "Say again?"

"I hacked Zeln's comms and blasted messages out," Silas's voice repeated through the speaker. "You want to know who answered?"

When he told her, her jaw dropped.

No fucking way.

51

"You've lost. Why do you keep fighting me?" When Zeln delivered a swift kick to Mal's ribs, Mal grunted in pain, and Penny wanted to skin him alive as more of Mal's blood soaked into the couch. *Bastard.*

As Zeln reared back to strike again, Penny sprang from her hiding place and hooked his wrist with her sickle, placing her knife at his throat. "Guess we just don't know when to quit," she said, and behind Zeln, she saw Mal flash a grin. "Sorry I'm late," she said to Mal, but her eyes never left Zeln's, and she took pleasure at the drop of blood running down his neck. "Told you I'd show you how to use a knife."

From outside, the shooting stopped as scuffling and shouts sounded from above.

Guards heading down here. Zeln must have triggered some kind of panic button. Better finish this quick.

"Where's Quentin?" she asked, digging the knife deeper.

"He's—"

"He's not here," Mal answered, breaths wheezing in his chest. "Not that I saw."

Zeln scowled, and relief rushed through Penny. *One less thing to worry about.* Tossing an extra knife to Mal, she said, "You want to kill him, or should I do the honors?"

Mal caught it with the hand that wasn't holding his bleeding side and he stood, towering over both of them. Her hand tensed around her sickle's hilt as she waited for his answer. *Just one twitch to the side, one flick of the wrist, and Zeln is bleeding out at my feet.* Taking lives had never been hard, and this one would be all too easy.

But she wouldn't take that away from Mal. His brand of justice was different from hers, and he needed to do this his way.

"I—"

The window exploded, raining bits of glass around them. Bullets lodged into the opposite wall as Zeln's bodyguards filed down the narrow stairs. Reacting on instinct, Penny dove beside the couch, Mal landing atop her, while Zeln ducked under the table.

Through the broken window, they had an unobstructed view of the ocean beyond and of the resupply cargo ship—the one not currently sinking—heading straight for their yacht.

Two lone figures stood at its bow, one with jet-black hair and a sniper rifle, the other bronze like pennies, hands waving frantically.

"Is that—?" Mal asked.

"Yep."

At least I found Quentin. He, Vick, and their soldiers had taken over the ship. Their plan might've been a good one in other circumstances—now they'd have extra lifeboats for the civilians. But big ships couldn't stop or turn on a dime. And the yacht was dead in the water.

They were about to be in a cargo ship sandwich, trapped between the incoming supply ship and the sinking refugee one.

Clutching Mal's arm, Penny said, "We have to get off this boat. Quentin can throw us a line, but can you climb?"

Her hand was wet with his blood, but his voice did not waver when he said, "I can do it."

Interrupting them, shots pinged off the wall—Zeln had grabbed a gun strapped to the underside of the table as he fired from behind some chairs.

Running to opposite sides of the small space, Penny and Mal fought their way through Zeln's bodyguards clogging the exits.

"Get to the bow!" she shouted, swiping her sickle. But these guys were good, and most of her attacks missed. *We don't stand a chance.* They fought like Zeln—trained, elite warriors—but to an extreme. Like they knew every move she was going to make before she made it. Like machines. This was something different than Pharmatrox's super soldiers.

With precious little time to get onto the resupply ship before it crashed into the yacht and even less time to evacuate the refugees, they had to move. Now. Glancing out the window, she saw the tugboats fishing people out of the water, almost at capacity.

As Penny grappled with her options, Zeln's laughter rang a dissonance in her ears. "You can't beat me, Penny. And you can't beat *them*. I've been doing some experiments of my own. No weapons," he said to his soldiers. "I want them alive. But bleeding."

Fuck, it's true. He's given them something we've never seen before.

From across the room, she locked eyes with Mal, and they shared a moment of understanding.

They all have to go down with this ship. This knowledge has to die here.

While Mal managed to dump some bodyguards overboard, Penny could tell his strength was waning, and he needed enough energy to climb up the rope to Quentin's ship. But she had her own problems. One of the soldiers grabbed her hair and attempted to smash her head against the wall, but she spun away, ripping her sickle across his neck in a deep cut, losing a good chunk of her hair in the process.

As she jumped over the railing and scrambled to the bow, Mal did the same from the other side, kicking back his pursuers. The incoming ship drew closer, and Quentin cupped his hands around his mouth and shouted something, but she couldn't hear over the sound of the drone passing overhead.

A rope flew over the side of Quentin's ship, reaching the water—but they'd have to swim to it. With the way Mal was sagging and bleeding though, he'd never make it.

Then she remembered the jet skis.

She'd punctured the fuel tanks, but maybe they'd have enough juice left to get them to that rope.

I only need it to work for one minute, tops.

"Mal!" She punched an incoming soldier in the throat. "Get to the lower deck. I have an idea." But when he didn't answer, she looked across—he'd slumped over the railing, a soldier pummeling his ribs with punches while Zeln aimed a knife for his throat. "No!" Flying to Mal's side, she bulldozed the soldier over the edge and spun her sickle in a wild arc, slashing until all the world was a blur.

He cannot have him.

Some of her strikes found Zeln's flesh, and she grinned at the sight of his blood—but she stopped herself from ending him. *Mal wouldn't want that.* Rearing back, she head-butted Zeln in the face and felt the satisfying crunch of bone, his blood exploding in a blinding cloud. After hefting Mal's arm across her shoulders, she dragged him down the stairs.

"Can you help me push this into the water?" she asked, unstrapping the jet ski from its restraints.

"Yeah. Right side is no good though," Mal said, holding his arm close. *He looks about ten seconds from lights out.*

Once they'd gotten the jet ski in the water, Penny climbed aboard and helped Mal sit behind her. Handing him a gun she'd stolen, she said, "Cover us." Dutifully, he held it in his good hand, firing at the yacht as the jet ski drifted away, but his shots were all over the place.

"Come on," Penny muttered as she turned the key, engine sputtering. The resupply ship was now a mere football field away from crashing into them.

"Penny?" Mal said.

"I see it," she said, hands shaking as she turned the key again. Finally, the jet ski rumbled to life, the scent of gasoline thick in the air as it leaked a swirl of rainbows into the water. Water sprayed as she gunned the engine, zipping just in front of Quentin's ship mere seconds from impact.

The wake pushed them away, and she twisted the handlebars, bringing them alongside the ship, where Quentin's rope awaited them. Looking up, she saw his bronze head appear over the side, like looking at a sunrise after the longest night.

Balancing on the jet ski, Penny grabbed the rope as high as she could. Beneath her, Mal took the rope's slack with his good arm, hauling himself up. Two seconds later, Quentin's ship careened into the yacht with a crunch of fiberglass, shouts arising as the yacht took on water.

When Penny whistled through her fingers at Quentin, the rope ascended, pulling them away from the wreckage below. *Must have rigged up some kind of pulley system.* And it looked like Quentin's ship would miss the refugees, but just barely.

After they reached the top and clambered aboard, ten or so crew members and Watchers held onto the rope—the pulley system, literally. But Penny didn't pay any mind to that, yanking Quentin into her in a fierce hug.

"You did it, Quentin. I'm so proud of you."

"And all without blowing anything up! Who would've thought. Was pretty easy to talk these guys into switching sides with Vick's knives to their throats," he said. But Penny barely registered his words as she shifted her attention to Mal, helping him to his feet.

Looking at the blood sluicing his skin-tight wet shirt, her chest felt like a fluttering bird was trapped inside it. To Vick, she said, "Please tell me you have medical supplies."

Her face was grim as she surveyed Mal's injuries, but she nodded and took off.

Penny gripped Mal's shirtfront, both to hold him up and hold him close, and pressed her face into his chest. "I'm sorry I didn't come for you right away. I'm sorry, I'm sorry," she chanted as her breaths rasped through her lungs. *Please don't die. If I'd gone for him sooner, he wouldn't be in such bad shape now.*

Then he cupped her face with his big hand and tipped it up. Warm, honey-brown eyes greeted hers, and even through the blood and bruises, a glint of pride shone through.

If he was looking at her like that, she knew she'd made the right choice.

But then Mal's gaze shifted and he staggered to the side of the ship, pointing below. "That fucker is trying to get away."

Zeln, swimming through the wreckage, heading for a boat speeding in from the harbor.

"Not on my fucking watch," Penny said, running for the rope and leaping overboard, rappelling down the side of the ship. Quentin and Vick poked their heads over the side as Penny barked instructions. "Vick, take a shot if you have it, but try not to kill him. I want that shit bag to face justice. Quentin, make sure Mal doesn't do anything stupid like try to help me. Give him an atomic wedgie if you have to."

"Aye, aye!"

Even Vick looked amused at Quentin's excitement, and Penny found herself smiling. But too soon, the frigid ocean water greeted her and she broke into a fast freestyle, chasing Zeln down. Every cut and gash burned like fire, and every single one of her injuries sustained over the past few hours made themselves known. But she pushed her body to its limits, ignoring the pain and focusing on the only goal that mattered now.

Zeln will not escape this.

Lungs burning, muscles aching, she caught up to Zeln just as he reached the small rescue speedboat. Grabbing his leg, she pulled him back into the water and shoved him under, dodging shots from his guards above.

It was a bad idea.

A hand around her ankle yanked her under, and the freezing water plunged into her lungs as she gasped in surprise. Fighting and kicking in a tangle of limbs, Zeln wrapped his arm around her neck, squeezing as more water forced its way down her throat. Panic was her only reality as she thrashed, not knowing which way was up. It was only her sheer stubbornness and inability to allow this asshat to best her that prevented her from giving up and remembering she had a knife in her belt.

Grabbing it, she stabbed wildly behind her, movements hampered by the cold water weighing her down from the inside out. The arm loosened, and Penny kicked her way to the surface, already vomiting water as she reached for the rescue boat's ladder with shaky hands, rallying herself to fight off the guards—

But the boat was full of dead bodies, bullets lodged perfectly in their foreheads. Barely able to think through the hacking coughs and vomiting that wracked her body, Penny looked around for Zeln, but he was nowhere to be found.

Until a fist in her hair yanked her backward, hauling her into the boat with a vicious twist. She cried out and rolled to get into a better position, but the water hadn't cleared her lungs and she coughed again, feeling a new round of barfing coming on.

A bleeding, soaked Zeln glared at her, murder in his eyes, as he held her black-bladed knife to her cheek, drawing blood. "You shouldn't have crossed me, Penny."

Something on the deck of the cargo ship behind him caught her eye, and Penny smiled, recognizing the telltale gleam of a sniper rifle barrel in the sunlight. "No, Zeln. You shouldn't have crossed *us.*"

He blinked in confusion, and Penny bucked her hips, flipping him off of her, as a bullet burrowed into his kneecap. He went down screaming as another and another lodged into his legs, shattering the bones.

Penny would never admit it to anyone, but his screams were music to her ears.

Well. Maybe she'd admit it to Mal. Because in the distance, she saw his hulking figure hobble beside Vick and Quentin, and she could have sworn he was smiling too.

But as she looked to the horizon, something else approached. Fast.

A trio of fighter jets, streaking toward them.

Shit. Her heart sank. *Zeln's allies must have come through for him. We're too late.*

But then she saw the look on Zeln's face. And it wasn't one of triumph.

It was one of unabashed horror.

As the jets looped around the scene, a Pharmatrox helicopter swooped in and hovered above the deck of Quentin's cargo ship, a lone figure climbing down the dangling rope ladder.

"What the fuck is going on?" she shouted, grabbing Zeln by the shirtfront with her knife to his throat.

But he'd schooled his features into neutrality and remained silent. If she hadn't seen the bullets hit his leg, she'd never have known he was in what had to be excruciating pain. In one swift move, she grabbed a guard's fallen volt rifle and slammed it into Zeln's head, knocking him out. With a growl of frustration, she steered the rescue speedboat back to the cargo ship and tied the rope around both of them, giving the signal to lift them up, ready to fight off whatever awaited them on deck.

As Vick pulled them both over the side, Penny asked, "What the hell happened?" A rustle of energy went up and the crew holding the rope parted.

And *Kev* stepped forward.

Her gaze locked on the rough-looking man, uncomprehending. "We thought you were dead," she said.

"I had to keep it that way. I can fully explain later, but right now, we need to get those refugees aboard."

"The fighter jets?" she asked.

"Canada came through," Kev said, gesturing to the crew who'd hauled the rope. "All because of you, Penny, and what you did here today. We saw everything. The whole *world* saw everything, exactly as it happened because of the drone footage. And they saw what you did for those civilians. Canada was the first domino. Once we had them, other allies who'd been on the fence followed suit." Placing a hand on her shoulder, his eyes crinkled in a warm smile. "You did this, Penny. We now have everything we need to finish this war and rebuild. You should be proud."

Proud. It had been so long since she'd felt anything other than rage and despair. But these past few months spent repairing her relationship with Quentin and Agnes, and building a new one with Mal and the others...maybe it was possible she could broaden her emotional spectrum and actually feel *good* again. Atonement for all the wrongs in her life was an impossibility, but she'd keep trying to be a little bit better every day. A big, warm hand slipped into hers and squeezed. Glancing up, she met Mal's gaze, happiness blasting through her and obliterating any lingering darkness.

And she'd keep chasing the feeling she got whenever Mal looked at her with those golden eyes that saw her for everything she was and loved her because of it.

Ducking his head to hers, he pressed a kiss to her forehead. "I'm proud of you, Pen. So fucking proud."

And for the first time, she let herself believe him.

52

"Y OU'VE GOT A FUCK ton of explaining to do," Penny said, kicking back in a chair in the stadium's war room.

Across from her, Kev took a seat, along with his Canadian contacts who had brought in the cavalry. "We'll hash it all out, but we have to rebuild an entire country. That will take more than one conversation."

"Better get talking, then," she said as she took a drink of boiling hot coffee one of the kitchen crew had brought for them. Around the table sat every critical member of their team who'd had a hand in their victory—Agnes and Derek huddling close; Silas and Ivan chatting; Lawrence and his newfound partner Naomi sharing a cup of coffee; Vick and Tara with their heads bent in a murmured conversation. She was pleased to see Tara and Ivan looking better after taking Chun's detox serum. *Hopefully it continues to work.* Beside her, Quentin fiddled with his latest invention. It always amazed her how his mind never stopped working, even in the idle moments.

A hand closed around her thigh, drawing her attention to the man seated next to her—*her* man, if she wanted him.

And holy hell did she want him. Now she just had to find the words to tell him.

Even weak with blood loss, Mal had stubbornly refused to miss the meeting. At his side, Ju Lee tended his wounds while chittering her disapproval. "I'm not going to stitch you up just to have you rip them out because you refuse to take a day off," Ju Lee scolded, tying off a suture in his shoulder. Judging by the blood soaking his shirt, his torso would need quite a few stitches too. "You *will* take it easy for at least a week, or you'll have me to answer to."

Cowed into obedience, Mal grunted his assent. "Four days."

"*Five.* That's my final offer."

"Deal."

Ju Lee huffed as she finished another stitch. "I liked it better when you were unconscious."

Breaking out of her conversation with Tara, Vick interrupted, saying, "I caught part of the ship through my arm earlier, if someone could give me a hand." She held out her arm, where a piece of metal the size and thickness of a pencil punctured straight through her bicep. "Haven't had a chance to make it to the infirmary yet."

Quentin covered his mouth, making a retching sound. Vick thrust a pair of pliers at Derek beside her, saying, "Rip it out. Immediately."

"You—what? Where did you get pliers?" Derek acted like she'd just handed him soggy spaghetti noodles.

"I always have pliers. Do it now, please. I can feel it knocking against my bone and it's starting to sting."

"What, no!" He held the pliers between two fingers like they might bite him.

"*Fine.* Didn't think you'd be so squeamish. I'll do it myself." Vick grabbed the metal bar with the pliers and *pulled*—

The rod came out and she tossed it aside, pocketed the pliers, then ripped off the bottom of her tee shirt and held it out. "At least tie me a tourniquet, someone."

Penny's eyes widened in an impressed look as Tara tied the cloth tight around Vick's arm with a beatific smile.

"You—you didn't even *yell* or blink." Derek swiped a hand over his face.

"I'll get to you next." Ju Lee sighed, shaking her head.

When everyone settled in, Kev cleared his throat, and the room quieted. "I'm sorry for letting you think I was dead. It wasn't my call." Cutting a glance at the Canadian emissaries, he added, "But it was the right one. I'd been having off-the-books meetings with Canada and other allies for a few months, but our gatherings started to get ambushed. My contacts ended up assassinated—Zeln's doing, we now know. Our potential allies were rightfully spooked. The only way they'd consider helping is if I went completely off the radar. And I agreed. Let the troxies think they'd killed me, lure them into a false sense of security, meanwhile I'm working quietly in the background to take them down. No one outside of a chosen few could know the truth, for risk of it leaking.

"That alone might have worked, if not for Zeln. Like you, we didn't realize his threat level until it was too late. We followed the soldiers bringing darts to the Capital, knowing something big was coming, we just didn't know what. I've been laying low in Baltimore in a Pharmatrox hangar under Faction control. I wanted to be close, should I need to move quickly. And then you came through for us, Penny. Once that drone footage hit the feeds and the emissaries saw what was happening, they pushed through an order to get the firepower we needed to browbeat Zeln's troops into surrender. Once Zeln was down, the rest of the operation crumbled swiftly."

"What are your plans for dealing with him and whatever's left of Pharmatrox?" Mal asked.

"Zeln will never see the light of day again, nor will anything to do with that wretched company," Kev answered with a hard expression.

Mal tightened his hand around Penny's leg, and she spoke up. "Zeln and Pharmatrox manipulated those people. Some of them might have taken up their cause willingly, and they should face the consequences. But not everything is always so black and white. If Agnes and Mal—*good* people—were troxies once, then I'm sure there are more like them in their ranks."

Steepling his fingers, Kev nodded. "You make a valid point."

"That's where Canada can help, maybe," Agnes suggested. "Setting up trials and rebuilding our government. Hold elections again and get some sort of parliament set up."

"Right," agreed Penny. "Because we're not going back to that sham constitution bullshit we had before Pharmatrox took over. This is our chance to build something that has *our* best interests in mind, instead of corporations. Maybe it's a pipe dream and maybe all forms of government eventually become corrupt in their own ways, but we should at least try to build a system that works instead of returning to the same broken status quo that has the rich getting richer and the poor getting poorer. But that's above my pay grade. Kev, I'm sure you know someone who'd be interested in running for office who is actually worth a damn."

"I have some people in mind, yes," he said with a small smile. She knew he'd been planning for this for years, and it was nice to fully pass the torch to him and his team.

Suddenly, the door hit the wall with a bang, a furious Dr. Chun standing on the other side of it accompanied by a frightened younger woman. "And you didn't think to fucking clue me in to the fact that you'd have to fake your own death?" Dr. Chun growled.

"Wanda, I—"

In two seconds flat, Dr. Chun flew across the room and pulled Kev into her, mauling him with a kiss, then smacked him in the face. "Cannot believe you, you insufferable—" Kissing him again, her protests were lost against his lips, and Penny couldn't help but chuckle, glancing at Mal out of the corner of her eye. She knew a thing or two about wanting to jump someone's bones *and* punch their lights out.

Agnes looked just as amused as she cleared her throat. "Excellent timing, Dr. Chun. I was just about to tell everyone about the cure."

Room was made around the table for the newcomers, and Dr. Chun sat at Kev's side, smoothing her hair. "Right. With Agnes's machine, Chandra and I found a detox serum formula that will work for any version of troxapine, as well as an antidote for the darts. We commandeered some of Zeln's scientists, and they're cranking it out as we speak.

"As for curing those who have already turned, we'll need some more time, but I have every confidence we can use what we've learned from the antibodies in Penny's blood to manufacture a serum to fully rehabilitate the turned—no matter how long they've been turned or what kind of troxapine is in their system. We successfully stopped Zeln from infecting the water supply, although his water-soluble serum is what I plan to use to widely distribute the detox serum—and the cure, once we have it."

"We have teams that can help speed up that process," said the emissary, a pretty middle-aged woman with dark brown skin and mahogany hair.

"From here on out, no harming the turned," Agnes said. But then she held her head with a sigh, a forlorn expression creeping across her face. "I just wish we'd known it sooner. There are so many we could have helped instead of killed."

Derek made a sound of protest. "There is no way you could have known. We did what we had to do to survive. Remember?" Something tender passed between them, and Penny felt as if she were intruding on a private moment. She'd never met two people more suited for each other, except maybe Tara and Vick.

"So where is this Zeln asshole now?" asked Chun.

"He's locked up in a holding cell guarded by our best," Mal said, and Penny laughed to herself. Raph, Sanjali, and Will were standing guard, even though the last still flirted with her, making Mal grind his teeth into a pulp. But even he could not deny Will was an excellent soldier.

"Mal said I could give him a nuclear noogie," Quentin said, looking up from his doodad with a serious expression, as if daring someone to deny him.

Mal ruffled his hair with a grunt. "'Course you can. It's less than he deserves."

Wrapping a hand around Mal's good arm, Penny said in a low voice, "And we'll make sure he gets what he deserves."

When Penny entered the holding room, Zeln glanced up. Even covered in dirt and blood with his wrist handcuffed to a pipe, he didn't give her the satisfaction of looking anything but implacable.

Until Mal stepped into the room behind her, and the temperature plummeted a few degrees.

"You thought I was dead," Mal said to the slight widening of Zeln's eyes.

"I don't know how you're not," answered Zeln, gaze roaming between the two of them.

The longer he looked at Penny, the angrier she felt Mal growing at her side. Threading her fingers through his, she gave his hand a soft squeeze, snagging his attention for a moment. The look that flashed across his face conveyed so many things it took her breath—gratitude, pride, lov—*fuck*. She'd barely come to terms with that last one. The two hadn't had a moment to themselves since the battle ended, but as soon as they did, they needed to have a conversation.

"So. You here to kill me?" Zeln asked.

Mal's hand tightened in hers, and she knew how badly he wanted to do just that. How badly she herself wanted to. But the same restraint that held her back from slitting the fucker's throat when she had the chance stole over her now.

This was Mal's battle, and he alone would choose its ending.

Emotions warred through Mal in little tics only she would notice—someone who'd been beside him through some of the hardest months of their lives. Finally, with a somber expression, he said almost to himself, "What have you become?"

"I am what they made me to be—ruthless. Unforgiving. *Inevitable.* The system was supposed to protect us, *save* us, but it beat me bloody and spit in my face. Did the same to you. So I destroyed it, board by fucking board, and made it my own. All great empires fall, Mal. And this new one you're building? It is no different."

Mal worked his jaw as he stared at a man who'd once been like a brother to him. "You killed my people. Hurt my woman. For that alone, I should kill you."

Zeln just waited, that same lazy smile on his face.

When Mal dropped her hand, tightening his into a fist around the knife in his belt, she thought he'd made his choice, and so did Zeln, who let loose a soft chuckle. "I knew it would end like this," Zeln said.

Mal's muscles tensed as he stared Zeln down. Zeln looked back with a taunting expression, as if daring him to plunge the dagger into his eye socket—something Penny was growing closer to doing herself the longer Mal stood there, but she held her ground.

Finally, Mal released his hold on his knife and turned for the exit.

Not even bothering to look over his shoulder, he said, "I have everything I want, Zeln. Your death—or life—no longer matters to me."

As Penny followed him from the room, calmness melted over her.

I have everything I want too. Almost.

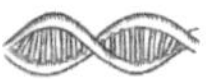

When Penny found Quentin, he was in a vacant room in the stadium organizing a small bookshelf with an array of knickknacks.

"What are you doing?" she asked as she walked inside and sat on a perfectly made cot.

"Just setting up my stuff," he said, placing another unknown object beside the others, twisting it to the side a half inch, then moving it back, nodding.

"Your...? But what about Maple Street? And there's no early morning training tomorrow, now that we have actual military aid."

He shrugged and continued unpacking his rucksack. "I know. I want to stay here more often. I like it. Plus, my sister lives here."

My sister lives here.

The words bowled her over with their power, her eyes burning. After everything they'd gone through in the past year, she'd longed for this day, but was never stupid enough to actually hope it would come true. She'd done too much, broken too much, to ever repair. Or so she'd thought.

But when Quentin turned his cheeky grin dappled with freckles on her, she knew. They *were* fixing their relationship. Had been for months.

And they'd keep doing it—together. A single tear escaped, and she clapped a hand to her mouth to cover the laugh-sob that escaped.

"Wow, didn't expect that to bring you to tears," he said, still grinning, but then grew serious. "Must really care about this brother of yours."

"I love him with everything I am," she said, pulling him into a tight hug.

Without hesitation, he hugged her back, and the best feeling, like liquid sunshine, poured over her. *We're okay.*

But there's one more thing I need to do.

"You seen Agnes?" she asked, breaking away.

She swore she saw a knowing twinkle in his eye when he said, "She's alone in the armory, sorting through supplies. Looked like she could use someone to talk to."

Sure enough, when Penny walked into the armory, Agnes was buried under a mountain of gear, inspecting things and tossing them over her shoulder, muttering. Unsure of what to say, Penny hovered by the door. So much had transpired over the relatively short time she'd known Agnes, and she knew she'd inflicted wounds that had cut deeply. Maybe wounds that would never heal. It would be a mark on her soul forever, and that would be okay. But not a day would go by that she didn't regret her actions toward the strong, smart, capable woman in front of her. The woman who had taken her little brother under her wing and saved him from injury and death many times over.

Clearing her throat, Penny said, "Want some help?"

Agnes's head shot up from her work, and Penny noticed the brief hesitation before Agnes smiled. Rightfully so, her reaction to seeing

Penny was still one of fear. *It will take time, but I'll be damned if I don't fix this too.*

But Agnes's smile was genuine as she said, "Sure. Taking a break from the sciencey stuff with Dr. Chun to do some monotonous organizing. Helps me think."

Penny sifted through a pile of volt rifles for ones that needed to be charged as she gathered her nerve. Apologies had always felt useless. They seemed to be more to the benefit of the apologizer than the person being apologized to, as a way for them to absolve themselves of the blame, meanwhile the person they'd hurt was still hurting. Words were only words, but sometimes they needed to be said—as long as they were followed up by the right actions.

"Agnes, I—fuck." Penny broke off, wiping a hand across her face. *Off to a great start.* "Words feel meaningless after everything I put you through. It was wrong. All of it. And I'm sorry. I feel like a shithead for offering something as useless as an 'I'm sorry' for getting you hooked on the dust, hunting you down, bringing harm to you and the others at the Outpost. I know I may never be able to make it up to you, but you should know, I'm different now because of you—because of *all* of you. Or, at least, I *feel* different. Thanks for giving me a chance to be better, and I'll continue to fight for that every day."

Agnes remained silent for a good thirty seconds, studying her with a pensive expression. The scrutiny almost had Penny fidgeting, but she held still as Agnes deliberated. The woman should want to punch her in the face, at the very least. Maybe this had been a bad idea. Maybe—

Agnes threw her arms around Penny and gave her a quick squeeze before pulling away. *Lots of hugs today.*

"Earlier, when you said not everything is black and white, I hope you know that applies to us too, Penelope. I'm not all white, and you're not all black. Your actions these past months have shown me that. I hope you can start to see it for yourself. And I think, if you keep on this track, you might find yourself with some new lifelong friends—besides me, I mean."

Friends.

Penny hadn't had anyone she could call a friend since Lexa.

And now, it appeared, she might have many. And she wanted it—badly.

"I think that sounds nice," Penny said around the lump that had formed in her throat.

Agnes gave her an unfiltered smile, one without the usual undertones of tension or fear. "Me too."

Now for the last thing I need to fix.

When Penny found Mal, he lounged on his bed with a creased paperback book open on his lap and a flashlight pointed at the ceiling illuminating the room in a dreamlike glow. Bandages wrapped his torso under his thin tee shirt and his hair was damp from a shower.

Penny watched him for a moment more, gathering her courage, before she knocked softly on the door. She'd been longing for and dreading this moment all day, hiding out in the armory with Agnes until she could no longer justify reorganizing the same pile of vests. When he looked up, his eyes crinkled as his face broke into a full smile—the smile he only ever gave to her. Setting his book aside, he patted the open space next to him, and she approached on shaking legs.

But all trepidation flooded out of her as she settled into the circle of his arms, fitting against him like a puzzle piece. *Look at me, already falling into the sappy cliches.* But she found she didn't care. Because of what she felt for Mal, she now understood the way Derek and Agnes looked at one another, all of that stuff she thought she'd never have because she'd never be worthy of it. But here was a man who refused to let her feel anything *but* worthy.

"How are you holding up?" she asked, her hand finding its way to his chest where she felt the reassuring *thump-thump* of his heartbeat.

Tracing a thumb across her jawline, he said, "Started to really feel it about an hour ago, but Dr. Chun hooked me up with some good painkillers and pumped me full of antibiotics. I'll survive. Where've you been?"

Hiding. Her feelings overwhelmed her and she didn't know how to put them into words. For the first time in ages, Penny could actually see the light at the end of what had been a never-ending dark tunnel. Not only had they started the wheels of war turning toward a resolution, she had Quentin back—up until a few months ago, salvaging their relationship had been the only thing she cared about. But now...she traced the tattoo on Mal's bicep, her heart clenching. *Now, I care about so much more.* "Today was...a lot," she said.

Warm air puffed against her face as he chuckled. "Understatement of the century."

Licking her lips, she steeled herself. "Mal, I—" *Jesus Christ, why can't I just say it?* Her fingers tightened in the fabric of his shirt as she battled with herself. Lies rolled off her tongue easily and always had, and she'd just said the same words to Quentin in a different context, but when faced with pouring out the one solid truth of her heart, the one thing she knew with utter certainty, and she couldn't fucking do it?

He thumbed her lower lip, a secret smile playing at his mouth. "Pen?"

As his molten gold eyes seared into her, the power of his gaze burned the truth out of her. "I'm not a good person, Mal. But I want to be. *You* make me want to be. Even when I was stuck in the dark dealing with the pain of being reunited with Quentin and facing my past, you saw something in me. You never gave up on me. Not then, not now. Not ever. I don't know what I did to deserve that kind of loyalty from you, but I'll never stop trying to earn it. I love you, Malosi. I—yeah. I love you."

The laughter that rumbled through his chest was bright and all-consuming, and she found a chuckle bubbling inside of her too. Wrapping his arms around her, he closed the breath of space between them, his soft mouth finding hers, his kiss igniting a swift heat that rushed through her with the power of a thousand suns.

There I go with the stupid cliches again.

"About fuckin' time, woman," he growled against her lips, capturing her smile. "Yeah. I love you too."

53

Agnes

Finally finished with her mind-numbing junk organizing, Agnes headed to return a box of cleaning supplies to the janitor's closet. About an hour ago, Penny had left her with a pinched expression and a vague excuse about having something to do, but she suspected she had some unfinished business with Mal. Smiling to herself, Agnes hoped the two most stubborn people she'd ever met would finally admit their feelings for each other and make it *official* official. Anyone with eyes knew the two of them had it bad for each other.

As she reached for the closet door's knob, a scuffle came from inside. Unsure, her hand drifted to her machete at her hip. Yeah, the war was in the process of being de-escalated, but that didn't mean there weren't still turned who wanted to eat her or other enemies unhappy with the ceasefire who wanted their pound of flesh. Wrenching the door open, weapon held high, she let out a yell—

"Puñeta! Agnes, what the fuck? Trying to give us a collective heart attack?" Tara said as she sprang away from Vick, who had her fingers tangled in Tara's hair, lips at her throat.

Danger abated, Agnes sheathed her weapon and shoved the box of cleaning supplies at them, smirking. "Why are you making out in the broom closet? Everyone already knows about you two."

Grumbling, Tara shoved the box on the shelf, still in the circle of Vick's arms. "We know," Tara said. "Just trying to get some privacy, but apparently that was too much to hope for."

Agnes snorted and Vick rolled her eyes, caressing Tara's cheek. "At least let us preserve the fantasy that we're sneaking around. Makes it more fun."

"You got it," Agnes said, shutting the door for them, but they were already back at each other and hardly noticed. Pleased that Tara had found happiness, Agnes made her way to the exit, an extra bounce in her step. It was late, but knowing Derek, he'd still be awake and waiting for her at home.

On her way past the cafeteria, she bumped into Silas. "What's got you looking so grumpy?" she asked. "Did Ju Lee steal your muffin again?"

"*No,*" huffed Silas. "But that annoying cockatoo stole my muffin of a man from me. Again." He tilted his head skyward with a sigh. "But I can't even be upset. Ivan loves training Quentin to be his deranged little protégé, and I'll be damned, but he's starting to make me rethink my no-kids policy."

"Woah," Agnes said, blinking. "That's *huge.* You despise kids."

"I stand by that. They're sticky and irritating," he said. "But nobody can despise Quentin."

"Sure they can," said Lawrence, sidling up to them with his arm slung around Naomi. "Especially when he leaves his wet towels wadded under your pillow and eats your last stick of beef jerky." Naomi chuckled, shaking her head. "Okay, yeah, maybe not even then. Because he'd just make some crack about how pillows are better when they're soggy and it's only the last stick of jerky because I already ate most of it. Damn kid winning arguments when he's not even here."

"Who's not here?" Quentin said, running over and launching himself at the nearest table, then sliding his butt across the top before coming to a stop next to them. Ivan jogged up after him.

Lawrence planted a noogie on Quentin's head, saying, "Just my favorite little pain in the butt."

"My official title," Quentin said with a mock bow as Ivan planted a tender kiss onto Silas's waiting lips.

"Sorry to keep him up so late," said Ivan. "He's been a big help with this project Kev has us working on."

"Hey, I don't have a bedtime. I'm practically an *adult*, after all of this," Quentin protested, looking around at the doubtful faces. "I'm more responsible than any of you! I hijacked a whole cargo ship *by myself* and had it rigged to explode in less than ten minutes." He sat back, crossing his arms with a dignified expression. "I'd like to see any of you wienerschnitzels do that."

Agnes could only shake her head and laugh, and she snagged Quentin into a quick side hug. "You're right. You certainly have earned a night of goofing off and copious junk food." Sobering for a moment, she gave his shoulder a squeeze. "We couldn't have done any of this without you. Love you, kiddo."

Beaming, he threw his arms around her in earnest. "Love you, Aggie."

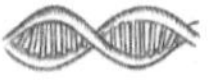

Finally stepping into her room on Maple Street, Agnes was greeted by the sight of a shirtless Derek, his tattoos in full display as he pulled on a hoodie, a pair of dark sweatpants clinging to his muscled legs.

"My eyes are up here." Derek smirked, and she snorted in response. "Get over here," he said, crooking a finger at her, her body already drifting toward him. Tucking a hand behind her neck, he dipped his lips to hers, but the quick greeting morphed into a lingering kiss as his tongue parted her lips, coaxing a sigh from her, before he pulled away with a grin. "Missed you too," he said.

She batted his shoulder as he towed her toward the bed piled high with blankets, and she collapsed into it, allowing him to scoop her into his lap.

"You must be exhausted," he said, pressing a kiss to her temple.

"I am." But it was a good kind of exhausted—the kind that came from working tirelessly toward a worthy goal. Helping people. Putting their world back together. Closing this horrific chapter of their lives. Suddenly nervous, she dipped her head. "I know we still have so much to do before we can move forward from any of this, but we haven't talked about what happens after."

"After what?"

"After we get the country back on track and can begin thinking about living normal lives again. Do we...will we...do you want to stay together?" she asked, nuzzling into his neck to avoid his gaze.

He raised her face with a fingertip on her chin, eyes blazing. "Did you seriously just ask me that?"

"Well, I thought you might want to go to your parents in Korea, and I didn't want to assume—"

"Stop fucking talking," he growled, taking her mouth in a punishing kiss that eliminated every niggling insecurity she'd ever had. When she was breathless, he pulled away with a sharp nip at her lower lip. "We're staying together," he said, but then a bead of uncertainty flashed in his eyes. "If you'll have me."

Chuckling to herself at the ridiculousness of both of them, she said, "I love you, you idiot. You're stuck with me."

"I like the sound of that," he said, pressing a soft kiss to her cheek, then tracing his nose across her jawline. "Love you." Which reminded her of her earlier conversation with Penny, and something must have shown on her face because Derek asked, "What's up?"

"I think I just told Penny that we're friends," she said, laughing at the absurdity of the statement, so diametrically opposed to her stance on the woman just a few months ago. But the true absurdity was—she actually meant it.

"You'll be good for her," he said.

Thinking about how Penny had trained her and her friends over the past few months, her leadership in the face of an absolute disaster, her sharp decisions under pressure, her fierce protectiveness of Quentin and everyone else, Agnes didn't completely agree.

"No," she said with a slow smile. "We'll be good for each other."

Epilogue—SIX MONTHS LATER

"F OR THE LAST TIME, *no*, Quentin, we do not have room for another half-finished project. The kitchen cabinets are already overflowing with the remnants of your abandoned experiments," Penny said, failing to hide her smile as Quentin rolled up his sleeves, preparing for battle.

"They're not *abandoned*," he protested. "Just shelved for the moment. Er, literally. But I'll get back to them, I swear. Agnes asked me to help her with some antidote delivery equipment first."

Penny shoved another experiment into the cabinet and quickly shut the door on it before the mountain of items could tumble out. "We need to get you your own workshop. Maybe you can share with Ivan? I'll ask Silas how he's dealing with the never-ending pile of projects. Between the two of you, we'll be buried in no time." The two-bedroom suite-style hotel room she and Quentin had been living in was great, but not fit to house Quentin's penchant for amassing piles of stuff.

"*Fine,* I'll go through everything this weekend and clear out some things. Happy?"

"Ecstatic," she said. "Go shower. Everyone will be here soon."

Muttering a *yeah, yeah,* he bustled off to the bathroom, leaving Penny to her own devices. She went about tidying up the small kitchen and gathering an assortment of snacks. Kev had given her first dibs on the recent shipment from Canada for the one grocery store in the Capital they'd gotten up and running, but she hadn't wanted to take advantage of his kindness too much. Although she did make sure to snag some Cheetos and beef jerky for the boys for their weekly movie night.

After Tara had mentioned her family's tradition of screening banned movies, the crew had happily taken up the routine in the hotel they all now lived in, along with the other civilians and refugees in the Capital. It was temporary housing until they could hold elections and decide how to get everything back on track. Quentin loved living next door to all of his favorite people, and Penny was happy to see him happy—and she enjoyed having the Outpost crew close by too.

On the countertop, her sickle, freshly polished, glinted in the faint fluorescent light as she picked at its worn wood handle. Her ritual of cleaning it every day held strong even though she rarely had reason to use it anymore. It was part of the uniform she'd been wearing for the past year or more—jeans, tee shirt, weapons belt, boots—so she'd carried it to her meeting with Kev earlier that morning out of habit. It felt strange to walk around without its familiar weight bumping against her thigh.

A knock at her door interrupted her thoughts and she answered it, smiling at the man occupying the majority of the doorframe. "Pen," Mal said on almost a growl, fastening his hand to the back of her neck and pulling her in for a devastating kiss that had her knees knocking together. When he finally released her, she held the wall for balance as she stepped back to let him in.

"Brought extra beef jerky," he said, plopping a bag on the counter.

"Trying to bribe Quentin?" she asked.

"Doesn't hurt. Maybe he'll let us have the room for the night if we get him hopped up on his favorite junk food," he said, looping an arm around her waist, his lips finding her neck.

His insinuation had bolts of heat shooting through her, and she curled her hands around his massive biceps. "All we have to do is make 'goo-goo' eyes at each other and he'll scram," she said. "But the junk food will definitely make sure we don't wake up to stink bombs in our socks or slingshots of slime."

He grunted a laugh, his exhale of breath tickling the hairs on her neck. Mal had been the first to offer being her roommate, but Quentin had beaten him out when he'd tossed his duffel bag onto the extra bed—how could she say no to the kid who she'd thought was forever lost to her? So Mal settled for the room next to theirs, even though he still spent most nights in Penny's bed, or her in his.

"How'd things go with Kev this morning?" he asked, sliding his hands into her back pockets.

"Good. We're still having a time training the civilians to handle the turned without killing them, teaching them how to shoot dart guns, all of that stuff. But we're making progress. About twenty-five turned so far this week got put into the stadium's rehab facility, and Dr. Chun says they should be fine after another few courses of treatment. But Agnes knows more about that than I do. You and Derek handling the new recruits okay?"

Mal grumbled. "Half of 'em don't know their asses from their elbows, but if they can hold a dart gun and hit a turned somewhere on their body, that's all we care about."

Chewing her lip, Penny broached the subject she'd been dreading. "Hear they're starting the trials soon. For Zeln and the troxies."

An unreadable expression crossed Mal's face and he nodded. "I'll leave it up to Kev and whatever powers that be to determine their fates. Hopefully they arrive at the right verdicts."

"I also hear some Pharmatrox supporters are planning a protest."

"Doesn't surprise me. They'll be hard to weed out, and it will take time for their anger and influence to fade. But if we refuse to give them media coverage and choke off their movement, it will be that much more difficult for it to spread. We can't make the same mistakes we did with Pharmatrox and the Leader all those years ago."

"We'd have to be morons to allow history to repeat itself," she agreed. But sometimes, these insidious ideals had a way of coming back around. Penny just hoped whatever new system they were building was resilient enough to fight it off.

Another knock at the door, and then it burst open, a flurry of activity flooding into the room. "Silas, you have the absolute worst taste in supernatural entities," said Derek, his arm slung across Agnes's shoulders, who rolled her eyes. "First it was wizards and now you actually like githyanki?"

"Are you saying you *wouldn't* want innate psionic powers?" Silas scoffed as Ivan towed him to the couch.

"I love that this argument has lasted over six months. Very entertaining. Not at all annoying," Tara said, plopping herself on the floor in front of the TV and digging in her backpack. Vick, Lawrence, and Naomi filed into the room last, the latter depositing a bag of chips and salsa on the coffee table, which Derek pounced on.

"Ooh, you got the good salsa! Kev must really like us," he said, unscrewing the lid and plunging in a chip. "Gotta eat your fill before Quentin gets here, or you won't get any," he said to the room, grabbing another wad of chips.

"Get any what?" Quentin asked, emerging from the bathroom and tossing his towel at a nearby chair.

"Uh-uh," said Penny. "Hang it up. Don't want it smelling even more like a boy's locker room in here."

Dragging his feet and rolling his eyes, Quentin did as she asked and then elbowed Derek out of the way of the chips.

"Oye, chavales! Those are supposed to be for everyone," said Agnes. "How about we share?"

Both with a mouthful of chips, Derek and Quentin froze in their snacking, shrugging, and the room erupted into laughter.

"What's the movie tonight?" Silas asked.

"*A Bug's Life,*" Tara said. "One of my favorites." Popping the ancient DVD into the disc reader, Tara hit play and settled next to Vick on the loveseat. There wasn't enough furniture to house everyone, so pillows were partitioned to the floor as they all crowded in front of the TV. Mal picked a spot on some cushions and patted the seat next to him, and Penny nodded, making a be-right-there motion. As she gathered up the snacks from the kitchen, Agnes appeared beside her to help.

"How's everything going out in the field?" Agnes asked, rifling through the grocery bag and organizing the different goodies on the counter.

"Really well, thanks to you and Dr. Chun," she said. "The darts are great and the cure is working. We just need to get it to everyone across the country more quickly."

"Right," Agnes said, but then her gaze snagged on Penny's sickle resting beside the sink, and her expression became pensive. "You know, for a while, I still carried my machete even though I only ever went to the lab. But after the trial dates were set and with the store getting regular shipments again, I put it away last week. Under the bed within easy reach, of course. It feels strange to hang up that part of myself. Strange, but good." Finishing with a small smile, she bumped Penny's shoulder and scooped up a platter of snacks. "See you out there," she said and went back into the living room to a chorus of applause for the array of junk food.

A warm glow stole over Penny at the embodiment of camaraderie occupying her living room. But not just camaraderie—*family*. They'd all been through hell a thousand times over, but they'd made it out on the other side, battered and beaten, but never broken. Not irreparably. She'd lost so much over the years, and everything in this room had been an incomprehensible impossibility a year ago. But now, she had Quentin back—and she had so much more than she ever could have imagined.

Part of her would always be the Faction's enforcer, the tough-as-nails woman who'd cut down anyone who threatened her loved ones. She'd never demolish that part of herself or try to hide it—without it, she'd never have survived any of the shit she'd been through. It had served its purpose and she was grateful to it, but...

Catching her eye from the living room, Mal gave her a slow, delicious grin that held the promise of pleasure later, and he again patted the seat beside him, the spot he'd saved for her. He'd been saving a spot for her well before she'd been aware of him as more than an eternal thorn in her side. He was absolutely still that, but he reminded her every day of what was possible when she trusted other people and relied on their strength as well as her own—everyone in this room did. But more than that, it was about trusting *herself* to make the right decisions—something she was still coming to terms with, but surrounded by these people—her friends—she had no doubt she'd get better at it.

Picking up her sickle, its smooth wooden handle perfectly formed to her palm after countless battles, she went to the hall closet and hung it up, then slid the door shut.

She didn't need it anymore.

Acknowledgments

And so we've reached the end. I hope you enjoyed Agnes's and Penny's journey. This duology started out as a standalone, but after writing Book 1, I realized I was not finished with Penny (or Mal hehe). The story would not be the same without this epic conclusion, and I hope you loved Penny's redemption arc and relationship with Mal as much as I loved writing it.

It will come as no surprise to anyone that Penny is my favorite character (and arguably the main character) of this entire series (shh, don't tell the others). Avatar: The Last Airbender is one of my top shows of all time, and Zuko has the best redemption arc I've ever encountered in any piece of media. It got me thinking about Penny's story... *What if Princess Azula had a redemption arc, too?* And thus, this book was born.

I'm moving on to other projects now, but I'll never forget this duology. These are the characters that first made me a published author. And you, my dear reader, were the first to experience them on the page. Thank you for going on this journey with me.

Writing is a lonely and solitary activity much of the time, but I want to give an enormous shoutout to those who helped me to get where I am today.

Cameron (Cee) Montague Taylor has been my developmental editor since day 1, and I would not be the writer I am without their guidance, advice, and rigorous brain dump sessions. Cee is an absolute treasure trove of ideas, and I highly recommend working with them. Nadara Merrill, my Comma Queen, is my line and copy editor (and I like to think my #1 fan? haha). Without her, I would have many more wildly incorrect commas riddled throughout this book. Thank you both for helping me to become a better writer.

Thanks to my cover and character artists for bringing my imagination to life (please go check them out on social media!): eilzianna.the.one, khazaaddum, lucielart, sweet_enetriss_, suusliks, bronwyn.psd, chelzd_art, trifbookdesign.

Thank you to my beta readers, Sarah and Jennifer, for your fast reads and early thoughts. It's always scary throwing a new book out into the world without any idea how it will be received, so thanks for being gentle with my fragile author heart and letting me bounce ideas off of you. I'm so grateful to you for your help!

My ARC team deserves a huge shoutout too—some people joined this series in Book 2 and had to go back and read Book 1, which I know is a huge ask, so it means the world that you would do that for lil ole me.

To my parents, thank you for your unending support and being my personal on-the-ground marketing team telling anyone and everyone to buy my books. Word of mouth referrals mean a lot, and it makes me smile to think that maybe a few people in our small town will read this very anti-fascist book series and have some kind of spiritual awakening. (A girl can dream.)

To my partner who had to endure countless mid-writing rants and my many menty b's, thanks for sticking by me and reminding me that no, I'm not insane; yes, you would still love me if I was a worm; and yes, I should keep writing because what I do matters. I love you.

To anyone who has taken the time to read, review, or chat with me about my book, just know, you all are the reason I do this. I think about quietly retiring and disappearing into the ether with alarming regularity, but then I'll get a message from one of you or I'll see a post about my book, and it reminds me of why I do this and why I must keep going even when it's hard.

In a world where it feels like the truth is not valued and where there are only dark days ahead, these kinds of stories are more important than ever. We must not be silent. We must continue to stand up for what is right. We must continue to be as loud as humanly possible.

Don't let the bastards get you down.

Meg

Leave a review

Thank you for reading! I'd love it if you could take a moment to jot down a quick review on Amazon and Goodreads. Reviews are so important, especially for indie authors, to gain more readers and reach a wider audience. Thanks and see you on the other side.

Review on Goodreads

Join my reader crew

If you want to keep reading the worlds I create, my next series will be an urban fantasy about a jaguar shapeshifter with a dark entity inside her threatening to take control and an alpha werewolf (...at least she *thinks* he's a werewolf) who are the supernatural guardians of a small town. Coming in 2026.

Subscribe to Megan Boley's newsletter

Separately, I will be publishing spicy romance books under the name M. Maddox, and my first book is *You, Me, & Après-Ski* coming out winter 2025. If you want to keep up with my alter ego, sign up below:

Subscribe to M. Maddox's newsletter

About the author

Megan Boley is a dystopian and urban fantasy author. She loves writing stories with badass women and a healthy dose of plot twists. If she's not planning out her next slew of books to write, she usually has her face stuffed in her kindle or is out hiking with her dog.

Connect with Megan

Instagram & Threads: @meganboleyauthor

Website: megboley.com

www.ingramcontent.com/pod-product-compliance
Lightning Source LLC
Chambersburg PA
CBHW031627310726
48974CB00003B/851